praise for rudy rucker

"Rudy Rucker should be declared a National Treasure of American Science Fiction. Someone simultaneously channeling Kurt Gödel and Lenny Bruce might start to approximate full-on Ruckerian warp-space, but without the sweet, human, splendidly goofy Rudyness at the core of the singularity." —William Gibson

"One of science fiction's wittiest writers. A genius . . . a cult hero among discriminating cyberpunkers." —*San Diego Union-Tribune*

"Rucker's writing is great like the Ramones are great: a genre stripped to its essence, attitude up the wazoo, and cartoon sentiments that reek of identifiable lives and issues. Wild math you can get elsewhere, but no one does the cyber version of beatnik glory quite like Rucker." —*New York Review of Science Fiction*

"What a Dickensian genius Rucker has for Californian characters, as if, say, Dickens had fused with Phil Dick and taken up surfing and jamming and topologising. He has a hotline to cosmic revelations yet he's always here and now in the groove, tossing off lines of beauty and comic wisdom. 'My heart is a dog running after every cat.' We really feel with his characters in their bizarre tragicomic quests." —Ian Watson, author of *The Embedding*

"The current crop of sf humorists are mildly risible, I suppose, but they don't seem to pack the same intellectual punch of their forebears. With one exception, that is: the astonishing Rudy Rucker. For some two decades now, since the publication of his first novel, *White Light*, Rucker has combined an easygoing, trippy style influenced by the Beats with a deep engagement with knotty (or 'gnarly,' to employ one of his favorite terms) intellectual conceits, based mainly in mathematics. In the typical Rucker novel, likably eccentric characters—who run the gamut from brilliant to near-certifiable—encounter aspects of the universe that confirm that life is weirder than we can imagine." —*The Washington Post*

"Rucker stands alone in the science fiction pantheon as some kind of trickster god of the computer science lab; where others construct minutely plausible fictional realities, he simply grabs the corners of the one we already know and twists it in directions we don't have pronounceable names for." —*SF Site*

"Reading a Rudy Rucker book is like finding Poe, Kerouac, Lewis Carroll, and Philip K. Dick parked on your driveway in a topless '57 Caddy . . . and telling you they're taking you for a RIDE. The funniest science fiction author around." —*Sci-Fi Universe*

"This is SF rigorously following crazy rules. My mind of science fiction. At the heart of it is a rage to extrapolate. Rucker is what happens when you cross a mathematician with the extrapolating jazz spirit." —Robert Sheckley

"Rucker [gives you] more ideas per chapter than most authors use in an entire novel." —*San Francisco Chronicle*

"Rudy Rucker writes like the love child of Philip K. Dick and George Carlin. Brilliant, frantic, conceptual, cosmological . . . like lucid dreaming, only funny." —*New York Times* bestselling author Walter Jon Williams

by rudy rucker

turing & burroughs

a novel by

RUDY RUCKER

night shade books
new york

First published in paperback and ebook by Transreal Books, 2012.

First Night Shade Books edition published 2019.

Night Shade books may be purchased in bulk at special discounts for sales
promotion, corporate gifts, fund-raising, or educational purposes. Special
editions can also be created to specifications. For details, contact the Special Sales
Department, Night Shade Books, 307 West 36th Street, 11th Floor, New York, NY
10018 or info@skyhorsepublishing.com.

Night Shade Books® is a registered trademark of Skyhorse Publishing, Inc.®,
a Delaware corporation.

Visit our website at www.nightshadebooks.com.

10 9 8 7 6 5 4 3 2 1

Library of Congress Cataloging-in-Publication Data

Names: Rucker, Rudy v. B. (Rudy von Bitter), 1946- author.
Title: Turing & burroughs : a novel / by Rudy Rucker.
Other titles: Turing and burroughs
Description: First Night Shade Books edition. | New York : Night Shade Books,
2019.
Identifiers: LCCN 2018041192 | ISBN 9781597809641 (pbk. : alk. paper)
Classification: LCC PS3568.U298 T87 2019 | DDC 813/.54--dc23
LC record available at https://lccn.loc.gov/2018041192

Cover artwork by Bill Carman
Cover design by Claudia Noble

Printed in the United States of America

acknowledgements

Four chapters of *Turing & Burroughs* appeared as stories: "The Imitation Game" in *Interzone* #2, 2008; "Tangier Routines" in *Flurb* #5, 2008; "The Skug" in *Flurb* #10, 2010; and "Dispatches From Interzone" in *Flurb* #11, 2011. "The Imitation Game" also appeared in *The Mammoth Book of Alternate Histories*, edited by Ian Watson and Ian Whates (Robinson, London 2010).

The description of Alan Turing at the Sunset Lounge in West Palm Beach is adapted from a scene in *Bird Lives: The Life of Charlie Parker*, by Ross Russell (Charterhouse 1973).

The passage about the Happy Cloak that my Burroughs character quotes is indeed from *Fury*, a novel by Henry Kuttner and his wife C. L. Moore. That novel first appeared as a 1947 serial in the *Astounding* science fiction magazine, and has been republished in numerous editions, including a 1950 Grosset & Dunlap hardback under Kuttner's name alone, and as a 2010 ebook from Rosetta Books.

My chapters in the form of letters are heavily influenced by the collected letters of William Burroughs, see *Letters to Allen Ginsberg* 1953-1957, (Full Court Press, New York

1982) and *The Letters of William Burroughs* 1945-1959, edited by Oliver Harris, (Viking, New York, 1993).

My chapter "The Apocalypse According to Willy Lee" draws not only on Burroughs's letters but on his novels *The Western Lands* and *Queer*. And my final chapter, "Last Words" is inspired by Burroughs's books *The Yage Letters* and *Last Words*.

The Author's Note includes material I wrote for interviews with Nas Hedron, Kelly Burnette, and Liza Groen Trombi.

Thanks to these readers for their help with proofreading and copy editing: Roy Whelden, Alex McLaren, Jon Pearce, Arthur Hlavaty, John Walker, and Sylvia Rucker.

contents

contents

"so how do you know rudy?"
an introduction by eileen gunn

I used to want to be the Hunter S. Thompson of science fiction, outspoken and outrageous, able to surf the sur-reality of life and politics in the late twentieth century and document it in my writing with weird gonzo chaos. But Rudy Rucker got there first.

At least that was my feeling some thirty years ago, when I read, in the cyberpunk zinc *Science Fiction Eye*, a short reminiscence in which Rudy recalled his two-year sojourn in Lynchburg, Virginia, undercover as a mathematics professor. In Lynchburg, as I read it, Rudy had been a proto-cyberpunk briefly trapped in the hometown of Jerry Falwell, and his insouciant encounters with the local evangelical celebrities were minor but emotionally charged. I thought the Rudy of the essay was as funny and paranoid and impulsive as Hunter Thompson at the Kentucky Derby.

Rudy, finding himself in the Middle-American heart-land during the culture wars, had fought the enemies of gonzo in hand-to-hand combat. He was even willing to feel ruefully regretful later, when he realized he'd exceeded the local parameters of neighborly hostility.

Reading the essay, I imagined a Hunteresque ending to the adventure, with Rudy fleeing Lynchburg forever, pursued by bats, leaving baffled evangelicals in his wake. I was impressed.

But I just finagled a copy of the magazine and re-read the original essay, and that scene, resident in my mind since 1987, is not there. No bats, anyway. No psychedelics. Looking at the magazine itself, however, I could see how I might have gotten carried away. *SF Eye* had a sort of *Rolling Stone* ambiance. As were so many of us in those years, I was hornswoggled by the typography.

Rudy *did* escape Lynchburg, though, and moved to California. He continued to teach and wrote a raft of stories, poems, and essays, and published several science-fiction novels and two books on the philosophy of mathematics for the casual reader. He furthered his cyberpunk creds, and teamed up with a software developer that explored cellular automata. He also formulated an approach to writing that he called transrealism, in which he sometimes appears as a character and combines details of his own life with science fictional elements.

Rudy's transrealism made a lot of aesthetic sense to me, though I was not so much an advocate of it as an inhabitant, someone who breathed its atmosphere and swam in its ocean. In the latter part of the twentieth century, it was pretty clear that we lived on the edge of a weird future. Putting ourselves into surreal fiction, as Hunter Thompson and the other New Journalism writers did with their reporting, was a way of acknowledging, and even welcoming, the transition.

In the early post-millennial years, I edited a science-fiction webzine with a political bent, *The Infinite Matrix*. I bought two Rucker stories, "A Dream of Flatland," and "Jenna and Me." The first was an excerpt from his novel *Spaceland*, and the second, a collaboration between Rudy and his son Rudy, was a brilliant and uproarious satire of the techno-political state of the US in 2003. (Google it. It's still online—or was when I checked this morning. Hilarious story, transrealist all the way, but now more nostalgia than science fiction. The future past reads as the present.)

In addition to transrealism, Rudy has formulated, over the past several decades, a sort of unified field theory of art, life, and computation. It describes a quality he calls "gnarl" that deals with the role of mathematical complexity in constructing our reality.

In 2005, I sat in an auditorium packed to the rafters with scholars of fantastic literature and listened to Rudy talk about the intricate whorls in oak burls and the patterns on cone shells and the existence of an underlying computational aspect to reality, accompanied by a distinctly non-gnarly slide show of diagrams and equations. He described gnarl as a degree of complexity—in nature, in art, in life. In terms of the movement of water, for example, he compared the motion of water in a cup of tea to that in a brook, and water flowing in a brook to that pouring over a waterfall, as examples of increasingly complex motion. In an aesthetic project, such as a novel or a story, this use of the word gnarly refers to an unpredictable process that, when examined, makes sense. Rudy likes a certain degree of gnarl in his books.

I have to confess that I understood only about a third of what he said that day, but I was fascinated. His talk defined and made sense of an effect I try to achieve when writing fiction: I want my stories to be surprising and strange, but not random, and I want them to contain complex associations that are not explicit. Some of the associations I deliberately include may be meaningful only to me, and sometimes the stories contain associations I notice only if someone else points them out. I thought all writers did this, but perhaps I am just modeling Hunter Thompson again. Last time I tried to explain my process to other writers, they looked at me as though I had a squid hanging out of my mouth.

What about the two-thirds of Rudy's lecture I didn't understand? Best if Rudy explains this himself. Check out his book *The Lifebox, the Seashell, and the Soul*, in which he writes about the mathematics that may underlie reality. Rudy explains it all, carefully and clearly, and in the course of his explanations you'll learn a lot about how a mathematician makes sense of the world—or, at least, how this one does.

A few years ago, Rudy and I wrote a gnarly story, "Hive Mind Man," with some transreal special effects and a hylozoic conclusion, which I won't spoil by telling you what "hylozoic" means. You can read the story for free on Rudy's website.

Why am I telling you all this? Because I think an awareness of transrealism and gnarl will come in handy when reading *Turing & Burroughs*, the book you're holding right now.

Alan Turing and William S. Burroughs were each brilliant and complex individuals. Turing was a mathematician, computer scientist, cryptanalyst, and theoretical biologist. He and his team cracked the German Enigma code, which helped the Allies win World War II. Burroughs was an experimental writer of the Beat Generation; in the long run, he was the most influential of the Beats. He was also well-known as a user and abuser of illegal drugs, and had accidentally killed his wife during drunken gun-play. Both Turing and Burroughs preferred sexual partners of their own sex and, until the late Sixties and early Seventies, both the preference and the acts were actively prosecuted in Great Britain and the United States. Turing, in fact, was found guilty and chemically castrated by the British government, despite his contribution to defeating the Nazis.

This book has gnarl to burn, and Rudy calls it "a biography with transreal elements." It blows the whole concept of "biography" out of the water and into a parallel universe, and yet it honors the real-world lives and sensibilities of its protagonists, each of whom lived outside what was safe and normal in their time. In building a happier ending for both Turing and Burroughs, the author used many fascinating—even jaw-dropping—details from his protagonists' lives, and you may want to read a bit about them after you finish this book, if only to re-set your reality levels.

My introduction here has tumbled down a rabbithole of chaos and gnarl and transrealism, and now is balanced precariously on an outcrop of rationality, so I will go no further. It's quite possible that there is no end to the scrolls of reality, complexity, and intellectual history that roll out when you ask someone how they know Rudy Rucker.

Seek the gnarl, as Rudy says. Read this book and seize the gnarl.

turing & burroughs

ONE
the imitation game

I t was a rainy Sunday night, June 6, 1954. Alan Turing was walking down a liquidly lamp-lit street to the Manchester railway station, wearing a long raincoat with a furled umbrella concealed beneath. His Greek paramour Zeno was due on the 9 p. m. train, having taken a ferry from Calais. And, no, the name had no philosophical import, it was simply the boy's given name—although it was indeed the case that at times dear Zeno could protract a seemingly finite interval of time into an endless sum of ever-subtler pleasures. Not that he'd think of it that way.

If all went well, Zeno and Alan would be spending the night together in the sepulchral Manchester Midland travelers' hotel—Alan's own home nearby was watched. He'd booked the hotel room under a pseudonym.

Barring any intrusions from the morals squad, Alan and Zeno would set off bright and early tomorrow for a lovely week of tramping across the hills of the Lake District, free as rabbits, sleeping in serendipitous inns. Alan sent up a fervent prayer, if not to God, then to the deterministic universe's initial boundary condition.

"Let it be so."

Surely the cosmos bore no distinct animus towards homosexuals, and the world might yet grant some peace to the tormented, fretful gnat labeled Alan Turing. But it was by no means a given that the assignation with Zeno would click. Last spring, the suspicious authorities had deported Alan's Norwegian flame Kjell straight back to Bergen before Alan even saw him.

It was as if Alan's persecutors supposed him likely to be teaching his men top-secret code-breaking algorithms, rather than sensually savoring his rare hours of private joy. Although, yes, Alan did relish playing the tutor, and it was in fact conceivable that he might feel the urge to discuss those topics upon which he'd worked during the war years. After all, it was no one but he, Alan Turing, who'd been the brains of the British cryptography team at Bletchley Park, cracking the Nazi Enigma code and shortening the War by several years—little thanks that he'd ever gotten for that.

The churning of a human mind is unpredictable, as is the anatomy of the human heart. Alan's work on universal machines and computational morphogenesis had convinced him that the world is both deterministic *and* overflowing with endless surprise. His proof of the unsolvability of the Halting Problem had established, at least to Alan's satisfaction, that there could never be any shortcuts for predicting the figures of Nature's stately dance.

Few but Alan had as yet grasped the new order. The prating philosophers still supposed, for instance, that there must be some element of randomness at play in order that each human face be slightly different. Far from it. The differences were simply the computation-amplified results of disparities among the embryos and their wombs—with these disparities stemming in turn from the cosmic computation's orderly growth from the universe's initial conditions.

Of late Alan had been testing his ideas with experiments involving the massed cellular computations by which a living organism transforms egg to embryo to adult. Input acorn—output oak. He'd already published his results involving the dappling of a brindle cow, but his latest experiments were so close to magic that he was holding them secret, wanting to refine the work in the alchemical privacy of his starkly under-furnished home. Should all go well, a Nobel prize might grace the burgeoning field of computational morphogenesis. This time Alan didn't want a droning gas-bag like Alonzo Church to steal his thunder—as had happened with the Hilbert *Entscheidungsproblem*.

Alan glanced at his watch. Only three minutes till the train arrived. His heart was pounding. Soon he'd be committing lewd and lascivious acts (luscious phrase) with a man in England. To avoid a stint in jail, he'd sworn to abjure this practice—but he'd found wiggle room for his conscience. Given that Zeno was a visiting Greek national, he wasn't, strictly speaking, a "man in England," assuming that "in" was construed to mean "who is a member citizen of." Chop the logic and let the tree of the Knowledge of Good and Evil fall, soundless in the moldering woods.

It had been nearly a year since Alan had enjoyed manly love—last summer on the island of Corfu with none other than Zeno, who'd taken Alan for a memorable row in his dory, a series of golden instants fused into a lambent flow. Alan had just been coming off his court-ordered estrogen treatments, but that hadn't mattered. In Alan's case the hormones had in fact produced no perceptible reduction in his libido. The brain, after all, was the most sensitive sex organ of them all. By now he'd suffered a year's drought, and he was randy as a hat rack. He felt as if his whole being were on the surface of his skin.

Approaching the train station, he glanced back over his shoulder—reluctantly playing the socially assigned role of furtive perv—and sure enough, a weedy whey-faced fellow was mooching along half a block behind, a man with a little round mouth like a lamprey eel's. Officer Harold Jenkins. Devil take the beastly prig!

Alan twitched his eyes forward again, pretending not to have seen the detective. What with the growing trans-Atlantic hysteria over homosexuals and atomic secrets, the security minders grew ever more officious. In these darkening times, Alan sometimes mused that the United States had been colonized by the lowest dregs of British society: sexually obsessed zealots, degenerate criminals, and murderous slave masters.

On the elevated tracks, Zeno's train was pulling in. What to do? Surely Detective Jenkins didn't realize that Alan was meeting this particular train. Alan's incoming mail was vetted by the censors—he estimated that by now Her Majesty was employing the equivalent of two point seven workers full time to torment that disgraced boffin, Professor A. M. Turing. But—score one for Prof. Turing—his written communications with Zeno had been encrypted via a sheaf of one-time pads he'd left in Corfu with his golden-eyed Greek god, bringing a matching sheaf home. Alan had made the pads from clipped-out sections of identical newspapers; he'd also built Zeno a cardboard cipher wheel to simplify the look-ups.

No, no, in all likelihood, Jenkins was in this seedy district on a routine patrol, although now, having spotted Turing, he would of course dog his steps. The arches beneath the elevated tracks were the precise spot where, two years ago, Alan had connected with a sweet-faced boy whose dishonesty had led to Alan's conviction for acts of gross indecency. Alan's arrest had been to some extent his own doing; he'd been foolish enough to call the police when one of the boy's friends burglarized his house. "Silly ass," Alan's big brother had said. Remembering the phrase made Alan wince and snicker. A silly ass in a dunce's cap, with donkey ears. A suffering human being nonetheless.

The train screeched to stop, puffing out steam. The doors of the carriages slammed open. Alan would have loved to sashay up there like Snow White on the palace steps. But how to shed Jenkins?

Not to worry; he'd prepared a plan. He darted into the men's public lavatory, inwardly chuckling at the vile, voyeuristic thrill that disk-mouthed Jenkins must feel to see his quarry going to earth. The echoing stony chamber was redolent with the rich scent of putrefying urine, the airborne biochemical signature of an immortal colony of microorganisms indigenous to the standing waters of the train station pissoir. It put Alan in mind of his latest Petri-dish experiments at home.

Capitalizing on his newly formulated theory of mor-phonic fields, he'd learned to grow stripes, spots, and spi-rals in the flat mediums, and then he'd moved into the third dimension. He'd grown lumps, tendrils, and, just yesterday, a congelation of tissue very like a human ear.

Like a thieves' treasure cave, the train-station bath-room had a second exit—over on the other side of the elevated track. Striding through the loo's length, Alan drew out his umbrella, folded his mackintosh into a small bundle tucked beneath one arm, and hiked up the over-long pants of his dark suit to display the prominent red tartan spats that he'd worn, the spats a joking gift from a Cambridge friend. Exiting the jakes on the other side of the tracks, Alan opened his high-domed umbrella and pulled it low over his head. With the spats and dark suit replacing the beige mac and ground-dragging cuffs, he looked quite the different man from before.

Not risking a backward glance, he clattered up the stairs to the platform. And there was Zeno, his handsome, bearded face alight. Zeno was tall for a Greek, with much the same build as Alan's. As planned, Alan paused briefly by Zeno as if asking a question, privily passing him a little map and a key to their room at the Midland Hotel. And then Alan was off down the street, singing in the rain, leading the way.

Alan didn't notice Detective Jenkins following him in an unmarked car. Once Jenkins had determined where Alan and Zeno were bound, he put in a call to the party who'd engaged his services. The matter was out of Jenkins's hands now.

The sex was even more enjoyable than Alan had hoped. He and Zeno slept till mid-morning, Zeno's leg heavy across his, the two of them spooned together in one of the room's twin beds. Alan awoke to a knocking on the door, followed by a rattling of keys.

He sprang across the carpet and leaned against the door. "We're just now *arising*," he said, striving for an authoritative tone. But his voice rose and fluted on the final word.

"The dining room's about to close," whined a woman's voice. "Might I bring the gentlemen their breakfast in the room?"

"Indeed," said Alan through the door, speaking more slowly than before. "A British breakfast for two. And please be quick. We have a train to catch rather soon." Earlier this week, he'd had his housekeeper send his bag ahead to Cumbria in the Lake District. And his wallet held more than enough cash for his and Zeno's expenses.

"Very good, sir. Full breakfast for two."

"Wash," said Zeno, sticking his head out of the bathroom. At the sound of the maid, he'd darted right in there and started the tub. He looked happy. "Hot water."

Alan joined Zeno in the bath for a minute, and the dear boy brought him right off. But then he grew anxious about the return of the maid. He donned his clothes and rucked up the second bed so it would look slept in. Now Zeno emerged from his bath, utterly lovely in his nudity. Anxious Alan shooed him into his clothes. Finally the maid appeared with the platters of food, really quite a nice-looking breakfast, with kippers, sausages, fried eggs, toast, honey, marmalade, cream and a lovely great pot of tea, steaming hot.

Seeing the maid face to face, Alan realized they knew each other; she was the cousin of his housekeeper. Although the bent little woman feigned not to recognize him, he could see in her eyes that she knew exactly what he and Zeno were doing here. And there was a sense that she knew something more. She gave him a particularly odd look when she poured out the two mugs of tea. Wanting to be shut of her, he handed her a coin and she withdrew.

"Milk tea," said Zeno, tipping half his mug back into the pot and topping it up with cream. He raised the mug as if in a toast, then slurped most of it down. Alan's tea was still too hot for his lips, so he simply waved his mug and smiled.

It seemed that even with the cream, Zeno's tea was very hot indeed. Setting his mug down with a clatter, he began fanning his hands at his mouth, theatrically gasping for breath. Alan took it for a joke, and emitted out one of his fun-house laughs. But this was no farce.

Zeno squeaked and clutched at his throat; beads of sweat covered his face; foam coated his lips. He dropped to the floor in a heap, spasmed his limbs like a starfish, and beat a tattoo on the floor.

Hardly knowing what to think, Alan knelt over his inert friend, massaging his chest. The man had stopped breathing; he had no pulse. Alan leaned over and pressed his mouth to Zeno's, planning to resuscitate him. But then he smelled bitter almonds—the classic sign of cyanide poisoning.

Recoiling as abruptly as a piece of spring-loaded machinery, he ran into the bathroom and rinsed off his lips. Surely this was the work of Her Majesty's spy-masters. A secret agent had been sent to murder Alan and Zeno both. In the authorities' eyes, Alan was an even greater risk than a rogue atomic scientist. His cryptographic work on breaking the Enigma code was a *secret* secret—the very existence of this work was unknown to the public at large.

His only hope was to slip out of the country and to assume a new life. But how? He thought distractedly of the ear-shaped form he'd recently grown in the Petri dish at home. Why not a new face? His recent progress with experimental morphogenesis had been extreme. The maddest notions seemed within reach.

He leaned over Zeno, rubbing his poor, dear chest. The man was very dead. Alan went and listened by the room's door. Was the agent lurking without, showing his teeth like a hideous omnivorous ghoul? But he heard not a sound. The likeliest possibility was that the operative had paid the maid to let him dose the tea—and had then gotten well out of the way. Perhaps he had a little time.

He imagined setting his internal computational system to double speed. Stepping lively, he exchanged clothes with Zeno—a bit tricky as the other man's body was so limp. Better than rigor mortis, at any rate.

Finding a pair of scissors in Zeno's travel kit, he trimmed off his friend's pathetic, noble beard, sticking the whiskers to his own chin with smears of honey. A crude initial imitation, a first-order effect.

Alan packed Zeno's bag and made an effort to lift the corpse to his feet. Good lord but this was hard. He thought to tie a necktie to the suitcase, run the tie over his shoulder and knot it around Zeno's right arm. If he held the suitcase in his left hand, it made a useful counterweight.

It was a good thing that, having lost some of his muscle during his state-mandated estrogen treatments, Alan had begun training again. He was very nearly as fit as in his early thirties. Suitcase in place, right arm tightly wrapped around Zeno's midriff and grasping the man's belt, he waltzed his friend down the hotel's back stairs, emerging into a car park where, thank you, oh Great Algorithmist, a cabbie was having a smoke.

"My friend *Turing* is sick," said Alan, trying to twist the vowels into a semblance of a Greek accent. "I am wanting to take him home."

"Blind pissed of a Monday morn," cackled the cabbie, jumping to his own conclusions. "That's the high life for fair. And red spats! What's our toff's address?"

With a supreme effort, Alan swung Zeno into the cab's rear seat and sat next to him. He reached into the body's coat and pretended to read off his home address. Nobody seemed to be tailing the cab. The agents were lying low, lest blame for the murder fall upon them.

As soon as the cab drew up to Alan's house, he overpaid the driver and dragged Zeno to his feet, waving off all offers of assistance. He didn't want the cabbie to get a close look at the crude honey-sticky beard on his chin. And then he was in his house, which was blessedly empty,

Monday being the housekeeper's day off. Moving from window to window, he drew the curtains.

He dressed Zeno in Turing pajamas, laid him out in the professorial bed, and vigorously washed the corpse's face, not forgetting to wash his own hands afterwards. Seeking out an apple from the kitchen, he took two bites, then dipped the rest of the apple into a solution of potassium cyanide that he happened to have about the place in a jam jar. He'd always loved the scene in *Snow White and the Seven Dwarfs* when the Wicked Witch lowers an apple into a cauldron of poison. Dip the apple in the brew, let the sleeping death seep through!

Alan set the poison apple down beside Zeno. A Snow White suicide. Now to perfect the imitation game.

He labored all afternoon. He found a pair of cookie sheets in the kitchen—the housekeeper often did baking for him. He poured a quarter-inch of his specially treated gelatin solution onto each sheet—as it happened, the gelatin was from the bones of a pig. Man's best friend. He set the oven on its lowest heat, and slid in the cookie sheets, leaving the oven door wide open so he could watch. Slowly the medium jelled.

Alan's customized jelly contained a sagacious mixture of activator and inhibitor compounds that he'd been tweaking and retweaking every day, adjusting the morphonic balance to match that of the womb. If he was truly on track, the latest stuff was tailored to promote just the right kind of embryological reaction-diffusion computation.

Carefully wielding a scalpel, Alan cut a tiny fleck of skin from the tip of Zeno's cold nose. He set the fleck into the middle of the upper cookie sheet, and then looked in the mirror, preparing to repeat the process on himself. Oh blast, he still had honey and hair on his chin. Silly ass. Carefully he swabbed off the mess with toilet paper, flushing the evidence down the commode. And then he took the scalpel to his own nose.

After he set his fleck of tissue into place on the lower pan, his tiny cut *would* keep on bleeding, and he had to spend nearly half an hour staunching the spot, greatly worried that he might scatter the drops of blood. Mentally he was running double-strength error-checking routines to keep himself from mucking things up. It was so very hard for him to be tidy. As a schoolboy, he'd always had ink on his collar.

When his housekeeper arrived tomorrow morning, Alan's digs should look chaste, sarcophagal, Egyptian. The imitation Turing corpse would be a mournful *memento mori* of a solitary life gone wrong, and the puzzled poisoners would hesitate to intervene. The man who knew too much would be dead; that was primary desideratum. After a perfunctory inquest, the Turing replica would be cremated, bringing the persecution to a halt. And Alan's mother might forever believe that her son's death was an accident. For years she'd been chiding him over his messy fecklessness with the chemicals in his home lab.

Outside a car drove past very slowly. The assassin was wondering what was going on. Yet he hesitated to burst in, lest the neighbors learn of their government's perfidy.

Sitting quiet in a chair, Alan wondered where he'd be right now if the killers had succeeded. All scientific logic said that death was a terminal halting that one wouldn't even experience. But yet . . . The most basic question about the world was, after all, unanswerable: *Why is there something instead of nothing?* An afterlife wasn't utterly out of the question. And if that were the case . . . As so many times before, his thoughts flew to his cherished, childish dream of meeting his first love in heaven. Christopher Morcom. Dead now for—good lord!—twenty-four years. Dragged into the depths of time's sullen, heedless river.

With shaking hands, Alan poured himself a glass of sherry. Steady, old man. See this through.

He moved his kitchen chair close to the open oven door. Like puffing pastry, the flecks of skin were rising up from the cookie sheets, with disks of cellular growth radiating out as the tissues grew. He'd jolted the flecks of skin into behaving like pieces of embryos.

Slowly the noses hove into view, and then the lips, the eye holes, the forehead, the chins. As the afternoon light waned, Alan saw the faces age, Zeno in the top pan, Alan on the bottom. They began as innocent babes, became pert boys, spotty youths, and finally grown men.

Ah, the pathos of biology's irreversible computations, thought Alan, forcing a wry smile. But the orotund verbiage of academe did little to block the pain. Dear Zeno was dead. And Alan's life as he'd known it was at an end, at age forty-one. He wept.

It was dark outside now. He drew the pans from the oven, shuddering at the enormity of what he'd wrought. The uncanny empty-eyed faces had an expectant air; they were like holiday pie crusts, waiting for steak and kidney, for mincemeat and plums.

Bristles had pushed out of the two flaccid chins, forming little beards. Time to slow down the computation. One didn't want the wrinkles of extreme old age. Alan doused the living faces with inhibitor solution, damping their cellular computations to a normal rate.

He carried the bearded Turing face into his bedroom and pressed it onto the corpse. The tissues took hold, sinking in a bit, which was good. Using his fingers, he smoothed the joins at the edges of the eyes and lips. As the living face absorbed cyanide from the dead man's tissues, its color began to fade. A few minutes later, the face was waxen and dead. The illusion was nearly complete.

Alan momentarily lost his composure and gagged; he ran to the toilet and vomited, though little came up. He'd neglected to eat anything today other than those two bites of apple. Finally his stomach-spasms stopped. In full error-correction mode, he remembered to wash his hands several times before wiping his face. And then he drank a quart of water from the tap.

He took his razor and shaved the Turing face of the dead man in the bed. The barbering went faster than when he'd shaved Zeno in the hotel. It was better to stand so that he saw his face upside down. Was barbering a good career? It would be risky to work as a scientist again. Given any fresh input, the halted Turing persecution would restart.

Alan cleaned up once more and drifted back into the kitchen. Prying up a paving stone just outside the door, he removed the bills that he'd stashed there in a screw top jar. The war years had given him a lasting distrust of banks. Combining this stash with his travel funds, he had a fine wad of bills.

It was time to skulk out through the dark garden with his travel funds and with Zeno's passport, to bicycle through the familiar woods to a station down the line, and there to catch a train. Probably his tormentors wouldn't be much interested in pursuing Zeno. They'd be glad Zeno had posed the murder as a suicide, and the less questions asked the better.

But to be safe, Turing would flee along an unexpected route. He'd take the train to Plymouth, the ferry from there to Santander on the north coast of Spain, a train south through Spain to the Mediterranean port of Algeciras, and another ferry from Algeciras to Tangier.

Tangier was an open city, an international zone. He could buy a fresh passport there. He'd be free to live as he liked—in a small way. Perhaps he'd master the violin. And read the Iliad in Greek. Alan glanced down at the flaccid Zeno face, imagining himself as a Greek musician.

If you were me, from A to Z, if I were you, from Z to A . . .

Alan caught himself. His mind was spinning in loops, avoiding what had to be done next. It was time.

He scrubbed his features raw and donned his new face.

TWO
the skug

When Alan Turing reached Tangier in June, 1954, the city's whitewashed lanes and towers seemed a maze of joy. He was elated with his escape from the shadowy agents who'd tried to assassinate him. And glad to leave the tedious, pawky computing machines of Manchester. He rented a comfortably furnished apartment and hid his money beneath a floorboard.

For now, Alan was free to do as he pleased—perhaps to idle, perhaps to push further with his startling new work on the chemical keys to biological morphogenesis. If he could fully fathom how Nature grows her knobby, gnarly forms, then he might well complete his lifelong quest to build a mind, to create a purely logical sentience by whom he could, at last, be understood.

He found that he loved Tangier on a visceral level. Every morning, Alan would take a long run on the empty beaches—the locals had little interest in the seaside. The quality of the light was uplifting. The muezzin calls to prayer were like intricately encrypted signals from a higher mind. And the cheeky street-boys of Tangier were a visual delight. For Alan, the Casbah was like a holiday fair with sweets at every turn—although, as yet, he hadn't quite dared to sample the boys. He was still in some fear of hidden enemies.

Seeking out fellow expatriates, he encountered the louche international café society of Tangier. At home, he'd rarely hit it off with mannered aesthetes, but in this odd backwater, everyone was hungry for companionship.

In his first month, Alan often spent the evenings at the Café Central in the Socco Chico square, enjoying the free-wheeling euphoria, the cognac, the mint tea and the kief. A dissipated Oxford poet named Brian Howard would hold forth on beauty, and then William Burroughs, a sexy, sardonic American of Alan's age, would send the group into gales of laughter with his scandalous routines. Alan noticed that amid the expatriates' merry intimacy there was no stigma in being homosexual.

One night the camaraderie loosened Alan's tongue to the point where he bragged to his raffish companions that he wasn't really the man whose name stood in his Greek passport.

"I'm *not* Zeno Metakides," Alan announced to the ring of smirking expats, his voice hoarsened by kief. "I only wear his *face*. In reality I'm a top-drawer mathematician who cracked the Hun's cryptographic codes. I won the war, don't you know—and now the Queen's mandarins want to *rub me out*."

The next morning Alan awoke with a start of horror. He must be suicidal, to be spilling his secrets to foppish wastrels who'd cut him cold, were they all back in London. He avoided the cafés from then on, going for his long runs along the sea in the mornings, visiting the market, and resuming his researches on computational morphogenesis.

To make his lab work more interesting, Alan had always preferred what he termed the "desert island" ideal. That is, he was in the habit of creating his experimental chemicals from substances that came readily to hand—things like foods or weeds or bits of offal that he found in the street. And so he began searching out suitable reagents and catalysts in the wares of the Moroccan street markets. Finding his way in the bedazzling maze of the souq was slow.

"What you look for?" asked a boy standing next to him at a shaded market stall one brilliant afternoon. He had sharp, crisp features and a friendly smile. He was about twenty—half Alan's age.

"Elixirs," said Alan, eying the youth. "Strong flavors."

"I am Driss," said the boy. One of his eyes was black, the other was hazel. "I can help you." He walked around Alan, studying him from every side. And then he puckered his pretty lips and clucked, as if calling a chicken.

Alan's heart fluttered within his chest. "I'm Alan," he said. "I've only just moved here."

"Ouakha," said the boy, meaning something like okay. "Well met, al'An. We'll cook dinner together, if you wish."

"Excelsior," said Alan.

Driss helped Alan pick out cardamom seeds, ginger root, pickled lemons, saffron, olives, semolina grain, lamb, incense, a small block of hashish and a bunch of odd-shaped vegetables. When they got back to Alan's room, Driss smoked some of the hashish, and, growing coquettish, let Alan make love to him. As the afternoon waned they cooked a Moroccan couscous with lamb stew.

"Wonderful," said Alan after the meal, feeling a rare moment of calm. "A feast for a sheik." The evening walls were amber with shadows of lavender. A cool dry breeze wafted in a scent of resin from the hills' gnarled pines. The muezzin wailed atop his minaret.

"You make medicine?" asked Driss, pointing toward the corner where Alan's chemical concoctions sat. "Perfume?"

"I'm habitually lonely. You might say I long to grow a friend."

Driss laughed merrily. "I am your friend, al'An. I am here and now. Full grown."

"But perhaps I want to grow a *gnome*," said Alan, getting to his feet with a spoon in hand. The rich food and the fumes of hashish had emboldened him. "Let me take a sample of your code. Open your mouth."

Driss parted his lips and waggled his tongue. Alan ran the edge of the spoon along the smooth pink lining of the boy's inner cheek, surely gathering up a few loose cells. And then he ran the spoon along the inside of his own cheek. He went and smeared the spoon against a layer of jellied mutton stock that sat in one of his flat pots.

"Our child," said Alan.

Driss watched from his chair, eyes alert. He was wearing Alan's bedroom slippers, his extra shirt and a pair of his boxer shorts.

"I must go home to my mother and my brothers," said Driss as Alan returned to the table. He gestured at his borrowed garments. "Do you mind if I keep?"

"Ouakha," said Alan with an extravagant gesture. "No matter." He was free of England for good.

Over the coming weeks, Driss became a regular visitor. He'd run errands for Alan or guide him around the town. And often he'd spend a morning or an afternoon in Alan's bed.

Fondly watching the youth's comings and goings from his balcony, Alan would scan for signs of a security breach, vaguely strategizing his plans for further flight. But so far, nothing he did in Tangier seemed to have real consequences. Perhaps he'd escaped Her Majesty's scrutiny for good.

Driss knew a fair amount of English, and he seemed to have a flair for abstract reasoning. Sometimes when they had an idle half hour, Alan would feed Driss a tidbit of mathematics. One day, for instance, he showed him a visual proof of the Pythagorean theorem—the figure involved a smaller square inscribed at an angle within a larger one. Another day he pasted together a paper Mobius strip, and got the youth to cut the strip down the middle with Alan's nail scissors.

"How many pieces will we have?" asked Alan in his role of maths master.

"Cut makes two," said Driss.

"Tallyho!" said Alan. "The phantoms of maths are more *wriggly* than you dream, young wizard. Snip and see."

"Only one piece!" observed Driss when he was done snipping along the length of the band. "The two are twisted into one."

"Like us, dear Driss," said Alan, venturing to caress the youth's cheek. Driss smiled and set the curling band of paper on Alan's head like a crown.

The golden days slid by. Though dwindling, Alan's hoard of cash was not yet exhausted. He pressed forward on his morphogenesis research. The smooth, fluid, self-generating mechanisms of biology were a relief from the electromechanical brains with their gears, wires, relays, electronic valves. The dabbling play in his make-shift lab was wonderfully unlike the communal politics of building an unwieldy computing machine. Thanks to his new biotweaking procedures, his cultured tissues would become programmable life forms.

The key was to create universal cells. The human body was known to have over two hundred distinct types of cells, all of them descended from the original cells of the early embryo. Alan's near-term goal was to coax the culture of his and Driss's cells into a primitive, Edenic state. These embryo-style cells would have great powers. By manipulating their morphonic fields, Alan would interact with them and train them to behave in desirable ways.

Patiently, and one small step at a time, Alan treated his burgeoning colony with delicate amounts of the catalysts that he'd found around Tangier. As well as the market spices, he drew venom from the jaws of a centipede he'd crushed, squeezed a drop of liquid resin from a lump of hashish, and even contributed a few drops of his own semen.

A bad smell was developing in the apartment, a nasty pong. When Alan first noticed it at, he thought it was the accumulating garbage.

Meanwhile he was finally bringing the little culture into a truly primordial state. These undifferentiated cells were theoretically capable of becoming any kind of cell at all—

skin, blood, bone, neuron, muscle—whatever. But Alan wasn't quite sure how he'd communicate with his undifferentiated tissue. As a way of getting started, he began talking to the culture when he was alone. Trying to teach it like a child or a pet seemed to make sense.

"Look what I have here," he told Driss, when the youth next appeared. It was noon, with the slanting sun lying on Alan's floor like a slab of iron. "Our offspring. A smart slug. Potentially smart, in any case."

Alan held out the dish, with the consommé supporting a thumb-sized glob of tan cells, longer than it was wide. The dish itself was glazed in labyrinthine patterns of blue and white.

"Skug?" said Driss, misunderstanding him. He hadn't been paying much attention to Alan's morphogenetic experimentation.

Alan laughed exorbitantly. "A *skug*, yes. The official name for our creation henceforth." He tried to enfold Driss in a hug, but the boy stepped away, as from a bad odor.

"This skug grows from our spit?" said Driss, peering at the bowl.

"It's powerful," said Alan. "Plenipotent." He leaned over it. "The skug hears me, I'm sure of it."

Ever so slightly the surface of the yellowish creature wriggled.

"What sorcery can the skug do?" asked Driss. He seemed uneasy with Alan today. Standoffish.

"I suspect it can merge with other beings," said Alan. "Let's test," said Alan, looking around the apartment. A dark red cockroach was skulking beside the overflowing kitchen trashcan. Tip-toeing over with exaggerated caution, Alan used a spoon to flick a droplet of some skug-flesh onto the roach—and the insect melted into a lacquered puddle.

"Wrong species," said Alan equably. "Too low in complexity to be worthy of our skug. How about—one of those *lizards* sunning themselves on the balcony railing?"

"As you like, al'An," said Driss, and fetched one of the little creatures. Alan used the spoon to smear a bit of the pink skug-jelly onto the writhing captive, being careful not to get the stuff on his or Driss's hands.

The lizard hissed and sprouted a pair of membranous wings, rising up from his back like a pair of rainbows.

"*Awwah,*" cried Driss, dropping the thing. The tweaked creature crawled and fluttered across the shadowed room, out to the balcony, and immediately fell off the edge and into the street. Driss ran down after it—but returned empty-handed.

"It's gone?" asked Alan.

"It's dead," said Driss. "I don't like to touch these behexed things." He sniffed the air and gave Alan a significant look. "You yourself—you are unwell, yes?"

Suddenly it became clear that the apartment's bad smell was coming from Alan's plastered-on Zeno-face. Odd that he hadn't realized this. Repressing the truth. The tissue-culture was losing its ability to integrate with Alan's metabolism. His face was dying.

"I'm fine," insisted Turing. He had a distinct feeling that Driss might not be coming back again. And so he pressed the youth into a half-hearted coupling.

Alan dropped off to sleep after his orgasm. When he woke alone, he saw that Driss had cleaned out the stash of travel money that Alan had hidden so well—he'd thought—under the floorboard beneath the stove. This time he knew better than to go to the police.

Alan set aside his pique and focused on his medical condition. There seemed to be no way to actually *remove* the dying Zeno face—it was too tightly integrated with his old tissues. And plastering a fresh new face over that was unlikely to heal the decay. His condition was akin to cancer. A challenge indeed.

His main hope was that he might reverse the necrosis of his Zeno face with an application of undifferentiated tissue, assuming the stuff were properly coached. The canny undifferentiated cells might migrate inward and replace the dying cells—like fresh players entering a game of rounders. Perhaps his face would take on the charming angularity of Driss's features.

But for now, Alan hesitated, unwilling to chance some brutal malfeasance on the part of the skug. In order to continue paying his rent, he found a part-time job in a repair shop run by an *opéra bouffe* fat man named Pierre Prudhomme. As if driven by theatrical clockwork, Pierre's treacly wife Marie flirted heavily with Alan, completely blind to his lack of interest.

"I hope I don't derange you," she might say in her odd English, meanwhile brushing her bosom and buttocks against Alan's muscular frame.

"I hope so too," Alan would reply, leaning over his bench of malfunctioning radios. "Dodgy work, this."

And then Marie would return to her kitchen, where she seemed to be continually boiling stews with garlic. To some extent the smell hid the advancing fetor of Alan's face.

Prudhomme took in all manner of appliances, but radios were Alan's specialty. He liked the heft of the electronic valves—the vacuum tubes. He was quite familiar with these devices from working on the Manchester computer.

Time passed, today and tomorrow, today and tomorrow. Alan's nerves were on edge from his continuing lack of success in programming the skug. In an impatient bid to halt the advances of the ruttish Marie Prudhomme, Alan told her that he was homosexual. It wasn't clear if she properly understood the word. She lifted her skirt and displayed her vulva. At this point Alan took to bringing the radios home to work on.

Fixing wireless sets in a rented room might be called a demotion from designing electro-mechanical circuits to search out astronomically large prime numbers. But Alan processed life's inputs as they came, scanning the days one by one. Given that universal computation lies within the humblest things, nothing was really more important than anything else.

In his notebooks, Alan worked out the precise changes that he needed to make to the skug's morphonic fields. Chemical tweaks weren't quite enough to get the job done. He was doing more than nudging an existing system into some predetermined state. He was, rather, driving the skug through a process of biological evolution— into the unknown.

Alan was struck by a sudden insight on how to speed things up. He'd use radio waves to reach into the lowest levels of the skug! Humming with excitement, he disassembled the two wireless sets on his workbench and repurposed the parts, creating an inductor-capacitor oscillator circuit with a feedback loop keyed to the inputs from a microphone that he'd abstracted from Prudhomme's cluttered work area. The radios' loudspeakers would come into play as well. Alan's resulting system was not unlike a voice-encryption system that he'd cobbled together after the War—it was a crude analog computer. They'd called it Delilah.

Confident that this new jury-rigged maze of electronic valves could open a channel into the putative mind of his little skug, Alan equipped his transmitter with a dish antenna. This item was fashioned from a hammered-tin tray that he'd picked up for a few francs at the market. A faded label on the tray's underside indicated that the metal had been salvaged from a gallon-sized olive oil can. Crimped and bent into a roughly parabolic shape, the antenna would focus radio waves upon the skug.

"Hullo," said Alan, beaming his output directly at the skug. "Cheers, bumpsadaisy, gadzooks." As he talked, he rotated a pair of control knobs, adjusting his broadcast's phase shift and frequency, searching out a resonant node, listening to a response from his radios' speakers.

And then, bravo! The crackle took on a filigreed quality. Delicately tweaking the knobs, Alan teased the sound towards a semblance of stuttering music. "I'm your mate," Alan intoned. "Goodie, hallelujah, prithee."

The skug-culture rippled and formed sprouts like snail-antennae, like the horns of tiny pink cows—dozens of tiny purple-tipped tendrils feeling the air. Guided by feedback, the musical tones from the radio sweetened into a warbling skirl, as of distant bagpipes heard across a heath.

"The horns of elfland," muttered Alan. "Sweetly blowing."

He set the microphone near the speaker, so as to intensify the feedback loop. The sounds thickened, as if groping their way towards speech.

Wondering if the skug were perhaps already talking, but in code, Alan set to work with pencil and paper, feeding test inputs into the skug and recording the responses. Unsatisfied with the results, he ran over to Prudhomme's shop and gathered in two more radios to cannibalize for his bio-analog computer.

Two days passed. It was the week before Christmas. Around suppertime, Driss appeared.

"Where's my money?" asked Turing sharply. "You stole it all. Ungrateful boy."

"I spent it," said Driss with a shrug. "I meant to buy a sack of flour and a goat to trade for a bride. But first I spent a little on a party. The stork waits a long time for the locusts to come. And then he eats. Dinner and kief and whores for me and two friends. It was wonderful."

"You spent it all? That's impossible. You saved no bride-money?"

"The police came. They beat me and took everything. They asked about you as well." Driss studied Turing. "Poor old man. Your disease grows."

"I'm close to a cure," Alan assured him. "Now apologize for your crime."

"The world is as Allah wills it. We do what is written. Do you have food?"

Alan offered Driss some of the dates and nuts that he'd been living on. And then he led Driss over to the corner of his stone room where the skug sat amid its chemicals and radio equipment. Ever since last night, Alan seemed to be hearing the skug directly in his mind rather than merely through his ears. And this wasn't impossible. The human brain was, after all, sensitive to electromagnetic fields.

"It has wrinkles now?" said Driss, leaning over the large, geometrically patterned bowl.

The culture of undifferentiated tissue was alive with slowly migrating ridges in the shapes of paired spirals, large and small. Nested scrolls. These were, Alan believed, the skug's biochemical memory storage system—brought into visibility by the electromagnetic stimulation of his radio waves. The culture had gone a bit luminous—the edges of the shifting furrows glowed in shades of curry and sand.

Responding to the harmonics of Driss's voice or perhaps to the spice of his breath, the culture rippled and formed a carpet of tiny snouts, writhing towards the dust motes that jittered in the slanting rays of the evening sun. A low jabber came from the radio, even more like a language than before.

"The skug *knows* you!" exclaimed Alan. "Think well of me, Driss. The skug needs to love me before it repairs my face. Let it feel your affection."

Driss held the bowl in both hands, crooning over it, intrigued by this new game. The kilogram of undifferentiated tissue rippled, as if enjoying the proximity of Driss's taut, tan face.

"Grow," said a wobbly thin voice from the radio speaker. Or that's what it sounded like.

Driss chanted back, and the phenomenon shifted to a higher level. The radio speakers themselves were silent, but Alan was hearing the skug's high little voice in his head. The skug was saying that it was hungry. It was sending out images and sensations to go with his verbalized thoughts—blobby geometric shapes and feelings of confinement. As the spell grew stronger, Alan seemed to sense Driss's thoughts as well.

Thoroughly aroused, Alan undid his pants and sidled closer to the youth—

A volley of knocks sounded. Alan and Driss stood in silence—the knocks turned to pounding. Alan's door shook in its frame, on the point of giving way.

"Calm yourself!" called Alan. He zipped up his fly and opened the door.

"I'm Pratt," said the man standing there. He looked athletic but soft, like a dissipated rugby player gone to seed. His skin was sandy with freckles, his eyes were colorless and bleached. He flashed what appeared to be a British passport, without actually opening it. "My credentials. I understand you're registered with the locals as Zeno Metakides." He cocked his head to one side, and peered past Alan at the lovely Driss.

"I no Brit," grated Alan, mounting his Greek accent. "You go."

Pratt sniffed the air. In his heightened mental state, Alan imagined that he could see the man stretch and flare his nostrils—cataloguing the odors like an inquisitive dog.

"You're in poor health, sir," said Pratt. "I'll make this short. I'm here to make you a proposition. It has to do with—Alan Turing?"

"No Turing," said Alan, feeling weak in the knees.

"Zeno Metakides was with Professor Turing when he died," said the rough intruder, wedging his foot into Alan's doorway. "Intriguing bit of data, isn't it." Pratt stared hard into Alan's eyes.

Silently Alan shook his head, wanting to refuse this entire conversation. It felt like being back at school, cornered by some bullying, unsavory older boy.

"The higher circles have a problem with the dental records. There was a secret autopsy, you understand. The face on the body—it was a flat tumor. A meat mask." Pratt's face split in a stark grin. "What say ye?"

"No know," said Alan hoarsely.

Pratt leaned closer, touching the tip of his tongue to his lips. "The higher circles are thinking Professor Turing is very clever. They tracked down his last paper. 'The Chemical Basis of Morphogenesis.' The boffins would be wanting some help from the man who wrote that. Especially if he'd perfected his techniques to the point of growing a face, eh? They'd offer Turing a clean slate, set him up in a lab, and pay him a good stipend."

"I see this Pratt with the police last night!" warned Driss. "He behave very raucous."

Alan tried again to close the door. Growing impatient, Pratt reached under his loose shirt, and produced a shiny revolver. "You help me, or I'll arrest you."

"Don't be an ass," burst out Alan, dropping his Greek accent. "You've no legal standing here."

"I can kill you right now," said Pratt, stolidly keeping the door half open. "Nobody cares. Either I kill you, or you accompany me to my employers. They're greatly chuffed on debriefing you—Professor Turing."

"Oh, very well, do come in," said Alan, moving to a new branch of his choice tree. His mind had cleared, he was thinking logically again. A conversation was really a kind of chess game. He stood to one side and made an inviting gesture.

As the sweaty Pratt pressed into Alan's room, Driss stepped forward and made a flipping gesture with the tessellated pottery bowl. The skug thinned itself, gliding through the air—and alit upon the intruder's face.

"Eat well, little brother!" sang Driss.

Pratt staggered and hoarsely bellowed, clutching his face with his free hand. Driss wrested the shiny revolver from Pratt's other hand and danced across the room, watching to see what would happen.

"Turing!" croaked Pratt, ineffectually clawing at the writhing leech of undifferentiated tissue. Tendrils of the pale yellow stuff were growing from his face onto his hands. "It's covering me, Alan! Oh god how it burns! Please don't—" Pratt broke off in a gurgle. The skug had occluded his mouth.

Moments later, Pratt's entire head was covered with the glowing slime, crazily bedecked with spinning saffron spirals. The undifferentiated tissue was spreading across Pratt's skin as rapidly as the water in an ocean wave. Pratt's flesh was an unexpectedly fecund incubation medium for the skug.

As a final act of aggression, Pratt lurched towards Alan—but it was no use. His soft legs buckled backward.

He fell onto his side, utterly helpless. With the last firings of his nervous system, he bucked his pelvis, finding a liquid, sexual rhythm.

Driss giggled, standing over the felled intruder, aping the motions of the man's hips. He waved Pratt's gun, making macho, overbearing gestures.

A glistening bubble formed where Pratt's mouth had been—and slowly the gas leaked from the bubble. Pratt's contours smoothed over, taking on the shape of a snail's body. He was a mound of muscle, his hide stippled with delicate grooves and filigrees, an archetypal mollusk, a giant slug. A pair of eyestalks poked forth from one end. The skug twitched, excreting the wadded rags of the agent's clothes and shoes.

Probing carefully with a table knife, Alan extracted Pratt's wallet from the damp bolus that had been the man's pants. The billfold held about two hundred pounds in twenty-pound notes. Wordlessly Driss stretched out his hand.

"You've stolen enough," Alan told the boy, handing over a single bill. "I'll need these funds. I think it's best I leave the country now. This may be the last time I see you."

He would have liked to hug Driss, but already the youth had turned away. And then he was gone, insouciant as a dream, insubstantial as a shadow.

On his own now, Alan studied the slug-shaped thing that Pratt had become. A skug. Sensing Alan's desire to communicate, the skug once again set a forest of tendrils to waving upon its surface. A chorus of tiny whistles emanated directly from the mound. Listening to the wavering rhythms, Alan again imagined thoughts taking shape in his sensitive mind. The skug was keying on Alan's brainwaves and his morphonic vibrations.

Mouth open in a lopsided grin, Alan did a slow-motion Indian dance around the skug, raising and lowering his legs, patting his hand against the mouth in a war whoop. He felt awed by the strange beauty of the room as sensed through the morphonic circuits of the human-sized skug. But he was careful to maintain a distance of at least two meters between himself and the beast.

Despite Alan's sense of mental contact, the skug didn't have much to say. Certainly it was grateful for the big meal. It seemed as if Pratt's personality was no more. Alan concluded that the skug's still rather rudimentary biocomputation was irreversible. For him to put a piece of the skug on his face at this time would be to suffer annihilation.

Further tweaks were needed, and there was no time like the present. Alan resolved to continue treating the man-sized slug with the healthful and educational rays that emanated from his radio circuitry. Aiming his disk antenna towards the mound, he cranked his transmitter to full power. He taped two disks of foil to his temples by way of giving the system an input device.

As night fell, Alan played telepathic tutor—thinking through the details of his epochal result on the unsolvability of the machine-halting problem, and mentally reviewing the partial differential equations that had appeared in his *Transactions of the Royal Society* paper on morphogenesis. Hopefully the arcane knowledge was hitting home.

Alan might have done more, but now the skug arose from its torpor. It tightened up its body and slid across the floor. A lisping chorus issued from the myriad of snouts upon the thing's surface—perhaps it was saying goodbye.

"Wait," called Alan, his voice harsh in the dark room. "I still need a sample of you for designing my cure. I still need to fix my face."

The skug extruded a meaty tentacle that waved in the air like a lariat. The base of the pseudopod pinched itself off. The liberated half-kilogram of skug-flesh dropped to the floor and formed itself into a compact sausage.

And now, flowing like lava, the bulk of the skug progressed onto Alan's balcony and began drizzling off the edge and into the filthy back alley below. Wanting to keep his distance but driven by curiosity, Alan went out on the balcony to watch.

The dripping skug-flesh was rising into a pair of stalagmites in the dim alley, two slanting limbs that joined at waist height tips and grew higher, slowly taking on the rudimentary form of—a naked man? A semblance of Pratt. The skug may have erased Pratt's personality, but, via the cells' genetic codes, it knew the man's shape. Jiggling at the waist, the skug-man waved a chubby arm and wobbled off.

Would Pratt's masters come looking for Alan again? It was past time to abandon this apartment. Using tongs, Alan maneuvered the remaining sausage of skug into a cloth sack. He knotted the top for safekeeping. Somehow he'd get a passport with a different name. But of course this all would be in vain if Alan couldn't heal his rotting Zeno face!

He bundled his radio equipment and a sampling of his home-brewed chemicals into a pillowcase. He cut his Zeno Metakides passport into pieces and burned them. He thumbed through the bills from Pratt's wallet.

He needed to fix his face, obtain a passport, and get aboard a ship. And for the short term, he needed a human ally. Someone dodgy, low-down, shameless. As if running on automatic, his mind turned to William Burroughs—the attractive oddball writer chap whom he'd met at the Café Central this summer. A Harvard man and a mor-phinist, Burroughs had a wonderfully jaundiced view of the world.

If anyone could sympathize with the surrealistic absur-dity of Alan's plight, Burroughs was the man. He'd seek out Burroughs, and something marvelous might result.

THREE
tangier routines

[These letters, and the ones reprinted in a later chapter, are said to have been written by the author William Burroughs. The letters in this chapter are variously addressed to Allen Ginsberg, Jack Kerouac, and to Burroughs's father, Mortimer. The letters date from December 22, 1954 to December 25, 1954; the first two are hand-written, and the final three are typed. Note that Burroughs uses a variety of spellings for "Tangier."]

To Allen Ginsberg
Tangiers, December 22, 1954

Dear Allen,

I been pounding my keys for a silo-fulla-queer-corn story this month . . . to the point where my typewriter seize up and croak. So I come at you direct through my quivering quill. Imagine a hack writer fixes with ink and he enters his personal Xanadu pleasure dream. But then the Great Publisher edit him outta Eden.

I've settled back into Tangier, they got everything I want. Each trip to the homeland drags me more. How did we ever let our cops get so out of hand?

If I ever started feeling sorry for my parents, I'd never stop. I'm a disappointment, but having gone thus far, I'd be a fool not to go further. My word hoard is compost to make lovely lilies bloom.

Too bad you and me didn't contact personal, but I couldn't make it to California with all them conditionals you were laying down. Why are you scared of mind-meld? Our buddy-buddy microscopic symbiotes do it alla time. Dysenteric amoeba Bil meets sexy-in-his-bristles paramecium Al, they rub pellicles—ah, the exquisite prickling, my dear—and *schlup*! My protoplasm is yours, old thing, the two of us conjugated into a snot-wad so cozy. I see me in a Mother Billie Hubbard ectoplasmic gown, tatting antimacassars to drape over that *harrumph* Golgi apparatus of yours.

"Just a routine," says Clem, standing bare-ass on the milking stool while the gray mare kicks screaming through the barn wall. "Sorry, old girl, I meant to use lard, not liniment."

The local worthies presented me with the key to the city—a nicely broken-in kief pipe stamped with arabesques. Ululating crowds of Spanish and Arab boys bore my pierced sedan chair though the streets. I'm installed in a Casbah seraglio, $23 per month, a clean plaster suite at Piet the Procurer's, with an extra bedroom and a balcony affording microscopic views of the souq.

Brilliant clear Mediterranean skies. I'm a myrmecophilous arthropod in the African anthill—a parasite/symbiote whom the Insect Trust tolerates on account of my tasty secretions.

I leech the sparkle of the sun from the waves, the Japanese outlines from the pines, the exquisite curls of steam from my cup of mint tea. These stolen vital forces are channeled into making me a citizen. Vote Insect Trust or die.

Kiki seems genuinely glad to have me back. What relief, to have a boy who cares for me. I've already given him some of my new dry goods. The pith helmet. The feather-duster. I'm this staghorn beetle lurches in, legs furiously milling, the ants swarming over me like slow brown liquid, flensing off my waxy build-up, a peaceful click of chitin from my sun-stunned den.

Eukodal back in stock at the farmacia. But dollies, M tubes and codeineetas still in short supply. Brian Howard is like to have burned down the place this summer. "I just don't *feel* right in the morning without I have my medication." Brian's gone home to the Riviera, buying a castle, my dear.

You gotta dig the Socco Chico when you and Jack come. The Little Market, the anything-goes interzone of Interzone. Maybe I write a magazine piece about it for *Reader's Digest*, you be my agent, and we retain intergalactic telepathy rights.

By way of Socco Chico color, I run into a Cambridge type at the Café Central last night, he say he used to be math professor. I know this character from the summer when he briefly orbited Brian Howard, but yesterday I hardly recognize him . . . his face all dead and gray. Talks like a full-on Brit boffin, with stutters and pauses like Morse code, and he shrieks key words for emphasis. "Ah, ah, ah, ah, ah, ah, ah, *Burroughs*!" Pathetically glad to talk to me, and I'm all ears, lonely Ruth amid the alien corn. He laughs inordinately at all my jokes.

After I stand him to a cognac and kief, he rush me outside to talk. This summer he called himself Zeno Metakides, but now he's shedding his character armor and says he's Alan Turing. As we walk, he's darting glances down the side streets in fear of, he says, a large man-eating slug that he's unleashed. And I'm digging the kicks, carrying a pipe and a bottle.

Turing say he's learning to program the processes of biological growth. His face, just as a for instance, is a fake, a meat disk that he cultured in a pan six months ago, and it's grown onto him like a lichen on a boulder. But it's rotting. While he's talking to me, he picks shreds of flesh off his cheeks,

Picking up on my visceral repulsion, the mad prof reassures me that his face-rot is akin to cancer and is therefore not a communicable disease. Says he's concocted a cure with the help of an angelic youth name of Driss. The cure itself have however gone metastatic on him and is the aforementioned slug that roams the Tangier alleys in search of boys.

But Turing's confident, and manful. He says that he's still quite fit, he goes running on the beach three miles every morning, trailing his flag of stink. It's a wonder the fellahs don't tear him apart bare-handed and roast him like a goat.

Turing has a third problem besides his rotting face and the escaped slug, viz. he is unable to return to his rooms because of some unspecified dust-up with sinister unknown agents who have penetrate the Zone. They are persecute him because he know too much. And then the evening breaks into blotches and streaks with a soundtrack of hysterical laughter. I leave Turing passed-out in an alley.

And now . . . oh the horror, Allen, the horror . . . I hear this character's voice in the street. Real-time message from the Burroughs memory unit: I offered to let the decaying math prof bunk in the spare room of this whorehouse suite where I hang my Writer shingle. He's coming up the stairs, his gray pieface aimed unerringly my way like a lamprey's toothed sucker disk.

Love,
Bill

To Jack Kerouac
Tangier, December 23, 1954

Dear Jack,

Jack, tell Maw Kerouac shut her crusty crack about me being a bad influence, of all the misguided abuse I ever stand still for. What you need is find you a decent woman, son. Marry the gash and tell your control-knob maw to wipe her *own* wrinkled ass alla time . . .

I'm practicing my winning sales pitch in case the writing game don't pan out and I am reduce to sell cooking gear like Neal. Ideas flap in my belfry like hairy jungle bats. Ah, don't turn away, my lad, I need you. Voice quavering from the darkness of Father Jack's confessional booth. I got confidential doings that I gotta spill or else I wig already. I buggered my typing machine, your grace. Commence Scrivener's Tale ...

Against my better judgment, I am temporarily lodging a shameless mooch who used to call himself Zeno Metakides, only he a Brit math prof in disguise. He was a code breaker in the War, and he say the UK authorities are out to liquidate him on account of he's queer. Or maybe it's KGB, CIA, or the Knights of Templar. His legit handle is Alan Turing, but that don't come from *my* primly pursed lips.

Turing is two years older than me, slim and fit, awkward and mechanical, with a robotic grating laugh I dig to provoke. Queer as a three-dollar bill. He has an endearingly bad attitude towards the powers that be. Dizzy with Wee Willy Lee's majoun-tea and sympathy, he's been pouring out his tormented heart. He's quite impressed with my pedigree, says he's had dealings with a giant artificial brain that use a magnetic memory unit from my grandpaw's Burroughs Corporation.

Turing says he's on the lam from England for some decryptional security breach. And now he's evacuated his Tangier squat to sponge off me. It's Strickly Platonic between Turing and me, at least for now, we're two logico-analytic brains in jars. But now and then I catch his brain stem schlupping across the counter and vining up my leg. There is, one allows, a certain mutual attraction.

But all this is nothing compared to the real-life routine my prof-in-residence is laying down . . . and this is the tasty part. Turing is wearing an artificial face, a meat-skin flesh mask that he pancaked on while escaping the MI5 Heat.

Says he grew the face from a sample taken from the tip of his deceased Greek lover's nose . . . that being the original Zeno Metakides. Seems the stumblebum Mystery Hit Squad poisoned Metakides instead of Turing. They used a pot of cyanide tea, how cozy. Whiz that Turing is, he quick grew copies of his phiz and of Zeno's dead pan, reassigned identities, and left the tarted corpse back home, escaping with the Metakides passport to . . . where else but old William Lee's trap in Tangier. It's like Allah sends him here special to be my gunjy muse.

Fed by Interzone's miasmas, his face-rot have turn galloping necrotic over the last six months, and now he's working on a cure. Yesterday all day he's tinkering with colored goo and radio tubes while I write out a new routine in longhand, reading some of the choicer bits to the wacky prof.

Passable fun, but around sunset, Turing drop all dignity and begin mewling and holding his face. "Oh how it aches, Bill, can you give me something for the pain?" My reputation have precede me.

I fix him with an ampule of Eukodal and I sit in my rocking chair watching the show. While Turing dreamy on the floor, this one particular centipede name of Akhmed crawl outta the crack by the toilet bowl to munch on his cheek. I break off a twitching bug-leg and smoke it in my tessellated pipe. And so we passed the night.

This morning Turing clarify that, the day before he moved in on me, the Interzone Heat have made him. He's rather shy on this point, but I gather he has offed a secret agent by feeding him to a shapeshifting slug that was originally to have been a special unguent for his horrible condition. And this thing is now on the loose.

Turing brought a pound of his alien mollusk's flesh in a cloth sack, and he set it out in a bowl on my counter. He call the thing a skug, he say it made of UDT or undifferentiated tissue, he talk to it like a pet. The UDT is subject to take root and grow anywhere. He very uneasy about using his skug before he's done doctoring the pet with, like, goat bile and radio waves, he brought a whole mad-scientist lab along.

Meanwhile, every time I turn around, Turing want more medicine. His horrible condition is make him a junk hog in record time. And this afternoon while I step out to fetch my mail, the situation reach the inevitable crisis.

As fate wills it, I was detain from my rapid return on account of three fellahs are immolating some kind of mutant monster in the lane that leads into my naberhood.

"This clumsy thing brings us shame," a boy explain, with weirdly fluid gestures of his arms—like maybe he a mollusk too.

Makes me feel so hot and nasty to see the flames lick across the rival mutant they've laid low, half-man/half-slug. The boys are goosing each other, laughing like hyenas, bending their faces into impossible grins.

When I finally sashay home, I find all my ampules gone, and my guest nodded out on the shitter floor. In a spasm of disgust I am compelled to remove his moribund facial tissues, using my scalpel-sharp shiv to sever the cap-illary-rich roots.

Liquidated Zeno's face in the bidet, I did, doused it in nitric acid. Hideous pungent stench. An Arab gendarme come pounding on my door, I yell that I'm making a pork couscous, and can I borrow a pint of piss. And then Turing arises from the Land of Nod and runs out to the balcony screaming like lobster lost his shell, blending his voice with the muezzin in the minaret across the way.

The stub of Turing's original face is red and raw like dysenteric buttocks. Taking pity, I squirt on some Vaseline and give him the last of my M tabs. He's asleep on the couch now.

I'm having a pipe, watching the skug-thing twitch on the counter. Maybe if I dip a dab onto my spine I sprout a lemur tail.

As ever,
Bill

To Jack Kerouac
Tangers, December 24, 1954

Dear Jack,

Turing fixed my typewriter, so now it's back to my novel, if it is a novel. *Interzone*. Maybe I just interleave the carbons of my letters with you-are-there descriptions

of my innaresting daily routines. "I live my art," says the
Author, smoothing his eyebrow with buffed-nail pinkie.
"Don't you?" What I need is a television camera broad-
casting me all day long. "You got an audience of like two,
Boss. A hebephrenic and a blind leper."

We find our protagonist in his louche Casbah suite . . .
the plot as thick as the goat offal simmering on his alcohol stove. Cook it up and shoot it, amigo.

Continuity note: House-guest Alan Turing was hogging
my junk to the point where I find my day's box of Eukodal
ampules empty before the Hour of Prayer. So I shave off
the dying Zeno face that was paining him. Made a man of
him, I did, only he look like lunch counter hamburger meat.
He planning to patch himself with questionable slime that
he call his pet skug. A larger version of his skug have eat a
secret agent and was burned by Arabs in the street.

This afternoon, while Turing fiddle-fucks with his
radio tubes and my broken typewriter, I watch a buzzard
circling the fellahin sky. I am one with the bird, taking in
the fragrant cedar of the souq braziers, the kief pipes' glad
exhalations, the drying jissom on pearly bellies, the slow
rotting of the black meat, and the persistent pong of the
parasitic Zeno Nu-Face that I charred with acid in my
bidet. Flashback of me stirring clotted filaments with my
double-jointed three-foot switch-blade.

Clickity-clack. Happy keys on my typewriter. I dance
the alphabet while my flayed-face professor putters at my
kitchen counter, less jolly than before. He plan to change
his looks yet again, and then to obtain a fresh passport—
not easy just now as the heat have close down the Inter-

zone paperhangers on account of a rogue con-man have pass himself off as the Norwegian consul and infect half of Embassy Row with coal-gas addiction which result in they metamorphose into scaly manila folders that smell of *lutefisk.*

"I am my papers."

Turing's company wears thin. In reaction, I'm compulsively pitching comedy routines at him, just to hear him laugh—a sound like a starter-motor on a cold morn.

I can't ascertain if he has hard feelings over my emergency surgery on him, his raw-meat phiz being somewhat hard to read. He still poking at his skug of undifferentiated tissue. He say he eventually need to let it grow all over his head for making a new face. But first he want to make it smarter.

Meanwhile he giving me the horrors with his boffin etiquette. "I say, Burroughs, could you possibly procure a pint of ammonia?"

He's sent me out to the farmacia twice today for like streptococcal infusion and bovine growth hormone, the latter come in glass icicle tubes that Turing crack open to drip yellow glow-juice into his little reagent vat . . . formerly my cooking-pan and now destined, I shouldn't wonder, for the Royal British Museum of the History of Bio-Computational Science.

Drip, stir, measure, mix, low mutter, squeak of pencil on paper . . . last night Turing sneak out and steal two car batteries he use to power a mad-scientist all-fluid self-generating magic-lantern show . . . he not care about making me felony burglary accessory after the fact.

The batteries connect to colored juice between two sheets of glass he cut out of my window. Seems like he's hand-crafted some kind of optical display, it's hooked into his radio tubes to make a show for his skug thing that sits on a cushion like a hairless cat—watching. Horribly the skug have grown a fuzz of snail-antennae, with a tiny black eyeball atop each wobbly stalk.

I fix M and settle in with the skug to watch Turing's show this morning for a few hours . . . jaguar yage visions, subdimensional towers, sea cucumbers of the hollow earth, branching tentacles of the Crooked Beetle, and then Joan's annulled face transitioning through the days and months of decomposition. Turing has the skug mirroring these mind movies on its own skin. He has probes all over it, he at his controls, watching me from the corner of his eye, his own raw face unreadable.

Despite all recent reverses, Turing remain manfully eager to emigrate to Amerika and set to work building morphogenetic slime processors for the Fatherland.

One thing Turing say this afternoon is very disturb me: "Tomorrow for Christmas, I want to be you." He say this with his voice flat and wistful like a prairie orphan, his teeth very prominent in his ruined face.

At this point, I'd gladly throw my boy Kiki off the sled and into Turing's slavering jaws, but Kiki don't come around no more. My lodger the Mathematical Brain is give everyone the creeps.

"Sorry to be a bother, Burroughs, but could you pop out for some turmeric and cayenne pepper? My display needs more *hues*."

Like I owe him endless favors. Just because I carved off his nasty rotting face. Classic mooch psychology.

I'm scared of him, Brother Jack.

As ever,
Bill

To Allen Ginsberg, Letter A
Tanger, December 25, 1954
Letter A

My original plan today: take a break from junk so's I can get my sex up . . . hit the Socco Chico and gift myself a Christmas boy . . . or eat majoun and be a centipede that wriggle along the endless maze of Tanger sewer pipes inspecting cheeks.

But I got this like house guest Alan Turing who spring a surprise routine of his own. He was working all night, and when I wake up this morn, there's no gay, bright presents . . . instead I see Turing's become a human-sized slug of undifferentiated tissue. What I'd call a *skugger*. The prof's gone viral on my ass.

He slime up onto the wall and across the ceiling, he move very fast for a mollusk, like a speeded up movie, *schluppp*, he drop down and assimilate me right in my bed. Now I'm a skugger too. Our skins quilt themselves together . . . all is one . . . everything is merged inside. We're filled with white light ecstasy, our four tranced eyes stare up like shiny puddles. Thinking fast.

Sexy the way our livers slide across each other, tasty how our bones bump the grind. With the orgone pleasure rush comes a nausea like I never feel it before, my trillions of cells in revolt against Turing's violation of the immune system code . . .

Feeling overly full, your humble correspondent lumbered down the stairs to his filth-strewn back yard and took a seventy kilogram dump . . . eliminating redundant units like a corporation resizing herself after a handsome acquisition. Mercy me, but I was shivers all over when I passed that gentleman's skull. Can't say as I actually looked back at what I crapped out, just scuffed some dust over the remains like a dog does, then hurried back inside for a festive refreshment—candied dates and hot black tea. For the first time in years, I'm feeling no craving for junk, booze or Miss Green.

I sat down at my well-oiled typewriter and began transmitting you this latest news . . . and then came the confrontation that every man fears and longs for the most.

The shambling thump of . . . something Burroughsian . . . huffing up the sun-sharpened stairs to my door, my fellow skugger dragging himself towards me like a canvas sack of black meat.

Taking a jiu-jitsu stance, I open my door to find . . . a lean, weathered man with thin lips and a sly smile, balding, horsy jaw, narrow nose, keen eyes, he's really quite dazzling this fellow . . . I might as well be looking into a mirror. This weasel Turing have absorb my chromosomes so he can lift my papers. Call him Alan-William Turing-Burroughs now.

The obvious question: do we make fucky-fuck? Fie! I'm not my type, dear. Instead we rustle up a brace of boys in the Socco Chico—my Kiki, and Alan's erstwhile soul-mate Driss. The big surprise is that the boys are already by way of being skuggers too. The transformation has had a bad effect on them, they seem a listless, limp. But once Turing lay on his hands and flow in his latest skuggy program tweaks, they peppy.

So we four while away a lovely Christmas afternoon in my digs, eating couscous and nibbling sweetmeats between tastes of the Forbidden Fruit, sometimes melting into a mound. Even when we're not in physical touch, we're reading each others' feelings and thoughts. It's richer than what I'd expected from telepathy—I call it *teep*.

Such expansiveness today, such laughter and joy . . . *luxe, calme et volupté*. And Turing—how rare to share the company of a truly intelligent and utterly subversive man. An oasis in the long caravan of life.

But then our hired boys leave, the sweets are all eaten up, and my opportunistic double want to sit in my rocker and use my typewriter even though I am still in mid-stream on this letter.

Over my shoulder, even now as I type, I tell him he's disloyal as a sheep-killing dog, and he think I'm joking. Even under the ameliorating influence of my genes, his laugh still very ugly and he enjoy to talk about like Diophantine equations yet. I have this suppurating anxiety he gonna burst open any second and release uncountable numbers of skug larvae to recruit the local citizenry *en masse*.

So I pull my shiv on him and explain it best he leave town tonight on the ferry to Spain. I'm giving him my passport and a letter of reference . . . just for the pleasure of seeing his questionable ass go out my door before he get me exiled from my Land of Nod. Still some details to wrap up . . . and then for The Novel. *Interzone.*

Love,
Bill

To Mortimer Burroughs
Tangier, Christmas Day, 1954

Dear Father,

The man who bears this letter and my passport has taken on my form as a way to avoid unjust persecutions of the sort that I myself am subject to. I ask you to assist him as much as you can.

He is a pleasant gentlemen of sober habits and considerable scientific skill. He hopes to find work in some technical field. I realize that you've long since sold your stock in the Burroughs Corporation, but perhaps you still have some contacts among the higher-ups. He feels he would do very well in a research lab.

I won't try to explain how it is that he took on my appearance. Suffice it say that the interaction had no bad effects on me . . . far from it, I feel livelier than usual, and I am full of energy for my next book.

Rest assured that I remain your true son Billy, and that I am indeed still in Tangier. I can arrange a confirming telephone call through the US Legation if you like. By no means should you discontinue my monthly payments. Love to Mother, and Merry Christmas to you both.

Billy

FOUR

aboard the phos

Alan left Burroughs's apartment with empty hands and a happy head. He patted his face, savoring its firm, healthy contours. The cure had worked. And it was still Christmas Day—although you'd never know it from these evening-shadowed Moslem streets.

He'd been so anxious about allowing the skug onto his body this morning that he'd taken a shot of Eukodal first. So his memories of the transformations had a hallucinated, fun-house quality. The skug had infected first Alan and then, at Alan's urging, Burroughs—with no harm done.

Alan chuckled to himself in the street, recalling Burroughs's whinnying scream when he'd dropped onto him from the ceiling. What a lark. And then he and Bill had melted together—intricate, esoteric, electric. They'd stumbled outside, divided in two, and regained human form, more or less their same selves, but both of them looking like Bill.

It was a surprise that Driss and Kiki were already skuggers as well. Evidently the preliminary tweaks that Alan had done on the Pratt zombie had brought the thing's biocomputations into a reversible mode—and thus the new converts hadn't had their personalities erased. But certainly the boys' affect had improved once they'd merged with Alan this afternoon. Alan's intricate feedback techniques had evolved his skugly processes to a high degree of elegance. And there was more to be done, much more. Alan's body was his laboratory now.

As he strode smiling down the street towards the port, he wondered how it would feel to break into run. But he didn't want to risk extra attention.

He now forgave Driss's drive to amass money by any means. But even though Driss was a skugger, it was still conceivable that he might shop Alan to the British agents. All the more reason to leave Tangier right away. This routine was done.

Alan would miss Burroughs, but he was keen indeed to exit this pest hole before some new leering jack-in-the-box popped up. He still had most of the money he'd gotten from Pratt, plus Burroughs's passport, not to mention a letter of introduction to Burroughs's father. Perhaps he'd be safe from the Queen's government in America.

Alan fully realized that both he and Burroughs were something slightly other than human now. The symbiotic skugs had altered them for good. Nearly all of the time he felt preternaturally alert.

Driss and Kiki said there were dozens or even hundreds more skuggers in the Casbah now—radiating out from Pratt. The Pratt skugger had been the only mindless one, and the boys had incinerated him as a matter of good public relations. In any case, Driss had said the local police were impounding whatever skuggers they could capture. Driss and Kiki were being very careful. Everything was in a state of change.

"Far out," said Alan to himself, drawing on Burroughs's subcultural vocabulary, and even managing to produce something like the man's dry Missouri accent. "Wild kicks."

Some of Burroughs's memories seemed to have migrated into Alan's retrofitted frame, perhaps at the cellular level. Sloping through the bustling last few streets by the pier, he even found himself wondering whether he ought to bring along some Eukodal for the trip. But no, no, this was an alien, Burroughsian thought procedure. Terminate it.

Alan took the short ferry ride across the strait that divided North Africa from Spain. As he debarked, he had a bad moment—he thought he saw a severed human hand scurrying down the ferry's gangplank behind him. It was up on its fingers. Alan looked away, looked back, and the apparition had either vanished or had lost itself in the clamorous crowd.

From the ferry port, Alan rode a smelly omnibus to Gibraltar, tormented by fantasies of something creeping under his seat to grab his ankles. He arrived in the colonial port town after midnight in a state of extreme nervousness and exhaustion. He got the night clerk's permission to sleep on a bench in the bus station, grateful to have his feet off the floor. Before closing his eyes he privily grew a pouch in his belly, tucked in his cash and papers, then sealed the pouch shut.

All night he dreamed of tunnels—and when he woke it occurred to him that these branching, narrowing passages had been his veins, arteries and capillaries. The skug's rudimentary mind was familiarizing itself with his flesh. It was as if Alan now had two souls.

Alan worried that he might have lost his shape overnight—that is, he might be looking more like Alan Turing than like William Burroughs. Still lying on the bench, he focused inwards upon his musculature, locking himself into the proper form. It was amazing to have such control over one's body.

An Arab boy began vigorously shaking Alan's foot. No doubt the urchin had searched his pockets for cash while he was sleeping. Alan was glad for the human attention, and glad for his hidden kangaroo pouch.

"Take to me to the harbor, and I'll tip you," Alan told the lad, sitting up. "You speak English, yes?"

"Breakfast first?" said the boy, rapidly miming an eating gesture.

"And then you'll find me an outbound ship for America," said Alan agreeably.

Alan ordered some raisin buns and white coffee from the bus station canteen. A low-class Englishwoman was at the counter, a ruddy virago with a hoarse voice like a jeering crowd. She cocked her head to watch as Alan reached under his shirt for some money—he only hoped she couldn't see his fingers sliding into his flesh. It was unsettling to be in an outpost of the Queen's empire.

Outside, the sun shone, with people taking walks and visiting each other, many of them carrying gifts. It was the second day of Christmas, what the English call Boxing Day. The sphinx-like Gibraltar Rock rose over the town, and the wild local apes scrounged garbage in alleys, chattering and baring their teeth.

A man in a black suit had collapsed in one of these cul-de-sacs. A few locals were leaning over him. The man looked floppy, practically boneless. For whatever reason, the skug within Alan wanted him to stop and help the fellow. But he had no time. The young guide was running ahead, leading the way to the steamers' docks.

In short order the boy had brought Alan to the gang-plank of a Portuguese liner, claimed his tip and hurried on his way.

Alan studied his really rather slender sheaf of bills, totting up his holdings.

"Welcome aboard," said a man loitering near the gang-plank, a roughly dressed fellow with a blue chin. "You going where, *Senhor*? We have one free cabin. Very commodious. Top side."

"I'm, ah, looking for passage to America," said Alan.

"We gladly take you," said the man, smoothly whirling his hand. "I am the ship's purser. She is the *Santa Maria*, top luxury, with ten ports of call, including Canary Islands and Venezuela."

"And how much to the United States?"

The man named a figure more than triple what Alan had on hand. Reading Alan's expression, the purser gestured the more expansively. "You pay me now for reserve, we bill the balance. Is no problems. I welcome you aboard. We go fetch luggage, yes?"

"I—I'd prefer something simpler," said Alan, uneasily glancing along the wharves that dwindled into the distance like an exercise in perspective. He wondered if this man really *was* the ship's purser. "Is there a chance of finding a freighter?"

"You want to travel like a pig iron, like a bale of ox-hide, like a sack of cement?" said the blue-chinned man. "No eat lobster, no dance big band?" He shrugged and pointed to the farthest end of the wharves, towards some smudgy ships like grains of rice. "You go down there, *Senhor*. A Greek ship called *Phos*."

"Thank you."

The apron of the wharves was cobbled and sunny. Nobody seemed to be watching Alan, so he went ahead and ran a mile to the end, unlimbering his Burroughs-shaped limbs, shaking out the kinks, reinvigorating his lungs with the cool, salty air.

While he ran, he imagined that his inner skug was conversing with him, not so much in words, but rather with flashes of color in his eyes, hissing sounds in his ears, twinges in his stomach and a tingling on his skin. Was the parasite urging Alan to spread the contagion? Or were these thoughts Alan's alone?

"We'll work all this out once I've got my cabin," said Alan, speaking aloud. "But don't expect me to go *inoculating* strangers." No answer. Perhaps he was going insane.

Looking at the less savory piers near the wharf's end, Alan spotted a Greek-flagged freighter whose name was *ΦΩΣ*, which he knew from his classics studies to be pronounced *Phos* and to mean *light*. This was the freighter that the Portuguese man had recommended. She was a lean, narrow ship, built for speed.

Her deck bristled with cranes, all quite still. Alan sidled up the companionway and found a solitary, dissipated man sitting on a chair drinking coffee. His feet propped on the ship's railing.

Alan hazarded a hello.

"Yeah, I speak English," said the man in a New York accent. "Merry fuckin' Xmas. What's on your mind, man?"

"I was wondering if I might book passage," said Alan. "To America."

"Find a bunk and hunker down," said the stranger. He had curly dark hair and brown eyes. "Squat and gobble. It's real slack on the *Phos*. Yesterday Captain Eugenio shit on the deck and wiped his butt with the flag. Now he's in town chasing whores."

"I wonder about the schedule and the rates," said Alan, not caring for the man's vulgar tone. "I'm William Burroughs, by the way."

"Vassar Lafia," said the stranger, lighting a hand-rolled cigarette that gave off the smell of kief. His unshaven face was oily in the sun. He cocked his head. "I could swear I've seen you before."

"I've a poor memory for recent months," said Turing. "I've been in the wars, rather. But I'm back in an approximate state of health. What can you tell me about this ship?"

"She's a tramp freighter," said Lafia. "A free agent with no timetable. She snags her cargoes as she goes along. Last I heard, the captain is planning to pick up wine in

Madeira, steam flat-out for Miami, then swing down to Havana for some cigars. We're loaded with olive oil and the man says feta cheese." He winked at Turing. "I've got a tramp cargo of my own. Socko from Morocco in the heels of my shoes. And don't look inside my toothpaste tube." Lafia paused, studying Alan again. "I've got it. You were in the Café Central. You weren't talking like a limey then. About four months ago?"

"I've been lodging in Tangier, yes," said Alan, not wavering from his usual accent. "So it's possible our paths crossed. But if you don't mind, I'd rather not delve into my private affairs."

"Visions of the past," said Lafia, his lips spreading in a grin. "Through the gem-encrusted glass. This August? You said we were dump dogs on a magic carpet—you wave it, Bill? Oh, never mind. I won't pry. We'll light off new bombs. And, hey, here comes Captain Eugenios after all. He'll book you onboard. Lunch is at one o'clock, most days, if the cook's in shape. Wiggy to have you here, man!"

The black-bearded captain was a hearty fellow with a short attention span. He offered Alan a price of a passage to Miami that was more than reasonable, leaving Alan with forty-odd pounds to spare. And then the captain disappeared for a nap. Alan retired to his own private cabin as well, number 17, a windowless steel cell below decks. The room had a sink and a mirror, a door that Alan could lock. A shared toilet and shower lay further down the passageway.

Alan lay on his bunk for awhile, sorting out his memories of Christmas Day. The skug had crawled onto him and melted into his flesh. It had been Alan's own idea to convert Burroughs. It wasn't yet clear to Alan if the skug had a true mind of its own. Perhaps he had been reading too much into the twitches and cilia of his tissue culture. He felt he was still his own man.

But, yes, his conjugation with the skug had changed him. His body was more responsive, more fluid than ever before. Perhaps this was how it felt to be a mollusk. Remembering a bit more from yesterday's hallucinatory segues, Alan stared at his hand and willed it to change shape.

With a slight sinking of his stomach, he saw his fingers warp and sag like melting wax. Focusing his full attention into his hand, Alan formed it into—oh, why not a duck's head, a shape fit for casting candle-shadows on the wall.

The hand drooped, the fingers fused, and—the tip became a shiny yellow beak.

"Quack," murmured Alan, opening and closing the beak. "Quack, quack, quack. Now resume being my hand."

His fingers returned to normal, leaving a tingling sensation in the muscles and the skin. He recalled what his Mum used to say when she'd find him making grimaces into the looking-glass. *What if you stayed that way?*

Alan went back on deck. There was no sign of a lunch, not that he was sure where to look for it. Everyone seemed to be napping or in town. And so he roamed the ship alone over the next hour or two—studying the intricacies of the cargo hoists, the radio antennas, and the smokestacks. He had the run of the *Phos*. He even made his way below decks and examined the engines.

It soothed Alan to analyze the workings of the ship's cranes, her communication channels, and her power systems. How clear and logical these devices were compared to the oozy growths of biology—or to the frantic vacillations of the human soul.

Quite aside from any issues involving the skug, Alan was a little concerned about the potential chain of cause and effect running from his street-urchin guide through that so-called Portuguese purser to Alan's booking passage on the *Phos*. Could this be an intricate trap? And what was the nature of Vassar Lafia's prior association with William Burroughs? Rummaging around in Burroughs's vague and partial memories, Alan could find no clues.

In any case, he couldn't face the tension of remaining in the Old World any longer. He'd take his chances with the *Phos*, and once he was in America, then—well, that was something else to worry about.

While Alan fretted and paced, the passengers and crew straggled in—perhaps thirty people in all. Some of the sailors were quite luscious, with dark eyes in olive faces and nicely muscled arms. The passengers were mostly forgettable: commercial travelers, neurasthenic students, retired couples. A mother and daughter pair were noticeable—plump and a bit comical, with identically protruding lips. The mother was pink and blonde, the daughter a bit darker, with a bob of auburn hair.

At the very last minute one more passenger appeared, a tall, pale-faced young American rushing along the wharf, sweaty in a tie and ill-fitting dark suit, his teeth bared with effort, his hair cropped down in a burr. Was that the man whom Alan had seen lying in the alley? He had a curious, undulating gait. Alan overheard the fellow's name as he booked a passage to Miami: Ned Strunk. Spotting Alan, Strunk gave him a hungry, blank-faced stare, and Alan turned away, repelled.

With hoarse, full-throated blasts from her steam-powered hooter, the *Phos* churned out through the Straits of Gibraltar and into open sea. Alan's heart rose to see the land slide away. He was in every sense a new man. Unimaginable adventures lay ahead.

As dusk fell, the dinner bell rang.

"Right this way, Bill," said Vassar Lafia, ambling by on the deck, eyes red. "Down the hatch." He led Alan to a low-ceilinged mess-room where the dozen or so passengers took their seats with the captain and three lower-ranking officers.

"Katje," said Lafia with an exaggerated yet courtly bow to the younger of the two women whom Alan had noticed. Even though her figure was so emphatic, Katje was dressed in a demure blue frock. "And Frau Pelikaan," continued Lafia, addressing the older woman at Katje's side. "May we join you? This is my old friend William Burroughs. Scion of a wealthy family and a sought-after tale-spinner. Bill, meet Katje and Frau Pelikaan from Brussels. They're headed for—was it Lake Okeechobee?"

"You will behave tonight, won't you, Vassar?" said Katje. She had a throaty Lowlands accent.

"Yesterday makes nothing," said Frau Pelikaan. "With so few passengers, we shouldn't hold the grudge. Sit, sit.

What does your family do, Mr. Burroughs?" She peered at him near-sightedly, her soft face friendly.

Alan groped for the Burroughs's memories—it was like catching carp in a muddy pond. "Business machines," he announced as he took a chair. "Originally, that is. And now they run a gift shop in, ah, Palm Beach."

"We're in sugar," said Frau Pelikaan. "My husband has an enormous plantation in Florida. Katje and I have been back to Brussels to renew our wardrobes."

"You two look very top-shelf," said Vassar. "Like stained-glass butterflies."

Frau Pelikaan looked down in a gesture of modesty, tripling her chin. And then she threw back her head and laughed. "Let's order champagne. Really, it's still Christmas."

"Apple cider for me," said Alan. Hosting a skug had rather put him off spirits.

The portholes showed the dark and moonlit winter sea, its swells as smooth as oil. The *Phos* was knifing through the waters at a remarkable speed. Candles lit the tables, and the steward served a very nice turkey velouté in pastry shells. Alan's apple cider went down well. The others started on a second bottle of wine.

Alan was glad to note that the disturbing Ned Strunk was off at the other end of the room, sitting with a Norwegian couple and a Spanish businessman. Strunk's face was empty, his long arms were like vines.

"Not bad for leftovers," Vassar said, as he spooned the last of his sauce off his plate. "You missed the rubber gut eat-orgy yesterday, Bill."

"I do hope they have more of that *bûche de Noël* cake," put in Frau Pelikaan.

"Are you single, Mr. Burroughs?" asked Katje.

"Indeed," said Alan. "A confirmed bachelor by now."

"Bill here was running wild when I met him in Tangier," volunteered Vassar, who now seemed quite drunk. Evidently he'd prepped himself before the meal. "Let me tell you girls about it."

"Are you sure this—" began Alan, but Lafia was not to be stopped. Gesturing for a third bottle, he leaned back in his chair, and began his narration.

"Bill here may not remember this tale, but I'll unspool it just the same. You ever heard of a magic carpet ride? There's a reason they talk about that in this part of the world. Those oriental carpets are windows, you might say, and travel devices as well. Bill and I rode a carpet to inner outer space. We started out at the Café Central. There's a bunch of drifters, con-men, expats, and degenerates that hang there—it's a party every day. I'd just come in from Gibraltar, and I found Bill here loading up a hookah with kief. The guy next to him, a chump name of Brian Howard, had tossed in a ball of opium. The tears of the poppy. Magic carpet fuel. I'm a student of the *Thousand And One Nights*."

Vassar's cheerful, reckless voice was filling the room. The subtle motions of Ned Strunk's head indicated that he was listening to every word. At one level, Alan was in fact delighted to see Vassar shocking the stuffy crowd. But, given Alan's peculiar circumstances, it seemed prudent to stem the flow. "Vassar, I'd really rather that you—"

"So Bill and me are blasting on the happy hookah, and suddenly there's this wild stink and I'm so wasted I think maybe I've crapped my pants," boomed Vassar. "But it's just a mangy dog has come in and is rolling on his back on the carpet by our table. Old cur's got his legs spread, wanting a friendly rub. And then Burroughs here gets down on all fours and starts sniffing the dog's dick! I nudge Bill with my foot, I'm like, 'Don't do that, man, they'll eighty-six us,' and Bill yelps back, 'We're dump dogs on a magic carpet! Come down here and *ride*!' You don't remember any of this at all, do you, Bill?"

Turing shook his head, fighting back a bark of laughter. He'd always found it amusing when someone's behavior was utterly beyond the pale.

"Now, really," interrupted Katje, her cheeks gone red. "These are no table topics."

"Well, it wasn't *me* did that to the pooch," said Vassar with mock primness. "It was Bill. I pulled him off the dog, moved the hookah down to the carpet next to him, and we sailed that funky rug around the Moon and Saturn too. When I came to, I was in Marrakesh. Mislaid Bill along the way." Vassar gestured extravagantly with his dripping spoon, mapping out the course of his imagined trip. "But let's turn to a more properly touristic topic. Did you ladies know we'll be in Madeira tomorrow night? We're allowed to go ashore for the evening. Charming town, Funchal, I passed through it this summer on my way out from America. I noticed a deluxe restaurant right by the docks there. *O Portao*. They say the scabbard fish is a pluperfect delight. Bill and I'd be happy to escort you there."

"I don't believe so," said Frau Pelikaan. "Maybe we see each other across the room and wave hello."

"Did I offend you just now?" pressed Vassar. "Katje, let me talk this over with you on the deck. We'll take a stroll in the moonlight."

"I have to wash my dress," said Katje, getting to her feet. Vassar had managed to flick several drops of velouté sauce onto her bodice.

"Can't we let the maid take care of that?" whispered Frau Pelikaan. "We haven't had dessert."

"Stay if you like, mother. I'll see you in the room."

"Oh, very well, I'll come with you. I want to be sure you hang the dress outside to dry. Our suite is so tiny." With curt nods at Vassar and Alan the women were off.

Vassar quickly ordered a brandy for him and a coffee for Alan. "This meal goes onto Frau Pelikaan's account. I charge the meals to my tablemates and write on a fat tip. The steward loves me."

"I must confess that it gives me an agreeable sense of irresponsibility to be in consort with you," said Alan. "You remind me of a school friend who was expelled for ragging the masters. But that story about the dog . . ."

"Could be I pumped it up," said Vassar, favoring him with a friendly smile. "Just to make them squirm. It was my *opinion* that you were sniffing the dog's dick, but it could have been you were merely lying on the floor. Seems like you've cleaned up since then."

"One could say that," said Alan. "This has been a very peculiar six months. And, as I say, I don't really mind your outrageous lines of talk. They hearten me. The social order is, after all, oppressive and absurd. So why not cock a snook?" Vassar seemed to have no idea that this meant to thumb one's nose, so Alan acted out the gesture, cheerfully waggling his fingers. Right about then, he realized that he could diddle his body's biochemistry so as to feel some of the same intoxication that Vassar felt. And this he did.

"Cock a snook," echoed Vassar, returning the salute. "It's what I do, yeah. I'm always on the edge of things. Grew up in Jersey City, started work on the docks during high-school, latched onto a mob widow and drove her to Miami. Switched to a music teacher down there, then broke off on my own. I see things my own way."

"How come you're called Vassar?" asked Alan, almost flirtatiously. "Isn't that a name of a woman's college?"

"My Mom's bright idea," said Vassar with a short laugh. "Really we're from Spanish Jewish stock, not that I go pushing that line in Morocco. Mom wanted to lay some class on me, so she picked that name Vassar. She knew it was upper crust."

Alan felt more and more attracted to this man. On a sudden impulse, he verbalized the emotion.

"I could fall in love with you, Vassar."

"Thanks, Bill, very kind of you to say that," replied Vassar, patting Alan's hand. "But I like my chances with that Belgian chick. Those beaky lips. Peck, peck! Maybe I could bring *Vrouw Pelikaan* into the mix. Squaaawk! I'm overdue for some action."

"I'm available," said Alan, who'd never been shy about pressing for sexual favors. But Vassar gave no answer to that. Mildly abashed, Alan made his way alone to his room.

His thoughts kept circling back to Katje Pelikaan's dress. Presumably it was drying unguarded in the night. Alan could steal it and wear it—and reshape himself into a woman! Why not?

Alan had already gone partway down that road two years ago. After he'd been convicted of having sex with a man, the Crown had sentenced him to their notion of biocomputational tweaking—injecting him with estrogens, supposedly to destroy his libido.

But that hadn't been enough for them. This summer the Queen's minions had sent a crew around to murder Alan with cyanide in his tea. He was well outside the tribe now, free to act according to his own lights.

Getting back to the subject of becoming a woman, Alan recalled that, while he'd been on estrogen, his skin had smoothed, and he'd begun to grow breasts. It hadn't been entirely disagreeable. He'd felt, at times, a rare inner peace. Now that he had the power of the skug within him, why not finish the job—and bed Vassar Lafia?

A big decision. But for starters, all he needed to do was to steal the dress.

FIVE
shapeshifter

A little unsteady on the rolling deck, Alan made his way to the clothesline that the passengers shared. There was Katje's gown, swaying gracefully in the night. Quickly Alan folded the garment into a bundle, tucked it under his arm and turned to start back towards his room.

"Hey, there. I've been wanting to introduce myself. I'm Ned Strunk."

Blast and damn. This, this—*yahoo* was standing much closer than Alan might have expected. He had some regional American accent. From the south? He'd popped out of the nearby passengers' lounge. And now he was intent on the absurd and unsanitary custom of shaking hands. Alan had to shift the blue dress from beneath his arm, with Strunk blankly gawping at him.

"Yes, I'm William Burroughs," said Alan, grasping Strunk's bony hand. "And I bid you good night."

"You're talking kind of funny." Strunk's eyes were like holes in his haunted face. "If you're supposed to be American."

"I'm an American who's lived overseas for much of his life," said Alan, moving away. "Not to be rude, but it's been a long day, and my head's like a wedge of cheese. Let's enlarge our acquaintanceship at a more propitious time, shall we? *Cheerio*, Ned!"

"I'd like to get kind of personal with you," said Ned, slinking after him. "I think you'll understand."

Was this a sexual proposition? If so, it was unwelcome. Giving no answer, Alan headed down the gray passageways to his room, his feet ringing on the metal floor. He double-locked the door, and set Katje's dress to dry on his chair.

Why deny your fellow? It was the voice of the skug within him, forming words in his head.

I want nothing to do with Strunk, thought Alan. *For all I know he's from the CIA. Like an American Pratt.*

He's like Pratt, but he's not an agent, said the skug. *Strunk's one of us. He needs your help.*

Possibly these were hallucinations. Cutting off the stream of thought, Alan splashed cold water on his face and went to sleep. He was much too tired to pursue Vassar tonight.

When he awoke the next morning he felt very strange. Where were his arms and his legs? His visual field was a mismatched pair of fisheye views.

Bending one of his eyes downward, Alan realized that, in his exhaustion, he'd relaxed into the form of a seventy kilogram slug. He was a glistening shade of ochre, with a darker zone along his slick, body-length foot. Two feelers bracketed his mouth, and his eyes were mounted upon short, muscular stalks.

Oh hell. Once again, Alan focused inward, coaxing his bodily structures into the desired Burroughs form.

"Stiff upper lip," he said aloud, as soon as he had something like a human mouth again. "One keeps up appearances."

He noticed that Katje's dress was dry. Carefully he folded it in two and hid it beneath his mattress.

Looking for a place to pass some time without being further importuned by Strunk, Alan made his way to the ship's bridge. The radio operator was a congenial Australian using the default nickname Sparks. Alan had a pleasant talk with Sparks about his equipment, and even offered a suggestion for healing a buzz in the system. The fix worked, and Sparks willingly lent Alan his circuit diagrams and his repairs manual. Alan loved reading about the latest kinds of radio tubes. Studying the possibilities back in his room, he began sketching out a design for a circuit that could send a signal to make his skuggy body still more malleable and easy to control.

At lunchtime, Alan dropped his researches to stake out the mess-room, watching from a perch on the deck. He managed to enter the mess just as Katje and her mother were leaving. Dexterously he seated himself at their now-empty table, and stuffed Katje's used napkin into his pants. Neither Vassar nor Strunk were around just now. After a quick bite to eat, Alan locked himself in his room with his treasure and began examining the napkin's stains. And there, yes, was just the bit he'd been hoping for.

With a sense of high ceremony, Alan undressed and lay naked on his bed, draping the napkin over his face. He dropped his perceptions down to a deep biological level and urged on the autonomic functions of his inner skug. *Make me into her.*

Katje had left a tiny fragment of skin from her lip on the napkin, and Alan was pressing it to his own mouth. His lower lip twitched and tingled, gathering in the scrap of Katje's flesh.

Alan's heart pounded, his ears buzzed with the happy chanting of the skug. His flesh and bones began to flow, subtly on the whole, but with occasional lurches, as when his pelvis broadened to being half again as wide. Cell by cell, Alan's tissues were learning Katje's genetic code.

After an indefinite period of time, he sat up and regarded himself in the mirror. He'd morphed into a very close semblance of Katje indeed, complete with breasts and a vagina. He wondered if the genitalia were shaped right. Although he'd been engaged at one time, and had even spent a couple of awkward nights with his fiancée, Alan had no clear image of the details. But surely Katje's genes knew.

It was very odd to be shorter and wider than before. And a little disturbing to have no penis—just that triangular little wisp of hair with a line at the bottom. Alan began thinking of the swarthy Vassar pushing his way into him, with his strong arms holding Alan tight. The image made him almost unbearably aroused.

There was a lot of noise from the deck, and it had been going on for some time. Alan realized that they'd maneuvered into the port of Funchal in Madeira, and were hoisting cargo on board. In due time, people would be going ashore for dinner. Excellent.

Slowly, almost in a trance, Alan donned Katje's dress, and sat on his bunk, studying himself in the mirror. It wouldn't do to appear as an exact copy of the Belgian woman. He rubbed and kneaded his face, guiding the features into a more foxy and feral form—effectively making the new face more like his own.

He had no make-up, nor any notion of how to apply it. But it was easy to amplify the redness of his lips from within. He wouldn't worry about underwear—the lack might well titillate Vassar. And as for shoes—oh, botheration. Certainly Alan's cracked old oxfords wouldn't do. There was nothing for it but to go barefoot. They were, after all, in the tropics.

When the voices and footfalls of the crew and passengers had finally damped down, Alan issued forth. The air was pleasantly damp and warm. And the decks were nearly deserted, save for the blasted Ned Strunk, who was sitting near the gangplank, doing nothing whatsoever, his expression as vacant as a dog's.

"Howdy, it's me again," called Strunk as soon as he glimpsed Alan in his womanly form. "You look all different."

Alan felt a pulse of interest from within. Something about Strunk appealed to his inner skug.

"I'm just a visitor," said Alan quickly. Although he was still using his native British accent, his voice was higher, with a bit of a purr.

"You're coming from Bill Burroughs's room, right?" said Strunk in a low voice. "Number 17."

"Don't ask a lady her secrets," said Alan, playing the belle. He had no time for this fool. He bent his lips in a simper, archly wagged his finger, and made his way down the ramp to the Madeira wharf, swaying his hips, comfortable in his bare feet.

Wait, went the voice in Alan's head. *Strunk needs you.* With a special effort of will, Alan muted the skug's signals.

Right down the block he found the lit-up *O Portao*—which looked to offer a rather pricey feed. Alan approached and peered in through the open cafe-bar. The maitre d' was eager to seat him in the dining room, but Alan saw no sign of Vassar. That layabout wouldn't eat here without a pigeon to pay his check.

And, oh Lord, there were Katje and her mother on the other side of the dining-room, tucking into a platter of—was that scabbard-fish? If Alan entered, the women might recognize the stolen dress. Alan himself had very little intuition about clothes—back in Manchester he'd sometimes gone to work in his pyjama shirt. But he knew he was atypical in this respect.

Leaving the *O Portao*, he dawdled along the quay, wondering where he might find Vassar. Perhaps it was best to leave it to chance. He'd wait and be found—just like a woman might do. Here was a pleasant, well-lit café. Alan took a seat outdoors by the sea wall, ordered fish and chips, and sat there peacefully listening to the wireless.

They were playing the Voice of America channel—a revue of swoony, romantic pop songs. A lament called "Till Then" flowed into a crooning dance tune named "Earth Angel." Alan felt very sensitive to the music. The plangent notes went right through him. As he sipped a glass of guava nectar, he began swaying his breasts, intrigued by their complex oscillations beneath the silky fabric of his dress.

"Hey there, Katje!" came a voice from behind him. "Want to dance?"

Alan turned and his heart leapt up. It was Vassar Lafia, drawn like a bee to the blossom, his golden-brown eyes alight. "Hello," said Alan, managing some sangfroid. "I don't believe we've had the pleasure."

"I'm Vassar. From the *Phos* ship. How wild, you look almost like a friend of mine. Her cosmic double, you might say. What's your name?"

"Abby. I—I live on Madeira."

"Are you a working girl?"

"Are you always so rude?"

"Do you want a date?" pressed Vassar.

"Let's dance. As you suggested." Alan reached up and took Lafia's hand. It was warm and strong. Gently they moved across the floor to the melding voices of a female trio singing "Mr. Sandman."

Alan's dance steps were a bit uncertain, but Vassar didn't mind.

"You're a tasty armful," he said, smiling down. "I'd like to get to know you better. I wish we had some time to maneuver in."

"I wonder if you could find us a warm spot to be *private*," said Alan, his pulse beating in his throat. "A place where we could lie down."

Vassar held him out at arm's length and grinned. "You're my kind of woman, Abby! Follow me. I'll sniff out a nook. I'm the thief of Baghdad, baby."

Vassar found a Mercedes parked in a dark alleyway, and somehow he got it unlocked. He was clever with his hands. They made love on the leather back seat, Vassar on top. It was spectacular. At the climax, Alan's skug wanted him to melt and to envelop Vassar's body entirely, but Alan held back from that. He didn't want to spoil this precious moment.

"You think you'll ever come to the States?" said Vassar, smiling down at him. "I'm gonna hate to say goodbye to a firecracker like you."

"Are you inviting me onto the ship?" said Alan, running the tip of his finger down the bridge of Vassar's fine nose.

"Well, I know you've got your own life here," said Vassar, backing off a bit. "Family, friends, the whole bag."

After a bit, they slipped apart and sat side by side on the car's leather seat, caressing each other. "What do you do here all day long?" asked Vassar.

"I raise orchids for export, and cultivate new hybrids," said Alan, saying whatever popped into his head. "It's quite a science, really, learning how things grow and how they take form." Gently he played with Vassar's penis, making it stiff again. "You've a lovely orchid yourself." He sighed and bent his head to the dear man's lap.

Neither of them wanted the night to be over. For hours they alternated love-making with conversation.

Vassar told Alan stories about his adventures in North Africa and the Mideast. He'd hitchhiked in hurricanes, broken out of jails, parachuted from planes. Or so he said. Spinning his tales in the dark, Vassar came across as touchingly insecure. He took at face value Abby's claims to be something of a scientist, and he offered praise. He bragged that he had a highly educated friend named William Burroughs aboard the *Phos*.

"He talks a lot like you, Abby. You two would hit it off."

Finally they said goodbye. Once Alan was sure that Vassar was back on the *Phos*, he crept aboard too.

At dawn the fully laden ship steamed into the Atlantic proper. Alan was too excited to sleep very much. He took on the shape of Burroughs again, and made his way to the mess-room for a late breakfast.

Who should he find there but Vassar Lafia, tired and triumphant.

"Did you have a jolly time in Funchal?" asked Alan.

"Wild sex, Bill. I met this girl in a café, name of Abby." Vassar turned his head, gazing out at the receding mound of of the island. "I need to see her again. Need it bad."

"Maybe you will," said Alan coyly. "I'm sure she wants more of you as well."

"I wish," said Vassar, not picking up on Alan's tone. "What a woman. I didn't have to chase her across hill and dale—none of that bashful doe routine. She knew what she wanted. And she's smart—she breeds new kinds of plants. I think she said orchids . . ."

"Mister Sandman, bring me a dream," murmured Alan.

"What's that?" Vassar shot him a sharp look. "Were you spying on us last night?"

"How would I?" said Alan. "But allow me a query. Did you find Abby's genitalia realistic?"

"What a question!" exclaimed Vassar with a burst of laughter. "You're a rare bird, Bill."

The passage across the sea lasted a week. The unsavory Ned Strunk continued making inarticulate overtures, vaguely sexual, but Alan resolutely fended him off. The man was, in principle, reasonably good-looking. But his odd demeanor made him as unappetizing as a hamper of dirty laundry. Alan almost wondered if the fellow were mentally ill.

He took to spending most of each day in his room, implementing a new radio circuit design. Sparks, who was short of funds, had sold Alan the radio shack's stock of spare parts in an under-the-counter deal.

Alan wanted to continue improving his symbiosis with his skug. He created another feedback transmitter, tuning its input to the faint electromagnetic signals from his brain, and beaming its output into his solar plexus. Using the device was, if you will, an advanced form of meditation. Or, looked at differently, a method of tuning the parameters of an intelligent network.

It was well to be working alone in his room as much as possible. This way he could avoid not only Strunk, but Vassar as well. After his night of love as Abby, Alan was finding it increasingly difficult to keep up appearances with Vassar. And he was concerned that Strunk might be some kind of agent.

Pondering his possible methods of defense, Alan had decided that the easiest way to handle an aggressor would be to convert them into a skug. Skugging Pratt had essentially destroyed the man. Now that he'd improved the skug's innate biocomputations, becoming a skugger was something much less violent. But even so, skugging a person definitely had the effect of bringing them onto one's team. Certainly this had been the case with Burroughs, and both Driss and Kiki had seemed the more pleasant for having become skuggers.

The question was, how difficult did it have to be to make someone a skugger? Thus far, Alan had been depending on increasingly heavy treatments. A thumb-sized skug for Pratt, a kilogram-sized skug for Alan, and, for the hapless Burroughs, a skug that was Alan's entire body.

Focusing in on his inner skug's processes, Alan was currently amplifying the virulence of his condition's communicability. Although he didn't care to start running tests in the confined environment of this ship, he was fairly sure that he was capable of making attackers into skuggers by inoculating them with microscopic scraps of his flesh.

In the daytime, Alan worked with his equations and his inner tweaks, now and then creeping out to the bathroom. And at night, he'd take on the form of Abby and strut back and forth, practicing at being a woman. And then he'd lie in bed and imagine Vassar embracing him again.

On the fourth night after Madeira, Alan snapped. Casting off all restraint, he left his room as Abby. Stalking down the ship's passageways, he smiled, thinking of himself as a hungry vampire on the prowl.

He found his prey in the passenger lounge, stretched out on a leather couch flipping through an illustrated catalog of propeller screws.

"Unreal!" exclaimed Vassar, sitting bolt upright. "How did you get here, Abby?"

"I stowed away," said Alan. "I wanted to see you again."

The gangly Ned Strunk was staring at them from across the room, clearly eager to join the conversation.

"We better get you under wraps," said Vassar. "How'd you like to see my cabin?"

"Very much indeed."

They made love till dawn. Amid the passion, it crossed Alan's mind several times that he was perfectly free to convert Vassar into a skugger. But he chose not to—at least not yet. It was somehow more flattering and erotic to have Vassar coming to him as an ordinary man. In the morning, Alan crept back to his windowless cell. He stayed in bed most of the day, keeping his womanly form. He couldn't face having Vassar address him as Alan again. He didn't want to hear the carelessly vulgar remarks that Vassar was likely to make about Abby.

Alan had a steward bring him lunch and dinner in his room, telling him he wasn't feeling well. It was December 31, and late that night the crew celebrated New Years Eve on the open sea, with the besotted Captain Eugenios firing off a series of red and green Very flares, normally used for signaling ship to ship. Alan prowled across the decks and found Vassar, his face glazed with unnatural hues.

Another night of love ensued.

"Where on board are you stowed, anyway?" asked Vassar as they lay in his bunk chatting.

"Don't be angry when I tell you," said Alan.

"I'll never be mad at you, Abby. You're my girl."

"Well—I'm staying with that friend of yours. William Burroughs."

"Him? That slimeball!"

"Oh, he's no ladies man. You've nothing to fear. I went to him because I didn't want to bother you. I don't like to be forward. But—after our night in Funchal—I had to see you again. I'm lost, Vassar. I hardly know who I am." Alan was taking an increasing pleasure in wild, emotional talk. He'd been too buttoned-up for too long.

Vassar made love to him two more times, and the second time, Alan lost all restraint and allowed his penis to grow out from his flesh just above his vagina, enjoying the rubbing of Vassar's belly against it. If Vassar noticed this, he didn't say anything.

After the sex, Vassar drained his brandy bottle. Feeling giddy, Alan altered his body chemistry to feel as intoxicated as his friend. And then, in the wee hours of January 1, 1955, he reeled across the deck towards his room, enjoying the intricate fringes that he was seeing around the ship's lights.

Suddenly there was a problem. The unwholesome Ned Strunk was leaning on the ship's railing, blocking the door to Alan's companionway, stubborn as a limpet.

"Get away," slurred Alan, still in his Abby form. "You've no business with me."

"Look here, it's time to lay my cards on the table," said Strunk, quite unexpectedly. "I know about you being Alan Turing and all. And I know you're William Burroughs too. And you're Abby. You're a shapeshifter. And I'm telling you I need some help. Come on, Alan. I'm not as dumb as you think. Stop being such a tight-ass."

"What are you talking about?" cried Alan, all but losing control. "You're mad!"

"I need your help, see?" said Strunk. "This creepy hand came crawling after me in Gibraltar and it slimed onto me. I'm an American sailor, a nuclear tech. I jumped ship and I stole this monkey-suit I'm wearing off a laundry line. The hand screwed me up, man, I don't know what's going on. That's why I seem like a moron. All I know is that voice in my head keeps saying you can fix me. So heal me, Professor Turing."

Frightened and disoriented, Alan didn't even pause to analyze the disturbing farrago. The man was nosing into his affairs? He was asking for trouble. Should Alan turn him into a skugger? Maybe not. Maybe it would be better to put Strunk entirely out of the picture.

Oh do help him, urged a voice in Alan's head. His inner skug. Fortunately Alan's latest tweaks to his system made it even easier to silence the wheedling tones.

With a savage, lashing motion of his arm, Alan lassoed Strunk around his neck and began choking him, pushing him back against the bulwark. The man's struggles were feeble—he was unwell. Hard luck on him. Alan had no thought of mercy, no thought of trying to make Strunk an ally. To devil with these parasites and persecutors. When Alan felt sure that Strunk was quite dead, he levered him over the railing and into the sea.

"What is?" called a tiddly crewman, making his way from his watch towards the forecastle.

"Nothing," said Alan, feigning a womanly moan, and leaning over the bulwark. "I'm a bit seasick."

The crewman stumped off, and now Alan moaned again, but this time for real. He was seeing something awful in the sea—a pale shape like a glowing dolphin, speeding along beside the ship.

Alan watched in silence, numbed by the onrush of events. In an abrupt motion, the glowing shape dove out of sight beneath the hull.

SIX
homecoming

Alan spent most of New Years Day hiding in his room. As his head cleared and his passions calmed, he reasoned things out a bit, reviewing his memories of the incident last night.

Though he'd been too intoxicated and panicky to analyze Strunk's words at the time, their meaning now came clear. The crawling hand that Alan had seen leaving the ferry—that had been real, it had been a small skug from who knew where. The man Alan had seen prostrate in the Gibraltar alley—that had been Ned Strunk in the process of being taken over by the skuggy hand. Evidently Strunk's personality had survived the assimilation, although perhaps imperfectly.

Strunk was a random American sailor, a deserter. And now he, like Alan, was a skugger—even though he didn't fully realize it. His inner skug was telling him to upgrade his altered body. He'd come to Alan as a victim of a plague that Alan had unleashed. For his part, Alan had strangled him and cast him into the sea. *Shabby*, said a voice in Alan's head. *Very shabby indeed.*

To make things worse, Alan's cold-blooded attack hadn't even accomplished its purpose. Judging from what had been visible over the ship's railing last night, Strunk had survived. And now he was hiding—like a subroutine awaiting a function call. Or, rather, like a bloody heart beneath a madman's cabin floor.

Alan rolled back and forth in his bed, moaning. His latest experiment with autonomous intoxication had left him with a terrible headache. He could hardly wait to go ashore and leave this botch behind. They were scheduled to reach the port of Miami before nightfall. Fumbling through his murky, second-hand Burroughs memories, Alan confirmed that the Burroughs parents ran a shop in Palm Beach, Florida. And he found the parents' home address as well. Quickly he jotted it down, lest he lose the memory.

Late that afternoon, Vassar came and knocked on Alan's door, whispering Abby's name. Alan stayed quiet, but somehow Vassar sensed he was in there.

"I want a replay," hissed Vassar. "I want a thousand and one nights with you, Abby. In the magic garden of love."

"Oh, Vassar," murmured Alan, nearly overcome. But he steeled his will and resisted opening the door. It wouldn't do to recommence the soap opera. He needed be working on his scientific investigations, not playing the trollop. This said, it was highly painful to hear his beloved's footfalls clatter away from his door.

Eventually the ship slowed, and voices called, each to each. A harbor pilot was coming aboard. Jolted to action, Alan took on the form of William Burroughs. He disassembled his jackleg radio system and stuffed the pieces into his pillowcase along with his soiled blue Katje dress.

The engines thrummed, the ship backed and filled. Soon the *Phos* had found her berth. Alan heard announcements from the wharf, and the soft thuds of hawsers being tossed down.

Seized by a sudden fear that he might never see Vassar again at all, he grabbed his pillowcase of vacuum tubes and ran up the companionway, taking a place on the deck near the gangplank, his Burroughs passport ready to hand.

On the deck, Alan had a dizzy sensation of being watched by an invisible, hovering eye. He was in rather poor condition today. He did his best to push the delusions from out of his mind.

Before long, Vassar appeared, his proud head smoothly turning as he scanned the motley crowd.

"Looking for someone?" called Alan.

"Abby from Madeira," said Vassar, coming close.

"Yes. A dear woman. She's mad for you."

"I'm wanting to say goodbye to her. And to set up a meet. Why didn't you tell me she was hiding in your room, Bill? I've hardly seen you on this trip."

"Abby and I weren't sure how you'd react. I'm not good at dissembling."

"So where is she?" said Vassar giving Alan a hard, calculating look. Could Vassar suspect that Alan and Abby were one and the same?

"She seeks to slip off the ship unseen," said Alan quickly. "She doesn't have any papers. But I'm quite sure she'd relish seeing you again."

"How would we work that, Bill?" Slowly Vassar ran his tongue along his lower lip.

"Abby can meet you at my parents' gift shop in Palm Beach. It's named Cobblestone Gardens. What day is it today?"

"January first," said Vassar. "Saturday. Happy new year, mad hermit."

"I'll tell Abby to meet you at noon on Monday," said Alan evenly.

"I'll be there," said Vassar. "If I can square it with the wife. Maybe we'll drive up together, me and her. Might be she'll dig it."

"You're married?" exclaimed Alan, his knees going weak with chagrin. His vision dimmed; he was seeing Vassar as if through a haze.

"Jealous?" said Lafia with an open-mouthed grin. "Now, now. You're not in the running, Burroughs. You know that. It's Abby I'm after."

With a half-hearted gesture of farewell, Alan walked off the ship. He needed to get over this mad infatuation. Vassar was like some ribald cartoon character, really quite lacking in empathy. How could he have let himself get so deeply involved?

The passport check was perfunctory, and the customs man didn't bother looking at Alan's pillowcase of radio parts. Nobody cared. It was Saturday evening, it was New Year's Day, it was 1955.

Asking around among the passers-by, Alan learned that Palm Beach was seventy miles north of Miami, that it would be impossible to get a bus or a train until tomorrow, and that there was no hope of changing money today.

Alan felt an intense pressure to get far away from the ship lest Ned Strunk reappear. And he still felt dogged by the sense of being observed. Could Strunk be somehow spying on him? It seemed best to proceed to Palm Beach immediately.

Alan was nursing a fantasy that the kindly Burroughs family would take him in. Surely, once he'd shown them Bill's letter of introduction, they'd understand why he wasn't exactly like their son. They'd want to help him anyway. Americans were fundamentally kind and generous.

Not so the cabbie whom Alan engaged.

"It's a three or four hour trip for me," the driver crabbed. "Going all the way up there and back. I want my cash in front, chum."

"I only have British pounds. They're worth very nearly three dollars each."

They settled on forty pounds, an absurdly high sum, and all that Alan still had. But booking a hotel would have cost money too. It was dusk now, with a rising breeze. Thunder-mutters and lightning-flashes were moving in from the Atlantic. This was no time to be walking the waterfront streets, which were splattered with vomit and teeming with rowdies and police.

The cab cut down a street of noisy dives, with jukeboxes blasting, women screeching, and men crudely hooting. Last night's revels had never stopped.

The sky had a greenish tinge, as if the neon lights were bleeding into it. An operatic clap of thunder sounded directly overhead. Abrupt sheets of rain lashed the windshield. Even now Alan had the oppressive sense of being watched.

Turning a corner at the end of the next block, the driver momentarily lost control. The cab swerved, skidded, and thumped into something. With a vile curse the cabbie pulled to halt.

"You've struck someone!" exclaimed Alan.

"You don't know that," snarled the driver. "Maybe a stumblebum." He lowered his window and peered into the heavy rain, not bothering to open the car door. "Don't see nobody. He must of run off. A junky or an illegal."

"What if the poor fellow's beneath your tires?"

"Put a cork in it, Lord Fauntleroy. We got some driving to do."

The cab rolled forward, with Alan staring out the rear window. He saw nobody in the street. And now the invisible watching eye seemed to be gone. Alan felt a sense of relief. The cab found its way out of the Miami maze, and the lurching turns diminished. Alan dozed off—only to dream of Ned Strunk importuning him, his voice hoarse and lonely, his arms sticky and long.

"Here we are, bub," said the cabbie, waking him. "End of the line."

"What time is it?"

"Eight or nine. Now beat it."

They were parked before a pale yellow house lit by the cab's headlights. The two-story stucco home was set on a sandy lot amid palms, cacti, and wiggly-branched flowering shrubs. The driveway seemed to be pebbles and shells. Everything was flowing with rainwater.

Alan stepped out with his pillowcase in hand. The cabbie gave him a final glance, ascertained that no tip was forthcoming, and peeled out, throwing wet gravel against Alan's trousers.

Faint light showed through the house's curtained windows, but no streetlamps lit the yard. Alan picked his way up the puddled driveway, his ears filled with the hiss and splash of the rain. Already he was soaked through. Hearing a scrape and scrabble behind him, he whirled and stared into the humid gloom. A long dark shape seemed to be lying on the ground where the cab had been. Could it be—an alligator? The beasts were said to be ubiquitous in Florida.

Alan ran the rest of the way to the front door, stumbling over a stone, frantically milling his arms to keep from falling. He was desperately afraid he'd feel the sudden impact of bone-crushing jaws upon his leg. He pounded on the door and rang the bell. Voices within quietly discussed the intrusion.

Alan stared anxiously at the gloomy shifting shapes of the shrubbery. Was the alligator coming closer? As he beat another frantic tattoo with the knocker, he felt a sliding in his flesh. Blast it, he'd just lost his Burroughs form, reverting to the familiar shape of Alan Turing—or was it Abby? Evidently his current system of body-organization had several local minima. A sufficient perturbation could nudge him from one valley to the next.

With an extreme focus of his will, Alan managed to regain his William Burroughs look—just as the door opened. A tall, balding man with a deep tan stood there in the light. By dint of his second-hand memories, Alan knew this to be Bill's father, Mortimer Burroughs, known as Mote. Mote wore a white shirt and chino slacks. He had a wary expression, but upon seeing the form on his doorstep, he broke into a smile.

"Bill! The prodigal returns! Come on in, son. You look like a drowned rat. Laura, Billy, come see who's here!"

"I'm delighted to arrive," said Alan, pushing forward into the entrance-way. He was wet to the skin, and his pillow-case was soaked. The tiled hall was furnished in the French manner, with a painted screen, a spindly white chair, a chandelier and a gilded mirror. "Please do close the door immediately," Alan implored. "There's an alligator."

"Got the DTs?" said Mote, as if playing along with a joke. "Time for some of those New Year's resolutions, hey?" He shut the door against the flowing night. "Let's find you some dry clothes to start with, Bill."

An older woman who looked a bit like William Burroughs herself came tripping down the white-carpeted stairs, her arms stretched out. She meant to hug him. And close behind her was a lively little boy with a shock of blonde hair.

"Daddy!" cried the lad. In a flash, Alan realized it was Bill's son, Billy. Somehow he hadn't noticed this memory record before.

"Wait," said Alan backing against the door as Laura Burroughs closed in on him. "Let me clear up a potential mis-understanding. I'm not actually your son, Mrs. Burroughs. And I'm not this boy's father." He fumbled in his pocket to find the letter of introduction that Bill had typed. "I only just happen to look like him—for the nonce. Please be so kind as to read this, Mr. and Mrs. Burroughs."

"Oh, what's wrong with you this time!" cried Laura Burroughs, implacably gathering him into her arms. She smelled like a white, waxy flower. She poked him in the side. "And now give little Billy a hug. Poor thing, he talks about you every day."

While Mote and Laura Burroughs examined the letter of introduction, Alan knelt down and faced Billy. The boy looked to be about eight. He had bright, intelligent eyes and a toothy mouth. "Stout fellow," said Alan, feeling a rush of sympathy towards him. "Well met."

"You're talking funny, Dad," said Billy.

"What's the point of this nonsense?" said Mortimer, tapping the folded letter against one hand. "I can't make sense of it."

Laura snatched the letter and tore it in pieces. "You show up with a stupid joke, Bill? Excuse my language, but it's like handing someone a card that says, 'Hi, I just farted!' Mote, I wonder if it's time to have him committed."

"He thought he saw an alligator outside," said Mote, lowering his voice.

"Oh lord. Is he in withdrawal again?"

"An alligator!" exclaimed Billy, perking up. "Let's feed him the roast beef bone. Race you to the kitchen, Dad."

With a mental sensation akin to slamming a car into a different gear, Alan recast his plans. Why had he even come here? It had been folly to suppose he could tell this family that he wasn't really William Burroughs. At this point the only winning strategy was, once again, the imitation game.

"What do you say I gnaw that bone myself," said Alan, letting a latent William Burroughs accent take over his vocal cords. "It's been a long, dry day. And to hell with the alligator. Sorry to come on so vaporous, folks. Did you say something about dry clothes?"

"What's in the pillowcase?" asked Laura, wanting to be mollified.

"*Radio* tubes," said Alan, drawing out he words. He was getting the feel of Bill's raspy, savory tone. "I've been fiddling with electronics. Learned the basics working in a repair shop over in Tangier." He shot Mote a look, gauging the man's reactions. "Maybe that's why I wrote that wild letter. My roundabout way of saying that I might yet end up in a research lab. Not that I'd expect to waltz in no questions asked. But you'd be surprised how much I've picked up."

"That's what I like to hear," said Mote. "A new leaf. Hope springs eternal."

"Get your father some of Mote's old clothes, Billy," said Laura. "I have a bag for Goodwill in the extra bedroom."

Billy ran partway up the stairs and waited for Alan to follow. "Did you *really* see an alligator, Dad?" he called down. "Sometimes they get washed down the rivers and end up in the ocean and crawl onshore. The salt water clouds their eyes. But they can rise up on their toes and run forty miles an hour. Could you wrestle an alligator, do you think?"

"The blind alligator scents his prey," said Alan squinting his eyes and charging up the stairs. Billy squealed and fled. They thundered into the spare room. Alan found a lightweight black suit and a tattersall checked shirt, both a bit large, but comfortable enough.

The family gathered around a table in the kitchen and watched Alan eat from the remains of their New Year's Day meal—black-eyed peas, kale, some very nice roast beef, and a chocolate pudding.

"Drink?" said Mote setting out a bottle of bourbon.

"Something non-alcoholic," said Alan in the dry Burroughs tone. "I'm a new man, I tell you. We'll raise a toast to 1955. Weren't we supposed to have flying cars by now?"

"I want one," put in Billy. "And a rocket ship."

"We've got a statue of Mercury with winged feet in the store," said Laura, pouring Alan a glass of Coca Cola. "Mote's been buying up graven images from Mexico. A gamble."

"They'll sell this spring when people start thinking about their patios," said Mote. He struck a classical pose, with his arms stretched to one side. "Gods and goddesses to rule your bathing beauties, your bartenders, and your cane toads."

"The neighbors had a toad as big as this," said Billy, holding his hands wide apart. "They said his skin was poison. The gardener hacked him with a machete."

"The toad used to make a noise like a squeaky wheel," said Laura. "*Eep eep eep.* All night. His doomed cry for love. Are you booked into a hotel, Bill?"

"I, ah, thought I might as well bunk here," said Alan.

"That would be nice," said Laura. "Instead of skulking off like a criminal."

"Sometimes a blind alligator likes a private wallow," said Alan, trying to lighten the mood.

"What brings you back to the States, my boy?" asked Mote. "Did you finish another book?"

"Not yet," said Alan. He had inchoate memories of typed pages, dense with mad routines. "I'm organizing my material. Bringing my files into full disarray. I thought I might show excerpts to my friends and push into a literary magazine." Names popped into his mind. "Allen Ginsberg can help. And maybe Jack Kerouac."

"Where are they?" asked little Billy. "Mexico? Louisiana?"

"The scene's in San Francisco right now," said Alan, channeling the Burroughs database that lay within his cells. Doing this, he could feel there was something bad about his past with Billy—something that he hadn't yet excavated. "Anyway I'd like to stay with you folks for a couple of days." He studied Billy. "How old are you?"

"A father should know that," said Laura.

"Where's his mother, anyway?" asked Alan carelessly. The air froze, shattered, and clattered to the floor. The sad faces of the family members were like smudged flowers. And now the troubling memory emerged like a maggot from a wound. Three years ago, William Burroughs had shot his wife in a moment of sodden horseplay.

"You're asking us where's Joan?" said Mote, his expression a mixture of pity and contempt.

Desperate to recoup, Alan feigned a poetic transport, and tried to frame his awkward question as rhetoric. Placing the back of his hand on his forehead, he quoted the first snatch of weepy doggerel that came to mind: "*Vainly I have sought to borrow / From my books surcease of sorrow— sorrow for the lost Lenore / For the rare and radiant maiden whom the angels named Lenore . . .*" He grabbed his glass of cola, drank deeply, and bathetically concluded: "*Quaff, oh quaff this kind nepenthe, and forget the lost Lenore!*"

"So let's be off to beddy-bye," said Laura after a long pause. She corked the bourbon and put it away. "Do you think you need to see the dentist or the doctor, Bill? I could make some appointments."

"Feeling fit," said Alan, getting to his feet. After Bill's many years of riotous living, Mort and Laura's expectations from their son weren't high. But tonight he was hitting new lows. "Sorry for the outburst. I'll be charming tomorrow."

"I'll show you your alligator wallow," said Billy, brightening up again.

The extra bedroom had a window looking onto the lush garden behind the house. The rain was abating; the temperature was pleasant. Alan opened the window and its screen by a small amount to let the fresh air waft in unimpeded—he'd missed this in his shipboard cell.

Alone again, tucked into his soft bed, Alan completely relaxed all control over his body. In seconds he'd slid into the form of a giant slug, homogeneous and boneless, a slimy yellow mollusk on the sheets, with his eyestalks drooping across the pillow. Cozy. He slept.

He awoke at the first light of morning. It was a fine day. Out the window, the southern sky was aglow with the ocean's reflected light. Something bumped and nudged against his window sash—pushing it wider open. The police? A thief?

With a quick pulse of will, Alan pulled his amorphous body into the shape of William Burroughs. Hopping out of bed, he saw a fleshy tendril come sliding through the window's open slit. Flowing inward like a time-reversed cascade, the glistening, doughy flesh accumulated on the parquet floor beside the window. A skug.

Holding its default mollusk-shape but briefly, the skug rose up from the floor and took on the look of the nude—Vassar Lafia?

"How—*how* did you—" began Alan, but the Vassar-like skugger strode forward and kissed him, cutting off all talk. Quite unable to control himself, Alan morphed into his womanly Abby form and let his partner's penis slide into him.

The bed was across the room, and having sex on the floor seemed somehow indelicate. As if sensing Alan's hesitation, his partner flung up one of his arms, letting it stretch into a thick tendril that *thwapped* against the high ceiling. Fully in synch, Alan glued his hand to the ceiling as well. Once he'd extended his arm that high, it should only be a matter of sending microtendrils from his palm to take hold of the lath and plaster—like the footpad of a housefly.

Softening their bodies, Alan and the intruder twined themselves around each other and rose off the floor.

Error. Plaster and splintered wood tore loose from the ceiling. They thumped to the floor.

Reset. Alan and the intruder wrapped fleshy tentacles around a now-bared rafter and rose into the air.

Bliss. Continuously copulating, they swayed and rotated—a soft chandelier. The sensations were exquisite, easily the equal of Alan's original merge with William Burroughs on Christmas Day. This was more than mere sex—it was cytoplasmic fusion.

During this intimate contact, Alan could readily perceive his partner's thoughts. The man wasn't Vassar Lafia at all. He was Ned Strunk, the very person whom Alan had sought to murder aboard the *Phos*. Strunk was finally getting what he'd wanted—an intimate conjugational contact whereby his body could adopt Alan's skuggy tweaks. Very well.

And, oh, but this was delicious! Alan was taking pleasure from every square millimeter of his body's surface—not only from the parts in contact with his new lover, but even from the bits that were bare to the morning breeze. The two skuggers jiggled in the air, embracing still more strongly—and now the mother of all orgasms washed over them.

In the final flash, Alan again had the disturbing vision of a distant eye watching him. But before he could ponder this, the bedroom door flew open.

Mrs. Burroughs was standing there amid the plaster dust. Perhaps she'd come to call her son to breakfast. Little Billy was at her side.

In seconds, Alan had released his hold on the rafter and had returned to his Burroughs form. The sated Strunk thudded to the floor, rose to his feet and scrambled out the window.

Laura Lee Burroughs could hardly have understood what she'd just seen. But she reached a judgment nonetheless.

"Out!" she cried, her voice a call to arms. "You've gone too far, Bill! I banish you!"

SEVEN
hanging with ned

Upstairs, Alan donned his borrowed dark suit and graph-paper shirt, abandoning his sodden old clothes and the radio parts. On a last minute impulse, he pinched off a thumb-sized fragment of his flesh. A skuglet. Via teep—Burroughs's word—he accessed the skuglet's tiny mind. He told it to lie in wait in a corner of the bedroom closet until it sensed the presence of the real Bill Burroughs in his parents' home, should the dear man choose to come after Alan. The skuglet could merge with Bill to relay Alan's memories of his trip thus far—and to tell him where Alan and his skug had decided to head for next.

Alan made his way downstairs empty-handed. Laura was in conversation with her husband, while Billy stood to one side, evidently pondering what he'd seen. Mote glanced at Alan with an expression of concern.

"Mother's on the war-path," he said. "Not that I care to sort out what's happened. I suppose it's better if you're in a hotel. Here." He pulled some bills from his pocket and pressed them into Alan's hand.

"That's the last cent you ever give him, Mote!" cried Laura. "We're not sending money to him in Tangier or anywhere else anymore."

Alan felt a pulse of anger from the invisible, spying eye that seemed to be watching him again. Mastering himself, he managed to say something polite to the Burroughs parents. "Thanks for your kindness. I'm sorry for the uproar."

"Go!" cried Laura.

"He was changing his shape like Plastic Man!" put in Billy. "I saw. He and the other man were hanging from the ceiling."

"Who's Plastic Man?" asked Alan, intrigued.

"My favorite comic book," said Billy. "Plastic Man can make himself into a dinosaur, or a hammock, or a lightning-bolt. Thanks to the mad scientists."

"That's enough chit-chat," said Laura. "Bill leaves or I'll scream."

"Goodbye for now," said Alan, patting the boy's shoulder. He felt sympathetic towards the lad, and wanted to say something that might help. "Live well. And—I'm very sorry about your mother. It was a horrible accident that I'll regret for the rest of my life. If I can ever find a way to undo it, I will." Alan forced a smile. "I know a few mad scientists."

"Fix it soon," said Billy softly. "It makes me sad."

Alan walked away from the Burroughs manse, heading towards the sun, towards the ocean beach. He felt another spasm of emotion from the ethereal mind that was watching him. The thing was furious with him. But now, blessedly, it withdrew.

Alan went ahead and flipped his shape back to that of Abby. He was done with Burroughs, and he certainly didn't want to risk looking like Turing.

His sleeves dangled and his trousers dragged. He paused, rolling up his cuffs. In order to take on Abby's form, his flesh had compressed itself. He was four or five inches shorter than he'd been a minute ago. Perhaps he should have kept Katje's dress. Not that it bothered him to look like a woman dressed in an oversized man's suit. In Manchester he'd been known to use a loop of twine for a belt.

Ned Strunk was at the first corner, leaning against the spiky trunk of a towering royal palm. He was dressed in the same outfit as on the ship, much the worse for wear. But his face looked tauter and cleaner than on the *Phos*. He was really quite handsome. Ned's conjugation with Alan had done him some good.

"Hi, cutie," said Ned, studying Alan's girlish form.

"Abby's the name," said Alan, reverting to his British accent. "You're looking well."

"Thanks to you. That voice in my head was right. I'm my old self again. But I still don't know what the hell anything's about."

"Look down in your mind," said Alan. "You'll find that you've acquired many of my memories. A side-effect of our recent *merge*." Alan paused, smiling. "For my part, I gleaned quite a bit of data on you. Not that I've gone over it yet."

"Are we still human?" asked Ned.

"We're *skuggers*," said Alan. "That's what I call it. It's a communicable condition. A contagious mutation."

"That hand crawled onto me in an alley in Gibraltar. Like I told you. It melted me and put the voice in my head. I had no idea. But now I know the hand was a—skug? And it tells me that you guys already converted two cops called Pratt and Hopper? And—and William Burroughs. And a bunch of street Arabs in Tangier?"

"Pratt was the first to be assimilated. The original skug began as a tissue culture that a young friend and I *developed*. We threw our skug into Pratt's face as a matter of self-defense. The skug was crude, and Pratt's personality was erased. Just as well. The man was a rotter. A cat's paw for the *Queen*. Britain has it in for me, you know."

"I'm on the run too," said Ned. "Nobody's even supposed to know about the big-ass cruise I was on. It was a secret test for a brand-new nuclear-powered sub." The young man paused. "I had a plan to sell that fact to some spies. If I could of found them."

"My concern is that the spies don't find *me*," said Alan.

"How did the skug get from Pratt to you and to me, anyhow?"

"After the skug absorbed Pratt, I adjusted the creature's biocomputations so as to make its actions less *dissipative*. I kept a bud of the improved tissue, and the rest of Pratt went stumping down the alleys of Tangier. I gather he made some converts. And one of them sent his hand after you."

"So the bud skugged you, and the hand skugged me?"

"*Skugged*, yes," said Alan. "Or might one say skugified? As you like. We were fortunate not to lose our personalities."

"I'm a stubborn guy," said Ned. "The skug hit me like a mule's kick. But I hung in there. I think of my personality as—as a story I'm always telling to myself. I'm not the feeb you thought I was. I worked my way through the University of Louisville as a mechanical engineering major, see? I'm not a math prof, but I love numbers and what they do. And I went in the Navy to learn about nukes. I figure it's the coming thing."

Ned's last remark set off a strong pulse of excitement on the part of Alan's skug. *This is why we need his knowledge*, said the voice in Alan's head. *He'll help our cause.*

Meanwhile they'd crossed a street, and were drawing near the ocean beach. Little Billy came pedaling after them on his bike. "Is that you, Plastic Dad? You turned into a woman! Wow. But I know it's the crafty William Burroughs, hee hee. Are you really gonna bring back my Mom?"

"I'll try, Billy," said Alan. "But, please, leave us alone now. My friend is worried about running into the police."

"If you don't have a room tonight, you can sleep in our back yard! I can leave some potato chips and pillows out there."

"I don't want to enrage your grandparents."

"I hope grandpa gave you enough money for a hotel. Or you could sleep under the pier. That's where the bums hang out. Will I see you tomorrow, Dad? What's your friend's name?"

"Ned," put in Strunk. "You're a force to be reckoned with, kid. Thanks for the tip about the pier. I'm surprised there's any bums here, a fancy place like this."

"Can you guys show me how to change my shape, too?"

"I don't want to do that to you," said Alan. "Please do go home."

"Don't forget me!" cried Billy, and was gone.

"How did you get linked up with this screwball Burroughs family anyway?" asked Ned.

"Well, right after I absorbed my skug, I went ahead and skugged *William Burroughs* in Tangier," said Alan.

"And you were playing at being him on the ship."

"Yes, he'd given me his passport, dear fellow. I was planning to pass a few days with his family here. Until your seedy antics got me *evicted*." Alan smiled at Ned, who looked more and more attractive to him. There was nothing like sex to spruce up a friend's appearance.

"It felt good," said Ned, sensing what was in Alan's mind.

"How did you hit upon the idea of dangling from the ceiling?" queried Alan, a blush warming his cheek. "It was—overwhelming."

"Well, that's how leopard slugs do it. We've got em living in our garden back in Louisville, Kentucky. They're what a carnival barker would call morphodites. Male and female at the same time. It was seeing you change into a woman that put me into a dangling-slug frame of mind."

"You aroused me by imitating Vassar," said Alan.

"I knew you had a thing for him. And I remembered how he looked. It's wild how we can change our bodies, isn't it? What a kick." Ned ran his fingers across his short crewcut.

Alan felt a sudden rush of empathy towards the youth. The fellow was much more interesting than he'd realized before. "I'm sorry I strangled you," said Alan. "And that I threw you overboard."

"Damn hard to kill a skug!" exclaimed Ned, brightening. "After I hit the water, I glued myself to the keel of our ship, with a sly tube running up along the side for air. I came ashore when you did, and morphed myself to look like a wino. Got in the way of your cab, and when it ran me over, I plastered myself to its underside. Hung there till you hit Palm Beach." Ned looked down at his dirty, wrinkled clothes. "I stored this suit wadded up inside my body. Not all that fresh-looking, is it?"

"I saw you lying in the driveway last night," said Alan. "I thought you were an alligator. You didn't say a word."

"I was too beat to start no hue and cry. I spent the night in the garden. And slimed into your window with the morning sun. That skug voice kept on saying I needed Alan's touch."

"Sound advice," said Alan. He felt safe and calm for the first time in a couple of days. It was good to be away from the ship, from Vassar, and from the Burroughs family. He needed to get back to thinking about science. This whole skug and skugger business was an epochal breakthrough. He longed to ascertain the best control techniques for these new systems, and to chart a path for integrating them into society at large. Ratiocination was a mode he found more congenial than the emotive vicissitudes of sex, friendship, and love.

"I'm commencing to feel all right," said Ned. The beach and ocean were in view. "All I need now is breakfast. And then, please, oh, mighty wizard of skugdom, some new clothes. I saw you getting money off Mr. Burroughs just now. You didn't count the wad, but I did. A hundred bucks. It's like I could see through your eyes."

"Remarkable."

They went into an aluminum eatery with windows facing the sparkling sea. A studiously poker-faced waitress took their order.

"Did you notice how she was looking at your get-up?" asked Ned after the waitress padded off on her crepe-soled shoes.

"I didn't," said Alan distractedly glancing down at his baggy coat with the rolled-up sleeves. He'd just now been thinking about continuous-valued feedback systems. "I do realize this isn't standard women's wear."

"Are you planning to keep being a girl?" asked Ned.

"The role suits me well enough," said Alan. "I'm a psychic morphodite—as you might put it. Although ideally I'd prefer man-on-man sex."

"They had some of that action on the sub," said Ned carelessly. "Part of the reason I deserted when we came up for air near Gibraltar. Slipped out at night and swam ashore. That prick of a chief was calling me a sissy. One guy dropped his soap in the shower and this other guy took him up on it. My supposed crime was to be standing near them, washing my hair, not giving a damn about what they did. Fact is, the chief wanted to bust me because I'd beat him at poker. Everyone gets testy in a metal coffin that's a hundred fathoms down. With a nuclear reactor for the engine." Ned wriggled his fingers, miming radiation.

"The sub's called the *Nautilus*?" said Alan, accessing his borrowed Ned Strunk memories. "It's not officially launched yet, is it?"

"This was the super-secret first cruise," said Ned. "Don't want reporters in case your tin scow goes off like A-bomb when the captain presses *start*."

With a clatter the waitress brought their food. "Is that everything you need?" she asked.

"I—I wonder if there's a clothing shop in this district?" Alan asked. "My usual things got ruined in the storm, which is why I'm wearing *these* sad rags." He fluttered his fingers at the lapels of his coat. He figured that, when pretending to be a woman, he could hardly go too far.

"Sure, hon," said the waitress, warming a bit. "Just down the block. But it won't open till afternoon, what with it being Sunday."

"We're frikkin' masters of disguise," gloated Ned as they dug into their ham and eggs. "The waitress is buying our routine. Like in a spy movie."

"How were you planning to get back to the States from Europe after you deserted?" inquired Alan. "Sailors aren't issued passports, are they?"

"I was gonna bum around the Old World like the rich college boy I never got to be. I've got the inside track on how that *Nautilus* reactor works. Figured I could turn traitor, sell info, and buy a passport. F-T-N. Fuck the Navy."

"I'm rather soured on the government myself," said Alan. "What with them attempting to *assassinate* me. The bright side is that my escape strategy led me to invent the skug."

"A partner organism, huh?" said Ned. "A symbiote."

"Exactly. You help your skug, and it helps you. I'm still working on perfecting the balance."

"Balance? I was like a goddamn zombie after I got skugged in Gibraltar. In the dark. You saw how I was on the ship. With the voice in my head saying I should merge with Alan to get my, uh, *wetware upgrade*."

"Wetware upgrade?" echoed Alan, savoring the phrase. "You coined that expression?"

"You know how it is," said Ned modestly. "The skug gooses up your mind." Ned paused. "And now I want a new face. When you copied that Belgian girl from the ship—how'd you imitate her so well?"

"I ate a fleck of skin from her napkin," said Alan. "A skug knows how to assimilate a tissue's genetic code. Lacking that, you can fake a look from memory. Like making a face in the mirror and wearing that to dinner. You managed quite a robust emulation of Vassar this morning."

"I wasn't all that close. You just saw what you wanted, old horn dog. It was a stretch for me to keep it up as long as I did. "

"You'll find it dead easy once you sample your target's *genes*. Your system settles down like a stone rolling into a valley. Look into yourself. You'll find you the gene codes for Pratt, me, and an Arab boy named Driss. And, come to think of it, now that we've conjugated, you'll have the codes for William Burroughs, Katje Pelikaan and, for that matter, Vassar Lafia. I've sampled Vassar's *effluvia* rather—"

"Hey! Spare me the slop. No offense, but I don't wanna copy any of you." Ned looked around the busy diner. "I want something fresh. Check that guy cleaning the table over there. I'll go Black! No way Uncle Sam will find me then."

Ned rose to his feet and headed towards the rest-room, brushing past the busboy. He feigned a stumble and ran his hand across the young man's hair. Sensing something amiss, the youth stepped back and frowned. Ned made an apologetic gesture and walked on.

On his return to the table, Ned displayed a commandeered fleck of dandruff—and proceeded to morph into the busboy's shape. Over coffee he tweaked his features a bit, peering at his reflection in the back of a spoon.

When the waitress brought their check, she noticed the mocha color of Ned's skin.

"Now look at you two," she said, cocking her head and laughing. "I'm serving a night fighter and a fairy lady. Where's my brain at? Let's cash you out before the manager starts in on us."

"You've been most kind," said Alan. He paid the check and led Ned outside.

Some of the passers-by were frowning at them, and a man in a car yelled something crude.

"That's the race thing," said Ned. "Florida's got rednecks out the wazoo. Make your skin color match mine. So we're not, uh, miscegenating and all."

"I suppose I could do," said Alan. He felt down into himself and found the channel for communicating with the melanin-producing organelles of his skin. A minute later he was browner than Ned.

"We won't be able to go into this clothes store here," said Ned. "We'll have to find the Black part of town. Shouldn't be far." He gestured at the mansions facing the sea. "All these rich people have Black servants. The deep South."

A police car came tearing down the beachfront avenue and made a squealing turn into the side street that Ned and Alan had come down. Peering after the car, they saw it pulling up before the Burroughs family home. Alan and Ned regarded each other uneasily.

"I wonder if that Mrs. Burroughs lodged a complaint on us," said Ned.

"Or it could have been someone else," said Alan. "I've been having this occasional sensation of being watched."

"What happens if the police nab us?" worried Ned. "I don't have any papers at all."

"We'll get new ones," said Alan. "I'll be discarding my Burroughs passport myself. Good show that we're disguised."

"But even so the police might somehow know that we're not, not—"

"Normal?" said Alan lightly. "Here's a secret. If we're cornered, we can always convert our captors on the spot."

"Break off a piece of me and let it crawl onto them?" said Ned. "Yeah. When that hand jumped me in Gibraltar, I went skugger right away. Not that I grasped that."

"I feel I've improved our skug processes to the point where the transition can be very nearly seamless," said Alan. "I've upped the virulence so that it requires no more than a pin-prick to your candidate's body—assuming the touch is empowered by your volition. Now that you've merged with me, Ned, you're in possession of my latest upgrades. We'll have no problem in skugging any particularly importunate pests."

"Okay, fine," said Ned. "But let's not go on any big rampage just yet."

The upgraded Ned was a good mixer. And his Kentucky accent went over better than Alan's Oxonian blither. Frequently asking directions, Ned led them to West Palm Beach, which was separated from Palm Beach proper by a narrow bay. Soon they were in the heart of the local Black community.

The first thing Ned and Alan did there was to buy clothes. Alan selected a maroon wool skirt and jacket with a cream-colored blouse. Ned bought tight slacks, a yellow shirt, and a poisonous-green sweater. The salesman was friendly, although he wondered at Alan's accent and odd garb.

"She's from Jamaica," Ned told the man. "My island girl."

Back outside, they sat on a park bench for awhile. Alan slowly tore his Burroughs passport into bits—shedding an identity yet again. The strolling Black couples and families smiled upon them. The park had a peaceful Sunday feel, with spots of light filtering through the palms.

Sitting so close together, Alan and Ned were able to synch their thoughts, although Alan wasn't yet sharing the full plan that he and his skug had formulated. It involved heading West—perhaps they should steal a car? Now that they were skuggers, society's rules meant less than ever before.

"But have I told you I'm meeting Vassar tomorrow?" Alan asked Ned, speaking aloud. "I don't want to depart before then."

"I've picked up some inklings of that," said Ned. "You call it teep? I wonder—am I supposed to be jealous?"

"How so?" said Alan.

"You're a woman, more or less. Vassar and I have both fucked you—more or less." Ned burst out laughing. "I can't believe this crazy trip." A little boy ran past carrying a ball.

"It's all quite mad," agreed Alan. "Really I should be working up a theory of *analog computation*. Putting my fortuitous advances onto firm scientific ground. But instead I'm playing the fugitive and nursing a schoolgirl crush."

"Oh, calm down," said Ned, leaning back so the sun hit him in the face. "Let's stay here all afternoon."

So that's what they did, enjoying the passing scene, not talking much, each of them thinking their own thoughts. Alan got himself a pencil and a pad of paper from a newsstand, and jotted down some electromagnetic field equations and chemical reaction rules. Thanks to his skugs he could program organisms like computations. His mind felt keener than ever before.

Night fell early. With the personable Ned in the lead, they found their way to a Black supper club called the Sunset Lounge. Alan ate his fill of fried chicken—a dish he'd never had before, although Ned seemed intimately familiar with it. After a dessert of pecan pie, the lights dimmed and a jazz band began to play. Sheer enchantment.

Alan and Ned danced a bit, and Ned ordered a second round of desserts. The sweets struck the two skuggers with the force of intoxicants. Relaxing into joy, Alan gazed at the hot-lit bandstand and the lavender haze of smoke that curled and wreathed above it. Not for the first time, he got the sense that being a skugger allowed him to absorb the world's information at a faster rate. As if his perceptual bandwidth had been upped by, say, fifty percent.

The Sunset Lounge felt immense. The bar, the polished glasses, the long mirror, the waitresses poised like blackbirds to fly to their customers, the tables, booths, dancers, musicians—everything was exactly where it belonged. The room was an inalterable pattern of space-time, and this moment was eternal. As the band swung and bopped, Alan began hearing tiny musical details, miniature sounds—the trumpeter's blue comments, the saxophone's half-notes astride the main line, the whisking of the bassman's fingers along his strings, the beats between the figures of the drum. The music was a shared sea in which they swam; a computation that chased its own tail.

Alan's thoughts grew ever more abstract until, without meaning to, he drifted into a reprise of a vision he'd had this morning. About an invisible eye that was watching him. The eye was a cupped disk at the center of a daisy whose petals were human flesh. The eye was angry.

Alan twitched spasmodically and fell over backwards in his chair, making a great clatter. Fortunately his doughy form took the fall without harm. And now Ned was helping him to his feet. People were laughing, not unkindly. The music played on.

"Something is *spying* on us," Alan told Ned, raising his voice to be heard. "A dreadful threat! Come away!"

"Who?" said Ned after Alan had dragged him outside. "What?"

"A type of eye," said Alan. "Far away. Tracking us, I reckon. I saw it this morning, too."

"How's any eye gonna see us?" protested Ned. "It's dark, man. You're batshit. Let's go back inside the club. I want a third piece of that pecan pie."

"The eye is rather like a radio antenna dish," said Alan, who could still sense the thing. "Open your mind, you besotted layabout. Snap to."

Ned leaned against the club's outer wall and gave the search a moment's concentration. And then he saw the eye too.

"Damn, Abby. That thing's made of skuggers all in a circle, with their heads wadded into a glob. Watching us for true. And now it knows about our new disguises." Defiantly Ned shook his fist at the empty air.

"I'll wager it's in Tangier," said Alan. "And that William Burroughs is involved. This morning the eye seemed disturbed—when Mrs. Burroughs dropped her bombshell about cutting off Bill's *payments*."

"Your pal William Burroughs is watching us?"

"My question is how the eye can work with such accuracy from Tangier," said Alan. "We're hidden by the curve of the globe. I need to understand the mechanism so as to—"

"I bet they're using the fourth dimension!" volunteered Ned. "I read about it in *Astounding Science Fiction*. Ordinary matter poses no obstacle in the fourth dimension."

"Utter bosh," sniffed Alan. "It's too absurd to have a rustic American preach crank science to me."

"Snothead," shot back Ned, undaunted. "The four-dimensional rays are carrying *telepathy*."

"He piles Pelion upon Ossa," said Alan primly.

"Which means the fuck what, professor?" said Ned.

"You're multiplying your improbabilities," snapped Alan.

In the distance a police siren wailed, slowly approaching.

"We've got a problem to solve, and you're busy crapping on me?" cried Ned. "That eye sent the cops to the Burroughs house, right? And now they're coming here! Let's haul ass!"

"Maybe it *is* some kind of telepathy," allowed Alan as they trotted along. "Admittedly you and I have had adumbrations of mutual mind-reading. And therefore—what?"

"We need to set up telepathy blocks," said Ned. "I've read SF stories about telepathy blocks. It's like you imagine a wall around your head. Something like a walnut shell."

"Or like a filigreed tapestry of pure mathematics," suggested Alan.

"Or a lead reactor shield."

"Or hebephrenic repetitions," said Alan. "And by this I mean *chants*."

"And now I'm thinking of a box made of wire mesh," added Ned.

"A Faraday cage," said Alan. "Quite reasonable. I'm sorry I was rude before, Ned. Let's imagine all of our blocking elements *at once*."

The ungainly recipe seemed to work—the nutshell, the screed of math, the lead wall, the gibbering mantra, and the imaginary Faraday cage. The spying eye or dish was no longer perceptible in any zone of their minds.

Two blocks behind them, the police car drew to a halt before the Sunset Lounge. Alan allowed himself a backwards glance. One cop was running around to the club's rear door, while the other pushed in through the front. They had their pistols drawn.

Ned led them down a side street.

"We need to find a safe bolt-hole for the night," said Alan. "Rather soon."

"I see a rooming house," said Ned, pointing. "You think that's safe?"

"I say we bury ourselves in the sand," said Alan. "Right nearby. I'm teeping that West Palm has a little beach on the bay."

"We'll worm into the ground like giant slugs," said Ned. "Yeah. The perfect end for the perfect date."

"Ever the ironist," said Alan, as they stepped onto the dark and empty strand. "Very well then. We'll leave nothing above the sand but our eyestalks and our breathing tubes. Be sure to make your skin extra thick and cold-proof, dear Ned."

The two of them melted into six-foot long slugs, their eyestalks glittering with pinpoint reflections of Palm Beach's lights. It was an odd moment. This might be how it felt to be an alien invader. No great change. Alan had felt himself an alien for his whole life.

Once they were buried side by side, Ned wormed a tendril through the sand to press against Alan's mid-section.

"How about if we merge a little?" suggested Ned. "To get us through the night."

"Lovely," said Alan, softening the barrier of his skin. "Snug as bugs."

And so the two friends slept as one.

EIGHT

dispatches from interzone

[The William Burroughs letters in this chapter are to
Allen Ginsberg and to Jack Kerouac. The letters date
from December 25, 1954 to January 3, 1955. The first
three are typed, and the fourth is hand-written.]

To Allen Ginsberg, Letter B
Tanger, December 25, 1954

Dear Allen,

No sooner have I seal up my Startling Holiday Letter
when a fresh wig fall off Santa's sleigh. And never mind
any pawky spoon-counting official take on what is reality.
Fuck that sound. My beat is Interzone, where any dream
is subject to shlup into fact.

So, awright, Turing's out the door, I close my first epis-
tle, and five minutes later I hear a lurker on my threshold.
I assume it's absentminded Prof T, who's doubtless forgot
an electromagnetic enema bag. I fling my door wide.

Of course it's a cop, his soul-sucking venality like a map
of London on his waxy young phiz. Jonathan Hopper,

pleased to meet, no time to natter just yet, he sniff around my trap, help himself to cognac, flop into my rocker. His demeanor a mix of Teddy boy and degenerate hipster. Flat affect, dull eyes. His every sentence like a parody of itself.

He say, "Our man's flown, what? Brilliant. My telepathy is a bit out of synch, I'll warrant. *You* know the score, Bill. There's a latency in orgone ESP. By the way, our agents just nabbed Turing's boy Driss. The Embassy is dead set on rounding up all the skuggers." He flash me an arch look.

I stand over him, in a quandary whether to pull my shiv or bare my crank. Hopper roll back his eyes, looking into himself. His face grows soft, his head pulsates. He's a skugger too, one understands.

"Chief Soames will be savage with me for letting Turing slip," he says, laying a soft hand on mine. "What can I give the old man? Trust me, Bill. *We* two want Turing on the loose." I feel a telepathic rush of sympathy.

"Turing's headed for the ferry now," I say. "He'll ship out for the States tomorrow."

"Avaunt!" say Hopper in a low, ironic tone. He stride to the open window and snap his arm like a whip. His hand—ah, Interzone—his hand flies off the end of his forearm like a pound of meat. Hand land in street, and scurries downhill towards harbor, very mincing and twinkly on its fingertips, a cunning little thing.

I am agog. I flash on a half-remembered film about a bum pianist who buy a dead goon's huge mitts for grafting them on. The night before the big operation, the hands crawl into the pianist's bed and strangle him. Close-up of his icon face, ecstatic in asphyxiation.

"I've instructed my hand to enlist a companion for Alan along the way," says Hopper, bringing me back into his narrative. "My little Twinklefingers will find just the right sort. Soames will be mollified if he hears I've put a tail on our man." Hopper's grin is several inches too wide and very wet. A tiny baby-sized hand wriggles pink on the stump of his arm. "Do make a happy face, Bill. I've half a mind to invite you to consult for Her Majesty's Secret Service. Cushy work indeed. But, I say, you look all in."

And then Hopper make with an oversized box of British bonbons—licorice drops, raspberry creams, ginger fondant, tamarind nougat, clove tapioca, and more. In my new state, sugar is a stim I highly crave. We jabber head to head, mixing words and teep, pastel sheets of saliva on our chins.

Backstory. A couple of days ago, Hopper is patrol the piss-fume alleys in search of missing agent Pratt, the first subject whom Turing have turn into a skugger. Pratt was on a zombie stomp, making skuggers in the Casbah, but then some of the fellahs burn him in the street.

Meanwhile Hopper have manage to eye-witness some conversions and his boss Chief Soames is rounding up all the skuggers he can. And then Hopper himself get slimed by one of the captives.

"Imagine the violence of my inner dialectic," Hopper tells me, very intense as he use a puddled finger to mop up the last crumbs of our indescribably toothsome English candy. "As a government agent, I want to exploit Turing like a slave. But as a skugger, I want him to spread his condition to your homeland. So how do I resolve my conflict? I make a bid for fuller communication."

Hopper teeps me an image of his hand Twinklefingers aboard the surging ferry to Gibraltar, lurking beneath Turing's seat—he hopes. We can't teep as far as the ferry direct.

Our conversation trails off, and I type this dispatch. Hopper watch me, blank, heavy into his insect-like sugar rush, reflexively grinding his teeth. Sexy muscles in his tough-customer jaws. Thrillingly banal.

We're due to conjugate, I ween. He need my skugger enzymes special to tone him up.

Shlup,
Bill

To Jack Kerouac
Tangiers, December 26, 1954

Dear Jack,

Biggest news is I've turned shapeshifter. I can mold my flesh like a cuttlefish do. *And* I'm a telepath, in my own small way. The teep signals are vibrations in the aether, sounds you feel but don't hear. They've always been around, but I didn't notice them before.

As a boy, I thought I saw with my mouth. I remember distinctly my brother telling me no, with the eyes, and I closed my eyes and found out it was true and my theory was wrong—or perhaps a bit previous. Teeping *is* like seeing with my mouth. I tongue my fellow skuggers' thoughts so toothsome. My range isn't only about a half mile, and you're not infested yet, so not to worry, I can't see you humping your pack. Hump it towards Interzone, baby. This scene is like, *snap*, wow.

And, oh yeah, I've kicked junk for sweets. Candied fruit fixes me special. Insect kicks.

I am become this weird mutant on account of my contact with Turing, who turned into a giant slug along the lines of the Venusian Happy Cloak so perspicaciously described in that transcendent ur-text for our modern times—I speak of Henry Kuttner's 1947 science-fiction novel *Fury*, which I am by way of finding in the hospital commons room the last time I kick.

> More than one technician had been wrecked by pleasure addiction; such men were usually capable—when they were sober. But it was a woman Blaze found, finally, and she was capable only when alive. She lived when she was wearing the Happy Cloak. She wouldn't live long; Happy Cloak addicts lasted about two years, on the average. The thing was a biological adaptation of an organism found in the Venusian seas. It had been illegally developed after its potentialities were first realized. In its native state it got its prey by touching it. After the initial neuro-contact had been established, the prey was quite satisfied to be ingested. A Happy Cloak was a beautiful garment, a living white like the nacre of a pearl, shivering softly with rippling lights, stirring with a terrible, ecstatic movement of its own as the lethal symbiosis was established. It was beautiful as the woman technician wore it, as she moved about the bright, quiet room in a tranced concentration upon the task that would pay her enough to insure her

death within two years. She was very capable. She knew endocrinology. When she had finished . . . the woman, swimming in anticipated ecstasy, managed to touch a summoning signal-button. Then she lay down quietly on the floor, the shining pearly Happy Cloak caressing her. Her tranced eyes looked up, flat and empty as mirrors.

So Turing have create what he call a skug, very like a Venusian Happy Cloak, and it crawl on him and make him a skugger. Then Turing crawl on me and I'm a skugger too, half Bill Burroughs, half alien jellyfish, happy with my lot.

Wild new career opportunities opening up. I am visited by a British secret agent man, Jonathan Hopper, and he a skugger too. We conjugated last night—but I don't wanna drag this in the gutter. Today, with our inner skugs urging us on, Hopper offers me a British passport and a bale of kale if I help him marshal a cadre of sixty-four street-skuggers into a living teep antenna to be housed in the basement of the British Embassy.

The skugs want to get our teep signals functioning for distances far in excess of ten feet. The official reason for our projected skugger hive-mind antenna will be to track the doings of Professor Turing four thousand miles away. One supposes that an *ahem* non-linear amplification is called for.

Last night Turing went to Gibraltar to catch a ship bound for the Land of the Free. Turing and I have this creepy plan that the Prof visit my parents in Palm Beach, having shapeshifted to look exactly like yours truly, and also he carrying my passport. So, Jack, if you meet me, it not me you meet.

A tangled tale, getting loopier by the hour. Hopper shares—or feigns to share—my feelings about the primacy of orgone energy. The orgasm is, I maintain, a flashbulb split-second reveal of the hieroglyphs on our shithouse wall. I *do* in fact have certain ideas about how to achieve the exponential orgone amplification requisite for the intercontinental detection of teep. It's gratifying to think that this Hopper's outfit actually wants my help. It's like my diffuse but wide-ranging researches are not in vain.

I just hope no local Holy Man get hold of our skugger antenna to blanket the Earth with non-stop Malignant Telepathic Broadcast. If that come down, tell the voices in your head you're a friend of Bill's.

I'm off now for a festive high tea at the British Embassy—where I'm to meet Hopper's boss. We'll feast on clotted cream and gooseberry fool. I'm all a-quiver.

As ever,
Bill

To Allen Ginsberg
Tangier, January 1-2, 1955

Dear Allen,

I'm sitting up late, writing you and metabolizing myself some endogenous opioids. Scoop bumpers from the wassail bowl and settle by my hearth, my poppet.

Tangier is alive with skuggers, that is, with biocomputationally enhanced shapeshifters possessing mild short-range telepathic contack with each other. My merge-partner Turing have skip town as planned, and is almost to Miami now. But his less than punctilious protocols have create hundreds of fellahin skuggers in the Casbah, with the hit-count rolling up like Chicago election-night results. You ever read *The Plague* by Camus—where the jaded Algerian croaker is alla time palpating buboes?

Not that we skuggers are in any sense diseased. It's only that I've welcomed a new symbiote into my system, and I'm thinking a bit faster than before. It's like joining the Communist Party, or coming out queer, or buying dope, or writing a poem, isn't it? We're everywhere, baby. Skugs in the rugs.

Goaded by a limey spymaster name of Chief Soames, the Tangier cops have gone apeshit, busting every skugger they can find, and walling them up in the British Embassy basement. A skugger is subject to ooze out through any hole larger than a fingertip. But Soames have leak-proofed his gaol real good. As of today, we have sixty-four subjects in our tank.

I might add that Soames's chief dick Jonathan Hopper is a skugger himself. But Jonathan and I don't share our secret proclivity with the others.

Chief Soames meets me at a tea-party and then, after two days of paper-shuffle, he agree to ignore my extensive criminal record—and put me the payroll of the Queen of England's Brain Police. It's hard to fathom this sudden change in my circumstances.

My remit? It's a plan that Hopper and I have cook up with our skugs. I'll use my deep familiarity with the Reichian theory of the orgone to meld the captive skuggers into a hive-mind capable of long-range telepathy.

Soames has agreed it's better to track Turing's progress rather than trying to arrest and repatriate him. He rather likes my remote teep plan. As a heavy drinker, often disoriented, Soames has a natural affinity for the woo-woo. "We'll get some use from these blighters in the basement," he says, smacking his lips. "We'll put the fear of God in that sod Turing."

Every day when I report for work at the Embassy, I remove my clothing, don a regimental-stripe necktie and go downstairs. The captive skuggers are a rum lot: cute boys, a few women, kids and geezers, all of them nude. "Booorows," they yell on my first day, several of them knowing me from the street. Turing's boy Driss is among them.

"Where is al'An?" Driss asks me.

"Gone to America," I tell him. "You can help me look for him."

"You take me there, Boo-rows?"

"Perhaps. Have you seen my boy Kiki?"

"He go to his mother in Fez. I your boy now?" Driss wraps a rubbery arm around my waist.

I introduce myself all around. My necktie, pale skin and enormous penis set me apart. Do remember I'm a shapeshifter. With sufficiently obsessive focus, I can be the biggest dick in any room. Naturally I push this too far, and by the end of the first day I am a bobble-head atop a pair of tiny frog legs holding up a Lincoln Log. Driss collapse laughing.

The second day, Driss and the fellahs tell me they're edgy at being in police custody. Only a few of them speak English or Spanish, but our skugger teep is working man to man. To perk the morale, I have the Embassy stooges to haul down a fifty-pound bag of refined white sugar. Everyone in the pit start feeling friendly.

The third day I double the sugar ration, and slime out some tentacles from my fingertips, plugging every navel in the room. Puppetmaster Bill. "Let's all get soft," I propose, teeping sexy images of mollusk reproduction. I chant whatever gone strophes come to mind, also feeding the skuggers' real-time reactions into the mix. Feebdack feedback. The Arabs are easy-going people, if you give them a chance.

On the fourth day, even more sugar, also a carboy of olive oil. Everyone feeling festive—we shining and sticky with sweet slick. I push my face against Driss's so our heads merge. *Plup!* Feels real wiggy. I use my squiddy arms to gather ye rosebuds. And then we're a starfish with a shared yubbaflop head on the Embassy basement floor. Our merged heads like the center of a wagon wheel.

I grow out a feeler with a lobster-eye to admire what we done. Our group face look like a gangland hit on President Eisenhower, a bald baby with slit-mouth scars and eye-puckers like 128 bullet holes. Hopper and his boss upstairs are abreast of our session, they very pleased.

On day five, I engage three footmen to haul in hods of wobbly British pastries, barrows of dates, heaped trays of kumquats. The skugger fellahs are increasingly admire me. "Booo-rows! Booo-rows! Booo-rows!"

Driss and I *plup* our heads together, the rest of the gang piles on. We make a parabolic monster face, a dish-shaped teep antenna pointing towards the floor. We vibe our mind-rays through the watery gut of Ma Earth. You wave, we wave. Hopper runs a droopy tentacle down the basement stairs into my spine.

And then—lo! We pick up on Turing in Florida.

For a minute there, I can see through T's eyes, he saying good-bye to this beefcake Vassar he's been romancing. He dither around and then he catch a cab. The scene is rainy, seedy, overripe. The cab ram into some mooch—and just then one of the fellahin boys pull out his head and start ululating the Call to Prayer. That time of day. Our trans-Atlantic confab break up.

"It's the *process*, not the *result*," feller says, fingerpainting the wall with his own shit.

I've been up all night, al'En, writing you. The sun rises, the stucco city glows with inner light.

It's a gas to shake my arms like wriggly dough, a rush to merge tissues with my new pals, wunnerful to host psychic vibrations in my head. I can even pick up a couple or three broadcasts. Radio Tanger with the Maghreb News. We're riding history's dragon.

Now I'll report to the Embassy and coax my skuggers into a teep star again. I'm on tenterhooks to see Turing at my parents' home. My son Billy living there too, you may recall. I wish I could be a better father.

Love,
Bill

To Jack Kerouac
Tangiers, January 3, 1954

So fuck this sound. I'm coming home. Scribbling on the Tanger ferry dock right now. I'm booked onto a chain of flights from Gibraltar to London to New York to Miami. Seven league boots.

I've been tied in with some Embassy officials here, and it turned sour. The upside is the Top Pig have write me a British passport and spring for my plane ticket as a parting gift. I'm quite mobile, being off junk.

My stoolie job was to telepathically spy on Professor Alan Turing, who's made it back to Palm Beach. Yesterday he go to my parents house and show his ass to the extent that Mother have terminate my monthly stipend forever. And he raising a ghoulish notion of resurrecting Joan. My wrath knows no bounds.

I run upstairs and drop a dime on Turing, that is, I tell Chief Soames, the head spy, that Turing is turn psycho killer and Soames need to sic the Palm Beach cops on the man right away. While Soames is slowly process my request, I go back down to my team of teepers.

It's time for their daily feast, and I hang there with them, mainlining the sweetmeats. We have a party, we singing songs and making our floppy, baggy bodyparts into skirly flutes and flubby drums. I'm getting into a North African sense of time. Around sunset, Chief Soames chief come down and tell us that by the time the Palm Beach cops got to my parents' house, Turing was gone.

I want to go right back to more spying then, but my skuggers are balky, also very jittery and disorganized from the sugar rush, also some of the boys are metabolizing themselves some endocannabinoids.

And then this boy Driss start petitioning me. He want to come to America. He say if the skuggers help me one more time, I should at least open a path so they can ooze out and slime free on the streets once more. I agree. The skuggers and I celebrate our new accord for some hours, wriggling like a basket of eels.

Finally around 3 am we restart the teep—which involves physically merging all of our heads. Right away we hitting it good. It's mid-evening in Florida. I home in on Turing, happy in a jazz club with some nobody name of Ned. Ned a skugger too. I'm oddly envious of him.

Turing feels my gaze, and suddenly he learns to put up a telepathy block. A formidable quarry. I rush upstairs and ask the security guard to let me use the Embassy phone and ring Chief Soames at home in his house. I want him notify the Florida cops again.

The guard balk at first, so, not standing on ceremony, I jab his gut and make him a skugger too. He turn very cooperative. I sit in his lap while I use his phone to give Soames his orders.

When I hit the Embassy again next day, my handler Jonathan Hopper want to talk with me.

"Bill, you've gone off the rails. The Chief's beside himself. You woke him for a wild goose chase. I fear you'll be dismissed."

I explain that Turing have terminate my family meal-ticket, and I don't like how he talk about dig up my dead wife. "Shooting her once was enough, already," I add.

"You're not yourself, Bill," says Hopper. "You're only saying these cruel things for effect."

I bull my way down to the basement and plug in with my skuggers again. We wobble our orgone antenna towards the Sunshine State for one last time, and I find Turing and Ned have dig themselves into the sand of West Palm Beach like quahog clams. Turing is asleep, with his teep-block around his ankles like wet underwear.

In his dream, he notice me and start teeping, sleepy and warm.

"Hello Bill. I rather miss you. Why are you persecuting me, brother?"

"Leave my family alone."

"You've caused them enough pain, eh? No matter. I'm leaving town."

"But, wait. I'll need to find you." And in that moment I realize that I'm in love.

"You don't really want me," Turing say shyly. "I'm odd." And then he fade into blobby visions of higher-dimensional skugs.

I sprint to the top floor and hammer like a maniac on Chief Soames's door.

"What is it, Burroughs? You've become excessively tedious."

"Call the Palm Beach police! We've got another chance to nab Turing! But I insist they capture him alive. The man's a find, a sport, a valuable mutation! We'll pin him down so I can debrief him!"

"Very well," says Soames. "One more call." He pause to study me. "And—Burroughs? Collect your pay and leave. You're sacked."

"Can you give me a British passport before I go?" I whine. "Turing stole mine, you see. And I need a plane ticket to the States. To wrap things up."

Soames make with a smelly yawn. "Snag a passport at Records downstairs. We stockpile the papers of our Brits who come a cropper here. And we'll issue you a two-day pass for the planes. And now I'll phone your beastly Florida bobbies, worse luck. It's like talking to jungle sloths."

I got half a mind to recruit Soames as a skugger too, but he careful to keep me on the other side of his desk.

Downstairs I ask the brittle woman in Records to give me *two* passports, wanting to do Driss a favor. She slap two on the counter, ready made. "The Jackson twins," she say. "Stanley and Daniel. Died here last year. A reckless pair—tried to hoodwink a sharif."

"They don't resemble me at all," I remark, studying the identical faces, coarse and dull.

"You're the India rubber man, innit?"

On the street, I engage the services of a farmer leading his donkey to market. We tie a rope from the donkey to the Embassy's barred and boarded basement window. The donkey pulls, and the window pop out like a tooth. The captive skuggers come oozing out, loose and wriggly. I rather doubt anyone will ever get a skugger antenna working again.

Meanwhile Driss rush to my side. "Ouakha," he say, batting his eyes. "Now we go to America, Boo-rows?"

"London for you," I say. "No further. America for me. Can you look like this?" I show him the mug-shot of Daniel Jackson. Driss wriggle right into form. I do the same dance. We're mirror-twins, me in my suit and he in his djellaba. We stroll off down the street arm in arm, Tweedledum and Tweedledee. Driss is quite a catch. But my plane ticket pass is only for one. His trip to London will come out of my personal funds, fond mentor that I am.

Hopper, my friend at the Embassy, come legging after us. "Burning our bridges, eh, Burroughs? I just now skugged Soames as well. Stick around, things are getting interesting."

"I have to see Turing face to face," I tell him. "And mend my fences with the parents. And check in on my son."

"I wonder if you'll have any trouble finding Turing."

"I'll find Turing in the West Palm Beach jail. That's why I turned him in. Once I've talked sense to him, he and I can take up where we left off."

"The police won't be able to hold him, Bill. Have some pride in the skugger team, old top. Tangier is collapsing around us now. And Palm Beach will fall as well."

I remain fixated on my pursuit. "If Turing breaks out, where does he go?"

"Unknown," says Hopper. "Look within. Your skug is as well-connected as mine. One straw in the wind: our Gibraltar agents reports that my prowling hand chose to recruit a sailor from a nuclear submarine to be Turing's shadow. A Ned Strunk?"

"Strunk is nothing," I rap out. "A hayseed. Not worthy to be Alan's friend."

"*Beware, my lord, of jealousy; It is the green-eyed monster which doth mock.*" Hopper lays his tongue roguish in the corner of his mouth, then holds out his hand. We shake, letting our flesh merge for a second, with the bustle of the market all around, and a muezzin calling in the distance. Driss watch us, alert to ebb and flow of control.

Back home I stuff my manuscripts and figurines into a suitcase. Driss put on my other suit and fill a bag with food. He excited to be going to London. Perhaps we meet there on my return.

And now I'm writing you as we wait for our ferry. Everyone I see here is a skugger already—some with three eyes, some with lariat arms. It's like we're inside a cartoon. Where I've always wanted to be. Whooo!

As ever,
Bill

NINE
cops and skuggers

Buried in the sand, Alan had a dream of Burroughs, speaking to him from within the spy-eye, oddly tender and wistful. Bill was coming to Palm Beach, just as Alan had hoped. Were they enemies—or in love?

And then Alan awoke to a police raid. A snarling German shepherd snapped at his eyestalks. Alan stiffened his tissues against the teeth, then transformed his slug shape into the copper-skinned Abby form. Perhaps the policemen would drop their initial impressions of Alan and Ned—it was, after all, wildly improbable to find a pair of giant slugs buried in the sand with their eyestalks sticking up.

"We're terribly sorry," cooed Alan, executing a womanly shimmy as he worked himself free of the sand and shrugged his dress into position. He held his shapely hands high in the air lest one of the police dogs snap at him again. Two cops and two dogs. "Is it unlawful to sleep on the beach?"

Meanwhile Ned, menaced by the second dog, was again wearing the body shape he'd copied from the bus boy.

"We're surrendering, okay?" yelled Ned. He wiggled his legs in a strange way, as if marching in place. Abruptly the hounds stopped barking and lay down.

"Don't you freaks try nothing cute!" called the shorter of the police officers, a plump man with a pale face and a smeary mustache. Although he was holding a pistol he seemed scared. "I'm Officer Norvell Dunn and you'll do what I say. Put the bracelets on 'em, Landers."

"They're disguised as a colored couple," muttered the other cop, a tall, weedy man. "Like the squawkbox said."

"These the ones," agreed roly-poly Norvell. "You saw how they was a-doing when we got here. Could be they already spread the disease to our dogs. Hurry up and cuff 'em, Landers, you long drink of piss. Make the arrest before the back-up gets here. So we get some credit."

Plain-faced Landers addressed Ned without moving closer to him. "I'll need to handcuff you and the girl," he said. "We got word about you from—where was it again, Norvell? Morocco?"

"Don't go tipping our hand," scolded Norvell. He was holding his gun with both hands.

"Let me talk to them in my own way, Norvell," said Landers, annoyed. "You're the muscle but I'm the brains."

"*I'm* the brains, nincompoop," yelled Norvell.

"Oh, silly me," said Landers with placid mockery. "I forgot." He remained rooted at Norvell's side.

"What all's supposed to be wrong?" called Ned at Alan's side. He'd dialed up his Southern accent.

"As if you didn't know," said lean Landers, dangling two pairs of cuffs. "You have some horrible disease that turns people into giant worms or whatnot. We saw what you looked like asleep. I wouldn't want to touch you. I wonder—could you clip on these bracelets yourself?"

"No need to shackle us," put in Alan, sweetening his voice, hoping to work his sexy-girl act. "We'll submit quietly. No need for concern at all. This is merely a misunderstanding." Sirens wailed in the distance.

All Alan needed to do was to touch the skittish bobbies. Perhaps he could rush them. Malleable as his flesh was, he could heal a bullet wound.

"She's like some sly goblin in a fairy tale," said Norvell, keeping his pistol firmly aimed. "How come you talk so fancy, girl? How about you show us a driver's license? Pull it out slow and don't be changing into no killer squid."

"Cool it!" interposed Ned. "We're locals. Me and my girlfriend Abby. We spent the night in the sand because Ab's folks won't let us sleep together. She grew up in the Caribbean, which is why she talks so high-tone."

The policemen looked almost mollified. But now, struck by a reckless whim, Alan flipped his wrist and let his fingers dangle, rubbery and two feet long. "Oops!" he giggled. Let the games begin.

Alan felt sure they could best these bullying fools. Malleable as his flesh was, even a bullet at close range should be manageable.

"Oh hell," said Landers, seeing the determination in Alan's eyes. He drew out his own gun as well. "We need to finish them off, Norvell. I say we lock the two of 'em in our car till the others come. And then pour on a few gallons of gas and burn the car." The approaching sirens had risen to a fever pitch.

"Let's say that's my idea," said Norvell, after a brief pause. "I get the credit." He gestured at Alan with his gun. "You first. Walk to our vehicle. And, Landers, you sic those police dogs on them again."

Alan and Ned exchanged a pulse of teep, and now Alan understood what Ned had done to the dogs. He'd sent tendrils from his feet, through the sand, and up into the animals' paws. He'd pricked their flesh and skugged them. The slightest infusion of skug tissue was enough. Reaching out with his teep, Alan could see a grayscale wide-angle view of the scene through the eyes of the nearest dog.

Landers let out a sharp whistle, and the skugged dogs began a charade of barking and nipping at Alan and Ned. Gun at the ready, Landers backed towards the cops' black and white station wagon and opened the rear door. Norvell stood to one side, his heavy pistol at the ready.

As if cowed by the dogs, Alan and Ned shuffled forward. But they were in teep synch with the dogs and with each other. Like a ballet. And now the dogs charged the policemen.

Ned sent a quick tentacle around Norvell's thick waist—and let the tentacle burrow into the cop's pale flesh. For his part, Alan lost a precious half-second watching Ned. And thus the shot from Landers's gun caught Alan by surprise. The bullet shattered his right knee.

As Alan fell, he let his right shin and foot come fully free—and he sent his lower leg dancing across the sand to spring onto Landers's face.

By the time the other police showed up, Alan and Ned had the situation well in hand. Alan had regrown his leg with no trouble at all, losing only a little fat from around his waist. He and Ned were sitting in the rear seat of the cop's station-wagon, as if in captivity. The dogs rested peacefully in a cage in back. And the now-comradely officers were standing outside.

"These ain't the ones," the skugged Norvell announced to the newcomers. "A false alarm like last night. These just a couple of vags. Landers and me gonna run 'em in anyway."

After a few minutes of tiresome American witticisms, the police dispersed. Norvell started the cop car and drove slowly down the West Palm Beach streets.

He glanced back at Alan and Ned, his pudgy face wreathed in a smile. "Being a skugger feels pretty damn good, don't it?" he said. "It's like I'm a touch sharper than before. I can't say as I'm sorry you infected us. So how can we help you on your way?"

"We need wheels," said Ned.

"We have a mint 1955 Pontiac Catalina in the impound lot back of the West Palm substation," said Landers. "Norvell and me took it off a dope dealer last month."

"You can run hog wild," said Norvell.

The four of them burst into a round of laughter—and the dogs joined in. Alan got perhaps too deeply involved in the laughing and yipping. He was modulating his sounds in frequency and amplitude, savoring the patterns of beats that arose as the joyful vibrations overlapped and bounced within the small cabin of the car, drawing the laughter out for as long as he could. Alan was no longer alone.

There were only four other police at the small substation. For the sake of appearances, Ned and Alan squeezed their flexible hands into those cuffs that Landers had. Leaving the dogs in the back of their wagon, Landers and Norvell herded the "captives" inside, talking roughly. It might have been okay, but Ned didn't like attitude of the booking officer at the desk inside the station, who referred to Ned as "low-tide Black trash."

In response, Ned grew one of his fingers out like a vine and skugged the white-haired officer on the spot. Exhilarated by the wild energy, the old cop let out a cracked hoot yelp and wriggled his arms like serpents.

"Did you see that?" yelled one of the other cops, drawing his gun. "All mutants!"

"You all right, Zeke?" a second cop called to the ecstatic convert at the desk. He drew out his gun and stood beside his partner. "Holy hell, that mutant-woman's arm is sproutin' like a kudzu vine—"

Growing rapid tentacles from his hand, Alan zapped both the cops before they could fire. But the fourth policeman, the substation's captain, had been been concealed in an office to one side. He appeared in his doorway and shot Ned in the ribs.

This was more serious than being hit in the knee. Ned curled on the floor, focusing into himself to put his body back in repair. In a state of panic, Norvell fired his pistol at the Captain, hitting the man smack in the middle his face. The cop went down in a nauseating explosion of gore.

So now there was a corpse in the substation. And seven skuggers. Alan helped Ned to his feet. Urged on by their inner skugs, the cops gathered around their dead captain, lying crooked in a pool of blood.

"So long, Captain Jackson," said one of them, with a hint of mockery in his voice.

Working on instinct, the skugger cops sent tangles of roots from their feet, sinking the tendrils into the body of the fallen Captain, rapidly absorbing his flesh and blood.

"Like mangroves growin' on a dead alligator," said Norvell.

Meanwhile a woman's voice was quacking from the phone on the dead Captain's desk.

"Damn," said Landers. "His wife. She heard all this."

He went over and hung up the phone. And then he turned his arm into a bouquet of tendrils that he ran along the Captain's desk, wall, rug, and ceiling like a feather-duster, cleaning up all signs of the execution.

"Captain should just have let us skug him," said Norvell. "Not that I'll miss him none."

"I'll be skugging Captain Jackson's wife in half an hour," said Landers, starting for the door. "I'll nip the trouble in the bud."

"I'll come too," said Norvell. "Captain's wife's a looker."

The five policemen burst into merry hooting, and the skugger dogs chimed in with howls.

"Don't forget our new car," put in Ned.

An hour later, Ned and Alan were back in the posh part of Palm Beach, driving their lavish populuxe car along the ocean boulevard. It was a mild, day, brilliantly sunny. The liberated Pontiac Catalina was a two-tone, maroon on the bottom and cream on top. America at her best.

By way of avoiding further confrontations with Southern police, Alan and Ned had their teep blocks up. And
they'd switched their skin pigment back to the pinky-tan
shade called "white." But Ned still wore the busboy's
facial features, and Alan had kept his Abby look, although
he'd plumped up his lips and breasts a bit. He was hoping
to stun Vassar with his sexual allure.

"Now we're all legal," said Ned. The skugged cops had
issued them driver's licenses made out to Ned and Abby
Smith, as well as a vehicle registration slip in Ned Smith's
name. "My keen skug-amplified mind noticed something
about the number on our license plate," Ned added. "Did
you notice, mister math prof?"

"Oh, let's not talk about numbers," said Alan, practicing
his Abby role. "Not on our *honeymoon*, Neddie dear." He
put on a simpering smile.

"I just hope those pigs didn't find some way to dou-
ble-cross us," said Ned. "And what if that Captain's wife
calls in the FBI?"

"One assumes that Norvell and Landers have dealt with
her in a timely manner," said Alan, going back to his usual
style of speech. "He peered in the car's side mirror, adjusting the shade of his lips. "You're so pessimistic, Ned. This
is a glorious adventure."

"I'm the one who got gut-shot," said Ned. "Not you.
If they chew us up with machine-guns, we might not
bounce back. Who's to say that eye in the sky won't send
a fresh wave of killer pigs?"

"I think the eye is gone," said Alan, remembering a bit
of his dream about Burroughs this morning. Had Bill

really said he was coming here? Did Bill actually care about Alan that much? It was good that Alan had left a messenger skuglet in the Burroughs parents' home.

"I don't care what you say, I bet the cops will be on us like stink on shit," said Ned gloomily. "We're public enemies. We started a wave of mutation. And we killed a police captain."

"*Norvell* killed the poor fellow," said Alan. "Not you and I. If we go gently, we can win our campaign in peace." The pleasant ocean air beat against his face, riffling his bobbed hair. He felt safe and powerful. And he was jazzed at the thought of seeing Bill Burroughs again. Vassar was sexy, Ned was nice, but only Bill was his intellectual equal.

"Win how?" said Ned, dogged in his pessimism. "Win what?"

"Oh, bother. My tweaks have made the skugly biocomputation exceedingly contagious, in case you hadn't taken that in. Tangier is ours, I'll hazard. And Palm Beach falls soon too. Before long I'll find a way to convert the whole world at one go."

"I'm getting these world conquest vibes from my inner skug," said Ned. "I think maybe the skugs are a little too gung-ho."

"I'm for them," said Alan. "Let's be double sure that our teep blocks are on before we discuss my plan." He surveyed his inner walls and found everything in order. It wasn't so hard keeping up the block once you'd learned how. "Right. You mustn't share my plan with anyone, Ned."

"I'll pile on the lead bricks," said Ned. "Tell me."

"My skug and I have reached the conclusion that we should proceed to the National Laboratories in Los Alamos, New Mexico," whispered Alan. "Stanislaw Ulam works there, a very fine mathematician. Ulam and I have followed each other's papers for years, not that we've never met face to face. He studies lovely mathematical arcana—nonlinear waves, cellular automata, higher infinities, and phase space. Along the way, he and that *fathead* Teller invented the hydrogen bomb. The bomb is the tool that the skugs really need." Alan pursed his lips, thinking. "I won't immediately tell Stan Ulam who I am."

"I know Los Alamos," murmured Ned. "I was there for my Navy sub nuke-training. Secrets of about uranium 238 and plutonium 239. The heavy-metal brothers, you might say."

"Excellent," said Alan. "You can help me worm my way in." He snaked a cheerful arm across the seat and chucked Ned under the chin.

"Back up a second," said Ned. "You're saying you want the skugs to get hold of an H-bomb? Doesn't sound like a real good idea."

"Think of a thermonuclear explosion as a short-lived sun," said Alan. "A source of health and *enlightenment*. A global revolution is imperative. Humanity has truckled to cretins for long enough. More on this later. Store our discussion in your deepest, darkest memory-crypt, dear boy."

"Okay, fine. But I may still want to argue with you."

"Agreed. Slow down now. We're almost at Cobblestone Gardens." Alan glanced at a gold ladies' wristwatch he'd nicked from the police evidence room. "Noon. Time for my—*tryst*. I do hope you're not insanely jealous."

"Definitely not a problem," said Ned evenly. "I'm glad to be your pal, Alan. You're the wildest guy I ever met. And we'll share wetware now and then with a morphodite slug-slime conjugation. But, no, I'm not hankering to carry you as any kind of steady girlfriend."

"Very well," said Alan, perhaps a little relieved. What with Vassar Lafia and Bill Burroughs he had enough romantic prospects.

Ned pulled into a parking spot beside Cobblestone Gardens, a medium-sized shop filled with fripperies. Laura Burroughs herself was visible within, arranging dried flowers. Noticing them, she smiled, as if eager for customers. For the moment she gave no sign of recognizing Ned and Alan in their current states.

An old black pickup truck rattled in next to Alan, with a high flat windshield and odd music wafting from within. Vassar was in the passenger seat, with a dark-haired woman driving. She peered at Alan, sizing him up, naturally taking him for a woman as well. The dark-haired woman smiled, with dimples forming in her pale skin. The smile wasn't entirely friendly.

"You're Abby? Hi there. I'm Susan Green. The wife. Your rival."

"Abby, baby!" called Vassar, hopping out of the old truck and hurrying around to the Pontiac. "We made it. Had to change a tire on the way up. Who's the guy?"

"Says Ned Smith on my license," said Ned, getting out of the car. Even though he was using the same first name, he looked nothing like the Ned who'd been on the ship. "And you're Vassar Lafia." He smirked knowingly and waggled his hand in a floppy kind of way. "What do you say we bring them into the fold, Abby?"

"Not yet," said Alan. "You behave yourself, Ned. And say hello to Susan Green."

"A natural born woman," said Ned, taking Susan's hand. She'd unlimbered herself from the pickup. "A thrill," continued Ned. "I've been penned up with men in a sub for months. Are you guys New Yorkers?"

"How would you know?" said Susan, cocking her head. "I thought I'd managed to go native down here. I'm wearing the jeans, the man's shirt, the tennie-pumps? A good old gal. Where are you from, anyway?"

"Kentucky," said Ned. "You have a New York face. That wised-up look. I knew some New Yorkers in the Navy. Before I deserted."

"All I ever meet are the problem boys," said Susan mildly. She glanced at Alan. "Go ahead and give Vassar a hug if you want to, Abby." She raised her eyebrows. "I'll bide my time."

Not quite sure how things stood, Alan gave Vassar a quick squeeze. As always, the man smelled wonderful. And then they edged apart, both of them alert to Susan's mood.

"I hope you play an instrument?" Susan asked Alan. "You should to know that music is my big thing." An unsteady sequence of clacks and chirps was issuing from the pickup's window.

"I don't play, *per se*," temporized Alan. But Susan Green seemed so intelligent that he wanted to offer a real answer.

"During the war I invented a voice encryption system based on a system of radio tubes. We called it Delilah. It made rather interesting noises. Not unlike—" He gestured at the truck. "Is that *musique concrète*? On your radio?"

"Susan's stuff, yeah," said Vassar. "On her tape recorder. She's a composer. Highly vibrational. Part-time teacher at the University of Miami. I'm proud of her. But back up for a minute, Abby. On Madeira you said you were an orchid breeder. Not an electronics whiz."

"Everything Abby's told you is bullshit," put in Ned, as if wanting to stir up trouble.

"I dabble in electronics," allowed Alan, not all that upset to see his old cover story start to fray. The best would be if Vassar loved him for who he really was. "You were saying, Susan?"

"I call my work acousmatics," said Susan, seemingly enjoying the conversation's twists and turns. "That shiny box with curved corners sitting on the truck seat? That's my Ampex two-track, playing my sounds. I work on tape, I use it to compose. First I sample things like water, birds, traffic, cafes, dishes, sex—anything interesting that I hear. I'm always paying attention. Once I have the tapes, I tweak the speeds, paste up snippets, and re-record." She smiled, happy to be talking about her work. "This part you hear now is Vassar snoring, only it's slowed down a hundred to one. It makes me think of, I don't know, hunting elephants in Africa." Susan glanced at her husband. "And now my big tusker is home."

"Yeah, Susan, yeah," said Vassar a little impatiently. "But why does that weird woman in the store keep staring at us?"

"Oh never mind her," said Alan. "That's just Burroughs's mother. This is her shop, remember. Cobblestone Gardens. She hasn't really met Ned or me."

"Well, actually she *has*," said the antic Ned.

"So where *is* Bill Burroughs?" Vassar asked Alan, ignoring Ned. "I figured he'd be the one to drive you here today, Abby."

"I wanted to get a look at Burroughs too," put in Susan. "He's kind of a legend."

"Bill's still in Tangier," said Ned, dead set on making trouble.

"You're wrong there," corrected Alan, wishing Ned would keep silent. "I think Bill's in London by now. Or already on the plane to New York. He wants to see me."

"The point I'm making is that Bill was *not* on the ship with Vassar," said Ned in a spiteful tone. "It's like I'm telling you, Vassar. Everything you know is wrong."

"What's *with* this guy?" Vassar asked Alan. "How did he glom onto you?"

"I'm guessing that you people are friends of my son's," said Laura Burroughs, suddenly stepping out from her shop. "I think I heard his name? I'm afraid we had a bit of a family drama yesterday morning."

"Oh, we're about to leave," said Ned hastily. "Sorry to be—"

"*You*," said Mrs. Burroughs, staring at him. "I'm sure I saw you yesterday in—you know—the guest bedroom. What *were* you doing? It was such a jumble. And the smell! I'm afraid I quite lost my temper." She stopped and pursed her lips. Getting no answer from Ned, she sighed. "My son is an irredeemable bohemian, and I have to accept him and his ways. I'm Laura, by the way."

"I'm Abby," interposed Alan with a bow. "And these are Ned, Vassar, and Susan."

"Do you know if my Bill's still in town, Abby?"

"He'll be with you tomorrow, I think," Alan assured her. "And he'll be more like his old self."

"Little Billy and my husband Mote will be so glad," said Laura. "Of course they're both making me out to be the heartless mother for ordering him out of the house. To make things worse, two policemen arrived after Bill left. They said dire things about plagues and mutants—they seemed quite unhinged. You're sure Bill's coming back?"

"Indeed," said Alan. "I had a conversation with Bill last night. Long distance. His main concern—perhaps I shouldn't mention this—he's worried about you cutting off his stipend."

"How typical," said Laura, shaking her head. "I won't ask you if Bill's at the drug hospital in Lexington. I don't like to be a desperate old hen." She paused, studying them. "Won't you four come in for a minute? I've got a pot of coffee in the back of the store. And endless left-over Christmas cookies. And many, many, many chairs."

Vassar and Ned were impatient by now. For her part, Susan was holding a microphone, apparently sampling bits of the dignified old lady's conversation onto her tape mix.

"I'm sorry, we're rather preoccupied," Alan told Laura Burroughs. "Ned and I are about to start a road trip. We'd only meant to use your shop as a meeting point with Vassar and Susan. A local landmark. I do appreciate your kindness, Mrs. Burroughs, and I'm sorry about that scene at your house. If I see Bill before you do, I'll let him know you're ready to forgive him."

"No use being angry with your crowd," said Laura with a sigh. "You live like seagulls. Swoop and gobble." Shaking her head a little sadly, she went back into her shop.

"There's something about this set-up that I'm not getting," said Vassar, glancing back and forth between Ned and Alan. "Like why was that woman talking about mutants? And what went down at her house? And why does this Ned know so much about me?"

"I'll explain it later," said Alan.

"After we all get to be real good friends," said Ned, still enjoying Vassar's discomfiture.

"Questions all around," said Susan. "Like why do I keep thinking Abby is a man? No takers? How about this one. Why is the bed of my truck full of boxes and bags?"

"So why?" said Ned, wanting to charm her. He mimed puzzlement with his hands out to either side.

"Why don't you go on and tell them, Vassar," said Susan, her voice a little cold.

"I, uh, screwed up," mumbled Vassar. "Ran my mouth. And we gotta bail." He leaned closer to Alan and hooked his thumb towards Ned. "Can I talk in front of this guy?"

"I'm wanted by the law myself," said Ned. "So come off the mystery man routine, Vassar. I suppose you're fretting about the hash you smuggled?"

"He's a secret agent!" exclaimed Vassar.

"Don't be daft," said Alan. "You told me about your hashish the moment I got aboard the ship. You told everyone who'd listen. I suppose I mentioned it to Ned while filling him in on your background. You've had some problem on this front? The customs inspectors seemed quite lax."

"My husband got in double trouble," said Susan. "The cops want to arrest him and the dealers want to stomp him. And this is all about a tiny little chunk of hash—maybe a few ounces. But Vassar had to go and start bragging to the boys at the neighborhood bar like he had a boatload, and the cops and dealers found out. So we're leaving town. Life gives you dancing lessons—do you know that expression?"

"I told you I'm sorry, Susan," said Vassar. "I don't know why you won't—"

"Oh, don't *worry*, even if my teaching gig might have been the only good job I'll ever get in my life. It's not like people are lining up to hire electronic composers. You clumsy idiot. I just hope we make it all the way to the west coast."

"We'll be lucky to make Louisiana in this bomb," said Vassar, patting the wobbly black fender of the pickup. "It's a 1936," he told Ned. "We haven't really been keeping it up."

"We?" cried Susan. "*You*. The car stuff is your job. But you've been off on your quest to the ancient world. Seeking the beyond. Plowing the fertile crescents!"

"I sure wish we had a car like your Pontiac," said Vassar, lowering his voice to talk under Susan's. "Did you two borrow it from the Burroughs family?"

"It's mine," said Ned. "We got it from the cops this morning. They even gave us papers. And dig the four-dimensional number on the license plate. 61296."

Although the last remark was obviously meant to impress Alan, he almost didn't feel like analyzing it. But it wouldn't do to let such a thing pass. One had to keep up appearances before the upstarts—ah, yes, 1296 was six to the fourth power.

Ned was still talking to Vassar. "We're the top-dog con-artists. You've got no inkling of the wild moves that Abby and me been pulling."

"So what if we join forces?" put in Susan, favoring Ned with a low-lidded smile. "We'll make it a party of four. Right, Vassar? I bet we could jam our stuff into Ned's car. The trunk's the size of an igloo."

Vassar didn't look enthused, but Ned did. Clearly he had a crush on Susan.

"What do you think?" Ned asked Alan. "The more the merrier? We can all be friends. Westward ho."

"I like the idea, yes," said Alan. "Safety in numbers. I just wonder if we'll be pursued."

Alan opened up ever so small a chink in his teep block and felt around for the emanations of Landers and—oh, good heavens. Something dire was happening at the home of Captain Jackson, some kind of ambush. Norvell was dead, and Landers was enslaved. And, damnation, now Landers had noticed Alan's teep! Landers was prying at Alan's mind, trying to winkle out his plans. Alan clenched his face, squeezing shut the hole in his teep block.

"Let's get rolling now!" ordered Ned, seeing Alan's distress. "Hump your crap into our trunk, Vassar. Susan, you can snag your that tape player and settle into the front seat with me. You can teach me all about, what was it called?"

"Acousmatics," chirped Susan.

"Dancing numbers," said Ned, moving with great speed and fluidity—opening the trunk for Vassar, reassuring Alan, courting Susan. "I had a job running a nuclear reactor in the Navy. I'm the Atomic Man."

"And we just ditch my truck here?" said Vassar, still doubtful.

"I'll give Mrs. Burroughs the key," said Alan, regaining his equilibrium. He wanted a last word with the woman in any case. His teep block was in place, and a good number of the local police were skuggers by now. All was not lost. Moving hurriedly, he plucked the key from the truck's ignition.

Laura Burroughs approached with alacrity when Alan stepped into the shop.

"Yes?"

"We're all going to ride in the car," Alan told her. "And Susan would like to leave her truck in your safe-keeping, if you don't mind. This is the key. Your son Bill is free to use the truck when he arrives."

"Well, that's very thoughtful," said Laura.

"And—and tell Bill that Alan hopes to see him soon," Alan said, momentarily forgetting his worries about the forces who'd captured Landers.

It was as if Laura Burroughs had her own kind of teep. She saw right into his soul. "*Alan* is another name for you, isn't it, dear?" She jotted her home number on the back of a Cobblestone Gardens business card and handed it to him. "Stay in touch."

"I'm glad you understand," said Alan. "Perhaps I'll give you a call in a few days. I do miss Bill."

Outside the three others were in the Pontiac, with Ned gunning the engine and honking.

"Happy trails," said Laura Burroughs.

TEN

four-way jam

The center of Florida was rolling countryside, with
many streams. Palms and magnolias gave way to pines
and scrubby trees that Susan called live oaks. Brambles
and honeysuckle filled in the spaces. In one spot an ambi-
tious vine had strangled a whole copse of woods.

"Kudzu," said Vassar, riding next to Alan in the back
seat. "The vine that ate Dixie. The dumb-ass road engineers brought it in from Japan."

"I'm an invasive species myself," said Alan. They were
too far from Palm Beach for him to pick up any fresh teep
from Landers or from the West Palm Beach police. Unless
you set up a group antenna like Burroughs had done, the
skugger teep only reached about half a mile. Going over
his mental records of Landers's distress call, Alan began
forming a better idea of what had occurred. Something of
a disaster. He and Ned would want to recruit Susan and
Vassar onto their team rather soon.

"You're talking about coming here from Madeira with
no passport?" said the out-of-it Vassar. "Hell, Abby, you're
welcome to this country. Isn't she, Susan?"

Susan gave Alan a long, thoughtful look. "I don't know what it is about this girl. By the way, Abby, do you have any money? A little dowry as it were?"

"I received about a hundred dollars from Mr. Burroughs," said Alan.

"Did you and Bill fuck?" asked Vassar. "Is that what his mother was saying?"

"Actually that was me and Abby in Bill's bedroom," said Ned. "Swinging from the chandelier. Ma and Pa Burroughs were glad to see us leave."

"But where was Bill?" demanded Vassar, growing impatient.

"Tangier," said Ned breezily. "Get it through your head." He studied Susan. "And of course you and hubby are stone broke?"

"Another reason we're skipping town," said Susan. She pushed her fine, dark hair out of her face and bent over to change the reel of her tape machine. Apparently she had many hours' worth in the stack of flat boxes by her feet.

"We've got Abby's money," said Ned. "And we'll prospect for more. And when it comes to motels—" Ned let the juicy word hang in the air for a minute. "How about if we share one room?"

None of the others wanted to touch that question. Sulkily, Vassar took out a little pipe and smoked a bit of hash. Alan was beginning to have second thoughts about his infatuation with this scattered man. Ned was younger and more attractive. Although, yes, there was a definite Romantic poet quality in Vassar's disarray. But on this front, Vassar didn't hold a candle to the mad writer, Bill Burroughs.

It was early afternoon, and with the winter sun over-head, the asphalt road began to shimmer in the heat. The tropical air beat against their faces. Alan dropped his teep block and had a telepathic conversation with Ned, fully discussing what he knew of Norvell and Landers. The feds had ambushed them—blowing off Norvell's head with a flamethrower, and sealing Landers in something like a giant glass jar. Landers was devoted to locating skuggers via teep. The best thing they could do was to hurry away from Palm Beach—and to be prepared to skug any pursuers who appeared.

The chirps and drones of Susan's tape-machine blended with the thrum of the car's big engine and the song of the tires on the road. Susan announced the topic or, no, the official title, of each of her compositions, her voice flat. "*Shopping For A Dress. A Pack Of Stray Dogs. What It's Like To Be Dead. Mom's Pearl Earrings. His Penis Bends.*"

In a way, the titles fit. Alan was amazed at Susan's skill at crafting these off-kilter compositions from ambient noise. Information everywhere. The more interesting Susan became, the shabbier her mate Vassar began to seem.

As they progressed northward through the state, the wild scrub gave way to big cleared pastures with cattle. The cows stood knee-deep in the dry winter weeds, munching the seedy stalks. White egrets stalked and flapped at their sides, spearing the insects that the cattle stirred up. Vassar continued smoking hash, but none of the others joined him.

"Those birds look like little old men with no arms, don't they," observed Susan. "Is anyone else hungry? We never had lunch. I don't like missing meals."

A diner with a gas pump hove into view on the right. "Let's stop here," said Ned. "Food and gas."

"Have you ever had a cheeseburger?" Vassar asked, escorting Alan from the car, his hand on Alan's narrow waist. "A cosmic mouth-trip."

"I've had them, yes," said Alan, recalling his time at Princeton University. "I'm due for another, I'm sure."

The place featured fresh-squeezed Florida orange juice, and was empty save for the owner. The four travelers sat on stools at a counter, and the stubbled host slapped heavy china plates with burgers onto the worn wood. And then he went outside to gas up their car.

"Here's to new beginnings," said Susan, raising her glass of juice. Her mouth was bright and cheerful against her soft white skin. "But, Ned, you never told us what you and Abby are running from?"

"The feds," said Ned, after a brief teep-check with Alan. It was time to start releasing info. "This morning it was just the Palm Beach cops on our tail. Abby and I took care of them, but one of the cops' wives phoned the FBI. And then, just as we were leaving town—how would you put it Abby?"

"The feds burned off this guy Norvell's head, and they sealed his partner Landers inside a glass jar," said Alan. "I'm worried they'll use him like a hunting dog. I suppose you might call him a skugsniffer. We'll want to maintain a brisk pace to remain out of range."

Vassar was doubtful. "Oh sure," he said. "The feds did that to two cops? And you know this—how?"

"I saw it in my mind's eye," said Alan, archly tossing his head. "Ned and I are telepathic, you see."

"Trying to freak me out, huh?" said Vassar, not believing him. "Maybe we can, uh, find a magic carpet to get away from the evil genie in the bottle."

"Telepathic?" said Susan, liking the sound of the word. "What am I thinking about, Ned?" She batted her eyes.

"I hope it's hanky-panky. But I can only see direct into the minds of people like Alan and me. People in this one special group. We're called—should I tell her, Abby?"

"In for a penny, in for a pound," said Alan.

"Tally ho," said Ned, gently mocking Alan's Britishness. "What it is, Susan, we're skuggers."

"I hope you're not out to recruit us," said Susan. "You have no idea how many evangelical Christians dropped by my office at the college after the local paper mentioned me. Scary, scary, a professor who's a Jewish woman. Reform her! I made a habit of taping their pinhead spiels, and I mixed them together into a piece called *Godwaters*. It's on one of the reels I've got here. But what are skuggers?"

"We're agents of change," said Ned, keeping it vague. "The march of progress."

"Mutation is the only way to go," said Vassar.

"Meanwhile this burger isn't doing the job," said Ned, looking at his empty plate. "Slide that box of candy-bars down here, Abby."

The owner came back in, leaving the door open. "We're in for a blow," he remarked, pointing to the west. "Clouds in a heap over the gulf. Like the walls of heaven fell down. See how they got gold rims?"

"Love it," said Susan, nodding her head to the unheard rhythms of the sun-gilded storm clouds. A window-shade flapped in the rising wind.

Alan's cheeseburger had gone down easily enough. His skug-enhanced body could digest anything at all. He felt greasy and cheerful, and a little relieved to have started the process of telling Vassar and Abby the truth. Who knew, perhaps those federal police wouldn't be able to track them after all.

Reflexively, Alan teeped around in the half-mile-wide radius that his mind could reach—but of course no other skuggers were in the vicinity. The short range of skugger teep was a bonus, if the feds were going to use the enslaved Landers to search for them. At least, with the skugs growing in awareness, there seemed to be little probability of anyone assembling a group-mind skugger antenna—like the one Burroughs had been using in Tangier.

Alan handed over one of his remaining twenty-dollar bills to pay for the lunch and the gas, taking his change in the form of sixteen candy bars. As a skugger, sweets meant more to him than they ever had before.

Back in the car, Ned and Alan each downed several candy bars. Vassar had one as well and, surfeited, dropped off to sleep. Susan rooted in her pile of tapes.

"Here it is," she said maneuvering the spool of tape onto her machine. "*Godwaters*. It's ninety minutes long."

A series of odd voices began jabbering about salvation and rebirth. Susan had looped and overlapped the words to produce a stuttering rhythm track that she'd overlaid with irregular squeals.

"Swine?" asked Alan.

"Seagulls," said Susan. "Pigs would be too obvious. And this way there's a shift in context, you see. The words are the surf."

Ned guided the maroon-and-cream Pontiac north-ward, temporarily ahead of the storm. By the time Susan's tape ended, the squall had overtaken them—violent Florida rain enlivened by stroboscopic lightning bolts and stumbling, drunken thunder. The steady-riding car was throwing up peacock-sheets of spray to either side. Alan felt exhilarated, happier than in years, on the loose in wildness of the American landscape.

"So beautiful," said Ned stopping at a puddled inter-section.

"Highway signs, yes," said Susan. "You'll be turning left on Route 8. That'll take us west into the panhandle."

"Eight's a nice number," said Ned.

They progressed westward along the Gulf coast, with the rain tapering off. Eventually Vassar awoke and they pulled over for a rest at the side of road. To their right was a cypress swamp. To their left a crooked moon sailed through the tattered storm clouds, casting radiance into the lagoon.

Alan savored the otherworldly scene—the tall bare trees with arched knees, the water obsidian black, the faint pale birds nested amid the veils of Spanish moss.

"Looks iffy," said Ned, who wasn't as reckless as he sometimes made himself out to be.

"I've heard people say that swamp water is good for you," said Vassar, crouching to splash off his face.

"Gator!" said Susan softly. "Look right there."

A bumpy dark form was lying just beneath the surface, half a body-length away from Vassar, the creature's nos-trils and eyes like gleaming knots on a silver log. He was utterly immobile, watching for his chance.

"Like a cop," said Vassar, taking a step back. He stretched and looked around. "My turn to drive? How far do you wanna go?"

Ned and Alan shared a pulse of teep. The great fear was that the feds had loaded Landers into a truck and were driving the skugsniffer after them—assuming they'd guessed which way to go. Alan wasn't quite sure how much information Landers had managed to glean from their final contact. In any case, it seemed wise to continue driving for many hours.

"Let's go for New Orleans," suggested Ned. "We'll take turns at the wheel and roll into the Big Easy at dawn. Find a room and have some fun. I've been there, you know. On shore-leave from the Navy."

"Vassar and I know some deep grooves there," said Susan. "We used to go the Vieux Carré for the music. Keep driving, yeah. It jolts me out of depression to stay awake all night."

"You're depressed?" said Vassar as if surprised. "Even though we're on an exciting adventure?"

"You nearly got arrested in Miami, Vassar. Tony El Tigre came by the apartment to shake us down. I gave up my nice job. And now we're in a car with your latest conquest, who seems more like a tranny than like a real girl—I'm sorry, Abby, but that's what I think. Yes, gang, Susan is depressed."

After this outburst, Susan ended up companionably dozing in the back seat with Alan. The two others sat in front, piloting their oversized an American car through the primeval night. Alan found it strange how easily

Susan had seen through his imitation game. A woman's intuition. Not that Vassar seemed to believe her.

Ned and Vassar took turns in the driver's seat, chatting and telling stories. They turned off Susan's tape machine and put on the radio, pulling in pop, hillbilly music, and, as the night wore on, jazz and the accordion arabesques of Cajun bands.

The sounds threaded through Alan's dreams. He saw chimerical ghosts like seahorses and flounders and cephalopods, with some of them bearing human faces on long necks. The ghosts peeped in from the periphery of his vision, slyly peering at him, always whisking out of sight when he gave them his full attention. Was his lamented flame Christopher Morcom among them?

But now images of the dead police captain appeared. First the captain was floating in a blackwater swamp being chewed by alligators, and then, oh horrible, the captain was rushing after Alan in vengeance, riding in a black hearse with a siren. Meanwhile the flickering ghost-things were chortling in the darkness behind Alan's head. Alan felt a sick conviction that these visions were real. But what did they mean?

It was a relief to awaken. Susan was leaning on his shoulder.

"You two look cute," said Vassar, smiling at them from the front seat. Ned was in the process of parking the car. They were in a city.

"Our bad boys," muttered Susan, rubbing sleep from her eyes. "We'll teach them respect, won't we, Abby? Let's make them our sex slaves."

"Perhaps," said Alan, embarrassed and a little aroused.

It was a wet dawn, still dark, the air filled with mist. They were in the French Quarter, among two-story buildings, very human in scale, with ironwork balconies supported by slender columns. A few of the town's legendary bon-vivants were passing by, only now making their way home.

A lean man with a cyst the size of a golf ball on the side of his face was singing the pop song that Alan had heard in Madeira. "Earth Angel." He moved his hands as if were swimming the breast stroke—dancing his way home. A gray-haired man in jeans and a billed cap was loading an eight-foot wooden cross into the back of his pickup truck, his night's preaching done. The cross bore the insignia, "Repent," along its cross-bar, the letters red and smeared. At the end of the block, a silky-voiced pitchman was cozening people into an upstairs after-hours bar.

"That's Zachary, isn't it?" said Susan. "This is the building where we stayed, remember Vassar? We had this wonderful room on the ground floor facing the garden in back. A little paradise. Hey, Zachary! Brother Squonk!"

"Square and root," said Zachary, a dark-skinned, well-knit man with tight curls. "It's Susan Green and Vassar Lafia. What you got for me, Vassar?"

"Smoke off the boat," said Vassar. "Straight from Sultan. Can we get the room by the garden?"

"The *looove* suite," said Zachary. "Vacant as of an hour ago. The night's dark suck and push is done. It's a spang new day. Feed my head and go to bed."

"Enjoy," said Vassar, passing Zachary a lump of hash.

"Can we, uh, score some sandwiches from upstairs, too? Muffalettas? Is the kitchen open?"

"I'll order two for you," said Zachary, examining Vassar's offering.

"And a six-pack of Regal Lager?" continued Vassar.

"Ned and I don't drink alcohol," put in Alan.

"Me either," added Susan. "Most of the time."

"Ginger ale for the others, and Regal Lager for me," amended Vassar. "I'm on a spree."

"We'll see," said Zachary, pocketing his hash. "Still playing with the acousmatics, Susan? Feed my ears. What's the latest?"

"*Bulldozer At The Dump*," said Susan in her flat, title-reciting tone. "*Wrong Supermarket. What It's Like To Be Dead. Orgasm Anyway. Godwaters.* I brought them all."

"This afternoon we'll jam. Your tape, my sax, and Nebuchadnezzar with his monstrous bass. Maybe Long John on the drums. Welcome to the Chateau La Pompe, y'all."

Their room was sizable and well-used, with overflowing ashtrays, empty bottles, and an enormous unmade bed. A door opened onto dim garden, faintly green in the burgeoning dawn. Feeling awkward, Alan found a trash can and tidied up. Ned got clean sheets from the cupboard and remade the bed. The food and drinks arrived. The little company recharged their energy.

"Let's bounce!" said Vassar now, bundling Susan and Alan onto the sheets.

"You too, Ned," said Susan, wriggling out of her shirt and pants. "Kiss me down low, sailor-boy. I know you want to. Be my slave."

"Susan, I don't know if—" began Vassar, his voice suddenly thin and righteous, even though he himself was jiggling Alan's large, bare breasts.

"In for a penny, in for a pound," said Susan. "Like Abby says."

So now they got into it, side by side. Vassar began hungrily pushing into Alan with short, quick thrusts, just like they'd done aboard the *Phos*. Alan reveled in the sense of being so easily penetrated. And Vassar had good staying power. Meanwhile Susan straddled Ned, rocked her crotch against his face for awhile, had an orgasm and switched to riding his cock.

Vassar kept looking over at Susan. He was aroused and somehow wistful. Alan rocked his womanly hips, wanting Vassar's full attention. Ned began to moan, a series of rising notes. Falling into rough synch, the four of them rushed the summit in unison. *Ka-boom*.

In the charged silence that followed, Susan slid off Ned and began kissing Alan on the mouth, thrusting in her tongue. He rather enjoyed this. Susan's antic creativity almost made up for her being a woman.

Meanwhile the overheated Ned, empowered by his skug, grew stiff again. He mounted Susan and plunged into her again.

"That's my wife," protested Vassar at this point. "Not some hired party girl."

"Oh hush, Vassar," said Susan, her voice tight and fast. "I'm into this now. Ned's the man." She let out a ragged laugh. "Let's yodel like we're in the Alps!"

"I said it's enough!" snarled Vassar. He sat up and

shoved Ned so hard that the taller man rolled off the bed and onto the floor.

"Time to zap you," said Ned, weary and annoyed. He swarmed across the bed, with his limbs like the bluntly flexing arms of a starfish. He elongated a finger and drilled it into Vassar's forehead—skugging the man on the spot.

Where Vassar had been all knotted aggression a moment before, now he was languidly draped in a posture of noble ease. Ned withdrew his finger; the hole in Vassar's brow healed over, and the drops of spilled blood sank into his skin.

Susan, shocked silent by Ned's assault, now found the breath for a scream. Ned abruptly skugged her as well, hooking his thumb into her temple.

Perhaps Alan could have intervened and stopped Ned. But he didn't care to. He was too fascinated by watching the situation unfold. And by now he was fully behind the skugs' cause.

A moment later, Susan had healed over, too. The four of them were in teep contact—that is, their skug-sensitized brains were exchanging subtle phase-modulated electromagnetic waves. Alan focused on Vassar, his rough-cut dreamboat.

Vassar was in his own world, staring at his hands, bending his fingers in odd ways, unsystematically exploring the qualities of his altered form. His inner mind was more oddly organized than Alan had realized before. The man's flashes of wit emanated not from chains of reason, but from surreal juxtapositions. A pair of images would collide and stick—and that would be the next thing that

Vassar said, heedless of any precise meaning. And then somehow a meaning would emerge. He had a great ability to turn off his inner filters. What Vassar thought, Vassar said. And, Alan could now perceive even more clearly than before, Vassar was somewhat unsure of himself. He knew full well that, on the world's terms, he was an ineffectual wastrel. Far from glorying in this, he nursed an abiding sense of regret.

"Astral radio rates you!" Vassar suddenly exclaimed, as if reacting to Alan's not entirely laudatory thoughts. Instinctively Vassar now veiled the deeper parts of his mind. "This is wild," he added, playing the rogue once more. "I like how you're staring at my dick, Abby."

"We'll grow comfortable with each other's inner ways," said Alan. It would only be a matter of minutes till Vassar saw down into the sexual secrets in Alan's mind. For now, Alan turned his attention to Susan, who was gazing at Ned, with a sea of stories in her eyes.

Susan's mind reminded Alan of when, as a boy, he'd creep into his mother's closet with its clutter of veils and feminine armatures, a place of mysteries. In Susan's head, sinuous melodies and sprung rhythms mingled with remembered voices and ambient noises—the slam of a door, a cough, the burbling of a percolator. Everything was in flux and under revision, as in some tootling cartoon landscape where every object joins in a communal jig. Susan was nothing like so blithe as he'd thought. Her psyche housed countless icons of how she had at various times imagined herself to appear from the outside. Her every utterance was a bravura performance to be pondered and stored. Her seeming opinions were to some extent in quote-marks, embroidered on samplers in mock-serious knotty-pine frames. Her actual opinions were harder to discern.

"It's okay, isn't it?" Ned was saying to Alan aloud. "That I skugged them?"

"We're four strange bedfellows," said Alan. "But, yes, we need a team if we're to spread the skugs worldwide."

"Complete global mastery, huh?" said Vassar. "Am I on board? Oh sure. Can I be, uh, the Duke of Jersey City?"

"And I'm the Duchess of Queens," added Susan. "Royal mutants on the prowl." Saying this, she twisted the last word into a musical tone, and warbled the sound up and down, her voice velvety. She stretched her arms like boneless tentacles, wrapping the four of them in a group hug. "All friends now? Even though you guys have destroyed our lives?"

"I hope this doesn't wear off," said Vassar. "I can stop even pretending to look for a job."

"We'll change the world forever," said Alan.

"Whoah," said Vassar, still sorting out the fresh scraps of data he was finding in Ned's and Alan's brains. "You're that same loser Ned who was on the ship? And, hold it— the Abby thing was a drag act? I've been boning a man?"

"And I'm not even William Burroughs," said Alan. "I'm Professor Alan Turing from Manchester."

"You might as well wear your real faces, boys," said Susan. "Let us see how you look."

Yes. Alan was dead sick of his imitation games. With a sudden flicker of his will, he was once again wearing

his original Alan Turing form—for the first time since
Christmas morning in Tangier. And Ned was back to
looking like he had on the ship.

"Alan, not Abby," said Susan, softly "Quite handsome.
The timid Prince Charming awakes from his spell. And,
Ned, you look even better this way."

"How do you feel, Vassar?" asked Alan. "I—I don't suppose you'll love me now?"

"I'll still run with you, big guy. I've got no problem with
queers. But—"

"You'll find the right man, Alan," said Susan. "Vassar
isn't the right man for anyone. He's a stopgap measure.
Even for me." Still naked, she cocked a roguish eye at her
husband. "And now that I can teep his complete record of
mortal and venial sins —"

"I like seeing your brain's insides, too," interrupted Vassar. "It's like I've made it into my teenage girlfriend's lacy
bedroom with the picture of a horse on the wall. We'll get
all snuggly and lovey-dovey, what do you say? A new leaf."

"I can be cozy if you can treat me right," said Susan.
"I've always gotten a thrill from you, Vassar. You know
that." She turned to Ned, who was rubbing against her
leg. "Back off, cad. I don't even know you."

"My dear wife," said Vassar. He yawned and sagged.
"Curl up with me, Susan, and we'll zonk some Zs. I feel
like I just had brain surgery. Or something."

"I'm *perky*," said Susan. "*Jazzed*."

"Oh, I'm for a snooze, too," said Ned. "Let's merge in a
mound. This'll be good for you, Vassar and Susan. Alan can
pass you a wetware upgrade to take off the rough edges."

Alan hung back, feeling himself on the outside once again. He feared that none of these three people would ever want to make love to him in a human way.

"Oh, stop feeling sorry for yourself and merge with us, Alan," exclaimed Ned, sensing his friend's thoughts. "This won't be mere sex," Ned added for Vassar's sake. "It'll be skugger conjugation. Very intense, very good for you. Alan is improving his metabolism all the time, and he'll share what he's got. The man's a genius, a mad scientist, the bullgoose wetware programmer in chief."

So, urged on by Ned and by Alan, the four of them piled up. Guided by Alan's teep, their tissues began to melt and flow, with tendrils from each body digging into the flesh of the skuggy flesh of the others. Alan was thinking of a topological paradox in which four endlessly ramifying solids share a single border.

But quickly the merge switched from the theoretical to the experiential. In some ways it was like sex, without being focused on the genitalia. They seeped, they shared, they shuddered, they slept as one. But Alan and Ned held back on the Los Alamos plan.

They woke in the early afternoon. Vassar gave Alan his extra shirt and pants. Led by Susan, they went upstairs into the on-rolling daily party in the Chateau La Pompe bar and grill. Zachary was improvising bebop bleats on his sax, with his jam-partners Nebuchadnezzar playing a lustrous wooden bass, and Long John on a red set of drums.

"Still no beer for you others?" Vassar asked as they paused by the bar. A golden-skinned woman named Bea was in charge.

"No need," said Alan. "You haven't half unpacked all the new wetware I've given you. Poke around in your *mito-chondria*."

"So, aha, I see that I can get myself high," said Vassar, staring off into space. "Makes life easier. You tweedle the bonk of the wiggle-doo."

"Putting it quite non-technically," said Alan.

"But we still need food," said Ned. "What kind of eats they got?"

"Crawfish?" said Vassar, leaning across the bar towards Bea, smiling and nodding. "You got? A giant pan of them, dear hostess. Enough for all of us. And I'll have a Regal Lager anyway."

"Feed our ears, Susan," called Zachary. "Jack us to the next level." While Long John played a stuttering tattoo, Nebuchadnezzar plucked suspenseful chords in a rising sequence that hinted at some dramatic conclusion.

"I'll be right back," said Susan. "I'll run and get my tapes and the machine from the car. Can you bring us a big pan of candied yams, too, Bea? Remember those, Vassar?"

Susan returned and got one of her tapes going—a giggly mix called *Orgasm Anyway*. And then Bea appeared with a rectangular pan of golden yam halves broiled with brown sugar, and a great round platter bearing a mound of boiled crawfish, dark dusky red, most of them about three inches long. Vassar showed Alan and Ned how to eat the tails of the crawfish.

Meanwhile the musicians played deedle-honk filigrees over the background of *Bulldozer at the Dump*. The tape contained sirens and the roaring of a lawn-mower.

"Highly agreeable," said Alan, his mouth full. "But what's wrong, Susan? I get a sense that—"

"I think some people have staked out our car. One of them tried to follow me. A thin redneck with a burr haircut. I cut through some alleys to shake him, which was a bitch, carrying my heavy tape machine."

"If we see the guy again, we can skug him," said Ned, his mouth full of orange yam. "And anyone else who's on our case. We rule."

"We're making it new," said Vassar. "You know how in all the SF movies, the fat cops and tight-ass scientists are working to control the giant ants or the twonky robots or the invisible aliens from space? We're turning the story around. We're the bizarre mutants, yeah—but we're the *heroes*."

"Should we feel sorry for the cops and scientists?" asked Susan.

"They get to be skuggers, too," said Ned. "So I like our new story better. It's time to break the system. The fat cats have been trampling the little guys for too long."

"And we're the rebel outsiders," said Susan. "Physical mutants. I always liked *playing* that role, but—" Her chin quivered ever so slightly. She was scared.

"Revel in your enhanced powers," said Alan, sympathetic to Susan's mix of feelings. "We've whole new worlds to explore."

"I hope we don't have to feel sorry for these *crawfish*," said Vassar, trying for a joke. "We're converting them, too."

"Converting the people and the crawfish and the yams," said Susan, perhaps a little too brightly. "It's all the same, huh? The flow of life."

"I've eaten *sixty-seven* of them now," said Alan, who'd been keeping track.

"He has a prime number in his stomach," said Ned.

"And now I need more sweets," said Vassar, finishing the last of the yams. "I'm realizing that from now on, sweets are what *really* get me high. Speaking as a shapeshifting mutant. Beer is piss."

"The light dawns," said Susan getting to her feet. She went to bop and dance beside Zachary and Nebuchadnezzar, and then she put on a new tape called *Granny Goose*. Bea returned with a half gallon of vanilla ice cream and a chocolate pie.

Perhaps everything was wonderful.

ELEVEN
on the road

R ight about then a skinny, weathered man came up the stairs.

"That's him," teeped Susan, shading her face with her hand. "The creep who followed me."

Without directly looking at them, the man had a quick shot of whiskey, then disappeared back down the stairs.

"*Stoooolie*," sang Zachary, the word long and low.

"I'll handle this," said Alan, feeling uncharacteristically tough. Bit by bit, being a skugger was changing him.

Making his feet soft and quiet, Alan hurried down the stairs like a nimble spider. He didn't have far to go. The spy was in a phone booth by the bathroom, talking into the receiver. Without over-thinking it, Alan pushed open the door and poked his hand into the saggy folds of the man's neck. He felt a slight tingle as a gout of skug tissue flowed into his enemy's body. And then the conversion was done.

"Rupert's the name," the man told Alan, placing the quacking phone receiver back into its cradle. "Rupert Small."

Alan's teep fed the man layers of information, although he made sure to block the new convert's access to the Los

Alamos plans. The fellow was an informer for the FBI, a part-timer rather than a fully employed agent. He'd gotten word from his contacts to look for a two-tone Pontiac Catalina, with a fifty dollar reward if he could finger the passengers.

"You was a few seconds late in tagging me," said Rupert aloud, baring his yellow teeth in a half-smile. "And now the heat's comin' down." He touched his neck. "Is it bleeding?"

"It's fine," said Alan, his mind racing. "How soon till they get here?"

"Ten minutes. This voice in my head says I should give you my car. A dark gray 1949 Hudson. It runs, once it starts."

"I'll call my friends," said Alan, sending them a teep signal.

"I feel like I'm shit crazy," said Rupert, stepping from the phone booth. An anxious frown shadowed his narrow face. "I don't like no voices in my head. That's what put my wife in the state hospital. The feds told me you was a cop-killer gang. But you more like Satanists, ain't you?" Rupert looked down at his arms which, in his nervousness, he'd begun twining around each other like vines. Jerkily, he straightened them out. "This thing that's possessed me—it's called a skug? I'm scared, Mister."

"You'll grow accustomed to it, Rupert. And the devil's not involved. Here come my mates. Let's go out the back door."

Ned, Vassar and Susan clattered down the stairs, Susan with her tape machine, and Vassar carrying the pile of tapes.

"It seems they extracted the information about our car from Landers," said Alan. "And Rupert here has phoned the FBI. We'd best roll on quite smartly."

"Who *is* this Landers, anyway?" asked Vassar petulantly. "I don't get what happened to him."

"He was a skugger and they captured him and they're torturing him to make him help," said Ned. "He's a skugsniffer. But he's not here in New Orleans yet. It'll be easy enough to skeeve away from the local clowns." He flashed a hard grin. "Dopes who'd hire someone like Rupert here."

"I was already sayin' your gang can take my car," put in Rupert, sounding aggrieved. "Although I will need a replacement. If your skug monsters can help with that."

"But our Pontiac was *beautiful*," wailed Susan. "Cream and maroon. And everything I own is in the trunk."

"We'll redeem your treasures, lady fair," said Ned softly. Alan could readily teep that, young and innocent as Ned was, he'd fallen in love with Susan as soon as he'd had sex with her. "And we'll make a clean sweep of the additional lowlifes staking out our car," continued Ned. "How many on your team, Rupert?"

"Three more," said Rupert, with a hillbilly cackle. "I'd relish to play a trick on those boys. They's a regular crew of crotch lice, horning in on my gig. We was playing poker when I got the call, you see, and they rode along in my car. It's parked right near yours."

The five of them exited the alley behind the hotel. It was three in the afternoon, a cool day, cloudy and bright.

"Look what somebody wrote on that pedestal, Susan,"

said Vassar, as they hurried past a statue of a saint. "*I am the light.* I'm gonna start saying that. Yeah, baby. I am the light."

"Illuminating every scene you're into," said Susan, enjoying her husband more than before. "My rebel seraphim."

"What we gonna do is slip through this little boneyard here," Rupert told Alan. "We'll motorvate over the back wall and skug them three boys in my car afore they know what's hit em. Make 'em slaves of Satan too."

"No black magic is involved," insisted Alan. "Skugs are *science*. A contagious and opportunistic biocomputational upgrade."

The vest-pocket cemetery was weedy and crumbling, with trash on the ground. As was the custom, the bodies were in crypts sitting atop the wet ground. A pale, fey woman in a ragged black dress slunk out from one of the tombs as if she'd taken shelter there.

"I'm Veronica Vale. You pilgrims lookin for a tour?"

"Sure," said Vassar, giving the woman the eye.

"We headin' straight through to the back is all," put in Rupert, who seemed to know the waif. "Go back in your hidey-hole, you."

"Your friends want me, Rupert," said Veronica, striking a pose. "*Noblesse oblige.* I'll show them my highlights. Hold your tips till the end." Very light on her feet, the spritely woman clambered atop the crypts, hopping from one to the next, staying abreast of the five skuggers, intoning a series of spontaneous effusions.

"Here lies Mamselle Bumpo de la France. Her poodle ate her frowny face. Over there is Doctor Patrice Congo.

He invented the inside-out trombone. Whoops-a-daisy, here's Marie Atomiste."

"You're great!" called Susan. She had her tape machine running, and she was pacing beside Veronica with her mike outstretched.

Veronica Vale hopped to the muddy ground, and skirted an overgrown structure. "Everything's glowing, you understand. With V-rays, eh? I see the future and the past."

"Where does it end?" asked Susan.

"New life for old meat," said the fey woman as they reached the cement wall at the back of the graveyard. "In Mexico City."

Rupert and Ned had already clambered onto a pair of headstones that leaned against the wall.

"Thanks awfully," Alan told Veronica Vale, handing her a dollar. And in that moment, he remembered his dream of this morning—the hearse with the flashing light, and the ghosts in the dark borders of his visual field.

"*Now* you see them," said Veronica Vale, with the preternatural sensitivity of the mad. "Now you don't." She waggled her fingers in Alan's face. "The crypts and the mud and the white winter sky." And then she'd danced back to her crypt.

Alan climbed up next to Rupert, while Susan and Vassar mounted a third gravestone.

"There's my Hudson," Rupert whispered, pointing to a stodgy gray car with a metal sun-visor like a cap's bill. It was less than fifty feet away.

"And the side-window's open," said Ned. "Here we go."

Ned's arm grew long and flexible, wriggling along the dirty pavement on the other side of the wall. "Oh!" exclaimed Susan softly. The arm crept along, drawing substance from Ned's shoulder and back—he became quite shriveled on his right side.

The three idlers in Rupert's car noticed the arm—Alan could make out the dark holes of their mouths in their surprised faces. The Hudson's engine made a frantic chuffing sound, trying fruitlessly to start.

Ned's arm rose like a cobra and struck—sending a finger into each of the vigilantes' heads.

"Quickly now," said Alan, slipping over the wall. Vassar helped Susan with her tapes and her machine, and then the five of them were on the sidewalk. The Hudson's struggling engine finally caught.

Rupert shooed his now-docile posse from his car and urged the others forward. "Go ahead y'all. The feds gonna be here any minute."

"Thanks, pal," said Ned, handing Rupert the Pontiac's key.

Rupert's newly skugged companions stood around him, a raffish, unlikely crew.

"I have it—the four of you should shape your bodies to look like *us*!" Alan said—speaking more to the skugs than to the skuggers. "Drive north to throw our pursuers off track."

With a rapid series of teep exchanges, their inner skugs organized the masquerade. And now Alan, Ned, Vassar and Susan were facing clones of themselves.

"So where all are you road-dogs headed?" asked the one who looked like Alan.

"I don't like to say," said the real Alan.

"West across Texas," said Rupert in a spiteful tone. "I saw that much in his head before he clamped down."

"Keep your trap shut about us," said Ned roughly. "Now beat it, and get your asses into that Pontiac down there. And before you leave, we'll move the stuff from its trunk into this crappy beater."

Ned took the wheel of the gray Hudson. Tentatively he tried revving the idling engine. It knocked and stuttered, with a bit of a roar.

"*Vroom!*" said Vassar as he, Susan and Alan got inside. "Go fast bad car." The Hudson was very worn inside, pale gray, with springs poking through the seat cloth.

Before any kind of police had arrived, Susan's goods were transferred, and the two cars were underway. As planned, Rupert headed north—and Ned found his way to a secondary road that ran along the bayou, that is, along the swampy border of the Gulf coast.

The Hudson's engine ran so roughly that a long push seemed unfeasible. Around sunset they veered off the main road, into a blue-collar settlement called Holly Beach.

The little resort was a congregation of trailers and dowdy, dinky plywood cottages, some with their windows boarded up. A line of power poles sketched a perspective against the jumbled silhouettes. Ned found a rickety two-story motel at the water's edge, run by a seedy rube named Oscar. As it was January 4, and a Tuesday to boot, the motel had no other guests whatsoever. Perhaps Oscar kept it open because he had nothing else to do.

The skuggers registered for a neighboring pair of rooms on the upper floor, Alan and Ned in one, Vassar and Susan in the other. They ascended to their quarters and surveyed the beach from a wobbly communal balcony that ran along the fronts of the rooms.

Alan was soothed by the rhythmic crashing of small brown-green waves. He'd been careening from one crisis to the next ever since stepping off the Phos four days ago. He needed some time to figure out an over-all plan. Where might the skug infestation lead? And why wasn't he more disturbed about the upheaval of his own inner life?

Voices and faint bursts of music sounded from a few of the cottages—some people were here year-round. Now and then a car or a pickup drove along the packed sand at the water's edge.

"Idiots," said Susan, observing a truck with a large flag on its rear.

"That's a bit like our Union Jack," remarked Alan.

"The Confederate flag," said Vassar. "Always a bad sign."

"I'm so glad we're leaving the South," said Susan.

"Check out the drillers," said Ned, pointing out towards the gulf.

The techno-smudges of a half dozen floating oil-rigs were on the horizon. As the night hastened in, the rigs lit up like Christmas trees, like spaceships. Alan wondered if the drilling platforms might learn to drift about on their own, prospecting for fresh oil pools, and even mining ore? What if the rigs learned to assemble behemoth copies of themselves—and began to reproduce? He imagined an Earth dominated by humans, skugs—and oil rigs.

"Shrimpers there," said Vassar pointing out a lit-up boat closer in. Long booms stuck out from its sides. "Dragging huge nets." The trawler moved slowly, laboriously, rocking from side to side, pulling the heavy weight of her catch.

"I'd be ready for more crustaceans," said Ned. "My skug's got my appetite dialed to high. That country boy downstairs—Oscar? He says there's a seafood depot down the beach. Open all the time."

They fed on memorably fresh and succulent shrimp in an unpretentious, knotty-pine-paneled nook off the seafood depot, which had coolers of frozen seafood along one side. They were the only customers. They topped off the meal with a massive bowl of bread pudding that Vassar cajoled from the twangy-voiced lady who ran the place. Reba. Her husband had seined these very shrimp. And she'd made the bread pudding—originally for her large family, who lived in a cottage out back

"I'll go make up another batch for them," said Reba. "If you can settle up the check now? Glad to see y'all enjoyin' yourselves. Just close the door on your way out."

They were quite alone now. Alan made a quick scan— no other skuggers were in range. Outdoors the wind was rising; the surf's tone was more insistent than before.

"Where exactly are we going?" asked Susan. "Across Texas and then what? You've been holding out on us, Alan. Hiding secrets. Maybe Ned knows, but I don't."

"It's better as a secret," said Alan. "Just in case."

"But I do know one thing," said Vassar. "Alan and our skugs want to turn everyone in the world into a skugger. All of us as one in the skuggy light."

"It's an opportunity for a lasting step forward as a race," said Alan. "Like when our ancestors left the water for dry land, or when they learned to walk on two legs, and to develop the power of speech."

"I keep thinking this is more like—I don't know—a virus that I caught," said Susan. "Even if the skug inside me says no. I keep hoping I'll be well by the time I'm in California. The real me."

"Becoming a race of skuggers is the path to an optimal future," insisted Alan. "The true path." For a brief moment, Alan saw himself as a Christ amid His apostles.

"In other words you've gone completely insane," said Susan, picking that image out of his mind. She got to her feet. "I've always hated cults. Religion sucks."

"I hear ya, girl," said Reba, reappearing through the back door. "Family's what matters. And good sex. No church at all in Holly Beach. Last year we had a preacher setting up shop to sponge onto us, and my husband run him off." She flipped off the lights. "Y'all go to bed now and work things out."

They didn't talk much on the walk back to the motel. Once they were upstairs, Ned went next door for noisy, confrontational sex with Vassar and Susan. Weary and bitter, Alan slept alone. Blessedly he had no dreams.

He awoke early, relishing the plash of the waves, the pearly gray light off the misty sea. Ned snored softly on the other bed. Often, in the empty interval of time at the start of a new day, Alan would get a clear sense of what mattered to him—before the usual worries and regrets came boiling into his mind.

Today the revelations were simple and clear: He loved William Burroughs. He wanted to be together with him. And he didn't want to die.

Next door a toilet flushed. Susan or Vassar was awake. Soon the four of them would be on the road again today, rushing further west. Alan realized he'd made an ass of himself last night. Jesus and the apostles? How gauche, how overweening. The skugs' influence was insidious, like a not-entirely-welcome drug. Why was Alan so eager to help these essentially inhuman forms of life? Was he really so resentful of society that he wanted to destroy it?

Standing in the bathroom, Alan looked sideways out the open rear window. A fit-looking man was studying their car, peering into the windows. Alan's stomach clenched. Surely this was another stool pigeon—or a federal agent.

Driven by an unexpected reflex, Alan vomited into the toilet. But—oh, how repellant—the vomitus was in fact a spawned-off skug. The slimy, orange-yellow thing sprouted a forest of tiny snail-antennae, feeling at the water and air, making a plan. And then it slithered from the bowl, smoothed over, paled in color, and took on the form of a seagull. The skug-bird hopped to the sill of the bathroom window and gave a peremptory caw. Hearing the sound, the snooper by their car turned his head. Too slow. The gull was already diving at him. The skug sank into the man's chest, enlisting him on the spot.

Alan pulled on his borrowed clothes and stumped downstairs. The new convert's name was Roland Gill, and he was indeed an agent for the FBI. Being a skugger now, Gill was basically on Alan's side, albeit with many inner doubts. The two of them had a low-voiced conversation, filling in some background details.

"I'm just surprised to find your gang here," said Gill. He was a solidly built little man, crewcut and with a mild Southern accent. Really quite cute. "Bunch of folks saw your car heading north on US 51. With passengers matching your group's description. English scientist, tall Southern guy, and a boho couple from up North. We're on track to capture them today. The agency only sent me out his way to follow up on that informer—Rupert Small? This here's his car. So I'm guessing you swapped. But—"

"Rupert and his friends changed their *shapes*," said Alan. "To look like us. They're all skuggers too."

"I can change my shape now?" asked Gill, staring critically at his right hand. "Get a little brawnier?"

"Whatever one wants," said Alan. "You saw the seagull. Moments ago, he was a foot-long slug. But do tell me what do you know of Norvell and Landers."

"Those West Palm Beach cops, yeah. The agency ambushed them at the house of the police captain they killed. We skuggers aren't going to win every round, it seems. I can't hardly believe I'm saying *we*."

"And they made Landers into—a skugsniffer?"

"Yeah. We got him locked down inside a glass contraption that trickles in just enough air and sugar-water to keep him going. Along with some electrodes to put a hurt on him if he won't help. He's our skugsniffer, like you might say. He uses this telepathic ability that we skuggers—"

"We call it teep," said Alan.

"Yeah," said Gill, squinting up at the pink sky. "Still getting up to speed. I can teep your three friends upstairs. Neddie's asleep, Susan's singing in the shower, and Vassar's spying on us. Comb your hair, Vassar. Grease it real good." Agent Gill looked back at Alan. "There's another problem we gotta face."

"What's that?"

"We got a government lab on the case, and they using Norvell's remains to culture an anti-skug vaccine. Should be rolling in production right about now. They inoculating the FBI strike force that's going after decoy crew you sent up US 51. They still think that's gonna be you. You lucky you got an agent on the inside."

"Quite," said Alan. "Do you have a secure line where I can phone you, Mr. Gill? It would aid us immensely to know how the hunt's progressing."

"Here's my office number," said Gill, teeping it to him. "But why not use telepathy?"

"The teep only reaches half a mile," said Alan.

"Oh, yeah," said Gill. "I did know that. The Bureau's milked a lot of intel from Landers by now." Agent Gill chuckled. "Might say Landers is spineless. Packed into that jar like a pudding."

"Canned pig meat," put in Vassar, who'd appeared at their side. "Crap in a can."

"Screw you, boho," said Agent Gill in a level tone. "Breaks my heart to be on the same side as a guy like you."

"I'm sorry, we're all a bit on edge," said Alan. "But don't forget the higher cause. And now, Mr. Gill, please go back to New Orleans and follow the hunt. And here's the technique for setting up a teep block so the skugsniffer can't suss you." Quickly Alan teeped Gill the info.

"Right," said Gill. "And I'll wait to hear from you. Meanwhile I'll tell the Bureau that nobody's seen Rupert's car out this way. And you'll be going—"

"The less you know the better."

"A foot soldier," said Gill, flexing his arms and making his biceps grow. And now, as if on a whim, he punched Vassar in the stomach. Smiling, he got in his car and left.

Meanwhile, Oscar, the motel owner, had stepped outside, obviously curious about what was going on.

"Ya'll boys in trouble?"

"All is in order," said Alan. "Correct, Vassar?"

"Might as well be," said Vassar, slowly straightening up. "I'm damn near indestructible."

Vassar went upstairs to round up the others, while Alan went into the lobby to settle accounts with Oscar. And then of course Alan skugged the motel-owner—and asked for his car.

"And you want to stick me with that whipped old Hudson?" griped Oscar, more concerned with the vehicles than with his new state of symbiosis.

"I'd advise you to repaint it and change the plates."

"Anyone with a lick of sense is gonna paint a gray car," said Oscar, tossing his head to get his lank, dangling hair out of his face. "Shit. And you're getting a 1951 Buick Roadmaster with those foxy little portholes in the side. Dynaflow."

"Is it two-tone?"

"Yeah, bo. White and green. And the roof's white, too. You care about cars? A limey like you?"

"My friend Susan cares. She's artistic."

"Ooo la la," said Oscar.

The four made their way through Port Arthur, through Austin, and into the heart of Texas. Alan and Susan rode in back and Vassar and Ned in front. Whatever had happened in the bedroom last night must not have been entirely satisfactory, as today Susan seemed to be on the outs with both Ned and her husband. Be that as it may, Alan was fully enjoying the randomness and oddity of this trip. The fact that he might very well be doomed gave it the more spice.

Lord, but Texas was big. They drove all day through a landscape like unfinished sketches for a world. Arid trails led up through stark, immense valleys into the red mountains. Unfinished, but lovely.

"There's so much more beauty than I can take in," Alan remarked to Susan. "I'm like a wineglass in a waterfall. I wish I could somehow merge with the flow. To *become* the landscape instead of making mental *models* of it."

"At least let's stop and take a better look," said Susan. "How about it, Vassar? Let's pull over."

Vassar drove them well off the road, a few dozen yards down a dirt track.

"You could drop the British Isles into this landscape and they'd hardly make a splash," said Alan, turning in a full circle. His attention fastened upon a huge single red rock, fluted on the sides. *Such* a mass of quanta. He felt a rush of ontological wonder sickness. Why did anything exist?

They wandered about, with little lizards lifting up their striped tails to run away. Alan admired the clumps of prickly pear cactus—the lobes with buds along their rims, and with yellow and red flowers sprouting amid the thorns. The cacti seemed so perfectly placed amid the grasses and the dry red rocks. All hail nature's unpredictable computations.

"It's like another planet out West," said Vassar.

"Do you ever feel that our language is too feeble?" said Susan, looking up from her tape recorder. She was capturing the faint sounds of the wind amid the rocks. "We have such a puny stock of words."

"And yet one imagines that human language *is* universal," said Alan, shifting into professor mode. "G. K. Chesterton remarks upon our presumption in supposing that we can represent the subtleties of nature and the mind with an arbitrary system of grunts and squeals."

Wanting attention, Vassar launched into a disturbingly lifelike imitation of a pig, starting with comfortable grunts and rising to frantic wheenking—and then, to top it off, using his shapeshifting skills to grow a disked snout and triangular, flopping pig ears.

"You're too much," said Susan, weakly laughing.

"Squeals about squeals," said Vassar, reverting to human mode. "That was *meta*, you dig? Art about art." Alan could never quite decide whether Vassar was stupid or smart. But at some level Alan loved him, even though he was all Susan's now.

When the sun began once more to set, they stopped in a roadside strip of a town called Gormly—gritty, sunblasted, wind-blown, positioned between a butte and a long hill leading up to some mountains. The weather had turned colder, with low wet clouds.

Now that they were skuggers, the four fugitives were always hungry. They made for the local diner. Alan was impressed by a mounted steer's head on the back wall; it was the size of a wood-burning stove, with immense horns protruding on either side. The waitress informed him that this particular longhorn's name was Old Gib, which was in fact the name of the diner as well. Old Gib had led numerous cattle drives from these parts to Dodge City—and in recognition of his service, his owners had mounted his head.

"That's *tight*," said Vassar. "What if our herders treat us like that, Alan? Once they've stampeded us wherever the hell we're supposed to go."

Despite their empathy for Old Gib, they all ordered steaks, in fact filet mignons, which cost little more than hamburgers here.

"This is is the first steak I've had in years," said Susan, as if proud of herself for eating one. She leaned back in her banquette, sticking out her stomach and patting it, gleeful as an eleven-year-old. "A skugger can eat anything!"

While the others were downing multiple orders of pie a la mode, Alan went to the phone booth outside the diner and phoned up Roland Gill. Instead of Roland, he got a woman who said she was Gill's assistant. Alan was a little leery of trying the alternate number that she gave him, but he steeled himself and went ahead. A strange man answered, but he passed the phone to Roland. Excited voices were in the background. A door closed, and now Gill was alone.

"Some bad news," said Gill, speaking very softly. "Our tactics squad caught up with Rupert and his pals today. The new vaccine works good—none of the tactics team got skugged. Landers did a bang-up job at picking Rupert's mind before our boys killed him. So now they fixin to chase you across Texas."

"Right *now*?" said Alan, a break in his voice.

"Leaving in ten minutes," whispered Gill. "We flew the team straight to Austin. We've got Landers in a long white ambulance car with a monster V-8. Police escort, sirens—we'll be coming up behind you, doing a hundred and ten. We got a whirlybird, too. Watch for it."

"And you're with the group in Austin?"

"Roger. I faked getting the vaccine and I've got my teep block. So far everyone thinks I'm on the up and up. It's thin ice, but the skug won't let me slack off. You know how it is. Maybe I'll save your life."

"Can I call you again?"

"That first number is secure. The girl you talked to, she's my assistant, and she's one of us too. We can pass messages through her. Tell her you're, uh—"

"Old Gib," said Alan. "I'll say I'm Old Gib."

"That works. All hail the skugs." Gill said this wearily, but without irony.

Rejoining his three partners in the quiet booth at the Old Gib Chuckwagon, Alan told them what Gill had said.

"We need teep blocks too!" exclaimed Susan. "Do they involve sound?"

"Sure," said Ned. "Listen here." He leaned back in his chair, tall and calm, looking like a Texan himself. "You imagine that your skull's a lead nutshell. And you occupy your mind with complex bullshit. Like math or sports records or musical scores. Down lower, you wallpaper your emotions with a chant—acousmatics would be perfect for this, Susan. And then you wrap the whole package in an imaginary wire chicken coop."

"What a load of crap," said Vassar dismissively. He wasn't fond of Ned. To clear things up, Alan simply teeped Susan and Vassar a simple, holistic sense of how to make the block.

"I'm covered now," said Susan, ever so slowly drumming her fingers on the tabletop. "With *Bulldozer At The Dump* on my mind. In case that ugly parade arrives. Do you know what they'll look like, Alan?"

It was dark outside now, with headlights whizzing by. A fine rain was falling, making the highway shine.

"They'll have Landers in a white ambulance with a siren and a light," said Alan. He paused, thinking. "The odd thing is that, day before yesterday, I dreamed about a vehicle of this type chasing me. But it was black instead of white. A hearse."

"This restaurant wants to close," said Vassar. "The lady at the counter keeps looking us. Like, *why are you still here*. But it'd be wack to get back on the main highway. We'd be like rabbits hippity-hopping down a railroad track, thinking we can outrun the locomotive. We gotta head off on a side road."

"Can't we go to a motel?" said Ned. "We need sleep."

"Dangerous," said Alan. "We lose our teep blocks when we sleep. Don't you remember how the police surprised us on the beach, Ned?"

"So let's bop way out into the range land and sleep in our car," said Vassar. "Ready to roll?"

"Do be careful," said Alan. "The driving will be dodgy in the rain."

He felt terribly uneasy. In his mind, the hearse and the ambulance had merged into a furiously puffing engine of doom, with a single blazing headlamp trained upon his pale face.

TWELVE
coyotes

On the way out to the car, feeling sick with fear and loneliness, Alan nipped into the phone booth again.

"Oh, what now?" snapped Vassar.

"Leave him be," said Ned, who'd already teeped what Alan was up to.

Alan had decided to phone the Burroughs home. Perhaps he was about to die. He needed to talk to Bill one last time. Grumbling but basically patient, Ned, Vassar and Susan stood beneath the entrance overhang outside the Old Gib, smoking cigarettes and watching the rain.

Lacking any large amount of coins to pump into the phone, Alan recklessly made it a collect call. He told the operator to say the call was from "Bill's friend Abby."

Fortunately it was Laura Burroughs who answered. Although it was nearly bedtime in Palm Beach by now, she was willing to take the call.

"Oh hello," said Alan. "You remember me from the chat at your store?"

"Yes I do," said Laura Burroughs. "The Abby who's an Alan. Lucky you, Bill is here. He turned up yesterday evening. I'll see if I can rouse him."

A moment of charged not-quite-silence ensued, with fifteen hundred miles of ticks and whispers chiming in. Perhaps some extra listeners were on the line? Alan didn't care. Nothing mattered more than speaking with Bill. Laura Burroughs's low heels clicked down a hall, a door opened, low voices murmured, heavier footsteps returned.

"Hello?" said Bill.

"It's me," said Alan, a bit of reproach creeping into his tone. "The friend you've been persecuting." The next words hopped out of his mouth unbidden. "I love you, Bill."

Alan heard Bill slowly clearing his throat. And then Bill spoke. "Pleasant words. Quite welcome. I got your message here. It crawled up my leg. I'll come where you said?"

"I'm still on the road," said Alan. "We're having difficulties."

"The heat?"

"Indeed," said Alan. "With luck I'll finish my trip tomorrow. You know the area." From having teeped and conjugated so intensely with the man during their Tangier interlude, Alan knew that Bill had attended the Los Alamos Ranch School as a boy.

"Right," said Burroughs tersely. "This line sounds tapped." Suddenly his voice took on an unexpectedly tender sound. "Sweet dreams, brave prince. I'll wing to your side." He cleared his throat and rang off.

By the entrance to the Old Gib, a dotty old man was talking with the others. "Yew ain't from around here," he rasped. "Are yew from East Texas?"

"Very far east Texas," said Susan. "Ultra super far east."

"Have yew visited the Gormly caves?" the geezer asked Alan. "If yew got time tomorrow, yew should see em.

They a world wonder. Just head up that road right across the street. It winds up to where they is."

"I'll keep it in mind," said Alan. "Good night."

The old man doddered off. To Alan he seemed sinister, a minion from the underworld. But Vassar liked his proposal.

"The Gormly caves!" said Vassar. "I dig it."

They were sitting in the car now, Vassar at the wheel, the rain running down the windshield. "I love caves," continued Vassar. "We can sleep way down deep, like in a bomb shelter. Nobody can teep us there. Let's do it."

"It's night," objected Susan. "They'll be closed."

"I bet some kind of guard lives up there," said Ned, taking to the idea. "A ranger. We'll skug him, and he'll let us in."

As it happened, the caves were atop a fairly long rise, at the base of some stubby peaks. They did indeed find a ranger living in a cabin near the caves' locked entrance. He was Cornelius Twiste, a gawky young bachelor with a prominent Adam's apple. Alan instantly, joyously, pegged him as a fellow exponent of the love that dares not speak its name. And a single shared glance confirmed this.

As gently as possible, Alan skugged Cornelius, and the young man readily agreed to lead them down into the caverns for the night. He rustled up five foam mats and sleeping bags for them—apparently it wasn't unheard of to have sleepovers in the cave.

As if by reflex, Cornelius gave them a bit of a tour along the way, turning the subterranean lights on and off as they passed. Alan was charmed by the names of the mineral formations: the striped beige draperies were cave bacon, the knobbly translucent growths were popcorn, the wrinkled, doughy slumps were flowstone.

They halted their progress beside a creamy, motionless cascade known as Moon Milk Falls.

"This is the perfect spot to camp," said Cornelius, laying his mat beside Alan's. "Dry and with sweet ventilation." Shortly thereafter he turned out the lights.

In the intense, velvety dark, Cornelius and Alan deliciously made love—ignoring the others' ability to hear them and to teep them. The others, as it happened, were *not* having sex tonight. Eventually Alan slept, falling into dreams of flight—with the ghost of boyhood flame Chris Morcom flitting along ahead of him.

In the morning Cornelius led them back the way they'd come, shyly holding Alan's hand. As a precaution, they put up their teep blocks well before they reached the surface.

"Some of those bulges look bigger now than on the way in," said Susan, merrily rolling her eyes at Alan

"A stalagmite could take a hundred thousand years to grow," said Ned, who was a bit slow this morning.

Alan briefly let himself imagine that the tingling dark night by the Moon Milk Falls had indeed lasted for a hundred thousand years. What brave new world might they encounter when they emerged?

But outside the cave, it was still raining, still 1955. Eight in the morning, wet and gloomy. As a parting kindness, Cornelius brushed Alan's cheek with his lips. A sweet goodbye. The low, dripping clouds seemed close enough to touch.

Soaked to the skin, Ned, Vassar, Alan and Susan motored down the hill to Gormly. The plan was to get breakfast at the Old Gib, and ask around about whether the police had passed through during the night. Perhaps Alan would phone Roland Gill's office to check for messages. And, depending what they learned, they might strike out along the back roads—not that any of them other than Ned knew of Alan's secret goal to reach Los Alamos, New Mexico.

Things felt wrong as soon as they coasted into Gormly. There was absolutely no traffic in either direction—and no people on the wet streets. They pulled up by the Old Gib diner. The place was deserted, with a CLOSED sign on the door.

"I'll try the phone again," said Alan, hopping out of the car.

Upon ringing Agent Gill's New Orleans number, Alan heard a new voice, cruel and mocking, not at all the same as before.

"Is this 'Old Gib'?" said the stranger, before Alan could even speak. "I'm Dick Hosty. You've reached the end of your trail, professor. Just like Roland Gill." The sound of the phone line was false, echoing, empty. A local tap?

Hands trembling, Alan hung up. The wretched, empty town felt like a stage set.

And now, sudden as a shout, a helicopter clattered in through the steady rain, hovering directly above them, a chopper with a full bubble canopy and a tail made of struts. From the passenger seat, a man was aiming a machine-gun at them, a heavy weapon with Swiss-cheese holes in the barrel's cladding. The first downward salvo, destroyed the Buick's engine.

All around them, as in a terrible dream, the streets came alive with flashing police cars. Nestled among them like a queen among drones was the dreadful shape of the long white ambulance—bearing Landers the skugsniffer within.

One man was in charge of the milling chaos—a tall Texan in boots and a ten-gallon hat, standing high in the back of a pickup truck, pointing, gesturing, and talking into a jury-rigged phone. With sudden conviction, Alan knew this was Dick Hosty, the man he'd just talked to. As if in confirmation, the behatted man pointed straight at Alan, wiggling his thumb like the hammer of a pistol.

The cops and agents opened fire. There were no skuggers among them—only the sullen, resentful Landers, sealed in his bottle in the rear of Hosty's ambulance.

The phone booth's sides collapsed in shards; the Buick's windshield and side-windows were punctured and cobwebbed.

In the car, the single-minded Susan she bent over her stash of acousmatic tapes, rapidly pressing them against her belly one by one, burying them in her skugger flesh.

Backing up to the car, Alan held his hands high in a gesture of surrender. The unrelenting rain was running down his neck and into his shirt. Ned climbed out of the car, and then Vassar, with his arm around Susan. Vassar was bleeding from his shoulder.

"You can still heal yourself," Alan called to Vassar, "Just focus, and you can grow the wound together." Alan called to him.

Vassar stationed himself in front of Susan, wanting to protect her. And dear Ned did the same for Alan.

"We're at the end of the road," Ned told Alan, his voice calm. "Remember me if you make it outta here, man. We had a good run."

"Maybe—maybe we can skug these bobbies," said Alan. "Dear Ned."

Two armored agents were striding towards them from Hosty's pickup, each of them wearing a backpack and carrying a gun-like metal wand. Flamethrowers! In teeped synchronization, Alan and Ned grew tendrils from their hands and ran them along the ground and into the legs of the advancing executioners.

But it was fruitless. The two cops had been vaccinated. From a skugger's point of view, their flesh was as infertile as glazing putty. There was no way to instill a symbiotic skug.

Hollering in fury, the agents pressed the triggers on their short-barreled wands and—here came the end—the nozzles blossomed with long tongues of flame. Crouching and moving closer, the killers played the cascade of burning liquid across Ned and across Vassar, moving the flames faster than the men could run away. Alan and Susan would be next.

Hosty's riflemen were firing with brutal precision. They knocked out Vassar's and Ned's legs from beneath them. Another shot drilled a hole in Alan's thigh. Vassar and Ned were screaming, their telepathic signals were horrible in the last degree.

Alan lurched over to Susan and manhandled her into the slight amount of shelter that lay the far side of the Buick. The helicopter remained directly above them, but for the moment they were shielded from the rifles and the flames.

Alan could teep the dying emanations of Vassar's and Ned's minds. The sensations were unfathomable, moving beyond pain and into a curious ecstasy. All the

circuits blown, the networks curling inwards, the sense
receptors gone.

"Save Vassar, you bastard!" said Susan, weeping and
shaking Alan by the shoulders. "Can't you feel it too? Go
out there and save him."

But there was no use. Alan lay down flat in the gravel
beside the Buick, working on his leg. Peering through
under the car, he could see Vassar and Ned very clearly.
They were charred stick figures now, their limbs waving
in a ghastly, insect-like parody of human life, their teep
signals coming from a purer and calmer place. The flamethrowers took a pause, their first task done.

"So horrible," said Alan, his voice catching. "I loved
them."

"Vassar was a gentleman all along. In his own way. I
should have told him that." Susan had flattened herself
by Alan's side. Suddenly her voice rose an octave. "Oh
god, Alan, look now—look, look, look—I can see Vassar's
soul!"

Faint patterns of lines were visible above their beloved
companions' charred skulls. Alan couldn't see them
straight on, he had to look a little to one side, picking
them up in his peripheral vision. Above Ned was an intricate polyhedron with faintly glowing edges, as if modeled
from pastel neon tubes. Dear Ned and his love of math.

And above Vassar was a plump glowing shape like a
thickened plate—hard to make out what it was. The
forms drifted upwards, just barely visible, mysterious and
promising. Souls? Who could say. By now they'd moved
beyond the range of view allowed by Alan's position—

lying on his stomach, peering though the narrow space beneath a car.

"Kill the other two skuggers!" Hosty was yelling, his hoarse, vindictive voice clear against the splash and hiss of the rain. "Do it now!"

Alan made his arm very thin and long, like a spider's leg. He grew his arm steadily upwards through the buffeting air-currents of the helicopter's prop wash, focusing all his attention upon the task. Meanwhile, on the ground, the men with the flamethrowers were circling around the side of the Buick.

High in the air, Alan's hand reached into the open door of the hovering chopper. He sank his branching fingers into the bodies of the pilot and his gunman. Blessedly these two hadn't been vaccinated. Sighing with relief, Alan skugged them.

"Hold all fire," bellowed the pilot through the helicopter's loudspeaker. "Hold fire, Agent Hosty!" Dropping rapidly from the air, the clattering copter thudded down in the lee of the Buick—right beside Alan and Susan.

The cops and FBI agents hadn't yet grasped what was happening. The skugging process was very new to everyone—and Alan's upward-reaching arm had been so thin as to be invisible in the heavy rain. The men with the flamethrowers drew back, faces stolid, awaiting further orders, imagining things were proceeding according to some official plan. For the moment, even Agent Hosty had fallen still.

With a crisp salute, the gunman from the helicopter disembarked, bearing his heavy machine-gun, which was trailed by a belt of bullets leading back to an ammo box on the copter's floor. Silently the barrel swayed left and right, as if defying anyone to challenge them.

Moving sullenly, as if in custody, Alan and Susan shuffled aboard the copter, Alan got the passenger seat, and Susan squeezed in between Alan and the pilot. The engine sound rose to a frantic roar. The skugged gunman from the chopper handed Alan the machine-gun and stepped away.

Alan broke into a wild grin as the chopper lifted off. He nudged the pilot, pointing his chin at the ambulance. "I want to shoot that!" he cried.

"You want to watch the kick on that Browning," admonished the pilot. He was a hatchet-faced, olive-skinned man with a black crewcut. "Try to dance with the thing. My name's Naranjo. Means juicy orange."

As the chopper leaned and circled, the policemen around the ambulance became uneasy. Dick Hosty began yelling orders again. One of his guards took aim at the chopper with his rifle. Leaning from the copter's door, Alan fired a fusillade towards Hosty and his men, sending the bullies scrambling for shelter.

And now Alan had the ambulance in the machine-gun's sights. His mind was running at high speed, watching for snipers, correcting for the helicopter's motion, planning the bullets' downward trajectory. With his arms poised like springs, he pressed the trigger.

The Browning bucked and jabbered like a live animal. The raindrops sizzled on the cooler-jacket around its barrel. Alan poured round after round into the bland, eggshell-white roof of the ambulance. Hosty's men were firing upwards. Fractures webbed the chopper's bubble-shaped windshield. Susan was making herself as small as possible, her eyes wide with fear. And now, oh no, a sudden blot of red appeared on her chest.

Alan exhorted Susan to heal herself—and kept on strafing the cops. Naranjo threw the helicopter into a tighter gyre. Alan poured still more fire into the rear of the evil ambulance—and finally the thing split apart. Its gas tank exploded, and a crooked ball of fire engulfed the foul cargo in the rear.

As the chopper slewed away, Alan had a final glimpse of the misshapen Landers twitching in the flames. Another victim in the war against the skugs. As innocent, in his own way, as poor Ned and Vassar. Alan sighed.

And now his attention returned to the helicopter's cabin. Rain was dripping in through the bullet holes in the canopy. Susan was bent forward, intent on healing the gunshot wound in her chest. Down below, Hosty was trying to follow them in a Jeep—but soon the chopper was alone above the cattle range, with a trackless wasteland of rocks coming up.

"Are you coping?" Alan asked Susan. "Can I help?"

"I'm patching my heart," said Susan with a tight little sob. "Knitting it up. So crazy weird. Anyone else would be dead. And I've still got all those tapes down in my belly."

"Nobody's really explained to me what's going on," said the pilot. "What exactly did you do to me back there, Turing? With that long-arm finger-poke of yours?"

"I made you a skugger," said Alan. "Gave you a symbiote. Like Susan and me. We have telepathy and we can shapeshift. That's why Susan can heal her wound. We're lucky."

"*Lucky*?" exclaimed Susan, her face a stark mask of grief. "You're killing us all! Ruining our lives. Poor Vassar! You thought he was just a toy to pick up and use. He was a man. He was my man. I want your horrible skug out of my body!"

"I'm with you on that," said Naranjo. "I don't like somebody reaching into me and changing me." He glared at Alan. "And now I have to help you whether I want to or not. So where you want to go?"

"There," said Alan, pointing northwest. "I'd like to make it to the northern part of New Mexico."

"You're talking about a five hour flight in my whirly-bird," said Naranjo. "And they'll be sending planes after us. Fighter jets with radar."

"Oh god," said Susan.

"You're scared of the *jets*?" said Naranjo, his thin mouth twitching in a slight smile. "Relax. You already survived the flamethrowers and the bullet through your heart."

"I have no interest in being all bluff and macho," said Susan. "And what do *you* know about grief, Naranjo?"

"Long story," said Naranjo shortly. He patted Susan's shoulder. "Didn't mean to harsh on you. You're right to be scared."

"I wish—" said Susan, her voice going thin and breaking. "I wish I'd hung onto my tape recorder. It would soothe me to be making some of this into art. Like I'd like to record the rackety thudding of this helicopter."

"Oh, it's a classical symphony in here all right," said Naranjo with a slight smile.

"You can remember the sounds," Alan told Susan. "Our minds are as good as any tape recorders now. And, if you try, I bet you can sing any sound that you can think. Maybe even by vibrating your skin."

"What do I care about your ridiculous opinions," said Susan. "You're a heartless robot."

"Right again," said Naranjo. "He wants us all to be mutant machines like him."

"We're on the same team," insisted Alan.

"In your opinion," said Naranjo. "Here's some good news. With this weather, if we fly low, the jets aren't gonna find us."

"It'll all turn lovely in the end," Alan said in his sunniest tone. "Maybe Ned and Vassar aren't really dead, Susan. Those shapes we saw above their bodies? Those could have been aethereal information patterns."

"Ghosts?" asked Naranjo, taking an interest. "I know some dead people I'd like to talk with."

"We saw their ghosts, yes," said Susan, happy with the thought. "Even though I can tell that Alan thinks we imagined it, and now he thinks he's talking down to me, even though I'm a professor too. Did you forget that, Alan?"

"Look here, it's not certain we saw those patterns," said Alan, truly wanting to comfort Susan, but remaining stubborn about bending what he considered to be the truth. "Everyone occasionally sees odd little shapes from the corners of their eyes, no? And ever since I became a skugger, these effects have been enhanced. My mind's clicking at a faster rate. I dream about pale monsters, undersea ghosts, wraiths of the air—"

"I saw Vassar's soul, goddamit. Just frikkin' admit it, Alan. I saw Vassar's soul and that makes me glad. Do you mind?"

"All right, I suppose it's possible. Perhaps the fact the we're skuggers makes us more perceptive. And perhaps the fact that Ned and Vassar were themselves skuggers made what you call their souls robust, active, and easier to see."

"So we don't have a thing to worry about," said Naranjo sardonically. "We've got glowing magic souls. Even if an Air Force fighter blasts us out of the sky. Oh hell, man, I should have stayed home in bed. But even that's no fun now that my wife left me."

Flying low, hugging the mountain ranges and the arroyos, Naranjo took them across Texas and into the southeastern corner New Mexico. The foul weather was moving with them, which was a plus, in terms of stealth.

The rain was turning to sleet. Fortunately the chopper had a primitive heater. And Alan found some rags to stop up the bullet holes in the canopy. A couple of hours went by. The engine seemed to be laboring harder than before.

"Ice on the blades," said Naranjo. "And we're low on fuel. I know of a crop-duster airport up ahead. We'll land there and tank up."

"Maybe we shouldn't stop yet," said Susan. "With the jets hunting for us and all."

"Got to stop," said Naranjo. "A full tank only carries my whirlybird about four hundred miles. Especially flying flat-out like we've been doing."

"What about the guys working at this airport?" said Susan. "What do we tell them?"

"We skug them," said Alan.

"Always the same answer," said Naranjo. "Recruit them to your psycho cause. We're crazed guerilla missionaries for a cult. So tell me how the skugging bit works, okay? In case I want to ruin someone like you ruined me."

As it happened, only one man was on duty at the little airfield, a pimply youngster in mechanics overalls, and he was on the point of locking the hanger. The sleet had given way to snow. An inch of the stuff lay on the ground. Pilot Naranjo shook the mechanic's hand and skugged him on the spot.

The youth's name was Earl. Earl, Naranjo, Alan and Susan ate all the candy bars that the airfield had behind the counter in its little store.

"Skuggers aren't exactly geared for running a store," remarked Naranjo, as he took half the bills from the till.

"Anarchy," said Earl, pocketing the rest of the cash. "Anarchy is cool."

Before leaving, Alan advised Earl about how to deal with the enemies of the skuggers. "It's vitally important not to be taken alive," Alan told the mechanic. "The authorities want to seal you in a jar and torment you into being a spy. But for a shapeshifter, there's generally a way to break free. Or—experience the illusion of death and ascend to the astral plane. Don't be limited by the old modalities."

And then the chopper was back on its way, beating northward into the veils of snow. The snow-filtered light was a warm shade, almost pale yellow.

"You said astral plane back there?" said Naranjo, giving Alan a quizzical glance. "Is that for real?"

"I wanted to express myself in a manner congenial to Earl's predilections," said Alan. "I teeped that he's devotee of fantasy tales. And the notion of an astral plane has an illustrious history. For instance—"

"Save it for the monograph, Professor Turing," said Susan. "Open your eyes and see how lovely this is. Beauty's all there is between us and death." The visibility was low enough that they couldn't see the ground or the clouds. They were centered in an unchanging snow globe of tumbling flakes.

"My own little world," said Naranjo as they continued to clatter along. "I like it like this. One time I was into a scene like this, and my chopper iced up and crashed."

"You weren't hurt?" said Susan.

"Landed in a tree," said Naranjo. "I'm lucky. That's a key requirement for being a pilot. And then I bought a new helicopter."

"But I still think we might ram into something here," said Susan, staring at the hypnotic dance of the flakes.

"Maybe it doesn't matter," said Naranjo in a level tone. He paused for a beat, then cracked his hard face in one of his slight smiles. "But I have instruments in the dash, Susan. And a map. And I pretty well know where we are. We're coming into the Pueblo lands."

"Are there mesas?" fretted Susan. "With sudden vertical walls?"

"This land is like my back yard," said Naranjo calmly. "My mother's people live here. Mom met Dad when he was stringing wires for the telephone company. Mom's brothers were cutting down the wires for the metal. Finally Dad worked something out with them. He gave them a giant spool of wire off the back of his truck. Family stories."

The storm was temporarily breaking up, with the veils of snow parting to show a brilliant blue sky above, sun twinkling on the crystals.

"My destination is Los Alamos," said Alan a bit officiously. "I can tell you that now."

"I already know," said the pilot. "You haven't been hiding it real well. Could be those cops saw it too."

"I'm overwrought," said Alan. "Are we close?"

"Couple of miles," said Naranjo, steering his chopper towards a field on the crest of a bluff. "But we're gonna land right here. No sense pushing our luck with the cloud cover gone. And it might be smart to hang back from Los Alamos for a day. They saw us leaving Gormly in this general direction."

"I was depending on you to take us all the way to our destination," said Alan, sounding tense and prissy again.

"But there's nothing at all down there," chimed in Susan, peering out the window. "Just some crappy shacks."

"It's my cousin's spread," said Naranjo, his voice gone cold. "An Eden, if you can open your eyes. But you can't. You're too white."

In silence, the pilot maneuvered the chopper to a spot beside the ramshackle structures. They touched down in two feet of snow. An Indian man appeared at the cottage door, his eyes crinkling, his smile a white slash in his weathered face.

"I didn't mean—" began Susan.

"We're done," said Naranjo curtly. "Cousin Ricky and I gonna cover up my helicopter so nobody sees it from the air. You go ahead and walk to Los Alamos. Take your chances. I'll be glad to see you gone."

So Susan and Alan thanked the stone-faced Naranjo for saving them, and set off, zipping their flimsy coats to their chins. The sun was low in the sky, and the snow was beginning once again to fall. At least their clothes were dry, and they had solid shoes.

In a last-minute gesture of mercy, Naranjo teeped them his memory of the trail. He said they ought to be able to make it to Los Alamos in two hours, even with the snow. Los Alamos was on a separate bluff, which meant they faced a climb down to the bottomlands, and a scramble up the other side.

The first part of the walk went well, with Naranjo's landmarks popping into place. But then it began getting dark. The snow was blowing hard, icing their faces.

"Something's following us, Alan!" exclaimed Susan. Doggy forms off to their right. "Wolves?"

"I'm hardly a native," said Alan impatiently. "And—blast and damn—Naranjo's out of teep range."

They came to a stop. They could see four toothy animals sitting on their haunches, about twenty feet off, yipping to each other in the dusk.

"Not wolves," said Alan. "Too small. Aren't there others kinds of wild dogs in the States? Like foxes or dingoes or jackals or—"

"Coyotes!" exclaimed Susan. "Of course. The fabled tricksters. I think they're scavengers? So we're okay until we slip off a sheer hundred-foot cliff and break our legs and have brain damage and bleed to death and freeze up hard as rocks."

"Maybe we just go back to Naranjo's cousin Ricky?" said Alan. "We could try again in the morning."

"Naranjo thought Los Alamos might not even be safe yet," said Susan. "The cops might be checking all the nearby towns. Are we really going to kill ourselves just because we had a tiny quarrel with Naranjo? But I can't think straight. You decide. I keep sinking into daydreams about my poor Vassar. You have to understand that he was brilliant. You did have sex with him on the ship, didn't you?"

"A couple of times, yes. And, as I said, I loved him too."

"But ever since New Orleans you were so cold to him. Contemptuous, almost. It was ugly of you."

"Once Vassar learned I was a man, I was cast into the position of being an importuning pervert. And so I withdrew. I meant no insult. Perhaps in Los Alamos, William Burroughs and I can be happily queer together." At the edge of a puddled shadow, one of the four coyotes moved closer, extending his dim muzzle to savor Alan and Susan's scent.

"I'm sorry I called you a heartless robot on the plane," said Susan, utterly whipsawed by her emotions.

"I do have tendencies in that direction," said Alan. "One of my uncountably many flaws." He pulled out his handkerchief and dried Susan's cheeks. "Silly or not, I don't relish the idea of facing Naranjo just now. What if we do try going a bit further?"

Soon they'd reached the crumbly edge of their bluff. The snow had let up again, and they could see straight across to the lights of Los Alamos on the facing cliff. Down in the bottomlands was an isolated cluster of lights. A heavy truck was driving down there. A military vehicle?

"If the weather's clearing, I guess we could push on," said Susan, thinking. "But it would help to shapeshift into coyotes. We'd be covered with fur, and walking on four legs. In synch for this landscape. I'd like to yip and howl, too. I'd like to howl for Vassar."

"I reckon we'd have to become three coyotes each," said Alan thinking it over. "To conserve our mass, don't you know. Giant coyotes wouldn't work. But, yes, I'm game. I'll be three coyotes, and so will you."

"Can we *do* that?" asked Susan, intrigued.

"Your pieces will stay in touch with each other," said Alan. "Like the nations of the British Empire. My skug says it's feasible." He sent a tendril out from his finger and sent it towards the closest of watchful canine forms behind them.

The coyote snarled at Alan's surprise touch, but he'd already extracted a tissue sample. He reeled in his tendril and passed some of the coyote cells to Susan.

"I use the doggy genes for, like, my flesh-knitting pattern?" said Susan.

"Indeed," said Alan.

"What if those coyotes attack us as soon as we're coyotes too?"

"We'll be ruthless in our self-defense."

Without any further ado, Alan slumped to the ground and broke himself into three pieces. A bit unsettling, that. Your head and shoulders here, your belly there, and your legs and bottom off to one side. But his skugger teep held his self-image together. Bristling and growling, he became three coyotes.

Susan followed suit. Spooked by the uncanny trans-formation, the real coyotes melted from view. And now, moving cautiously, the Alan-and-Susan pack of six made their way forward.

"Lovely," Alan teeped to Susan. "I'm my own good company."

"Make way, you," teeped Susan, one of her muzzles nip-ping one of Alan's legs. "Here's where we have to scram-ble down. I smell the path. This is fun."

As they picked their way down the steep cliff, the snow and wind returned. The sky clouded over, and it was utterly dark. Even on four legs, it was all the Alan-and-Susan coy-otes could do to keep from sliding off a ledge. The small cluster of lights on their left had made for a beacon—but now the heavy snow masked it from visibility.

In the bottomland, they stumbled around, bewildered and blind. At some point they began mounting a bluff.

"I think we got turned around and that we're climbing up onto Ricky's side again," teeped Susan after a while. "I smell our old tracks. We're going in a circle. That's how lost hikers always die. They see, like, a door in a snowbank that opens into a room full of steam-heat and opium. The grave. I don't really care. I'm ready."

"Let's gather our wits," teeped Alan, setting his three coyote bodies on their haunches. Barely visible at his side, Susan's coyote bodies threw back their heads and howled. Alan joined in, mourning Vassar and Ned. Answering howls sounded—and not so very far away. The real coyotes.

Very uneasy, Alan strained at his mind, hoping to pick up a flash of teep from the sulky Naranjo. The pilot wasn't to be found, but there was something else in the psychic channels, a nearby sense of warmth from a sacrificed friend.

"Vassar," teeped Susan. "He's with us."

A flapping gold blob flickered at the edges of Alan's visual fields. It had a thin tail at its rear.

Putting their heads down against the storm, the pack of six followed the spirit guide towards a hoped-for shelter.

THIRTEEN
the apocalypse
according to willy lee

[This double-length chapter is the entire text of an unpublished memoir fragment by William Burroughs, hand-written in January, 1955.]

A t fourteen I'd study myself in the mirror, practicing "looks"—the dreamy waif from famine-land, the lonely succubus lapping sex spills, the noble on the nod.

Evidently I was queer. I'd watch my friend Peter's delicate hands, his beautiful dark eyes, the flush of excitement on his cheeks, and I'd project imaginary psychic fingers, caressing his ears, smoothing his eyebrows, pushing the hair back from his face, my soul an ectoplasmic amoeboid that strained like a hungry blind worm to enter Peter's body, to breathe with his lungs, to see with his eyes, to learn the feel of his cock and balls.

Reviewing these states of mind before my mirror, I'd notice that, as I heated up, my mouth would fall slightly open, with my teeth showing in the half-snarl of a captive animal. The social limitations upon my desires were the bars of my cage. Every day I was looking out through those bars, watchful, alert, waiting for the keeper to forget to latch the door.

Eventually, of course, I broke loose and showed the more receptive boys how the cow ate the cabbage. "Bear down, Peter. You'll fit."

I liked to imagine merging with my lovers. One of my first routines. "Wouldn't it be booful if we should juth shlup together into one gweat big blob," I'd say in baby talk, lying at ease with a boy. This never went over well— until I met Turing.

Montage—pages fly off my calendar. When I was thirty I began cohabitating with Joan Vollmer, nine years younger than me. She knew I was a queer junky, but we were on the same wavelength, to a telepathic extent. I've always longed to be so effortlessly understood. Seven years Joan took care of me. *Faute de mieux*, sex with a woman isn't bad.

I failed Joan in innumerable ways. Addicted and indicted, I drifted through New Orleans, Texas, and down Mexico way. And there, one autumn evening in 1951, I shot Joan in the head. A William Tell act—with an empty glass for the apple. I say that the gun's aim was crooked, that I was possessed by an ugly spirit, that Joan telekinetically drew the bullet towards her brain. Poor excuses.

For any number of years I'd been developing my routines—crazed and menacing rants like a drunken out-of-control burlesque comic might lay on the rubes. I'd spring my spoken-word art on friend and foe alike. My goal? Free-flowing laughter—at least for me—rollicking hyena kicks to break the grip of my frightened flesh.

While in Mexico City I'd progressed towards a complete lack of caution and restraint. It was like I thought nothing must be allowed to dilute my routines. I'd once been shy about approaching boys, for instance, but I could no longer remember why. My centers of inhibition had atrophied.

In the months before I shot Joan, my routines had led to ostracism, eviction, and threats. The routines bubbled forth like mephitic gasses from a sulfur spring. "Pardon me, Señor, you should have made that one a fart." All too often, a routine could slop over into real action. Go into a bar and call a policeman a moronic baboon, petition his partner for sexual favors, wave your gun in the bartender's face—metastasized madness.

When I shot Joan I was pretending to be drunk and criminally reckless. But I only *imagined* I was pretending. Drunk is what I was. Joan fell with my bullet in her temple. The unbroken glass rolled in a circle on the floor.

The sinister musical-chairs opera of Mexican justice closed in. I skipped town and landed in Tangier, devoting myself to debauchery and the literary arts. Wouldn't you?

I'd see Joan's sad ghost at any time, always from the corner of my eye, never straight on. I'd awaken with her at my side, puffy and tattered, or in the bloom of youth—with the slow oozing blue hole in her temple. Joan at the edges of the real. Her lips would move. I'd hear a terrible, slow buzz.

Over time her shape began changing to something less human. Something with tentacles. She spun and swooped, she'd dive at me. I'd flinch and twitch. A nut on the street, an expat scribe.

As I continued my bohemian investigations, a number of the people in Tangier took a violent, irrational dislike to me. Especially the people who ran bars. You want I should kill myself already?

I found that any prior, calfskin-bound notion of a novel was radically inadequate for expressing what I needed to say. I wanted to write routines. Note that it falls flat to run a routine through the voice of an "eccentric" character. The routines have to emanate direct from the unseen unreliable author. A transcript off a cuneiform tablet off a UFO.

Sometimes I'd lie in bed and see grids of typewritten words, moving and shifting, a haunted crossword puzzle. I'd try and copy it down. Other times I'd take dictation from voices in my head. As Allah wills.

If you're writing routines, you can't try to control what you write. The blind poet jacks his bone at Mount Olympus, *wheee*! Typed and scribbled sheets accumulated on my floor. I was writing my way out.

My relationship with Professor Alan Mathison Turing began in the final days of 1954. The man had fallen on hard times and, against all better judgment, I allowed him to move into my Tangier digs for a week.

Turing was a British mathematician who'd done code-breaking work during the war, later turning to the design of giant electronic brains. By the time I met him, his kick was programming the processes of biological growth. Not unloath to experiment upon himself, he'd infested his face with something vile.

Why did I fall for him? He was two years older than me, which would normally put me off—I like the young stuff. Not to mention that he appeared hideously diseased. But, as Turing's experiments unfolded, he gained a seemly, pleasant look—in fact, for a time, he looked exactly like me.

I enjoyed Alan's intellectual companionship from the start. If he came on like a Martian, this was only his protective comedy routine. His oddness was his bulwark against the world's hale cretins. Like me, Alan was a born outsider, frankly and unapologetically queer. And he hated the authorities—with good cause. The British secret service was bent on assassinating him.

By way of breaking the ice, Turing told me he was planning to become a human-sized cancer tumor. His plan was to cut down on the need for all those body-organs and be a shapeshifting slug of undifferentiated tissue. He'd brought with him a culture of undifferentiated tissue in a cloth sack. He called his protosentient sample a *skug*, and he addressed it like a pet.

Initially I took this for a mere routine. But Turing was bent on pushing his jape to full fruition. He amended his skug with odd compounds from the souq, and tutored the creature with radio waves. And on the third day, lo, the miracle occurred. Turing merged his doctored skug with his body and became a *skugger*.

And a few minutes later, Turing transformed me as well.

At least initially, I found it very agreeable to be a skugger. I seemed to be vacuuming up inputs at a quicker rate than ever before—as if under the effects of a stimulant, but with no subsequent come-down.

More interestingly, as skuggers, Alan and I were shapeshifters, capable of molding our flesh into whatever mad form. To start with, he mirrored me. We had fabulous sex that segued into full-body conjugation. At last I'd truly shlupped with a lover.

Added attraction—we were telepaths as well.

The brain is a bioelectric orgone system, one understands, and it gives off signals akin to radio waves. Teep. A skugger is exquisitely sensitive to teep signals, and is adept at generating them in coherent form. Skugger-to-skugger telepathy extends for as much as half a mile.

From the very start, we skuggers were a social menace. The authorities viewed us as mutants, as disease vectors, as nihilists. Each of these assessments was in some degree correct. But—let me repeat—being a skugger was a delicious pleasure that one longed to share.

During the coming skirmishes, the cops would occasionally capture and subvert a skugger, making a spy of him or her. But the skugger quislings never lived long. To use your telepathy as a tool of repression is to become an orgoneless automaton, a clay juju doll.

Soon after Alan and I became skuggers, he left Tangier for the States, bearing my appearance and my passport. He was fearful of the British operatives and their ongoing plans to terminate him. After Alan's departure, the British Embassy somehow drew me into an ill-starred attempt to spy on him—via a skugger-hive-mind parabolic-dish antenna. I cooperated, I suppose, out of curiosity. And for the pay. And for a fresh passport.

I've mentioned that skugger teep reaches only half a mile or so. But a shlupped combine of skuggers can achieve a hyper-resonant state with Earth's orgone-pool, making it possible to send and receive teep halfway around the world.

For a few days I was remotely observing my new lover for the British heat—Alan was in Florida by then. Still looking like me, he'd had gone to visit my parents and my son in Palm Beach. Even now, I'm not sure why he did this. I was angry.

My pique escalated into a psychotic fugue state when I overheard Alan telling my son Billy that we might find a way to bring my dead wife Joan back to life. As if by dream logic, I knew right away that this was inevitable. And I was terribly afraid.

As an additional affront, Alan had enlisted another skugger, a rustic American named Ned, and they'd behaved in such a debased fashion at my parents' that Mother had resolved to cut off the monthly allowance that had been my mainstay for my whole adult life.

Flipped into vengeful-demon mode, I prevailed upon the British Embassy to finger Alan for the Palm Beach police. But the sly Turing and his new friend Ned turned the cops into skuggers as well.

At this point I myself set off for Palm Beach. My plan was—what? It's hard precisely to recall. Certainly I wanted to get my family allowance reinstated. And perhaps I longed to chastise Alan in the broadest possible sense. Sexually speaking, I wanted him more than ever.

On my plane trip to the States I reached a level of equanimity. A salubrious side-effect of becoming a skugger was that I could inwardly dose myself with endorphins that had the feel of opiates. I'd attained the goal of the adept's quest: the Man within.

Stepping off my plane in New York City, everything looked sharp and clear, as if freshly washed. Sensations were hitting me like tracer bullets. I felt as fabulously alive as an electric eel. Walking with the King and nothing to declare.

I'd morphed into an beefy Brit to match my passport, but once I cleared immigration, I reverted to the Burroughs Classic look. I felt like a dog rolling in offal after his bath—savoring the filth of being his true self.

My parents frowned and clucked when I arrived in Palm Beach. Mother's kind face simmered with unspoken questions. At least my son Billy was openly glad to see me. He enjoyed the weird science-fictional vibe of my two back-to-back visits—the previous visit having been, of course, Turing's hoax. Billy liked to see reality warping into a comic strip.

There was a newspaper in the kitchen, with the head-lines were bewailing the outrages that certain unknown drifters had perpetrated—including the deaths of cops. The full particulars of Alan's visit came clear to me when I went upstairs. A tiny skug crept into my trouser leg, and leeched onto my calf. Alan had left this creature as a mes-senger—to fill me in on his doings.

And thus I learned that my mother and my son had witnessed Alan and Ned enjoying sexual intercourse and skugger conjugation while dangling from the guest bedroom ceiling. The details filled me with an irrational chagrin. I'd given my heart to a science boffin—a socially inept and ordinary-looking man—only to be jilted? *Quelle horreur*, my dears.

Dutifully I made peace with my family. My stipend would continue as before. And that evening, Alan phoned me at their home. He was conciliatory, but frantic. The feds were on his tail. He had some hopes of escape. He begged me to meet him at his destination—which his messenger skuglet had told me was Los Alamos, New Mexico. And so I flew after this oddly enticing man, promising Mother that if I managed to settle down with my friend, I'd have son Billy come out for a stay.

Landing in the Santa Fe airport near Los Alamos, I picked up no teep. Where was Alan? And I had a distinct impression that I was being tailed by a rat-faced man who'd pushed onto my flight when I'd changed planes in Chicago.

Using my shapeshifting powers, I changed my look in the men's room. Staring into the mirror, I imagined myself growing very, very old. Wrinkles enmeshed my eyes. My face sagged, my teeth melted into my gums, my slack lips hung open, my body frame dwindled and warped. I pushed it further than reasonable, ending up in the condition of a ninety-year old man. I turned my jacket inside-out and hobbled across the lobby. The rat who'd been tailing me walked right past. People don't like to see their future.

Stepping into the whirl of snow outside, I saw a peripheral flicker of light. A shape that seemed continually to be edging into view without ever coming into clear visibility. A ghost.

"Is it Joan?" I asked aloud.

"No, man. It's Vassar Lafia." The answer came via teep, the voice hoarse and clear. "I was a skugger too."

"You?" I replied with harsh disdain. I'd gathered from Alan's skuglet-shared data bank that the dissolute Vassar had been another of Alan's sex partners—this during the sea journey from Tangier. "You're dead?"

"The pigs fried me this morning, man. Incinerated me and my man Ned with an Army-surplus flamethrower. The war on skugs. Alan's still alive. I'll take you to him. Get one of those truck Indians to drive you."

The ghost was near my ear, as if perched on my shoulder. But if I turned to stare at him, he moved on behind my back.

There were indeed a couple of pickups idling at the curb. I hobbled over to the closest one, very elderly in my gait, digging the geezer routine, swaying my pelvis with vim.

"I'm skittish as a hog on ice," I exclaimed to the Indian at the wheel. "Can you carry me somewhere?"

The driver gestured me into the truck, seemingly oblivious of Vassar's ghost. Parroting the ghost's teep, I told the Indian I wanted to go to Ricky Red Dog's ranch on the next mesa. The driver—his name was Ken Kiva—said he could do it for ten dollars. To cement our deal I offered to buy us two pints of whiskey. "We'll make it a dang fool joyride," I cackled toothlessly.

As we pulled off into the blizzard, heading for the liquor store, I returned my appearance to its customary youthful vigor. Ken Kiva slid his eyes over, checking me out, and grinned. "El brujo, man," he said. "Very smooth move."

I gave him a twenty and he went into the package store. I waited in the truck with Vassar's ghost twinkling around the edges of my vision—he was a gold, fluttering shape, thick in the middle. I'd gone on a kief binge with this Vassar Lafia in the Café Central last summer. I'd performed public fellatio on a dog on the floor. A highly evolved routine.

My Indian driver returned. By choosing a generic brand, he'd managed to get us two fifths rather than two pints. Although, as a skugger, I could get as high as I wanted by internal effects, I enjoyed the flare and burn of the whiskey in my mouth. The snowflakes, as seen in the truck's single working headlight seemed festive and rare. The truck had no heater, but I found a verminous blanket.

As we traversed the deserted back roads, the whiskey began taking its toll. It developed that Ken Kiva didn't precisely recall where Ricky Red Dog's ranch was. So, for the rest of the drive, every now and then I'd wiggle my fingers by the sides of my head, stirring up the action in the borders of my visual field. Vassar's ghost would light up and feed me more directions. I'm not sure if Ken Kiva could see the ghost or not—I asked him, but he didn't like to say.

Sometimes we'd have to wait several minutes at a questionable road fork, companionably drinking while I made my summoning gestures. Vassar's ghost was at times slow on the uptake—he told me he was alternating between guiding me and helping Alan.

Ken Kiva fishtailed his truck up the final grade to Ricky's with some difficulty, arriving at low farmhouse buildings, smoothed and rounded by the drifts of snow. "Ricky Red Dog's," exclaimed Ken. "I'll sleep here too."

In the house I met a handsome Indian named Naranjo. He was smoking tobacco with his cousin Ricky, who lived here with his family. Ken muttered briefly with Ricky Red Dog, then flopped down on a blanket and passed out, fully at ease.

"Where's Alan?" I asked Ricky and Naranjo. "Alan Turing? I'm to meet him here."

"He left with the girl," said Naranjo curtly.

Staring at Naranjo, I realized he was a skugger too. And I could teep that he was holding something back. His cousin Ricky spilled the beans.

"Naranjo sent them into the storm," said the round-faced Ricky. "They're to walk to Los Alamos. The next mesa over." The difficulty of the task seemed to amuse him.

"Greenhorns," said Naranjo, shaking his head. "They thought they were too good to stay here."

Obviously Naranjo held a grudge against Alan and Susan. But rather than asking more questions, I listened to Vassar's ghost, glowing at my side. I could see him better all the time. He resembled a small stingray. He said he was making progress in guiding Alan and his friend Susan Green. Susan was Vassar's widow.

"It's wild in the canyon between the mesas" said Vassar's voice in my head. "One of those cave doors is glowing with ghost vibes. Like an apartment window lit by TV. Shit, man, I should be in New York. Not dead in a snowstorm being a St. Bernard."

I didn't answer Vassar. I'm not one for talking back to the spirit voices in my head. I sat there with Ricky and Naranjo for a time, quietly staring at the fire in the stove, passing around the rest of my whiskey, and me enjoying my Man within.

I probed Naranjo's mind some more, feeling a little sexed by his rough look. He was a small-plane pilot with gangland links in Mexico City. Sometimes he smuggled junk across the border, sometimes he did contract jobs for the U.S. heat. A man for all seasons. He was angry at Alan for skugging him, and at Susan for denigrating cousin Ricky's ranch.

"Can you do me?" Ricky Red Dog asked me, interrupting my reverie.

"Eh?"

"Make me, what do you call it?"

"He wants to be a skugger, too," said Naranjo, curtly. "But I won't be the one to infect my cousin, not me. It's bad."

"You're a very sulky boy," I said, just to needle Naranjo.

"Ken Kiva said you're a brujo," Ricky told me, his moon-face credulous. "He said you changed your face and talked to ghosts. Come on, Bill, I want to be a skugger. Why you and Naranjo holding out on me?"

I would gladly have sent a tendril into Ricky. But now I was distracted by the vibes of Alan and Susan. Only a few hundred yards away and coming closer. Something weird about their teep.

A minute later, we heard a frantic scratching at the door. Ricky rose to open it, and a pack of hairy beasts came rushing in. I had a nasty moment in which I imagined they were supernatural demons. Anything seemed possible.

The six doggy animals raced around the room, sniffing, yipping, shedding clots of ice.

"Mad coyotes!" yelled Ricky, pulling his rifle from the wall. "Rabies!"

"Wait!" I cried, dog's best friend. I sent my arm out like a python, snatching the rifle off Ricky and, while I was at it, sinking in my finger to skug the guy already.

Meanwhile three of the coyotes bunched up by my legs, and pressed their snouts together. *Plup, plup!* The three heads fused—and their bodies merged like being zipped together. The ill-shapen combine shuddered like a contortionist—and became Alan Turing. Out in that blizzard he'd shapeshifted into an archipelago.

I felt an unexpectedly strong rush of affection. Like a schoolboy crush. I wrapped my arms around Alan and kissed him.

Meanwhile the other three coyotes merged into this dark-haired pale woman Susan Green. Ricky's wife and kids boiled out of the sleeping quarters, everyone in a tizzy. Ricky Red Dog cool everyone down.

So Naranjo lay down on the floor by the stove beside Ken Kiva. And Susan, Alan and I settle into a side room.

Our room had gaps in the log walls, lice in the blankets. Susan lay on her own, gently vibrating, in tears. Possibly she was making it with Vassar's ghost. With, like, his tail plunged into her spine.

Alan and I launched into a full-body conjugation, even better than sex. We shared our recent memories—and I scored some boffo wetware upgrades.

In the night I rose to piss, and here came something swooping at me. A spectral flying cuttlefish—a creature with W-shaped pupils and a wad of tentacles for a face. About a foot long, colored in shades of mauve and ultraviolet, just visible at the edge of my vision. My wife Joan.

This was the first time I'd seen Joan's ghost since turning skugger. She'd tightened up her appearance, and her vibes hitting me much more intense than ever before. I teeped her voice in my head, a gibbering screech.

"You killed me, I hate you, I'm stuck—" Like that.

"It wasn't really me," I teeped, deploying my stock defenses. "I was aiming very carefully five inches above your head. Towards the top of the glass. But as I pulled the trigger—something moved my arm."

"Your hateful, selfish brain moved your arm, crumbum," said Joan, her voice as clear in my head as if we were back in our kitchen drinking coffee. "I'm going to pay you back." And now she went back to dive-bombing my head and screeching. The same old bum kicks.

Now that Alan had upgraded me, I could do teep blocks and, thank heavens, I could wall out Joan's ghost. Still in a tizzy, I put on my coat, relieved myself off the porch, and stood there mooning at the moon. I wished I had some H. This bullshit about a Man within wasn't fully making it. My skug had no real concept of what it meant to get properly high. I wondered how soon I could score.

In the morning we gathered in the main room, and Ricky's wife made us a breakfast of hominy and, like, goat kidney on the wood stove. A strikingly fresh and delicate woman with two shiny-eyed kids in tow. I sat at on the floor with Alan, Susan, and the three Indian men.

"Vassar spent the night with me," Susan told Alan, "He'd rather be with me than go to heaven." She looked so happy that I found myself wondering if she were unhinged. Even though I'd seen glimpses of Vassar myself.

"This guy was murdered yesterday?" said Naranjo.

"But he's not really dead," insisted Susan. "My understanding is that ghosts hang around on Earth for a while and that then they go to some higher level. If they want."

"I know about the hanging around," I put in.

"Ned's already moved on, and Vassar's still here," continued Susan, all beatific. She was fiddling with a little drum of Ricky's, tapping intricate beats. "The pigs killed Ned and Vassar with flamethrowers. Ned went on towards—paradise? Vassar says that's the most dangerous road of all. Hardly anyone makes it to the highest heaven. Vassar wants to look around here some more before he leaves. He told me he noticed a far-out Indian ghost in that canyon between here and Los Alamos. He wants to talk to him."

Alan was silent for a moment, staring off into space—and then he got into one of his talking encyclopedia routines.

"I'm developing a theory regarding ghosts," intoned Prof Turing. "Granted that they're real—what are they, physically speaking? I rather suspect that ghosts are based on exotic microtubule structures in the air, vortex filaments linked in a mesh. And I posit that the nodes of the mesh are exotic particles that we may as well call *memnons*. One's memnons waft forth upon one's dying breath, carrying an encoded representation of the soul. Microtubules spring up among the memnons—and you've risen from the dead. Your ghost is a gossamer *lacework*. Think of a spiderweb glinting with dew. And, it goes nearly without saying, this phenomenon is very highly enhanced in the presence of skugs." Alan smiled, the very image of the enlightened engineer.

"Think of a flying cuttlefish instead," I said, putting my hands under my chin and twiddling my fingers like tentacles. "That's my wife Joan. She was ragging on me last night. With enhanced soundtrack."

"William's *better half*," said Turing. "Nature's bachelors are fools to marry."

"Where's Joan buried?" asked Susan, still eerily perky. Like so many hipsters, she knew the lurid William Burroughs backstory.

"Mexico City," I said shortly.

"What if we go down there and lay Joan's soul to rest?" suggested Susan. "Instead of rushing straight into Los Alamos. The cops could be setting up another trap."

"How about we raise Joan from the dead?" I said sourly. "Like Alan here was promising my son."

"That goes too far," said Susan, shaking her head. "That's black magic."

"Beige magic," I said. "Eh, Alan? Your mnemnons might turn wizardry into an office job for government flunkies."

"I'm nobody's flunky," said Alan, taking offense. "And, yes, I say we *can* raise Joan."

I found myself intrigued. "It wouldn't be any quaint, fusty table-turning scene. Not ye merrie Englande. Think of Aztec scorpion gods and man-eating centipedes. Remember this—I shot Joan in the head and she wants revenge. But if we could pull it off—it'd be a relief to reach the end."

"Let it come down," said Naranjo, taking an interest. "Yeah. You boys want to go to Mexico City for a day instead of rushing to Los Alamos like sheep. And I know a little plane we can borrow. This forest ranger has a snow-plowed strip out in the wild here. Ricky can drive us there."

Across the room, Ricky guffawed. "You're talking about Ranger Rob the Smuggy Bear. Yeah, man."

"I'm for it," said Alan. "It'll tangle our trail. And we'll circle back to Los Alamos when we're done."

"What's so special about Los Alamos?" I asked Alan. "They build bombs. Why you want to make that anti-life scene?"

"Alan wants a ray-gun for skugging everyone at once!" said Susan.

"Nuclear telepathy," I said. "Holocaust enlightenment."

"These are inaccurate characterizations of my plans," said Alan stiffly.

"Will the magic ray-gun make a sound?" said Susan, laughing for the first time. "*Uhn, uhn, uhn.* I'd love to tape it."

"Or tape Alan's last words while the feds fry him up," said Naranjo. "*Th-th-th-that's all folks! Quaaaaaaak!* Hey, enough chatter, let's get the plane. I'm in the mood to make a pickup down South. If it's okay with this goddamn parasite that Alan infected me with."

Getting the plane wasn't hard—Ricky Red Dog drove them to the ranger's place, and Alan skugged the fat, hairy man who lived there. Ranger Rob the Smuggy Bear. A nasty old pedophile. It made you feel dirty all over just to look at him all wrapped in oily beaver pelts.

The plane was a Cessna four-seater. Naranjo and Susan sat in front, Alan and me in back. We flew straight through, staying low as crop-dusters, unseen by the pig's radar eyes, stopping twice at rural airports for food and gas, skugging the people we dealt with. It took a heap of eating to maintain our skugs.

The first airport sold a line of flight and work clothes, and we got ourselves outfitted with rough-trade khakis and leather jackets for when we'd go back North, Susan too. Naturally we cleaned out the cash register as well.

And at the second airport we got all feisty and robbed a nearby bank, scoring a city pay-roll in a cartoon canvas sack, enough pesos to match three thousand dollars US.

I was glad to be flying into Mexico City. I always dug the freedom of the place, the effervescent high-altitude air, and the sky's pitiless shade of lapis lazuli blue. Goes good with circling vultures.

But by the time we'd parked the plane, it was dusk. The streets were sinister and chaotic—with the special chaos of a dream. Naranjo split off from us to score some weight with his canvas sack of pesos. Skugger or not, the man was determined to work his old routine.

"Look for me when you want to go home," Naranjo told the others. "Burroughs will know where."

I guided Alan and Susan to the Bounty Bar, a scurvy dive where Joan and I used to hang. Like wading into a nightmare swamp of stasis. The faces had changed, but the gestalts were the same.

Flush from our crime spree, I got the bartender to rent us an upstairs room unseen. This way we'd have a place to close the deal with Joan's ghost—if it came to that. We had a few drinks, Scotch for me, Mexican soda-pop for

Alan and Susan. The place was filling up. I was very high off the endorphins from my Man within, but it didn't feel quite harsh enough. I started talking about scoring something real.

"Remember why we're here," admonished Susan. "For poor Joan's memory. We have to help her soul find liberation." She dragged Alan and me around the room, and we let her. The faces flowed past, and Susan's voice gabbled at everyone. I'd dialed up my high to where I was just seeing colors and shapes.

At some point, Susan zeroed in on this gaunt, long-haired cat with an air of arrested development. Like a waxwork in a museum of mental aberration. He was sitting alone with an empty, sticky-looking glass and an ashtray full of butts.

"I hear you are muralist, Señor Cortez?" said Susan, in a corny stage accent. She leaned over him and stuck out her tits. "I am composer."

"What kind of sound?" asked the guy. He didn't seem Mexican at all.

"Sound like *thees*," said Susan amping the corn. She dragged a chair back and forth so that it screeched against the floor. She made wild grunting noises at the same time. "Acousmatics, *vato*!" She flopped down in the chair she'd been flinging around and pointed her finger at her chest. "Susan *Verde*. And this skinny *maricon* is my friend Bill."

"Far out," said Cortez the loner. "But don't talk that way. I'm from Texas."

"The, uh, bartender says you're doing a mural at the Panteón Americano," continued Susan, not missing a beat.

Hearing that, I turned off my buzz and started paying attention. The Panteón Americano was where Joan was buried.

"Yeah, babe," said Cortez with strange, sinister jocularity. "A mural in mosaic. I'm copying a work by Salvador Dali, *Young Virgin Auto-Sodomized by Her Own Chastity*. It's highly erotic, you dig, but as long as it's got the word 'Virgin' in the title, I figure the archbishop gives me my hall-pass. Even though what the clerics really wanna see is a dying man with an hourglass and a scythe on the floor, and the man's reaching up ecstatic towards a triangle of white light, it's like God's eye, or Mary's snatch more brighter than a harp of gold. I work at night when nobody's there to run the Inquisition on me."

"You, ah, have the key to the main gate?" I asked, getting aboard our hell-bound ride.

"Sure," said Cortez, looking us over and reaching a conclusion. "And you three want me to let you in, right? Helping freaks set up necro sex parties is by way of being a profitable sideline." His face folded into an expression of contented depravity. "No problemo."

"No party," I said. "We're here to visit my dead wife."

"Sure you are, Bill," said Cortez. "You've got a bone to pick." It was as if he and I knew each other from somewhere, and his words referred to private jokes from our period of intimacy. Like in a lucid dream.

"Let's do it," I said, handing Cortez a sheaf of bills.

Rising to his feet, Cortez seemed to float a few inches above the ground. I saw him as an airborne jellyfish, torpid and predatory. "Get me a bottle of tequila, too," he burbled.

It was quite dark out. Cortez, Alan, Susan, and I walked towards the Panteón Americano cemetery. It wasn't very far. On the way, we passed some outdoor markets. I felt numb and cold, like a condemned man on his way to the gallows. For his part, Cortez made a side deal with Susan Green, selling her a nasty little pistol that he had in his coat pocket.

"Fuck the pigs," said Susan, striking a tough pose with her dinky gun. I doubted she'd know how to reload it.

Cortez keyed us through the graveyard gate. Images of Joan's burial and the cops and the reporters were streaming from the dusky borders of my visual field. Joan's corpse. Her parents. My brother. The morgue. My lawyer. Joan's face.

Cortez was overly loud and animated, swinging his flashlight in reckless loops. Rather than helping us find Joan's crypt as required, he dragged us to the chapel to show off his bullshit mural—some bobby-soxer girl with a rhino's horn between the cheeks of her butt, completely vapid. Cortez was executing his work using tiny squares of tile tinted in the properly hideous hues of conventional religious art.

"The tiles are like atoms in matter," Cortez intoned, warming up to an artist's brag. "The tiles are like people in a crowd. We're puzzle pieces, man. Who fits?" He laid his dark hand on Susan's waist.

I was very edgy by now. My skug's candy-ass endorphins weren't softening this scene at all. I made my arm into an anaconda and gave Cortez a bone-rattling shake. "You go back to the gate and don't let anyone in," I told him.

"Yeah," sneered Susan, getting very cocky with her shabby little gun. "Make it snappy or I'll blast you."

Cortez picked up a heavy hammer from his bench, glaring at us with bloodshot eyes, fully set for a showdown. Susan really was ready to shoot him. It was like, with her husband murdered, she didn't care what she did. I liked that.

"Here, here," interposed Alan. "Let's be civilized, Mr. Cortez! We did pay you, but—" Alan passed him another bill. "Do take your tequila and sit by the front gate. That'll suit us very nicely."

So Cortez reeled back towards the cemetery entrance. I bagged his hammer and a screwdriver as well.

Now that I didn't have the besotted artist yammering at us, my head cleared and I was able to find Joan's crypt. I'd walked here in my dreams often enough. It was January, but the Mexican graveyard was lush with poinsettia shrubs and the stylized cypress trees. The moon was peeping out. I could hear the yowling of cats.

With Alan's help, I pried the plate off Joan's unlabeled spot in the wall. A wild smell. She'd been dead over three years. I'd feared her ghost would dart from the tomb, more vengeful than ever before. But nothing happened.

"Any bit of tissue will do," said Alan, bustling at my side. He reached bare-handed into the funerary niche, his arm deep in the dark. A madman. "I'm touching her," he reported, and made an abrupt, twisting motion, as if snapping desiccated sinews.

Alan displayed his prize to me, cradling it in the palm of his hand, dramatically lit by a moonbeam. A withered

finger, with dried skin and strands of dark flesh. It bore a
fingernail. Alan remanded it to my custody.

"Joan," I said, my voice weak and strange. I clutched the
finger tight in my hand.

We blew through the gate without talking to Cortez at
all. Endless traffic clogged the night street.

"Are you all right?" Susan Green asked me.

"I'm imagining Joan trailing back from her finger," I
said. "Bobbing in the air like a lifesize balloon."

"We'll go to that room you rented?" coaxed Susan.

"Right-o," put in Alan. "Above the Bounty Bar. But we
need some *material*."

We were nearing the all-night market that we'd passed
on the way to the graveyard. Alan trotted over to one of
the butchers there and—how horrible—purchased a hun-
dred-pound skinned calf, draping the creature across his
shoulders. Uncut protein for Joan.

I'd asked the Bounty bartender for any old room. But—I
could hear the unerring ping of synchronicity—he'd given
us the very room in which I'd shot Joan in 1951.

It seemed the room was currently in use as a short-
term flop for whores and johns. Where once the lodging had held books, rugs, and a circle of friends, it was
now reduced to a bed, a chair, a light bulb, a glass by the
sink. Alan threw the slaughtered veal calf onto the dirty
floor. A church bell tolled midnight. I closed the door to
the hall. The intense silence peculiar to Mexico engulfed
us—a vibrating, soundless hum.

Moving in a trance, I spawned a skug off my stomach
and laid it upon the veal calf. The bony flesh shuddered

and took on life, forming itself into a featureless loaf. By way of orienting itself, the skug carpeted itself with tiny snail antennae, each stalk with a black bead eye at its tip. The thousand eyes watched me and made way as I laid Joan's finger down in their midst. I was like a bishop installing a reliquary bone.

To promote the transformation, Susan Green sang to the skug, running her odd voice up and down an archaic scale. Susan was weirdly vibrating her throat to add dark, low overtones. And now, guided by the genetic codes in the dead finger, the skug morphed into a crude human form, then tightened into a replica of the final, spindly Joan.

Not daring to think too deeply about what I was doing, I set to work on programming the simulacrum's mind via teep. I was in effect reconstructing Joan's personality from my memories. I remembered the early days—Joan and I camping on her vaguely oriental bed with coffee and benzedrine, two youths chattering about decadence and nothingness, Joan quite alluring in her silks and bandannas. I thought of Joan catching a June bug outside our shack in Louisiana, and tying a thread to the bumbling bug's foot—Joan called it the beetle's hoof, and she flew the beetle in a circle around our heads. I thought of more and more.

Even in the last days in Mexico City, Joan had kept her slant humor, seeing adventure in our squalor. The week before she died, she'd perched herself atop a pile of six mattresses we'd found in the street—and she'd called herself the princess and the pea. A phrase from Allen Ginsberg's *in memoriam* poem popped into my mind.

> She studied me with
> clear eyes and downcast smile, her
> face restored to a fine beauty.

And now it was so. Joan's body sat up and blinked, very jerky, very robotic. This wasn't going to work. She wasn't really alive. But then I saw the glinting ultraviolet cuttle-fish of Joan's ghost, dawdling at the fringes of visibility, twiddling her tentacles and flipping her hula-skirt fin, making up her mind. She dove into the skugged meat.

Still sitting on the floor, the Joan-thing shuddered like a wind-riffled pond. She fixed me with her eyes and began talking, her voice languid and intermittent, like music down a windy street.

"I want to leave. I want to go to paradise. But I'm not done with you, Bill."

"I'm agonized by regret," I said. "I writhe abjectly. Go up to heaven, Joan. You deserve it. Forgive me and go."

"What about little Billy?" asked Joan, rising lithe to her feet. She seemed taller than I remembered. Reaching out, she laid a cool hand on my face.

Immediately I had a physical sense that I was carrying a large covered basket. I'd been carrying it in my arms for a long time. Our son Billy was in the basket. He was going to die.

"I'll help him!" I cried. "It won't happen that way." I stepped back, breaking Joan's hallucinatory contact.

"You won't save him," said Joan, bleakly mournful. "I know you." She looked around as if only now recognizing this as the spot where I'd shot her.

I stood frozen in place, awaiting her next move, more than ever wishing I hadn't set this in motion.

"*Ooooo!*" said Joan, her voice purring up through an octave. "*I know*. It's time for our William Tell routine."

Without moving her arms or her shoulders, she poked her head out on a snaky tendril, scanning the room. Of course she spotted Susan Green's gun.

"No," said Susan, guessing what lay ahead. It was like we were playing out a script. Joan held out her hand. In thrall—or maybe just curious to see what came next—Susan passed Joan the pistol. Turing sat goggling like a mute imbecile.

"The glass, Bill," said Joan, her voice low and firm.

I moved across the room like a fish in heavy water. I set the glass on my head.

A few paces away from me, Joan raised the pistol.

"Don't," I said, faint and husky. "Don't shoot me, Joan."

She fired. I flinched to the side. The bullet struck my temple. I slumped to the floor: deaf, blind, undead. I could sense things via teep.

"It's over!" breathed Joan, with a fading lilt of summer in her voice.

Her ghost wriggled from her skugly flesh and fluttered in the air, still like a flowing cuttlefish, but more—peaceful than before. Flying around the borders of my teep, Joan's ghost shrank as if moving far away.

Her spurned new body reverted to being a skug. It raised one end, as if sniffing the air, then humped along the floor and slid out the window.

Brain-scrambled as I was, I hallucinated that I humped

my own body after Joan's skug. Fully into the invisible zone of the astral plane, I slithered out the window and— just for jolly—levitated myself fifty feet high in the air. See me fly?

Downstairs at the Bounty Bar, Cortez was coming back from the cemetery. I lifted a pinky and Cortez ran amok with his razor-sharp tile knife, wounding a photographer and killing three poets on the spot. But when Cortez surged across the bar for a fresh bottle of tequila, the bartender beheaded him, using a Aztec *maquahuitl* edged in volcanic glass.

La policia kicked in our rented room's door, inevitable as reek on rot. It was a straight-on replay of 1951, but with me in a new role. The victim. They took me to the morgue and laid me naked on a marble slab. With a spongy erection.

"We need acousmatics," said Susan, sidling in. "I memorized the sounds of a race riot in Miami. I'll pump the replay from my skin, mixing in the shrieks of swine at the slaughterhouse. We'll raise Bill from the dead and rectify those *policia*."

My head was splitting in unbearable pain. I retracted my limbs, blanking things out.

"Bill?" said Alan, leaning over me and shaking me. "Bill?"

Reset. We were still in the room where I'd been shot. I sat up and spit the bullet from my mouth. The sun was high.

"What a burn," I said. "Let's split this scene."

"Agents everywhere," said Susan, leaning out the open window. "Like shit on shit. We need more acousmatics." She emitted a fresh torrent of noise. It was a collage of every sound I'd ever heard in my life—thrown into a rock-tumbler.

The sky went pale green. Hailstones fell past, big as hens' eggs, shattering on the street. Elephants trumpeted frantic at the drone of an approaching twister. The room's wall rocked twice and exploded out. Turing and I slid helpless across the floor, pissing our pants. Cars tumbled through the air with clown-cops behind the wheels. A striped circus tent swept upwards, drawing me into a whirling shattered midway of bleachers and shooting galleries, of sugar skulls and Socco Chico queens.

Poised at the virtual tent-peak of the vortex was Joan, far and wee, the bride on the funeral cake, luminous white, bidding farewell, giving me the finger. Behind her glowed the light of a Missouri sunset, the clouds like bruised flesh.

I twitched and vomited, turning myself inside out. I was an eyeball on a transfinite spinal cord, shooting up like Jack's beanstalk, slipping through the same clenched hole as Joan, the atomic pucker, the tiny pinprick between purgatory and paradise. My eye in heaven gazed upon a radiance beyond our wan spectrum—vivid, vital, vibrant.

The core spake unto Willy Lee: "I am. I am the V-bomb." And as yet, your prophet knew not the meaning of these words.

Second reset. I was still in the flophouse room we'd rented, on the floor in a clotted crust of blood. I'd been in a night-long seizure, reflexively regrowing my brain. The sunlight lay like pig iron on the ground. The police had dispersed—if they'd ever been there at all.

We got a cab to the Mexico City junk neighborhood and teeped Naranjo. He'd scored two kilos of coarse brown H.

Back on the plane, with Susan in front with Naranjo, and Alan in back with me, I tore into the corner of a brick, and told Naranjo I was keeping an ounce for my own. He didn't care. I stashed my junk into the cellophane of a cigarette pack. Alan watched disapprovingly.

"Hardly prudent," he said.

Skugged, shot in the head, back from the dead, I wanted to be on the nod, skating the edge of OD, in blank oblivion. But when I went to snort my junk, my inner skug wouldn't let me. So I dialed up the inner stim and declaimed unto my fellows a Sura.

"Hearken unto me, Alan, Susan, and Naranjo. I am the man. I was there. I snaked the hole to heaven. Death can be conned. There's a higher level, my dear ones, a paradise beyond the shrieking sea of ghosts. Yea, wouldst thou attain immortality, thou shalt—"

"Shut your crack, Burroughs," said Naranjo. "Unless you want another ride on that deathbed rollercoaster." He'd turned around in his pilot's seat. He had an oily 45 automatic pointed at my forehead. He looked utterly resolute. "I'm not about to listen to your bullshit for ten hours."

"How about I suck your cock instead?" I said, just to push him a little further. I like to see people go over the edge.

"Degenerate," muttered Naranjo, stashing his gun and turning back to the plane's controls.

"Don't bully Bill," said Alan at my side. "He's had a rough night of it."

So I held my tongue during the long flight back to Ranger Rob the Smuggy Bear's strip, leaning on Alan's shoulder, staring freaky out the plane window, continually amazed to be alive.

I was done with Joan.

los alamos

"Y ou have *got* to change your look," said Ranger Rob as Alan, Bill, Susan and Naranjo debarked from the plane on his snowy, tree-shrouded landing strip. "The word is out. You're in the news."

Ranger Rob was a fat-faced man with too much hair—a gray pouf on top, nasty muttonchop sideburns and a lumberjack beard with pancakes and bacon. And he was a skugger too, thanks to Alan. The little TV in his tiny, vel-vet-curtained cabin was jabbering away. The story of the Gormly ambush was a national sensation. Newscasters and politicos were ranting about witchcraft, satanic cults, communist cells and anarchy. Alan's and Susan's faces were on endless replay, shown in a news film shot during the attack, with occasional glimpses of Naranjo, labeled as a hostage. The high point of the film was a grainy, slo-mo loop of Alan deforming his body in a skuggy way, reach-ing up for Naranjo's helicopter.

"Funny they're not talking about a mass vaccination," said Alan. "Using that anti-skug vaccine Roland Gill was telling me about. He was the FBI agent I skugged?"

"I bet that vaccine is hard to make," said Susan. "Expensive. They're saving it for the elite. For the police. Meanwhile it's open season on us."

"We'll shift shapes," said Alan. Driven by a mixture of nostalgia and a desire to agitate Bill, he took on a form remembered from his boyhood.

"My first flame," explained Alan, cocking his now-narrow head at an impudent angle. "Christopher Morcom. He died of TB at nineteen."

"That's young even for me," said Burroughs sourly. "And I don't dig fantasies of boyish innocence. We're all little shits from the start."

"I'll *sophisticate* myself for you," said Alan, running his hands over his slender cheeks, and aging himself into his mid-twenties.

"I'll match that play," said Burroughs, reducing his apparent age from forty to about twenty-five. But still he kept the same Burroughs face. He could afford to. As yet he wasn't on the U. S. skughunters' radar.

Meanwhile Susan took on the look of a strong-browed, short-haired woman with full lips. "Bebe Barron," she said. "She's an electronic composer who's a friend of mine. She and her husband Louis are making the soundtrack for a science-fiction flick. They're awesome. Louis wires up these crufty, dirty circuits, and Bebe finds the music."

For his part, Naranjo made himself starker and fiercer, with slashes of facial tattoos along his cheeks. Like a warrior-spirit version of himself. "I'm heading for Santa Fe," he announced, fitting the two bricks of heroin into a knapsack. "Meeting a guy. With any luck, this is my last deal. Straight arrow from here on in. Give me a ride, Ranger Rob. You can drop the others in Los Alamos on our way."

So the fat, oily Ranger Rob drove Bill, Alan, and Susan to Los Alamos. The ranger gave Alan's bottom a lingering pat as the computer scientist disembarked. And then he continued towards Santa Fe with Naranjo.

"I remember a good diner along here from when I was a kid," said Burroughs, as he, Susan, and Alan tramped along a slushy strip of drive-ins. They were dressed in the sturdy aviation clothes they'd lifted along the way, each of them in a leather flight jacket. Like a team of acrobats.

"The Big Bow Wow," continued Bill. "Specializing in chili and sopaipillas. These puffy Southwestern pastries? Unspeakably toothsome with honey. We'll kill some time at the Bow Wow with a newspaper, and comb the classified ads."

"Looking for what?" said Susan.

"Aren't you teeping us?" said Burroughs. "Alan wants to get a job at LANL. The Los Alamos National Labs. And I'm thinking we ought to find an apartment."

"All three of us together?" said Susan.

"Cheaper that way," said Burroughs. "And we men can protect your dank furrow."

"So delicate of you to say that," said Susan, her voice modulating to a harsh shout. "So refined. It's been all of two days since those pigs incinerated my poor husband."

"Have you seen his ghost again?" asked Alan.

"Not since that first night," said Susan. "After he saved us from the blizzard, he dropped out of sight. Even though he could have helped us in Mexico. But you know Vassar. Always gadding about. Always a new idea." She looked tired and wretched in the day's fading gray.

"I'm sorry," said Bill with atypical empathy. "I overplay the tough guy routine. I'm jonesing because my skug won't let me get loaded on Naranjo's brown nod."

"I'm willing to be your friend," said Susan. "And Alan loves you. So I wouldn't mind living with you two boys till the Apocalypse comes down. Might not be long."

"Were you really playing acousmatics last night?" asked Bill. "After Joan shot me? To drive off the police?"

By way of answer—on non-answer—Susan distended her skugger mouth into a duck-leg trumpet and made an impossibly weird sound. Alan echoed her. For a moment, the two of them stood there blaring like Judgment Day angels.

They made their way to the Big Bow Wow and sat dipping their sopaipillas in honey and scanning the *Los Alamos Monitor* for rentals and jobs. A black and white TV on the wall was pumping out news updates, a steady flow of aggression and fear. Some pundits thought the skuggers were saucer aliens. The FBI's J. Edgar Hoover pegged them as marijuana addicts.

The waitress was a chatty woman with a halo of dark curly hair and a pink round-collared blouse.

"Looking for a place to live?" she said, noticing them reading the ads. "With the world coming to an end? I'm Tina. Maybe I can help."

Bill didn't respond to the overture. Instead he asked for more coffee.

"The three of you want to rent together?" pried Tina when she returned with the pot.

"Bill and I are homosexuals," said Alan. "And Susan's a widow. A *ménage à trois*. Do you mind?"

"Haw," guffawed Tina. "Putting it right out there." She leaned over the table, lowering her voice. "I spotted you boys for queers. So, guess what, my girlfriend and I have a granny cottage to rent! Half a mile down the road. We'd be glad to take you in. You're the right kind of grannies. You got jobs?"

"Not yet," said Alan. "That's quest two."

"They're hiring some tech staff at the National Labs," said Tina. "Some big-ass LANL project gearing up. It's about those skug things?"

"The Venusian sea-slugs, you might say," said Bill. "The Happy Cloaks. We're experts on them. From way back East."

"I want to apply to be a skug-hunter," said Alan. "Yes indeed."

"Me too," said Susan. "But I wonder if LANL will hire us. Since we're from out of town. There seems to be lot of paranoia just now."

"LANL needs warm bodies," said Tina. "They're so gung-ho that they're doing interviews tomorrow, even though it's Sunday. I hear they've got a special watchdog thing to keep out any skuggers who try to sneak in." Tina gave them a cool, thoughtful look. "It's called a skugsniffer? He's a captive skugger, and he uses telepathy to detect any other skuggers among the applicants."

"You know all that?" said Susan, taken aback. "What kind of blabbermouth security people does LANL have?"

"Los Alamos is a company town," said Tina, twinkling. "Everyone knows everything. Or tries to. It's kind of a status thing. And if you're a waitress . . ." She gave a cute shrug.

"So where's this granny cottage of yours exactly?" said Alan, not wanting to get any deeper into secret-sharing.

"I'll draw you a map," said Tina. "Maybe you passed my place on your way in. My girlfriend's at the house right now. Sue Stook. She runs a vet business out of the house. I can phone her. Blonde, tough like a cowhand, cute. She's a top."

"I'm a top these days," said Alan, enjoying the word. "Right, Bill?"

"And I'm the lowliest baboon of them all," said Bill, bending his long, thin lips into an imbecilic, self-satisfied simper. "My dance-card filled in by my superiors."

"Is that really true?" asked Tina, leaning closer. "About baboons?"

"Why do you think they have those hairless, mauve rear-ends?" said Bill. "It is as Allah wills."

By nightfall, they'd settled into Sue and Tina's granny cottage. Even though it was snowing again, Alan was grilling them a steak on the open porch in back. It wasn't so much that he was hungry as that he enjoyed performing so traditional an American activity.

"Feels like a vacation," said Susan. "Vassar would like it here. In the flesh." Her round chin quivered. "Oh, Alan, How can a human body disappear from one day to the next? And the Earth just keeps rolling on?"

"I like the idea that Joan made it all the way up," put in Bill.

"But Vassar's gone," wailed Susan. "I want him to visit me again." She raised her voice as if calling to someone in the next room. "Vassar! Vassar!"

Silence. "Ned made it all the way up, too," put in Alan, just to say something.

"Up to *where*?" said Susan, almost in tears. "What are we even *talking* about?"

"The ancient Egyptians called it the Western Lands," said Bill, slipping into his own kind of academic mode. "The high heaven beyond the ordinary afterlife."

"Did you see the high heaven while you were dead on the floor in Mexico City?" asked Susan.

"I saw a cyclone in a circus tent," said Bill. "And at the tip-tiny top I saw a bright hole. If a ghost makes it through, they're off the slaving wheel for good. And Joan did go through." He scowled at Susan. "After she shot me with the dime-store cap-gun you handed her, Susan, and thanks very much for that, by the way."

"Joan had us ensorcelled," said Alan. "It wasn't Susan's fault. And anyway you needed to pay your karmic debt, Bill. I'm just glad your brain *healed*."

"Wal—I'm used to harsh rushes," said Bill, with an assumed air of pride. He jiggled the ounce of brown heroin he was still carrying in a cellophane cigarette pack. "I could ride a harsh rush right now. Too bad I can't execute the physical motions to snort this fine Mexican H. I'm, like, paralytic. My skug's like an internal parole officer. And that, in my measured opinion, is a sufficient reason for annihilating all of the skugs on Earth. Not that I feature working for the US Army here."

"I am most assuredly going for those LANL job interviews tomorrow," said Alan. "The National Labs are the blokes who built the hydrogen *bomb*, you know. Top-drawer mad scientists. I'll be in good company, albeit as a fifth columnist."

"Fifth columnist meaning that you hope to undermine the LANL project and turn everyone into a skug?" said Bill, drily. "As I've asked you before: Doesn't this strike you as anti-human?"

"You're only playing the spoiled child because you can't sniff your silly heroin," said Alan. "But think it through—surely you don't expect that opiates do wonders for your personality? Or for your sexual performance? Do remember that we're here together as lovers, dear." Alan stretched out his shapely arms. "We've *yummy* young bodies, too. Fresh and pert. We should enjoy them."

"Indeed," said Bill with a grudging smile. "I only wanted to make the point that the skugs are mind parasites. I didn't quite grasp this at first. But we've seen the skugs' ilk before. Hypnotic propaganda loops. Addiction demons. Possession by ugly spirits. The skugs are an unusually virulent type of mind parasite—as biologically real as typhus bacilli. Opportunistic creatures sliming into us like liver flukes."

"Timid *goooooose*," said Alan, stretching out his neck to a length of three feet in mime. "What's so wonderful about our current society, Bill? The rulers are set on to murdering me, and I shouldn't doubt that you're on the kill list too. If we can spread the skugs planet-wide, we'll be safe, and we'll raise humanity to a new level. Why must the masses remain stupid and dull?" Alan glanced over at Susan. "Which side do you plump for, my dear?"

"I'm a composer," said Susan. "Not a yakker like you two. One real plus about being a skugger is that I can use my body as an instrument. As for LANL, I want to get my hands on their big new computer. It's called MANIAC?"

"Operated by Alan's hebephrenic mad scientist peers," put in Bill.

"By the way, *MANIAC* is a joke name," said Alan, setting the steak on the kitchenette table. "Purportedly it's an acronym for Mathematical Analyzer, Numerator, Integrator, and Computer. In reality, the engineers wanted to cock a snook!"

"Way too British," said Bill.

"Like I say, I want MANIAC to run some sound-synth programs," said Susan. "Higher acousmatics. We'll simulate musical instruments weirder than anything anyone can build."

"Do as you like, you two, but *I* won't be carrying the bomb-factory lunch pail," said Bill. He gestured at the pastel plywood kitchen with the speckled linoleum floor. "I'm a lord of this mountain redoubt. Restored from exile. As you know, I attended the Los Alamos Ranch School when I was fifteen. I still remember our school song."

Bill cleared his throat, then sang with raspy energy, throwing back his head for the final line, savoring it.

> *Far away and high on the mesa's crest*
> *Here's the light that all of us love best*
> *Los* Aaallll-*amos.*

"What was the school like?" asked Alan.

"I had to do exercises before breakfast, clean my plate at meals, stay out in the cold all afternoon, and ride a sullen, spiteful horse. In the school song, the light on the mesa's crest—that prefigures the atomic bomb, you understand. Note that in 1942, the Army tore down my school and set up their Manhattan Project right where I used to have my oatmeal. All of time is one instant, no? I learned this in the Beyond, my little ones. The atomic bomb is the orgasm, is the bullet, is my brain."

"So, *oookay*," said Susan, rolling her eyes. "Alan and I go off to apply for work tomorrow. And you'll be here alone, Bill, and—?"

"Well, if I can't get loaded, I might as well write a fresh segment of my perennial memoirs. I'll lead off with some snappy boyhood sex-talk, milk my routine about shooting Joan, segue into multiple degeneracies among the skuggers, and culminate with Joan's apotheosis. Coda: my mad, bony, street-preacher rant about seeing beyond the veil. I found a pen and a pad of paper here already. *Mektoub*. It is written. Or will be soon."

"Let's go to bed, my darling scribe," said Alan.

The next day was clear and sunny, colder than before, and with the mountain skies a pale manganese blue above the coruscating snow banks. Sunday morning. Their landlady Tina appeared at the door of the granny cottage, bearing a pan of home-made cinnamon buns.

"I'm on second shift this week," said Tina. "So I thought I'd nip back here and nose into your plans. I see you found the spare nightgown, Susan. Very yummy. I'm glad you three are here. I noticed you guys through the Bow Wow windows yesterday before you came in. In the slush, with your matching coats. No bags. Like gunslingers."

"Sinister fugitives," said Bill, lighting a cigarette.

"Glamorous," said Tina. "You have no idea how dull and straight Los Alamos can be. Oh, I should tell you that over the years some used clothes have accumulated in your closets. Businessy kinds of things. Help yourself. And the interviews are at the LANL main auditorium at 10 am. They've definitely got that skugsniffer I was talking about. So be ready for him."

"We've had dealings with a skugsniffer before," said Susan carefully.

The sentence hung in the air for awhile, nobody wanting to touch it.

"I sure hope you're not scheming to rat someone out," added Susan.

"I'm no kind of straight arrow," said Tina with her frank, country smile. "I'm for letting it all come down. I don't care what you guys are."

"Just as a matter of interest, let me tell you a little about the skuggers versus skugsniffers thing," said Susan. "One of the big deals with skuggers is that they have telepathy with each other. A skugsniffer is an enslaved skugger who teeps the presence of any nearby skuggers. And then the cops know to kill the skuggers."

"Is there any way to trick a skugsniffer?" asked Tina, intrigued.

"If skuggers know a telepathy scan is coming, they can put up a mental block and the skugsniffer might not notice them," said Alan.

"I'd be surprised if that move still works," said Bill. "Respect the slyness of the pig, Alan. The twinkle of the trotter. A mental wall—that could be seen as a tip-off."

"Perhaps one could run a second-order imitation game," mused Alan, thinking aloud. "An inner emulation. And—" He stopped himself. "But, as Susan says, this is all quite hypothetical. No point rattling on ad infinitum, eh? Did you say 10 am, Tina? Perhaps the widow Green and I will be on our way."

"I'm writing today," said Bill with a let's-get-down-to-it air of anticipation.

"I love all this bohemian stuff," said Tina.

"I'd be grateful if you could bring me a sandwich, a tot of bourbon, and some coffee later on," Bill told Tina. "I'm happy to pay."

"Sure," said Tina. "I can do that. I'll come around noon." She took her leave. "Good luck, you three." She paused and turned back. "Oh, one more thought for you, Susan and Alan."

"What?"

"Don't tell the LANL security where you're actually living. In case they were to come for you. Give them a fake address. Say you're at, I don't know, the Cowboy Motel up past the Big Bow Wow."

Alan and Susan dressed up like office drones and set out on foot along the two-lane highway that bisected the town. It was hard, packed snow embossed with tire tracks. There wasn't much traffic.

"So what about the skugsniffer?" asked Susan.

"We'll get ourselves an alternate pair of personalities," said Alan. "We'll pose as normal people."

Susan laughed. "And don't forget we need new ID."

"I have an idea for that. See the filling station ahead? We'll kidnap a brace of sojourners and glean what we need."

"Kidnap?"

"I'll teep you the details."

Alan and Susan picked their way along the road's pleasantly crunching snow to the gas-station. While Alan bought a red metal can and filled it with gas, Susan watched the flow of customers. And then she teeped Alan that she'd found the right pair: a sportive boy and girl in their mid-twenties, adventurers in a station-wagon with knobby tires. They had rough wooden skis on the roof, a duffel-bag in back, and Colorado plates.

"Oh, please can you help us?" called Susan, mincing over to them. "My husband and I ran out of gas, and we need a lift down the road, it's just a mile." Not pausing for an answer, Susan turned to Alan. "Come over here, dear! I've found our saviors."

The raffish blonde couple were named Peter and Polly Pfaff. Everything was fine with them. "We're heading for some back country further on," said Peter cheerfully. He had sunglasses and a short, blonde beard. "But we thought we'd put in a day near Los Alamos first. You know about Nordic skiing?"

"I'm more the espresso and jazz type," said Susan. "It must be nice to be so vigorous."

"We pack up some food and camping gear, and then we're into the boonies with a topo map," said Polly. She had her hair in a long pig-tail wrapped around her head. Her lips were white with waxy balm. "But today we're just going for a day-trip. A stony, twisty canyon-run at the Bandelier National Monument. We'll go in overland. The army has the main road into Bandelier blocked up. Maybe we'll ski up the river, if it's solid."

"Epic views of the ancient cliff-dwellings," added Peter, driving along. "Very spiritual. People say you can feel the ghosts." He glanced back at Alan and Susan in the back seat, sitting with their red can of gas on the floor between them. "How much further is your car?"

"Take the next left," improvised Alan. "We're on that side-street."

"Okay . . ." said Peter, pulling slowly into the snowy lane. "But I don't see any car? Or tire-tracks?"

"Now," said Alan.

Alan and Susan grew out their forefingers and sank them into the backs of Peter and Polly Pfaff's downy necks, with Alan linked to Peter and Susan to Polly. At Alan's direction, the car pulled over to side of the lane and stopped. They weren't in the direct view of any houses.

Rather than fully skugging the pair, they used their bio-hookup to soak up the two ski-bums' memories. A whole life in a minute.

"Give us your wallets," said Alan.

Moving sluggishly, with blank eyes, they handed back their wallets.

"Watch this," Alan told Susan. Using his left hand, he opened his leather coat and khaki shirt and laid the Pfaffs' Colorado driver's licenses on his belly-skin. The patterns transferred over to Alan's flesh, as if stamped on. The skin thickened up in two rectangles. Alan peeled them off like scabs. *Both* sides of the documents had been copied.

He handed Susan her new ID. If not exactly paper, the cunningly textured skin felt close enough to it. Alan copied the skiers' Social Security cards as well. And now he put the originals back into the wallets and passed them forward.

"We release them now?" said Susan. She and Alan still had their fingers in the backs of their hostages' necks.

"Yes," said Alan. "But before we unplug, we tell them to sleep for half an hour, and to wake with no memory of meeting us. They pulled into this side street for a nap. We'll let them think they bought the can of gas as a backup supply. A prudent precaution."

It was an easy walk to the entrance to the Los Alamos National Labs, whose main entrance was about a half mile further along the main road. On the way, Alan and Susan made themselves blonde and blue-eyed—to match what it said on the new driver's licenses. At least the licenses didn't have pictures, so they wouldn't have to change their features again. Alan still looked like his unforgettable first heartthrob Christopher Morcom; Susan still looked like her fellow electronic composer Bebe Barron. But blonde.

"Remember that we're a married couple now," said Susan. "Mr. and Mrs. Pfaff."

"I don't care to be *married*," said Alan. "Brother and sister! Cousins!"

"No, we're married," said Susan, teasing him a little. "That's what our records say, if anyone looks them up. And its what the memories we'll be showing off say, too. I'm such a Polly Pfaff. Ski, ski, ski."

"Right-o," said Alan, taking a breath. "We'll slip into our borrowed personas, giving off the wholesome scent of ski wax and fresh rye bread." One of the Los Alamos National Lab's buildings was visible up ahead, a brick structure with a glass and steel walkway along one side.

The LANL gate guard directed them towards a different building, a faceless concrete auditorium. For now, Alan was no longer thinking his own thoughts; he was fully absorbed in being Peter. It was a life-or-death imitation game.

He had a rough moment when he saw a tall man in an asinine hat leaning against an ambulance outside the auditorium entrance. Although Alan wouldn't consciously formulate the recognition till later, at a subliminal level he knew this to be a man who'd tried to kill him, and that the creature inside the ambulance was—

Alan threw his whole soul into the Peter Pfaff persona. "Nice slope over there," he said to Susan, pointing a mountain peak in the middle distance. "We'll earn some bucks here, and go ski-camping for a week."

"I'd love to meet some of the local Indians while we're on the mesa," said Susan in a her sappiest tone. "Maybe join a kiva ceremony? Why's there an ambulance?"

"Not for us!" said Alan, squeezing Susan's hand. "We're tiptop. Let's go in and see about a gig." In his role as Peter, he was speaking the American idiom.

They entered an echoing lobby with a few tables. It was by no means a mob scene. Less than a dozen applicants had appeared. They looked like housewives and mechanics.

"The job you want is tape puncher," a rangy, talkative woman told Susan. "That's what I do. It's like being a typist. You look like you'd be fun to work with. What we do is poke holes in paper tapes that tell MANIAC how to act. The test is over there." She pointed to a machine with a small keyboard. "I'm Tilda. Come on. I'm recruiting you."

"Okay," said Susan. "I'm Polly Pfaff."

In his less than scholarly Peter Pfaff persona, Alan felt no confidence about being able to punch the tape reliably. "What are the other jobs?" he asked the chatty Tilda. "I'm Polly's husband."

"You might go for tube tech," said Tilda. "It means you run around the back of the MANIAC changing radio tubes when they burn out. The test for that one's inside the auditorium."

"Okay," said Alan. "See you later, Polly."

It was interesting inside the auditorium. Rather than exposing the delicate and highly classified MANIAC's machinery to every ham-handed job applicant, the engineers had decorated the stage with a rickety array of colored lights. The flickering bulbs were red, yellow, green and blue. The assemblage gave the concrete auditorium a festive, holiday air.

As Alan watched the blinking lights, he noticed an interesting flow of forms, as if on an illuminated night-club sign—although the patterns were more like twirling paisleys than like, say, leg-kicking showgirls or flying champagne corks.

"Tube tech test?" inquired an engineer with a clipboard, walking up the aisle to greet him. A second engineer was down on the stage, a silhouette against the flowing patterns.

"Yeah," said Alan.

The man handed Alan a shoebox holding some small colored lightbulbs. "The idea is to keep the network on. It's a complex circuit. When one of the bulbs fails, some of the others go black. And we'll be timing how quickly you can figure out which bulb is dead. We'll do three runs."

"I used to fix my Oma's Christmas lights in Denver," said Alan, running his Peter Pfaff routine.

"Good for you," said the engineer, setting down his clipboard. "No peeking now." He cupped his two hands over Alan's eyes. His fingers were pleasantly warm. "Zap it, Joe!" he called.

When the engineer uncovered Alan's eyes a moment later, he saw a wobbly, irregular blotch of darkness in the flowing patterns of lights. He hurried down to the stage and got started, reasoning as well as he could while maintaining his protective mental simulation of Peter Pfaff. Joe, the junior engineer whose job it was to screw up the circuit before each run, was sitting on the edge of the stage with his legs dangling.

Seen close up, the network was more complicated than Alan had realized. Each bulb was in a small fixture holding four bulbs in all. A rat's nest of cables tied the fixtures together, and each of the fixtures was about six inches from its closest neighbors.

The fixtures were continually turning on and off, sometimes red, sometimes blue and so on. Waves of color jittered across the network like nested scrolls, with the elusive zone of outage a dark cloud against a spinning sky.

By the time Alan found the dead bulb, he had flop-sweat rolling down his ribs. He went back up into the auditorium and let the man with the clipboard cover his eyes again, while skinny Joe put another dead bulb into the system. The second run went faster than the first.

At the end of his superb third run, Alan paused on stage, staring contemplatively at the melding patterns, letting a little corner of his Alan Turing mind begin working on the question of what algorithm was being used. It seemed very like an activator-inhibitor rule.

Right about then he noticed a third LANL engineer—a man in a suit sitting in the shadows at the back of the stage, twiddling a little console board of controllers, perhaps exploring the possibilities of the network's behavior. The shadowed man looked familiar. But—still aware of the skugsniffer outside—Alan didn't allow himself to think too deeply about it. He turned away from the secret master of the network and gazed up at the engineer with the clipboard.

"How'd I do?" Alan called.

"You're in," said the man, beckoning. "Just let me copy

the info off your ID, and we'll get you a gate pass. Your first shift can be tomorrow, 1 pm to 9 pm. We're running around the clock, three shifts a day."

Out in the lobby, Alan found that Susan, too, had done well. She was a tape puncher, with the same work hours as him.

The pressure of imitating Peter and Polly Pfaff was so strong that they didn't talk much until they were back downtown in Los Alamos, at the Big Bow Wow, out of the skugsniffer's range. Tina had brought them coffee, cheeseburgers, and apple pie.

"I assume you realize who those people at the gate were?" said Alan.

"The asshole in the cowboy hat was Dick Hosty," said Susan. "Right? And he killed my husband with a flamethrower. We're going to get him, Alan. We'll pay him back. He's going to die."

"Of course," said Alan in a soothing tone. "No worries."

"Who was the skugsniffer?" asked Susan. "I couldn't get a read, and I was scared to be too obvious."

"Roland Gill," said Alan. "That was the FBI agent who I skugged in Holly Beach. He was almost a friend of mine. Poor Gill."

"Why are we screwing around inside LANL anyway?" demanded Susan. "Why don't you get a gun and shoot Hosty right now? Or sic Burroughs and Naranjo on him. Those guys don't care."

"Think bigger picture," said Alan. "I need to worm so far into LANL that I meet with their top brain. And that's probably Stan Ulam. Have I ever mentioned him to you?

No? Anyway, LANL is cobbling up a nuclear weapons project against the skugs. It's our role as skuggers to prevent that."

"I'm amazed I got hired there at all," said Susan, her mood shifting as she ate her pie. "I don't know anything that they care about."

"Stan Ulam," repeated Alan, his mind running on its own track. "That's who was sitting in the shadows at the back of the stage! I was so busy imitating Peter Pfaff that I didn't realize it. Yes, yes, of course. It's as I said. Ulam is the chief designer. You have to help me meet him, Susan. It'll be natural. I'm keeping his machine in trim, and you're turning his code into holes punched in tape."

"I just wonder where Vassar went," said Susan, staring out the window at the rolling, sunny fields of snow.

nonlinear feedback

It took Susan less than an hour to learn her job—which was converting the head designer's handwritten instructions into punched tape. She used a nice little tape puncher with about a dozen keys. Her new friend Tilda worked next to her, showing her the ropes.

Their overseer was a bland, doughy woman named Dora. Dora wore colorless Army-issue spectacles, with her hair in a bun. Three hard-featured younger women filled out the roster. Susan was the only new hire on this shift.

After Susan had converted her first page of written code into rows of holes on a small spool of paper tape, Tilda smiled and told her to feed the tape into a reader beside her desk. The reader scanned through the tape, one row of holes at a time, then initiated a frantic burst of activity among some other machines—well-worn metal devices that created subsidiary rolls of punched tape on their own, spooling the tapes to and fro according to some hidden logic.

"Dora says the feds used machines like this for the last

census," Tilda told Susan. "I always think of falling dominos. One thing leads to another."

"I like it a lot in here," said Susan, savoring the aural filigree of clicks and clacks, the tapping of the solenoids, the hum of the rollers. She felt proud for having initiated this cascade. "I wish I'd brought my audio recorder."

"You're a musician?" exclaimed Tilda. "Sister! I play fiddle in a western band—Diamonds And Spades. We do weddings, funerals, and shitkicker BBQs."

"I'm more a composer than a performer," said Susan. "Not that I write out notes and clefs and all that razzamatazz. I do—acousmatics? Means I tape tasty noises and paste them up."

"This isn't a coffee klatch, girls," said Dora, suddenly looming over them. "Punch more tape."

"Sure thing, boss," said Tilda. "But tell Polly here what's going on. Polly punched her first spool of tape, and fed it into the reader, and the whole room went batshit. Why for? Huh? Huh? Huh?"

Dora solemnly scanned over Susan's tape. "This tape told the tabulators and the unit record machines to create a tape that's a ten-thousand-line model of a hollow ball," she said. "A spherical shell." And now she widened her bulging eyes, as if to look more commanding. "Back to work! No lollygagging."

"I'm, ah, also wondering if the MANIAC can make music," ventured Susan.

"I'm sure Dr. Ulam can answer that," said Dora. "When he has time to talk to you. For now please don't bother him. Dr. Ulam is brilliant, but he's very distractible."

"Not that he ever talks to us anyway," put in Tilda. "He likes to go into the machine room. Warms his hands at the holy vacuum tubes."

Dora strode across the room to ride herd on the other three. "Pick up the pace, girls. Mankind's future is in your hands!" The young women met this with jeers and giggles. One of them made a jacking-off gesture. Quietly Susan folded and pocketed the hand-written sheet of instructions that she'd just encoded.

Over in the MANIAC's room, Alan's job was slow-paced—until it wasn't. He was to sit on a stool behind the MANIAC cabinets not doing much of anything until one of the two engineers running the machine would yell something like "Failure in sector Yankee-Foxtrot."

And then Alan would have to find and replace the bad tube. The MANIAC wasn't more than ten feet long—and the rear panels on the cabinets were open. He had easy access to the innards. But the thing had over two thousand tubes, and even with the sector advice, Alan would have to decide among at least four or five possible culprits.

The guys running the machine were engineers whom Turing might ordinarily have befriended—one of them was Joe, who'd been helping with the job test yesterday. But they weren't interested in talking to Alan. He was a pawn, a tool, an inferior. Alan remembered his own inability to properly see the low-ranking techs when he'd been in power at Manchester.

Time dragged as the late afternoon shift wore into night. Alan would have liked to be scheming about how he might meet Ulam and find out the details of the big

anti-skug project being set into motion here. But, more
so than Susan, Alan was cautious, even paranoid, about
thinking his natural thoughts. He kept worrying that
Hosty's skugsniffer might direct his attention inward to
the occupants of the lab—and ferret Alan out. Not that
there were any signs of that.

Staring blankly at the gently glowing thermionic tubes,
awaiting the next circuit failure, Alan drifted into the trance
of an invisible man. And that's when he saw Vassar again.

In the snowstorm on the mesa, Vassar had been a fluttering rhombus, vague at the edges of Alan's field of perception. But now the ghost was center stage. He resembled a meter-wide manta ray, with lambent wings of the
same brightness and tint as the filaments of the vacuum
tubes. The long cord of the ray's tail led deep into the guts
of the MANIAC.

"Wake up, spaceman," teeped Vassar. "I'm back. Can
you get me in touch with Susan?"

"Failure in Sector Romeo-Zulu!" called one of the
engineers just then, and Alan sprang to work. When he
had a moment to think again, Vassar was gone. Perhaps
Vassar had by now found Susan on his own.

Alan's and Susan's shifts were over at 9 pm. The LANL
security was quick to herd them and the other workers
out the gates. The two caught a ride to the sketchy, mea-
ger core of Los Alamos.

Once they were alone, Alan told Susan about seeing
Vassar. Susan hadn't seen Vassar herself, but she told
Alan what she'd heard about Ulam. They grabbed some
sopaipillas and chili verde at the Big Bow Wow. Alan was

very interested in the instruction sheet that Susan had bagged—he claimed he could reconstruct the system's whole programming language from these few lines.

"I've a knack for these things," he told Susan. "Like a paleontologist modeling a brontosaurus from a tail bone."

After their meal, they headed back to the granny cottage, bringing some take-out food for Bill Burroughs, in case he was awake.

Bill was more than awake—he was fully wired, snapping his limbs like a marionette, going full bore on his memoir. He'd set up a typewriter on the kitchen table. His output pages were scattered across the table and the floor.

"I'm a soft machine," exulted Bill. "A meat teletype from Atlantis."

Alan found it sexy to see his boyfriend writing. He went over and gave Bill a reckless kiss on the mouth. Delicious. "How far along are you, dear?"

"Jumping around," said Bill, teeping his pleasure at Alan's attentions. "One hard pop per page. Right now we're skugging hicks at nowhere airstrips."

"And—are you finding your inner skug of use?" asked Alan. He was still trying to decide whether his parasites actually provided a true creative boost.

"The inner light," said Bill in a sardonic tone. He stretched his hands upward as if towards a blazing sun, then ran trembling fingers across his face. "Wearing the Happy Cloak!" Now he paused and shook his head. "Why do amateurs always think that artists depend on drugs, or demonic possession, or biocomputational implants? It's all me, Alan, straight or high. But I will grant that my skug is quite encouraging. It views my chronicle as a gospel. *Exodus* perhaps, or the *Book of Revelation*."

"Have you seen Vassar here?" interrupted Susan. "Alan saw him at LANL."

"I was writing about his ghost today," said Bill, pointing at some pages that had ended up in the far corner of the kitchen. "In my deathless prose, your man burns more brightly than ever before. Be a dear and put my pages into some kind of order."

"Kiss my ass," said Susan amiably.

"We're ready to bunk down," said Alan. "And, Bill, if you'd care to join me for a tussle, I'd be more than—"

"No time!" cried Burroughs, leaning over his typewriter like a race-car driver at the wheel. "Further communications incoming."

"I envy you," said Alan. "I'm feeling dull as dog meat." He set the bag of food from the Big Bow Wow beside Bill's typewriter. "Burnt offerings for the high scribe."

"You're kind," said Bill, looking up, his eyes frank and mild. "I like that."

Alan felt a pulse of teep harmony. "I'll sit with you for a bit before bed."

"But not too long," cautioned Bill. "I don't want any sense that you're silently petitioning for preferential treatment in my Akashic records."

Alan laughed and got himself a glass of juice.

Alone in her bed, Susan was lulled by the nested rhythms of the typewriter keys, the ding of the bell, the thunk of the carriage return, and the ratcheting swoop when Bill scrolled in a fresh sheet of paper.

All the while, she stayed focused on the idea of Vassar—summoning him, on the verge of of sleep. And then he was before her: a large, translucent manta ray. His tail led to the socket in the wall. His voice in her head was clearer than before, more energetic.

"Hey, babe."

"Why did you leave me?" teeped Susan. "I thought maybe you'd gone up to heaven. Or that you'd—fallen apart."

"I've been hanging with one of those local cliff dwellers. The ghost of an ancient Tewa Indian. I call him Xurt. He looks like a raven, but with some feathers falling out. He's been dead for five centuries in those caves. He's hungry and he's pissed off. We're helping each other. I want to get even with Dick Hosty. And he wants to stop those war-pigs from building a monster bomb in his canyon."

"Bomb?"

"The army calls it a V-bomb. Project Utopia. Xurt and I found a way to follow the war-pigs' info trails into their sty."

"You mean the Los Alamos Labs? Where Alan and I are working?"

"Xurt and I made a nest in their giant computer. I'm like Aladdin in his cave. I'm branching out from there, drawing energy from the circuits of all Los Alamos. The computer, the phone systems, even the power lines. Xurt digs the hook-ups. He wants to haunt the whole lab." Vassar flexed the winged delta of his body. "Me, I'm setting the stage for the takedown."

"Of Hosty?"

"If Alan has the guts to help me, Dick Hosty is going to die." Vassar flickered and was gone. And the weary Susan was asleep.

Bill wrote all night, alone in the kitchen. At dawn he gathered up his pages to shuffle and reshuffle them. Gradually a stable configuration emerged. On a whim he wrote *The Apocalypse According to Willy Lee* across the top of the first page.

Bill felt drained and shaky, as if seeing the world through a layer of plate glass. Finishing any project was horrible—like driving off a cliff at a hundred miles per hour. First came the abrupt come-down, and then the immediate worry that the work wasn't as good as it had seemed while he was *in medias res*.

This come-down was particularly harsh. Bill was seeing blurs in his perception, like trails and smears when he turned his head. Even the modest sounds of Alan waking up and showering had an unpleasant boom and drag. Should he load up on those soothing endorphins from the Man within? No—that was starting to feel like being given brainwash meds in a psych ward.

Alan strode into the kitchen, chipper in his boyish body and, truth be told, too British to bear. "You look all in, Bill," he fluted. "Is the masterpiece done?"

"You sound like a magnetic tape that's being dragged at irregular speeds past the read-head," said Bill irritably. "Horrible."

"I suspect you've overdosed on your endogenous neurotransmitters," said Alan, his kind face filled with concern. "You need a nice lie-down, Bill."

"Don't try to nurse me!" Bill felt a sudden and deep revulsion with his current status. He'd been mutated by a slug and he'd fallen into a sexual relationship with the parasite's designer. He'd followed the stooge back to small-town America, and now this new lover was playing footsie with the government pigs.

"Perhaps you'd feel better if you phoned your family in Florida?" said the maddening Turing. "You mother and little Billy would love to hear from you."

"*Fuck* that sound," spat Bill. And then he felt ashamed of his coldness. His voice cracked. "Why can't writing be enough? Why are you physically coming on to me?"

Now Susan was awake too, standing in the door of her room. Susan, Alan, and Bill. Three zombies.

"I want out of here!" yelled Bill. He snatched up the phone and dialed Allen Ginsberg's number in San Francisco. Thanks god he knew it by heart. The phone rang for quite some time, and finally Ginsberg answered, sleepy but alert. It was maybe 4 am out there.

"Make this good," intoned Ginsberg, right there in the moment. "I'm having a drunken night in my house with a boy."

"It's Bill. You have to rescue me." While saying this, Burroughs shot a hostile look at Turing and Susan. Teaching them a lesson. He felt spiteful as a toad. "I'm in Los Alamos, New Mexico. Imprisoned by religious fanatics."

"Cultists?" asked Ginsberg, mildly interested. "Any Peyote?"

"No, man, these are mutants. They implanted a new organ in me."

"Are you high?"

"I've been up all night writing a memoir, Allen. Get me out of here today. I'm behind enemy lines."

"Long road, Bill. Los Alamos where they build the bombs?"

"New bomb on the way. The V-bomb."

"I'd dig seeing a test," said Ginsberg. "Intolerable light and radiance, and afterwards the grey world is a ghost, with the juice sizzled away. Maybe I can ask Neal to drive me out. He's on a tear. Entangled with a madwoman. He needs a break."

"Cassady? That motor-mouth Okie? Don't drive, Allen, take a plane. I'll pay. I'm fat with kale. Gangland deals in Mexico."

"Neal's not an Okie, Bill. That's just an accent he finds amusing. You're so jealous of Neal. Open your heart."

"All right, I'll pay Neal's ticket too, Mother Superior. Anyway, I'm young now. Irresistible. You lowlifes rent a car in Santa Fe. I'm in Los Alamos in the granny cottage behind the house of Sue Stook the vet's. She has a statue of horse out front. If you pass the Big Bow Wow, you've gone too far."

"Smallville," said Ginsberg. "The town where Hiroshima was born! Strange ancient America."

"I want out of here, Allen. Before they inculcate me into the Higher Mysteries. They'll trepan my skull, shave my balls, play the thigh-bone trumpets and drag me up the ziggurat. Maybe you bring me a dime bag of junk?"

"We'll chant, Bill. It'll fry your hot dog for fair. I've learned to overlap the short and the long breaths." A boy's voice interrupted Ginsberg, and he ended the call in laughter. "We're riding to the rescue, Captain Burroughs."

With Bill as agitated as he was, Susan and Turing left the house early. They stopped by the Big Bow Wow.

"I saw Vassar last night," Susan announced. "You and I didn't really get a chance to talk or teep yet today. Thanks to that wacko Burroughs."

"He's gone spare," said Alan. "I fear I'm not enough for him. I'm a boring wonk. Not a writer." Alan sighed and shook his head, crestfallen. "So what did Vassar tell you?"

"You're not boring, Alan. You're the archenemy. Give yourself some credit."

"Archenemy?" said Alan, slightly puzzled. "Oh, you mean my skugs. I've started taking them for granted, rather."

"World leaders *definitely* view you as the archenemy," insisted Susan. "Anyway. The main thing Vassar told me is that LANL is building a bomb against the skugs in that canyon between here and the mesa where Ricky Red Dog lives. The V-bomb. Project Utopia."

"Those lights we saw when we where lost in the storm," mused Alan. "That was the bomb site. Why V-bomb? And how would *Burroughs* know?"

"Not sure about that," said Susan. "At first I thought Burroughs had teeped the name from me. But there's that vision he had when he was dead in Mexico. He saw something in heaven?"

"God knows all," intoned Turing. "Very strange if any of that religious bosh proves out to be true." As so many times before, he thought of his lost love Christopher Morcom. Safe in heaven dead? Waiting for him? For now, Alan himself was wearing Chris's face.

"You better make your move on Ulam today," said Susan, showing him the designer's handwritten instructions again. "Make a plan, Alan. We can't just be reacting to events. We have to get Hosty."

"Dora said this was the code for a spherical shell?" asked Alan, looking at the instructions.

"Her very words," said Susan, mopping up syrup with her last bit of French toast. She signaled the waitress for seconds.

"Presumably the shell is the shape of the charge they're going to use in this new bomb," said Alan. "This V-bomb. They're simulating the explosion on the MANIAC. Trying to predict how it'll behave. And if these particular handwritten instructions do all that . . ." His voice trailed off and he was quiet for a few minutes.

The clattering, humdrum diner faded away. Alan was where he most liked to be, in the land of pure abstractions. And now the answers came into his head. He understood how the computational patterns were tethered to the little knobs of the symbols. With wry amusement, he saw a simple way to throw a monkey-wrench into the MANIAC.

With his pen moving as rapidly and evenly as a mechanical plotter, Alan inscribed twelve lines of code on the back-side of Susan's sheet of instructions. He read them over one, twice, three times. No margin for error.

"So you want me to punch these onto a tape?" asked Susan, in tight teep synch with him now.

"Right. And this first line ensures that when you feed the code into the reader, the signals go directly over to the MANIAC. Without printing out any intermediary tapes."

"And then what?" asked Susan.

"I meet Ulam," said Alan.

Sure enough, around three in the afternoon, the MANIAC went into a frenzy. Its lights flashed with rising intensity; its tape spools whined at a frenetic speed. So viciously crafted was Alan's logic knot that Joe the engineer had to cut off the computer's main power switch.

Five minutes later, Stan Ulam appeared. Like the other men, he wore a jacket and tie. He was nearly bald, with thoughtful wrinkles, a large nose, and a slight smile.

"What's up, Joe? Why has the shit hit the fan?" Although Ulam had a noticeable Polish accent, he made the most of the American idioms he knew.

"A problem with the program, Stan," said the skinny engineer at the controls. "I can't quite nail it down. I fetched a copy of the program tape."

Alan piped up from his stool beside the tube cabinets. "An endless loop, I'll wager. A jump to a previous program point. An infinitely nested recursion."

"Advice from the peanut gallery?" said Ulam, mildly amused. "Who do you think you are, Mr. Tube Tech?"

"I'm, ah, Peter Pfaff. I don't have any formal degrees, but mathematics and computer science are hobbies of mine."

"Computer science," said Ulam, as if the phrase left a bad taste in his mouth. "A discipline that explicitly calls itself a science is a pretender. Social science. Political science. Military science. And car science for the grease monkeys in the garage."

"Ah, but remember Turing's use of the Halting Problem to solve Hilbert's *Entscheidungsproblem*," said Alan smoothly. "That's science about computers, Dr. Ulam."

"Your tube tech is speaking always this way?" said Ulam, turning to the two engineers at the controls. He held his hands stretched out to his sides like a comedian delivering a punch line.

"He only started here yesterday, Dr. Ulam," said Joe, who was rapidly flipping through the MANIAC's program tapes. "He never said anything at all so far."

"There's the glitch!" cried in the other engineer, who was looking at the paper tape over Joe's shoulder "A bad jump and an endless loop." He scowled at Alan. "Suspicious."

"I made a simple deduction," said Alan shrugging his shoulders. "I can't help being clever."

"Fix the program tape and restart the run," Ulam told the engineers after a moment's deliberation. "And call in a replacement for this tube tech. He's off the job. And tell Dora to fire whoever it was who punched the bad tape. We are not needing practical jokers." Ulam turned his intent gaze full upon Alan. His eyes were gray-green. "I want to talk to you in private. Come."

Alan followed Ulam down a hall, not sure what was in store. The two of them took a seat on a couch at a bend of the passage, and Ulam asked Alan an escalating series of questions about maps in operator space, nonlinear wave equations, and the practical implementation of cellular automata upon computing machines. He seemed greatly to enjoy Alan's answers, and when he was done, he beamed and patted Alan on the knee.

"I am hoping you're not so intractable a spy that we have to execute you," said Ulam. "I'm deeply in need of an intelligent person to talk with. No such individuals are working at LANL just now. Come, we'll let the security men pick your bones."

Alan had been through the security office for his clearance to be a tube tech. This time, however, he had to offer up his fingerprints, pose for two photos, and submit a blood test. Once more the agents scrutinized the Peter Pfaff ID that he'd grown from his stomach skin. So far as Alan knew, the real Peter and Polly Pfaff had finished their Bandelier day-trip and had moved on to gnarlier slopes by now. Good to have them out of the way. As before, Alan told the security he and Polly were lodging in the Cowboy Motel—and nobody checked. The security office wasn't very well organized.

Meanwhile the FBI and the CIA sent background information on Peter Pfaff over the teletype—fortunately with no photos attached. Alan was still wearing Christopher Morcom's face. Above all, Alan was grateful that they didn't wheel in the skugsniffer. Apparently the security staff didn't want the skugsniffer inside the secure zones of the lab.

"Can you rush the approval?" Ulam asked the security agent. "I would need Pfaff today and tomorrow."

"Says here he's been a folk singer," said the fat agent, tapping his finger on one of the print-outs. "Questionable."

"As you know, I'm chief scientist on Project Utopia," said Ulam. "Crash priority. This colorful character's input could be a key for keeping the project on time. I am taking my inspiration where I find it."

"We'll give him a temporary clearance," said the security chief, unimpressed. "He'll have to apply for an extension in three days." With a flurry of paper-stamping, the man put together a new identity card.

"You are passing now to the inner sanctum," said Ulam, hurrying Alan along. "We have a better cafeteria. Classified food. And now for my office. You can be yourself in here and talk freely. They are sweeping the place for bugs every week. Even the skugsniffer isn't nosing in here."

In Ulam's lair, shelves of math and physics books filled one wall, with scores of journal reprints mixed in. A massively boxed cathode ray tube sat in a corner above a bank of switches and dials. A heavy wooden table held a fascinating collection of mechanical devices that Ulam must have cobbled together himself, very rough and handmade. A blackboard was bedecked with arcane formulae and odd diagrams. Alan's idea of paradise.

Ulam picked up a gimmick the size of a shoebox, with a piston on one side and a pair of wooden mousetrap-style levers linked to eccentrically mounted gears.

"Can you make a wild guess what this is?" asked Ulam puckishly.

"A mockup for the initiator cascade of the hydrogen bomb," said Alan after a moment's hesitation. Ulam waggled his expressive eyebrows, impressed by Alan's acumen.

And this was the moment when Alan's inner skug could wait no more. A tendril shot out from his finger and into Ulam's belly as if to skug him.

But the finger could find no purchase in Ulam's flesh. The long extension shriveled to a wisp and dropped away, leaving as a stub—Alan's original finger.

"I am vaccinated," said Ulam. "Naturally. Like all of the higher-ups. I was of course suspecting you to be a skugger. Smelling a rat, no?"

Alan looked frantically around the windowless office. The only way out was through the door. Ulam would sound an alarm and the guards would be firing at him. As a skugger he was relatively immune to bullets—but if they had a flame-thrower, he was done for. If only he could make it outdoors, he'd change his form and find a way to slip away, perhaps as a snake beneath the snow. But—how odd—Ulam was simply standing there smiling at him.

"Aren't you going to do anything?" Alan had to ask.

"Keep your friends close, and your enemies closer," said Ulam. "Machiavelli. Who better to advise me on project Utopia than a skugger? If you can play along with me, Mr. Pfaff, there may be an opportunity to tell your fellows the details of our plan to exterminate all skuggers."

"Why would you help us?" asked Alan, bewildered. "Why would you create a security leak?"

"I know the situation from both sides," said Ulam moving his hands up and down like the pans of a scale. "Approximately my entire family was dying in the Holocaust. Exterminated for being Jews. Safe in America, I fight our enemies by working on the atomic bomb and the hydrogen bomb. I helped create the instant holocaust of Hiroshima—and the potential for much worse. I am the exterminated and the exterminator. Both sides." He dropped his hands.

"I'm—I'm glad you're willing to talk," said Alan, damping down the wild skug-chatter in his head. "I should tell you that I'm not Peter Pfaff. I'm Alan Turing."

"In wonderland!" exclaimed Ulam, his eyes keen. "If true. You and I were once exchanging letters, yes? About what?"

"About Turing machines and the van Kampen characteristic of a continuous group," said Alan readily. "Fifteen years ago. I pointed out a flaw in your reasoning."

"Most excellent," said Ulam, shaking Alan's hand. "And I was thinking Turing is dead. A suicide, they were saying."

"The British security's lie," said Alan. "The filthy MI5. They wanted to exterminate me for being homosexual."

"It never stops," said Ulam. "Persecution upon persecution."

"I used a biocomputational technique to elude them," said Alan, still proud of his maneuver. "And this led to my skugs."

"You the father of the skugs!" exclaimed Ulam. "And I the father of the H-bomb. An apocalyptic partnership. Do you feel you can you work with me, Alan? Is your skug symbiote granting you sufficient free will?"

"My skug is eager to win your confidence," said Alan. "As am I. But of course you can't fully trust me."

"Understood from the start," said Ulam. "A risk worth taking. You have an unparalleled record in merging mathematics and practical technology. I am knowing of your classified work on breaking the German Enigma code."

"So set the score even and tell me about Project Utopia," said Turing hungrily. "The V-bomb in the canyon,"

"Not quite yet," said Ulam, perhaps surprised that Alan knew even this much. "I need to weigh the risks and benefits. For today—let's tinker. To warm up. And tomorrow we get to work. First play—then pounce. One day is enough for any job."

"Fine," said Alan. "But there's one more thing. That woman whom you told them to fire. She works as Polly Pfaff in the tape punching room. Posing as my wife. Everything I know, I share with her. Bring her in here with us. I'm concerned about what Dora and your security might do to her. Let her play with us too."

"She is another mathematician?"

"She composes electronic music."

"Aha. We are fiddling while Rome burns."

Ulam picked up a telephone with an elaborate hood over the mouthpiece that kept Alan from hearing what he was saying. The hood was wired to a black box on the floor. It was an electronic sound-cancellation device— Turing himself had built one for the British Navy. You could block a sound by emitting a counter-sound that was precisely out of synch. You needed the hood to send the counter-sound into the room rather than into the mouthpiece with the message-sound.

After a few minutes Ulam set down his hush-phone. "The security chief is flipping his wig. He was very eager to offer this woman to the Grand Inquisitor."

"Dick Hosty!" exclaimed Alan, his stomach tight. "Please tell me Polly's safe!"

"She's on her way here. Frog-marched by two agents who'll stand guard outside my office. Just in case you two are going bananas." Ulam pulled a lever on his H-bomb model and the piston snapped up. "*Boom!*"

Ulam took a liking to Susan, and the three of them had a wonderful afternoon together. For today, Ulam didn't seem interested in working on whatever it was he was supposed to be doing for Project Utopia. Alan knew the feeling. Sometimes it was best to let subterranean rivers do the preliminary excavation.

Ulam's cathode ray display was directly wired to the MANIAC, and he was able to route programs to the big machine from the controls on his console, displaying the outputs as slowly moving dots and lines on his screen.

At first the patterns reminded Alan of oil slicks or—come to think of it—the patterns he'd seen in those Christmas-tree lights during his tube tech test in the auditorium. But soon they switched to something else. Orderly-looking waves that unexpectedly pushed up their peaks, took on lumpy, unnatural shapes, and occasionally exploded into chaotic fuzz.

"Nonlinear feedback," explained Ulam. "Normally a spring is pulling back in proportion to how far you've pulled it. It's linear. But what if it is pulling back in proportion to the third power of its displacement? It's cubic then, nonlinear. It's not well known that I was using nonlinear wave equations to design the hydrogen bomb. And now, for Project Utopia, I take a step beyond. Instead of reasonable exponents like three, I am looking at crazy exponents. Like negative seven, or pi, or the square root of minus one."

"And these exotic nonlinear waves have to do with V-bomb?" said Alan.

"I call these waves *V-rays*," said Ulam. "Return tomorrow for our exciting conclusion. But for today, our Mata Hari here has been asking me for—how did put it, my dear?"

"Vile vibrations," said Susan.

"Yes," said Ulam. "In the key of V." He rooted through a cabinet of equipment and managed to wire a speaker to the back of his cathode ray display. Immediately the room was filled with radically ugly sounds. "Vile," said Ulam, nodding his head to the irregular rhythms. "And I think *voluptuous* in some way."

"Can we tape-record this?" Susan asked.

"Why not?" said Ulam. "We are all going bananas. Perhaps in two days the world ends." He used his hush-phone to call for a reel to reel tape recorder. The security men may have thought it was for documenting confessions from the two questionable employees. In any case, the machine appeared at Ulam's office door within minutes. Laughing and joking as if they didn't have a care in the world, Susan and Ulam taped a half-hour's worth of increasingly gnarly material.

Near the end, Ulam ran a wire from the speaker inputs back into the inputs that led to MANIAC. The sounds grew wondrously dire. And then—like some eldritch jack-in-the-box—Vassar's glowing manta ray peeped out at Alan and Susan from the back of the cathode ray cabinet.

"Nonlinear feedback," said Ulam, oblivious of the watchful ghost. He glanced at his watch, weary from the long day's diversions. "It's seven in the evening. You two can go."

"Can I take the reel to reel recorder?" asked Susan boldly. "I have a lot of acousmatic tapes that I want to play."

"An enterprising woman," said Ulam. He thought for a moment. "I don't see that security will object. Although they may want to be sure there's nothing hidden inside the machine."

"Can I take this new tape too?" said Susan. "The one we just made? I'm imagining a piece called *The Dance Of Two To The Pi*."

"You say *dance*?" said Ulam. "Not death? I'm hoping you're right. You can try to take the tape. But good luck getting it past security." Ulam clicked his heels and offered a mock salute, pretending to be an agent.

"Oh, smuggling something small is easy for a skugger," said Susan. She pulled up her sweater and pressed the reel against her bare belly. The reel sank in like a coin into dough. "This is how I saved my old tapes at the Gormly ambush," she remarked, her voice tightening. "But let's not get into that. We'd better go."

"I thought you'd have some scientific questions for me," Alan plaintively reminded Ulam on his way out. "I *did* offer to help you."

"Come alone tomorrow," said Ulam. "Tomorrow is the work day. The big showdown."

Alan and Susan pumped up their Peter and Polly personalities, and walked down the hall, Susan carrying the tape machine. The security office carefully vetted the machine. And the two guards stuck close to them until they'd reached the front entrance. It was snowing again. A white ambulance was waiting there in the dark with— Dick Hosty at the wheel, wearing a pistol in a shoulder holster.

"Ya'll need a ride into town?" he called. "Dick Hosty's the name. You're Peter and Polly Pfaff, lest I'm mistaken.

Heard you just lost your job, Polly. Rough deal. Hop on in. It's started to snow again."

A low chatter of police talk emanated from a squawk-box on the dash, and a microphone hung near Hosty. The back of the ambulance was filled by a great dark cylinder. Alan didn't dare let himself think about that. He only hoped that Susan was keeping her guard up as well.

"Thanks, Dick," said Alan, squeezing into the middle of the bench-style front seat, his voice folksy. "Come on, Polly. He can drop us at the Big Bow Wow." Alan looked around the ambulance as if in awe. "You get many emergencies out here, Dick?"

"Aw, I don't use this ambulance for no life-saving, Pete. I got a sick friend in back I like to haul around."

"Real sorry to hear that," said Susan, her voice wavering. Alan could feel the tension in her frame. "Your friend's in an iron lung?"

"Sump'n like that," said Hosty, pulling onto the road. The headlights carved snow-speckled cones in the night. "Makes some people feel funny when my friend's around. Right, Roland?"

An extra speaker in the dash crackled. A voice from the cylinder in back. "Right, Dick. I find traitors for you."

"But Peter and Polly Pfaff here are okay?" asked Hosty, glancing over at them, his face hard and mean.

"AOK, Dick," said the speaker. "I don't teep a thing."

"You *sure*?" said Hosty, jabbing a jerry-rigged red button on the dash. Alan heard a slight crackling sound behind him, and the speaker emitted a yelp. Hosty had sent an electric shock into the captive skugger.

"Don't *do* that, Dick," begged the skugsniffer. "It hurts more than you know. I promise I'd never hold out on you. If I sniff any skuggers, you're going to hear about it."

"Alright then," said Hosty. "Just makin' sure." The ambulance fish-tailed a little as Hosty accelerated towards town. The cop chatter on the squawk-box continued.

"I'm very, very upset that LANL fired me," said Susan, having a little trouble with her voice. "Peter and I are practically broke. All I did was goof up on one tape-punch, and *bam*! That Dora's a bitch. At least my Peter's still working."

"Kicked him upstairs, what I heard," said Hosty in a coz-ening tone. "Working as a special assistant to Dr. Ulam."

"Lord knows why," said Alan, playing the bedazzled rube. "He's an odd duck, that Dr. Ulam. All I did was mention that math's a hobby of mine, and he was all over me like a cheap suit. I guess he's lonely and needs some-body to listen to him. I'm glad to help. Seems like it's a mighty important project he's on."

They reached the sparsely lit center of Los Alamos, lit-tle more than a wide place in the road. "You can drop us off by the Bow Wow, Mr. Hosty," said Susan. "Right here. Now."

Frozen-faced, the two of them went into the diner, got some take-out food and walked a half-mile further down the highway to Sue Stook's granny cottage, Alan carrying the reel-to-reel machine, Susan carrying the food, both of them watching their footing in the accumulating snow. They played Peter and Polly Pfaff all the way, talking about Nordic skis. Alan was afraid to say how glad they he was that Hosty and his skugsniffer had headed straight back to LANL from the Big Bow Wow. And Susan didn't dare vent her hatred of Hosty.

They snapped out of their Pfaff routine when a huge Cadillac pulled up behind them in the cottage's driveway. Two-tone of course—turquoise on the bottom, cream on top—and with a front grill like a hall of mirrors. The horn was stutter-beeping hello.

"Oh my god," said Susan, glad for the distraction. "They actually came. Things are going to change."

"Looks like a couple of *natives* here with old Bill Burroughs," whooped the driver, hopping out. "Nine hours door to door, Ginzy. Thanks to the aeroplane."

"Feeling a little woozy," said the passenger, levering himself out of the humpbacked whale. "But otherwise a delightful drive from Albuquerque, Neal. Hello all. I'm Allen Ginsberg." The steady snow crowned his long hair with a halo. "The chains were beating on our fenders, Neal. The owner warned you about that. I hope we don't get billed."

"Bill Burroughs is paying!" said the driver, staring at the cottage. "He's rich, even if he won't admit it." No lights shone within. "Where's the buffet with the roast turkey? Is our boy on the nod?" Dressed only in jeans and a T-shirt, the handsome man sprang over to Susan, grinning and holding out his hand like a salesman. "Neal Cassady, and pleased to unseat you."

"Susan Green. And this is Alan Turing. We're undercover spies." She held up the Big Bow Wow bags. "You can share our food."

"Mormons?" said Neal.

"How so?" said Turing.

"Bill said he was imprisoned by religious fanatics," said Ginsberg. "Not that I always believe what Bill says when the flat horrible reality of morn closes in after a night of spectacles." He smiled. He had a warm aura.

"We were debating on the plane whether Bill's captors were from the Apocryphal Satanists, the Voodoo Vindaloo, or the Shekinah Glory Uncircumcised," said Neal.

"It's something else entirely," said Turing. "Maybe I'll try and recruit you when we're inside. But no worries, we're not raving maniacs, and membership is, where possible, voluntary. Do let's get in out of the snow. It's shaping up for a storm."

"We had a blizzard in Colorado one year it got so deep the horses on my girlfriend's uncle's sister-in-law's farm could barely stick their snoots above the powder," said Neal. "The frosty snoot-bumps looked like puffball mushrooms."

"Wonderful image," said Ginsberg, gazing lovingly at Cassady. Now he turned his attention to the granny cottage. "These houses seem so primitive, with their poor television antennae tacked on to the patched up chimneys. Is Bill really here?"

"He's probably asleep," said Alan. "He was typing all last night. A memoir about our trip to Mexico this week. We saw Joan's ghost down there."

Seemingly unimpressed, Ginsberg leaned back his head to stare up into the sky. "Spirits as multifarious as snowflakes. Ubiquitous. Every two the same. Eddies in the aether without end."

"This Joan ghost wasn't aethereal at all," said Susan. "You're missing the point. We reconstituted her from a bone and a skug, and then she shot Bill in the side of his head with a pistol." Cheerfully jingling her keys, Susan unlocked the cottage door.

"And Bill survived because he's a skugger," added Turing, stamping his feet and snapping on the kitchen light. He studied Ginsberg and Cassady. "I assume that Californians know about skugs and skuggers?"

"On radio/TV/newspaper around the clock," said Ginsberg. "Hot flash for the nation who eats her own vomit. New pariahs! The queers, the commies, the Blacks, the dope fiends, the jazz musicians, the mad, the abstract painters, the unions, the Beat poets . . . and now the skuggers."

"Go, Ginzy!" exclaimed Neal. "Unzip the zap. So Bill's a telepathic, shapeshifting semi-human slug? Bad-ass old bookworm that he is." He thumped the kitchen table and raised his voice. "We're here to rescue you, Burroughs! Extrude those slimy stalk eyes, my man! And hand me your works and your wallet. This is for your own good."

Bill appeared in his bedroom doorway, squinting against the light and coughing. "Like I'm running a halfway house for recidivist criminals." He peered at the dark windows. "Slept away the day. I like being out of synch with the clone world."

"It's an objective correlative for your unparalleled alienation," said Ginsberg, embracing his friend. "Dear Bill. Back from Tangier and his oriental fountain of youth, twenty years younger. A fairy tale. What mad narratives unspool amid you skuggers? Whence, whither and yon?"

Pleased with the attention, Burroughs kissed Ginsberg on the mouth for so long a time that Turing grew uncomfortable and then jealous. Cassady looked over at Turing and waggled his eyebrows.

"Disencumber yourself of those Bow Wow vittles, Susan," Neal told Susan, and took a seat at the kitchen table. "We'll gobble and snarf. Later I'll run out for more, skidding my monster Caddy down the street. You can come along if you like. I'm legendary for taking young ladies for rides, you understand. This turquoise DeVille is ordinarily rented only for weddings." Neal mimed a leer. "A mobile bower. There's a four hundred BTU heater to drive off the morbid chills from the pinched-ass Great Plains."

"You sound exactly like my husband used to," said Susan, strangely giddy. She was setting out the Big Bow Wow food, also some cold-cuts and beer from the fridge. Careless about revealing herself to be a skugger, she made her arms long and snaky to quickly move things around. "My husband's name was Vassar Lafia. Sorry, Neal, but I'll be in the market for a different style of man this time around." She bent her arm into corkscrew curve and chucked Neal under the chin. "Not that I utterly rule you out. I like the raw confidence and the wavy hair. And I'm known for breaking my resolutions."

"Is being a skugger a good high?" asked Neal as he began devouring a hamburger.

"Kind of," said Susan, inflating the size of her left hand and studying it. "I've been thinking about this particular question. Being a skugger speeds up your vibration rate. The world is One and Many, I'm sure you'll agree. Normally

I would vibrate at about thirty pulses per second, oscillating between the One and and the Many, that is, oscillating between viewing myself as merged into the cosmic reality, and viewing myself as a little ant who fights her way alone. My informed estimate is that being a skugger has kicked my natural vibe rate from thirty up to fifty cycles per second. I know about vibrations because I'm a musician." As punctuation, Susan snatched Neal's hamburger from his hand and set it on his plate before he could even see it happen.

"Gawrsh," said Neal, pretending to be a hick chewing the air. "Sign me up for your cult and I'll be your pageboy, Lady Green."

"Fascinating physical arcana," said Ginsberg, who'd been pondering Susan's words. "This notion of a personal vibration level—it's runs through all the secret mystery teachings. The minstrel is the god, the god is the minstrel, the song is the song."

"Feller says de Broglie's matter waves explain the duality," put in Burroughs, clearing his throat. He fixed himself a bourbon and joined them at the table. "Our essence lies in certain giant hereditary molecules. The gene codes. If you regard these molecules as matter waves, you have a precise meaning for your personal vibration. Your insect buzz is the quantum-mechanical frequency of your genome."

"Flabbergasting erudition," said Ginsberg, enjoying Bill's words. "The wise man with his myrrh. Alert the tedious dullards at the Guggenheim Foundation. A new star gleams! Were you hitting musty, foxed stacks of science journals in a bookish Tangier detox, Bill?"

"I teeped all this from my new lover," said Bill, looking

directly at Alan for the first time since their quarrel this morning. "It's as if Turing has built an extra room onto my head. I'm afraid I've been rather ungracious to him today. I was wrung out from my long night of writing."

"If you love me, why did you kiss Ginsberg in front of me?" demanded Alan.

"I saw the opportunity," said Bill with a shrug. "I'm taking advantage of looking young. I've always been greedy for sensation. You know this, Alan. And please don't sulk. Sit next to me, dear. Have I told you that you look lovely today? Youthful and world-weary at the same time. Your Christopher Morcom look."

"Meanwhile," interrupted Susan, drawing out the word for jokey emphasis. "Was Bill saying that a normal person's actual genetic molecule actually vibrates at something like thirty cycles per second?"

"I can't be bothered to calculate that for you," said Burroughs, insouciantly swirling his drink. "Ask Turing."

"No need to get into the niggling minutiae, Susan," said Alan, loath to spoil the fun. "But thirty and fifty *trillion* might be closer to the quantum-mechanical molecular vibration rates. Let's suppose that one's psychic perceptions chunk the oscillations by the trillion. So we're both right."

"I relish the literal specificity of thirty," said Ginsberg. "What does thirty cycles per second sound like, Susan?"

"Well, fifty is basically speaker hum," said Susan. "An annoying buzz. Thirty is deeper, almost granular." She opened her mouth with her chin drawn back and let out a deep *awww* sound. "Thirty is mellow." Susan took another deep breath and continued the *awww*.

Ginsberg chanted along like a monk, his voice smooth and deep. "One Many One Many One Many One Many One . . ."

Turing was distracted from all this by the clamor of his inner skug. It wanted him to make some new recruits. Now! The skug was like a vampire hungry for blood.

So Alan focused on Cassady. "Are you serious about wanting to be a skugger, Neal? I can set you up immediately." Without Alan even willing it, his finger grew out like a vine to twirl in the air before Neal's chest. "Do it now?" importuned Alan.

"Bring on the rush," said Neal, leaning back his head with a reckless air. "Dial my vibrations to fifty, Doctor T."

"Don't do it, Neal," rasped Bill, interposing his hand. "It's slavery. The skugs are parasites. Like tapeworms. Imagine a ruthless street preacher who lives in your spine and uses you for kicks. Although there is the one big up side that you can change your shape."

"Maybe worth trying," said Ginsberg, thoughtfully combing out his full beard with his fingers. "And the skug kicks become your kicks. A karma yoga. Anyway, Bill, you're a skugger, for good or ill—and you managed to write a substantial memoir fragment, was it last night? Would you say that it's crafted at the same egregiously apostolic level as your Tangier routines?"

"*The Apocalypse According To Willy Lee*," said Bill. "I hardly remember what I wrote."

"Auspicious sign," said Ginsberg. "Read it to the group after dinner?" He tugged one of the Big Bow Wow bags towards himself. "This food *is* communal, I trust?"

"Skug or no skug?" Alan asked Neal, still wanting to make his new convert.

"Go," answered the handsomely profiled Neal, and Alan sent his finger forward.

Things calmed down a bit after that. Neal liked being a skugger. Appetite redoubled, he raced out to the Big Bow Wow, bringing back great staggering armfuls of food.

"Hup, hoop!" said Neal, eating his final Bow Wow Burger. "The mighty loaves and the wee fishes. "You should turn skugger too, Ginzy. Don't falter on the shoreline. The ark of the new goof is come."

"I find it more interesting to continue as before," said Ginsberg equably. "I'm an ongoing thought experiment in the history of poesy." He yawned. "Where do we sleep? There's only the two bedrooms?"

"I suppose I could fit Neal in," said Susan demurely. It was like she'd decided to take a break from her grief.

"Far be it from me to disturb you two or, for that matter, Turing and Burroughs, the young mutant lovers," said Ginsberg, making himself pitiful. "I suppose it's the sofa for old Allen. The cheese ripens alone. Slumped on a mound of rags. The match girl in the driving snow."

"Oh come in with us," said Bill.

"We'll find a way," agreed Alan. "We're highly flexible."

"I have some new acousmatics to play for you guys," said Susan, yawning as well. "Nonlinear feedback. I smuggled out a tape from the lab. But I'm beat."

"Me too," said Burroughs. He gave Alan a smile. "Even though I've only been up for two hours. I might tinker on the memoir later in the night. And present it tomorrow."

Susan stole a shy look at Neal. "Will all of you still be here tomorrow?"

"Do stay on, Bill," put in Turing.

"I'm in no rush to split," said Ginsberg. "It would be worthwhile to see a nuclear blast, the better to stand as witness to history. When's the next pop coming up?"

"I think day after tomorrow," said Turing. "They're calling it the V-bomb. I'll know more tomorrow."

"They plan to set it off in a canyon near here," added Susan. "Where the cliff dwellers lived."

"*Maaaa*," said Neal in his best Okie voice. "*I wanna to see them Wild West fahrworks.*"

SIXTEEN

wave mechanics

Alan awoke to the jabber of Neal, Susan, Ginsberg and Burroughs in the kitchen, gay and lively. Neal was cooking a huge breakfast and Bill was drinking whiskey. The kitchen air was a haze of cigarette smoke. Outside the snow had let up again.

Last night Ginsberg had dropped off to sleep right away, leaving Bill and Alan to have a proper make-up session on the floor beside the mattress. Being skuggers, any surface felt relatively comfortable to them—particularly while making love. For her part, Susan showed every sign of having been intimate with Neal.

"Dig," said Neal, turning towards Alan. He shrugged his left shoulder and popped up an extra head that wore a copy of Ginsberg's face.

"This is in poor taste, Neal," said the Ginsberg head.

"Teach you a lesson!" said Neal. He formed his right hand into a fat mallet and *bonk* struck the fake head. It squealed and sank back into his flesh.

Sitting at the kitchen table, eating oatmeal, the real Ginsberg smiled and shook his head. Evidently he'd already seen this routine several times.

As if competing to be the more bizarre, Bill Burroughs stretched out his arms at the sides of his head, and flowed into *ugh* the form of a ten-foot long centipede, glossy dark maroon on its back, pink underneath, and with scores of wildly twitching ochre legs. Bill's long body bent forward and he snapped his dripping mandibles in Turing's face. The fluid gave off a pungent smell of musk and bourbon.

"Feeling chipper, eh Bill," said Turing, half-amused. "Let me get a spot of tea, and I'm off to save the world."

"Can I help?" asked Susan.

"Not yet. Ulam wanted me to come alone today. Have you seen Vassar?"

"I'm hoping he's behind the scenes," said Susan. "Or it could be he's jealous now, and in a sulk."

"The Cassady curse," said Neal, preening a bit.

"I'm using you as much as you're using me," said Susan sharply. "This girl is wise—my little *pageboy*."

Neal actually looked abashed.

"I'll be on my way now," said Turing, shrugging on his coat. This was all too intense. He could get breakfast at the Bow Wow. "Bye, Bill." The centipede waggled his head, Ginsberg bowed, and Neal winked.

Susan followed Alan to the door. "What about Hosty?" she asked, all merriness leaving her face. "When are you going to kill him?" She seemed almost like a nagging wife.

"The moment will come," said Alan, expressing more confidence than he really felt. "Vassar will help me. We'll have to disable Hosty's radio."

"Do it today," urged Susan, going back inside.

Alan paused for a moment, gathering himself for the big day. For now, the sky was clear and sunny.

The two-tone Cadillac was a smooth hump beneath a drift of snow. There was an empty barn behind the cottage where one might in principle garage a car, but that wasn't the kind of precaution that a Neal Cassady would take. No matter. The drifts were sculpted into lovely higher-degree surfaces—quartics or quintics at the very least.

Tina was on duty at the Big Bow Wow. She brought Alan tea in a pot—a rarity in the States—and a nice breakfast of coddled eggs with muffins.

"Some creep was asking about you this morning," Tina confided to Alan when she brought the check.

"Asking about the extra guests in the Cadillac?" he said.

"Hadn't noticed those yet," said Tina.

"You will," said Alan. "A poet and a rowdy."

"I think the guy asking about you was from the LANL security staff," resumed Tina. "He said he'd seen you eating here and he wanted to know where you live. I didn't tell him, but be careful."

"I appreciate this," said Alan.

He put on his Peter Pfaff personality and hitched a ride to LANL. A security guard walked him to Ulam's office. Ulam was at work looking very disheveled. He'd pushed aside the gadgets on his table and was standing over a trove of diagrams and calculations. Yesterday's orderly blackboard had become a palimpsest of erasures, drawings, and wiggly symbols.

"Tomorrow is the big blast," said Ulam. "I suppose you know. Our security stinks."

"What will the V-bomb do?" asked Alan.

"Oh, you've guessed by now," said Ulam, beginning to pace around his office like a prisoner. "It kills the skugs.

How? The V-bomb creates rays that attack some large proteins that are particular to skugs. These V-rays are pushing the molecules into unstable high-energy states, and the molecules collapse into junk. *Pffft*."

"How strange," said Alan, feeling a dizzy sense of unreality. "You're talking about boosting the personal vibrations of the skugs and, I presume, their skugger hosts. My friend Susan and I were discussing something very similar last night. A convergence of thought."

"It's a strange time," said Ulam, still pacing. "I myself have been glimpsing a ghost the last few days—a thing like a manta ray. We approach the world's edge. It was like this before Hiroshima. Sit down if you like, Alan." With that, Ulam returned to his document-laden table. "Tell more more about what this Susan says. She has the artist's intuition. And a beautiful face."

"Susan says that skuggers vibrate at a rate faster than normal humans."

"Our V-bomb is no bohemian elixir," exclaimed Ulam with a short laugh. "I think Susan and I are talking about very different things."

"Well, yes," said Alan, embarrassed to be caught out. "Of course I know this. But as a metaphor—" He stopped himself and began again. He should be on the attack, not defending himself. "If you kill the skugs, you kill the skuggers. Including Susan and me. You're talking about an American genocide!"

"I am aware of this issue," said Ulam shortly. "This is why I toss at night and see ugly ghosts. And this is the reason number one why I am glad to be confiding in you. I want you to avert the deaths of the skuggers."

"Me!" exclaimed Alan, dismayed. "But *you're* the one setting off the V-bomb!"

"I want you to compose a warning we can spread to the skuggers," said Ulam. "We must tell them to expel their skugs by noon tomorrow. And then these people are safe. And my conscience is lily white."

"How are we supposed to *expel* our skugs?" asked Alan, growing angrier. "You have no idea what you're talking about, Stan. A skug is completely integrated into a skugger's metabolism."

"Use your noodle," said Ulam, falling back on one of his newly learned American idioms. "I give you twenty-four hours." He lowered his voice. "Understand that I am acting independently here. I have no authorization from the higher authorities. But if you can find a deskugging method, I'm sure the authorities would disseminate your instructions for good press. As if offering civilians a chance to leave a targeted zone. Our military is not wanting the bad press of a domestic Hiroshima."

Alan tried to consider the offer in a rational way. But his thoughts were muddled by the angry clamor of his inner skug. And when he tried to push the skug down, the room began to spin. His vision blurred, his knees wobbled, and he dropped to the floor.

The next thing Alan knew, Ulam was helping him to sit up, and offering him a glass of water. "You fainted, Alan. You steer between a Scylla and Charybdis. As do I. We'll help each other through."

"I'm afraid," said Alan, reassembling his scattered thoughts. The moment of unconsciousness had been like a jump-cut. A literal experience of the void. "I'm terribly afraid."

"I have a second motivation for cooperating with you and the skugs," said Ulam, gazing at Alan in his chair. The scientist resumed pacing, as collected as if he were ticking off points on a list. "I know all too well how polarities can flip. Perhaps the V-bomb is a big flop. Perhaps the skugs win and everyone on Earth is a skugger. In this case, I am hoping you will stand up for me and, above all, for my family."

"Of course," said Alan readily. "We're both mathematicians."

Ulam nodded in agreement. "You are a brilliant man, Alan, and I'd like you to go over my calculations with me. I'm terribly worried that I've gotten something wrong. And what I'm telling you about the V-bomb may help you in seeking a way to expel your own skug."

Of course this kind of talk set Alan's inner skug to ramping up for another rebellion. "Let's not even talk about such things," said Alan quickly. Already he was seeing spots before his eyes.

They sat in silence for a minute, until Alan's vision cleared. And now he posed a different question. "Can you explain why you think I'll help you build the V-bomb at all?"

Ulam tapped his diagrams and gave Alan a knowing smile. "For the same reason that I corrected that fool Teller's botched design for a hydrogen bomb. You and I like to know. We like to make things work."

"Yes," said Alan, nodding his head. "I do want to know the secrets of the V-bomb. What *are* the V-rays? How do you make them? How do you tune them to the frequency of the skugs?" His skug was cautiously in favor of this line of inquiry. Knowledge is power.

Ulam drifted over to his blackboard and began drawing

lines. "V-rays are a style of radiation that's associated with living organisms. Not an electromagnetic wave and not a particle. A purely quantum mechanical wave of contingent probability. The V stands for vitality—and for the element vanadium, which happens to potentiate the ray production. By shaping a vanadium-doped bomb's core to certain peculiar specifications of my own design, we can produce a burst of V-rays with very specific properties."

On the blackboard Ulam drew a kind of circle with dents in its edge. He gazed it for minute, then erased it and went to lean over his table again, poking at his diagrams and his pages of tightly written equations. "Come see."

"How far can the V-rays travel?" asked Alan, peering over Ulam's shoulder.

"This the beauty part," said Ulam. "My V-rays resemble neutrinos, in that hardly any form of matter impedes their motion. They sail through concrete or lead or the body of a cow, but if they are stumbling upon a living skug—*tzack*! A kick in the pants."

They pulled up chairs to be more comfortable and spent the rest of the day poring over Ulam's work. The hours flew by. The reasoning was remarkably lucid, the formulas very clean. And by late afternoon, Alan had an idea about how to pervert the design for his skug's purposes. But he still needed to know how one would go about physically tweaking the bomb.

Ulam went across the room to fetch them some cookies and a couple of glasses of apple juice. "My working lunch," he said, handing Alan his share. "Or supper. So now—your verdict. No problems?"

Feeling the old lust for intellectual battle, Alan began

savagely picking at the construction's weakest point. "Shouldn't you be using the Hermitian conjugate of this Hilbert space operator?" he said, tapping one of the sheets of formulae. "Perhaps you know better than I. But it hardly seems obvious that the V-ray operator is self-adjoint. Can you truly be sure that your detonation process will produce a discrete spectrum with a single, unique eigenvalue?"

Ulam's lips began soundlessly to move. Repeatedly he ran his hands down the sides of his face.

Alan pressed harder. "If there were to be a multiplicity of points in the discrete measurement spectrum, then the V-bomb might annihilate quite a wide range of life forms. Even more dire: If the spectrum were in fact continuous, then your V-rays could disintegrate the planet Earth itself."

"Already I think of that," muttered Ulam. "Thinking about this all the time. Pipe down." He clawed a fresh sheet of paper over to himself and went into a frenzy of calculation. "Another bump in the core shape," the mathematician murmured after about five minutes. He was scribbling at a tiny, crooked diagram and talking to himself. "A bump at azimuth thirty-seven, elevation forty-nine, and then we're safe, please dear God. Then we are being safe."

"Stout fellow," said Alan.

Ulam glanced up as if he'd forgotten Alan were there. "I have to go on-site now," said Ulam. "Project Utopia. Down in the canyon. This evening is my last chance to be making adjustments. I would not be going near that bomb tomorrow. It will be on countdown starting at midnight, and from then on in a risky condition."

"Can I come along now?" asked Alan. "I'd like to see it." His skug wanted him there. He already had a rough outline for a method to make the thing into a universal skugging ray. Perhaps he could overpower Ulam at the Project Utopia and—

"No, no, no," said Ulam. "Only me. I am the only one with clearance to go down there. Well, I suppose that Dick Hosty has clearance as well. Just Hosty and me. None of the other LANL scientists is understanding what's going on with Project Utopia—and none of is wanting to risk any blame. We'll leave my office together, and I'll be bidding you farewell out front."

On the way down the windowed hallway, they saw that it was twilight and that the snow storm had returned with new force. The sky was yellow-gray with the teeming flakes. A security agent ordered up a tracked snow vehicle to ferry Ulam into the canyon.

Ulam almost forgot to say goodbye. All that was in his mind was correcting the Hermitian conjugate error in his V-bomb. But at the last minute he focused on Alan and again exhorted him to find a deskugging routine while there was time. The tank-like vehicle clanked off with Ulam aboard. Alan was on his own.

His mind was in turmoil. The skug was pressing him to pursue the path towards universal skugification, but by now Alan longed to somehow free himself. Not that he could safely think about these issues right outside the lab. He had to maintain his Pfaff cover.

The despised Dick Hosty appeared in his white ambulance. He had heavy, knobby chains on his tires, and he wore his pistol even more prominently than before. He wanted to drive Alan home. And once again he wouldn't take no for an answer.

Although Alan had his tiresome Peter Pfaff personality firmly in place, Hosty seemed even more suspicious than yesterday.

"Where are you actually staying?" he asked Alan as soon as the ambulance pulled away from the curb. As before the squawk-box was tuned to a police channel, and a hand-held microphone danged near Hosty's head.

"Well, I *was* at the Cowboy Motel," said Alan uncertainly.

"I checked there, and they don't got any record of you, Pete," said Hosty. "So I asked around at that Big Bow Wow where you like to eat. Waitress wouldn't give me the sweat off her butt, but a good old boy eatin a steak said you was rentin a cottage from a vet lady down the road. Sue Stook? The waitress is Sue's girlfriend, what I hear. I hate shit like that."

"How is this any of your business at all?" said Alan, mustering his gumption. He needed to put an end to this conversation. It would be a disaster if Hosty and the skugsniffer got near his cottage.

"Aren't you wanting to renew your security clearance tomorrow?" taunted Hosty. "Way you're goin', I don't see that happening at all."

"Frankly I don't give a ruddy fuck," said Alan, at the end of his rope. "Set me out at the Bow Wow and we'll part ways for good."

"Nice talk for a tech," said Hosty. He addressed himself to the skugsniffer once again. "Hey, Roland, you really sure this guy ain't a skugger?"

"No skuggers in sight," said the skugsniffer in a weary

tone. "This man checks out the same as yesterday. And don't go shocking me for nothing."

"Like this?" said Hosty, sadistically tapping his shock button. The skugsniffer in the tank sent out a howl of pure agony.

"That's so you'll keep your sniffer primed real good," said Hosty. He motored past the friendly lights of the Big Bow Wow with no reduction in speed. "We gonna deliver Pete direct to his abode. Just in case he's got something to hide. We got jeeps and soldiers on the ready at the labs."

All the old fears and resentments came boiling up within Alan. Proctor Whitsitt caning him, Detective Jenkins arresting him, the MI5 men poisoning Zeno—always more enemies—Pratt in Tangier, Landers in Palm Beach, Rupert Small in New Orleans—and now Dick Hosty, who'd killed two of Alan's ex-lovers with a flame-thrower.

"Skuggers up ahead!" blared the skugsniffer's speaker. "A nest of them—a woman and two men."

A calm golden light filled Alan's head. Vassar was with him, giving him strength—the aethereal manta ray's tail was plugged into the ambulance's cigarette lighter. Everything seemed outlined with bright beads. The squawk-box police radio had gone dead. Vassar's easy voice sounded in Alan's ears.

"Go ahead, man. This is it. Even up the score."

The next thing Alan knew he was choking Hosty, his hands gone huge and massive, digging into Hosty's flesh, breaking his windpipe and snapping the vertebrae of his neck. Hosty clawed at his microphone to no avail.

In his final spasms, Hosty may have formed an idea that his skugsniffer had betrayed him. Pressing a hidden control with his foot, he sent a lethal bolt of power into the skugsniffer's tank. Alan could smell the burnt flesh. Hosty was dying at the wheel, and poor Roland Gill was dead in back.

Meanwhile nobody was driving the ambulance. It lurched to a harmless stop in a roadside snowdrift. Fortunately no other cars were out in the storm. There in the dark, Alan saw Hosty's soul, a small writhing turnip thing that drifted out the window and dwindled down to nothing against the snow-smeared sky.

"No curtain calls?" challenged Alan. "After all your honk and menace?" He heard no response, and he was glad. As for Roland Gill in back, his ghost has found its onward path unseen.

Alan laid Hosty's corpse on the seat , took the wheel, and restarted the stalled car. He drove through the streaming flakes to Sue Stook's and parked in the empty barn behind the lit-up granny cottage. He covered the ambulance— now a hearse—with tarps.

Now what? Go indoors? Alan studied his hands. The hands of a killer. He wasn't quite ready to face his friends.

For their part, Neal, Susan, or Bill could readily have teeped Alan's presence, but they were otherwise involved. An unobtrusive telepathic scan showed Burroughs to be necking with Ginsberg on the couch. Susan and Neal were having sex in Susan's bed. To add spice to the love-making, Neal had grown an extra penis. And the wanton Susan had a second vagina. The couple were linked together like puzzle pieces.

The anatomical extravaganza was hardly Alan's cup of tea. Unnoticed by his friends, he withdrew his telepathic tendrils. He was starting to shiver from the cold, and from his stormy emotions.

Neal's fat Cadillac was only lightly coated with snow—presumably he'd cleared it off and taken it on the road for a drive today. Hopping into the behemoth, Alan fired up the engine and the heater. He sat in plush comfort for a bit, gathering his wits.

He did feel some slight remorse for so ruthlessly killing Hosty. But more than that, he felt pride, and a sense of safety. His greatest enemy was gone.

How he wished that he could do as Ulam had urged, and find a way to expel his skug. Ulam didn't fully grasp, however, that working on this wasn't an option for Alan. Not as long as a skug lived within him. Testing the bounds, Alan let himself wonder if some process along the lines of a hush-phone could be of any—

Instantly he felt disoriented and short of breath. His temples were pounding in pain. In another moment he'd be—

Dutifully he switched to his plan for a skugging ray. This was what his skug wanted him to think about, and it wouldn't do to defy his ever-more-watchful master. Very well then.

Whether or not Ulam took the notion seriously, there was something to Susan's remark about personal vibrations. She'd grasped the basic principal of skugging rays. It was a matter of nudging the human genomic vibrations to the level of skugger vibrations. And this was something that a V-ray ought be able to do.

Of course there were intricate theoretical details—having to do with a non-commutative quantum-mechanical operator that renormalized the symmetries of the genome kernel in Hilbert space. But Alan had already solved this bit in his head. The issue now was to design the implementation details.

His approach would be to deform the V-bomb's blast charge in a fashion that he was in fact designing even now, sitting alone in the DeVille, tracing curves in the haze that his breath made on the car's windows.

At this point Susan teeped the fact that Alan was outside in the Cadillac—and that he'd killed Hosty. She threw on her clothes and rushed out to embrace him.

"You're a hero, Alan! You avenged Vassar! I've had such a broken heart."

"I teeped what you and Neal were doing in there just now," said Alan, a little embarrassed.

"Just a game," said Susan. "A pastime. You men take sex too seriously. Come on in and let's celebrate the fall of Hosty. You'll freeze to death out here!"

Back in the granny cottage, Neal was out of bed, cooking a steak and smoking a marijuana cigarette. He'd driven to Santa Fe in the Cadillac that afternoon, loading up on supplies.

"I met with your man Naranjo," Neal told Turing. "Sniffed him out with my skug-brain. He steered me to some weed."

"How's Naranjo faring?" asked Alan.

"Unloaded his stash, flush with cash, wife back at last, and he's buying a plane," said the cheerful Neal. "Turning legit. He survived his last deal. In the movies that's when the reluctant gangster always gets popped. One last bank job, Louie, one last job. *Bam*! But Naranjo's all dapper and hale."

Meanwhile Susan and Burroughs were teeping Turing's thoughts, learning of his plan to create a ray to turn everyone into a skugger—and spotting his forlorn and forbidden hope of expelling his skug from his own body. Alan could sense that these two would have enjoyed getting into a discussion about how to get rid of their skugs, but the parasites were clamping down on them all—more so than ever before. The scent of a final victory was making the skugs less tolerant.

"You're talking behind my back," said Ginsberg, sensing the ebb and flow of the teep. "Like I'm the crazy person who *doesn't* hear voices in his head. So here's my brain-wave feed." He launched into a Hindu chant.

Susan got into playing acousmatics recordings on her new reel to reel, rather softly and solemnly, as if at a wake. Summoned by the sounds, Vassar's ghost reappeared, a cheerful, golden manta ray fully six feet across. Everyone could see him but Ginsberg. For Ginsberg's sake, Neal danced over and sculpted the shape of Vassar, running his hands along the flanks of the twinkling manta.

"Thank you, Neal," said Ginsberg. "You populate the void."

In an unexpected gesture of hostility, Vassar now flew right through Neal's chest.

"Oof," said Neal aloud. "Here comes the husband."

"I don't like you moving in on my wife," teeped Vassar, banking around for another pass at Cassady. "Bonehead."

Turing jumped to his feet and waved his hands to distract Vassar. "Come on, Vassar, you and I fought Hosty together just now. Help me some more. Tell me how Ulam's been physically tweaking the V-bomb. I bet you saw."

"I bet I did," teeped Vassar, settling down to a slow ripple of his wide golden wings. "I'm omnipresent, almost. Me and my ghost buddy Xurt."

"Hemisemiubiquitous," said Neal aloud.

"Ulam gets *inside* the bomb," teeped Vassar. "Kinky as that seems. Like a guy inside a clown car."

"I see a round metal shell resembling a submarine to be lowered into an oceanic trench," interpolated Burroughs, also speaking aloud. They were running the live commentary for Ginsberg's sake.

"The bomb is soft like lead and I can see radiation coming out," continued Vassar's teep. "Ulam pounds the stuff with a ball-peen hammer. Sculpting it, like. He wears a lead-foil suit, and then he showers off. "

"I'll go in there myself tomorrow," said Turing aloud. "I'll undo what Ulam did."

"In where?" said Ginsberg, a few steps behind.

"Inside the V-bomb," said Turing.

"I have no idea what's going on," said Ginsberg.

"Neal has two dicks," Burroughs told him.

"Side to side or one atop the other?" asked Ginsberg. "Like a whale or like a kangaroo? Show us, Neal."

"I'm various," said Neal making magician gestures with his hands above his crotch.

Vassar wrapped his wings around Susan and bid her a last farewell. A final tenderness filled the two. Susan's face showed a calm that Alan hadn't seen in days.

And now the parting scene was done. With an odd motion, Vassar withdrew towards heaven. It wasn't that he went up or down or left or right. He went—elsewhere.

When Alan had seen Hosty's ghost do this, he'd mistaken it for shrinking. But it was something other than that. It was a motion into a higher dimension.

As an elegy, Susan turned up the volume on her machine and put on the tape they'd made in Ulam's lab—the sounds of higher-order nonlinear feedback.

"I'm getting a fine high buzz off this," said Ginsberg. "Maybe I feel like a skugger."

"Here's an appropriate visual track," said Alan. Drawing on his experience in the Tangier radio repair shop, he took off the back of the granny cottage's TV and tweaked the tubes until a wave of outré blips and zags began rolling across the screen.

Burroughs stood by Turing, quite taken by the images.

"Puts me in mind of those glass plates of slime you were experimenting with in Tangier," said Bill. "Your orgasmatronic all-meat TV."

"Where it all began," said Alan. "Our Xanadu." He gave Bill a hug. "I never thought it would end at a nuclear weapons lab." His throat tightened. "I—I hate to say this, Bill, but I feel our romance is very nearly at an end." He held his friend out at arm's length, then kissed him. "Consider yourself free of me, Bill. No strands of guilt."

"Dear Alan. Can we win the war against skugs?"

"We'll skirt that issue, no? Look at this some more." Turing busied himself in showing Bill how to diddle the TVs adjustment knobs to make the patterns dance with Susan's sounds.

Perhaps jealous of the lovers' moment of intimacy, Ginsberg went back to chanting, more insistently than

before. For his part, Neal was circling around Susan, tootling a trumpet solo through the spaces of his cupped and
reshaped hands.

Bill once again lifted his unlovely voice in his Los Alamos school song:

> *Far away and high on the mesa's crest*
> *Here's the light that all of us love best*
> *Los* Aaallll—

He broke off abruptly, pressing his hands to his chest.
"What?" said Alan. "Are you all right?"

Bill looked at Alan in silence, locking eyes. Faster than
thought, Alan felt an encrypted teep message flit into him.
Bill's expression told Alan not to unpack the message as yet.
It was a secret to be used later—and somehow Alan was to
know when. Not yet in any case. Don't think about it.

Alan went to bed early, leaving the others to continue
their party. Washing up in the bathroom, he studied himself in the mirror. His face was very like Chris Morcom's
indeed—jaunty, with a narrow head and a crooked smile,
with kindness and humor in his eyes. As the long day's
final surprise, a diaphanous copy of the face rose from the
mirror and spoke to Alan.

"You'll be with me soon," said Chris's ghost. "I'm glad.
It'll be lovely."

Before Alan could answer, the apparition had vanished.

He slept soundly, barely waking when Burroughs and
Ginsberg tumbled into the bed.

SEVENTEEN
v-bomb

In the morning the sky was pale blue, with a new round of potential snow clouds humping on the western horizon. The highway had been plowed, leaving a great wall of snow across their driveway. Sue Stook used a yellow tractor to clear the entrance.

Alan and his friends had a quiet breakfast around the kitchen table. It felt like the end of something. Neal put on a juggling act with a bag of oranges—at one point he had four in the air.

"You lot had best clear out," said Alan finally. "There's a slight chance that the V-bomb will kill everyone."

"Everyone on Earth?" asked Ginsberg. "Our government would risk that?"

"Maybe just everyone in Los Alamos," said Alan. "Or in New Mexico. I say you get in Neal's car and drive fast."

Alan was a little surprised by how readily the others took him at his word. All four of them got up from the table, preparing for flight.

"The rental guy in Albuquerque said I could keep the DeVille for two weeks," said Neal, pulling on his coat.

"Long as Bill pays the daily rate when I bring it back, including tax, wax, and pro-rate denture adjustments. You come too, Turing. We'll drive to New York and come back here, if here's still there, now or then. I'm due to make a surprise inspection of Ellen Sue Bonham in the Village."

"I have to stay," said Alan, wretchedly alone at the kitchen table. "I have no choice. So do this rapidly, please. Rip off the bandage. Bundle up, grab groceries, go."

"Greenwich Village is perfect for me," said Susan, already at the fridge filling a shopping bag. "The one true audience for my acousmatics! I'd like to get some shows and to sell some recordings. Maybe I'll even teach again, if all else fails. As it usually does. Whatever. I'm ready for a fresh start. Assuming the world doesn't end."

"I'd like to go back to Tangier," said Bill, rummaging through his belongings and pulling on a second layer of clothes. "This whole continent drags me. America isn't young, you know. It's ancient and evil. With aluminum siding."

"Going to Tangier?" echoed Alan wistfully.

"All of our plans being contingent upon the whip and lash and whim of our rulers, the skugs," added Bill, coming back to the table to lean over Alan. "But maybe the humans can win in the post-V-bomb world." He shot Alan a heavily significant glance.

"I don't dare think about rebellion, Bill," said Alan quietly.

For now he had no choice but to play the role of skugly slave. But later—who knew. He hadn't forgotten about Bill's encrypted teep message, whatever it was.

Of course the envious Ginsberg had to stick in his oar with some high-minded verbiage. "People should find their own paths towards the cosmic light. The skugs are essentially corporate. A psychic prison camp."

"Yas yas," said Cassady, rushing outside with a broom. He brushed the snow off the Cadillac and jumped inside. Roaring the engine and burping the clutch, he rocked a preliminary launch ramp into the snow. "Susan!" he called. "Come sit in front with me, sweet cakes. We'll chauffeur the esteemed Beat authors in the back. Ready to roll, boys? You sure you're staying here, Turing? There's no real need to go up in gamma ray smoke with the V-bomb blast, is there?"

Alan shrugged and gave Bill Burroughs one last goodbye kiss. He couldn't voice his many questions lest his skug start nosing in.

"Follow Alph to find the key," said Bill, subtler and hipper than any mutant parasitic slug would ever be. The kiss came and went, and then Burroughs was in the car with Ginsberg.

"Bless you, Alan," said Ginsberg, folding his hands at his chest and bowing. "You're the true hero. Forgive any false steps."

"I love you, Alan," Susan told him, blotting at her eyes. "You're so wonderful. And a hero. More than you even know."

By the time the four reached the end of the driveway, Burroughs, never loath to play the curmudgeon, was already yelling angrily at Neal for his perceived recklessness in driving. Turing couldn't help but notice that Bill had taken his unused stash of brown Mexico City heroin along. And then the carnival was gone.

It was very quiet alone. Alan wandered around the little cottage, picking things up and setting them down, hardly noticing what he did. His mind spun. He had plans within plans within plans. First and foremost, he needed to make physical contact with the Project Utopia V-bomb.

Ulam had said he himself wouldn't be going down there today, because it would be too dangerous, now that the countdown had begun. But Alan was heedless of the danger. He was driven by his skug, and by his secretive longing to save the world.

Thinking of death, Alan remembered his vision of Chris Morcom last night. Perhaps it was really true that he might find his loved one in heaven. How strange if the most treacly and conventional notions of the afterlife turned out to be true.

What time was it? 9:10 am. And the V-bomb was due to go off at 10:00. How was he to get at it? Well—it wouldn't do to phone Ulam for help. Ulam wouldn't want an interloper fiddling with his baby.

Could Alan simply push his way into the site? Perhaps he could form his body into the shape of a giant bird, swoop down upon Project Utopia, skug the guards, and begin his work? But, no, the guards would have received the antiskug vaccine. And if Alan came on too forcefully, the flame throwers and helicopters would come.

Thinking about LANL's defenses against skuggers, Alan suddenly realized that he had the perfect method for breaking in. He'd go the Project Utopia site as *Dick Hosty*. Ulam had said that Hosty was the only one besides himself with the clearance for access to the V-bomb. And Hosty was right here. On ice.

Not wasting any more time, Alan hurried out to the barn behind the cottage. Hosty lay frozen on the front seat. Presumably the sad contents of the skugsniffer tank were frozen solid as well. No scent of decay.

Alan managed to start the engine, then turned on the heater. Working from his memories of Hosty, as well as from the figure beside him, he shapeshifted himself into a perfect replica of the man.

And now for the hard part. Making the most of his skuggy fingers, Alan worked Hosty's clothes off the stiff corpse—and donned them himself. And he made damned sure that he could find Hosty's ID in his pockets. He dragged the naked corpse to a corner of the barn, piled tarps on it, and got the ambulance on the road.

Bandelier and Frijoles Canyon were only fifteen minutes further than LANL. The road had been plowed all the way there, and the ambulance's tire-chains were holding up well. The landscape gleamed in the mild sun. Alan's skug hummed with joy at the prospect of making the V-bomb into a skugging ray.

Alan had no problem at all with the Project Utopia security—the guards leaned over, recognized the features of Hosty, scanned his ID, and waved him through. They didn't even ask what he was doing. Dick Hosty was the top cop. And the guards were eager to get back into the shelter of their block house.

The road zigged and zagged a few times. So far, the ambulance's chains were holding traction. And there at the bottom of the canyon was a little tin shed, all alone. Alan glanced at his watch. 9:45. Fifteen minutes till detonation.

The snow was very deep by the shed. The ambulance slewed to a stop, axle-deep in a drift. Alan walked the last bit of the way, then used his shapeshifting fingers to pick the lock on the shed's door.

And now he was inside. The V-bomb was no torpe-do-shaped cartoon bomb with fins. It was a roughly spherical casing the height of a man, with a maze of heavy wires snaking around the case, prepared to deliver the sparks of ignition that would ignite the dynamite that would propel the nuclear material into a critical mass that would unleash the mighty avalanche of V-rays.

The V-bomb had a small round door in its side, like the hatch on a one-man submarine. Hanging in the hut near the bomb was a white radiation suit of rubberized canvas, with an air filter, a view plate, and a watch on its wrist. Alan shed his Hosty clothes, feeling the bite of the frigid air.

He slipped on the radiation suit, half-wondering why he bothered. It was 9:52, and the bomb was programmed to detonate at 10:00. He'd soon be past the point where radiation sickness mattered.

Alan opened the door in the side of the V-bomb and peered in. Tarnished puzzle-pieces of plutonium lined the inner shell, looking a bit like lead. Resting on the bottom of the tight chamber was a cushion with a flashlight and hammer beside it. Ulam's workbench.

Holding the flashlight, Alan wriggled inside the V-bomb, seated himself cross-legged, and closed the bomb's door. He felt himself at the still center of the world.

He hefted the hammer, tapping at the soft gray metal of the bomb fuel, making the first of the adjustments that might make the V-bomb irradiate the planet with skugging rays.

Although his skug was in an ecstasy of approval, it harbored a trace of concern that Alan's physical presence might somehow hamper the smooth detonation of the device. The skug was urging him to hurry.

Alan sighed and set down the hammer. "I can't possibly do this if you're jabbering at me," he teeped to his skug. "Rest assured that you're getting everything that you want. Do back off now and let me concentrate. I'm sure you understand that I have limited time." Alan glanced at his watch. "It's 9:56. I have four minutes to make the adjustments, to get out of the casing and, perhaps, to grow wings and fly away."

On figurative tiptoes, giggling like an excited child on Christmas Eve, the symbiotic mind crept down into the recesses of Alan's subconscious. Alan was, after all, the skug's maker, and he still held, to some extent, the status of a father figure.

Finally alone, Alan unpacked the encrypted file that Burroughs had bequeathed him. The decryption key was of course *Xanadu*.

And what was in the file? A complex wave form—Bill's precise memories of the overlaid sounds of Susan's tape of nonlinear feedback, Ginsberg's chant, Neal's tootling, and

Bill's own cracked voice—and something else. The resulting pattern was a wave whose shape was the precise opposite of the organic vibrations within a skug. Scaled to suitable speeds, the two patterns could cancel each other out.

9:59.

How might Alan code Bill's wave into the V-rays? As a start, he filled his chest with air and chanted the intricate sound aloud. With superhuman flexibility, he chirped the same sequence faster and faster—until it locked in on the vibrations of the skug within him—and melted the thing away. One less skug.

A molting raven seemed to be here inside the bomb casing with Alan. It was Vassar's friend Xurt, the ancient ghost of a Tewa Indian, cocking his head and making a friendly caw. Xurt was instilling Alan with shamanic powers.

With a single gesture of his will, Alan dematerialized. That is, he unlocked his body and became an intricate matter wave, dancing out a sped-up version of Bill's sound sample. Alan was resonating within the V-bomb's cavity—like a fat note in an organ pipe, or, more accurately, like a light wave within a hall of mirrors. He was poised to modulate the V-rays when they emerged.

The last thing that Alan sensed before the blast was the smile of Christopher Morcom, beckoning from the beyond.

EIGHTEEN
last words

[This section transcribes the soundtrack of a videotape by William Burroughs. A label on the tape reads "WSB. Last Words on Turing. Jan 13, 1997." Only Burroughs appears in the tape. It seems likely that he recorded it himself, aged eighty-two, in his house in Lawrence, Kansas, eight months before his death.]

My regrets besides Joan? I wish I'd been a better father to Billy. A better son to my parents. I failed everyone in my family. The price of making my literary career. I've been over this a million times.

Something new today. Professor Alan Turing. I've left some papers regarding our adventures together. Long story short, Turing's suicide in June, 1954, was a fake, a botched assassination.

Having escaped murder at the hands of his nation's security forces, Turing invented a contagious parasite called a skug. On Christmas Day, 1954, he infected me with a skug in Tangier. I rather enjoyed it. Alan and I became lovers.

How to describe the man? Reckless, youthful, carefree, mathematical, sweet, unconventional, eager, intimate, awkward and utterly devoted to the life of the mind. I never met his like again. Perhaps I was foolish to let him go.

I miss him.

But it's too stultifying telling my feelings to a glass eye. With my voice echoing in this empty room. I'll cut to the climax.

The authorities in Los Alamos, New Mexico, designed a doomsday device called a V-bomb. It was supposed to beam out V-rays that would kill not only the skugs, but also kill anyone who harbored a skug in his or her body. We called ourselves skuggers. For background details consult my unpublished memoir, "The Apocalypse According To Willy Lee."

At the end, in January, 1955, Turing and I were holed up in a cottage in Los Alamos along with Allen Ginsberg, Neal Cassady, and an electronic composer named Susan Green. All of us but Ginsberg had turned skugger.

A local security asshole named Dick Hosty was on the point of busting us. Turing strangled Hosty and hid him in our garage. It was evening and we were celebrating, I suppose. Susan Green put on one of her peculiar sound tapes. Ginsberg began chanting, Cassady was making noise as well, and I began obliquely wondering if there might be a way to make the ambient mélange of noises into a deskugging song.

I couldn't think about this explicitly, as the skug within me was opposed to such a line of thought. But I managed anyhow. I'm a devious man. And my skug wasn't riding very close herd on me. It didn't take my intellectual powers seriously.

It was of course Turing upon whom the skugs were fixated. He was a famous mathematician, he'd helped invent the electronic computer, and he'd made a high-level contact in the Los Alamos National Laboratories. Turing was looking for a way to protect us four from the V-bomb. Indeed, the skugs expected that Alan would in fact doctor the V-bomb so as to turn every human on Earth into a skugger.

Getting back to our celebration party, we were rollicking amid a storm of sound. On a vagrant impulse, I began singing in my rather poor voice, drunkenly braying some drivel that I remembered from my days at boarding school in Los Alamos. And here's where magic comes in.

As skuggers, we'd become so sensitized that we were seeing ghosts. In particular, I was at this moment aware of a five hundred year old Tewa Indian ghost called Xurt. He resembled a tattered crow with mangy feathers, enveloped in a pale green glow. Xurt added a squawk to my song—and this was the final tweak of discord that my impromptu fugue required.

I felt the moorings of my skug loosen within me. And at this point—for reasons which I'll explain momentarily—I chose to draw back. I piped down so quickly that my skug wasn't aware of what I'd come across. I'd privily created—and opportunely memorized—a pattern that could function as a deskugging routine.

I could have deskugged all four of us then and there—Neal, Alan, Susan and me. But my vanity stopped me. How so? The key point is that, as a skugger, I'd been able to make myself appear twenty years younger. At this point, for once in my life, my twelve-years-younger friend Allen Ginsberg was interested in having sex with me. I'd always had an unrequited passion for Allen, you understand, but he'd demur.

During those wild days in Los Alamos things had been different. I felt myself the cynosure of every eye. I was having sexual relations with Ginsberg, and I had my affair with Turing as well. Although I disliked my skug, I wanted to harbor it just a bit longer, so as to make the most of an upcoming road trip to New York City with Allen and Neal Cassady.

But I didn't want to waste my discovery. Having been Turing's companion for a few weeks, I'd picked up a knowledge of cryptographic techniques. I encrypted the powerful pattern that I'd just memorized, and I sent the pattern to Alan Turing via skugger telepathy. The key for my encryption was taken from the first line of Coleridge's mesmerizing, opiated verse.

In Xanadu did Kubla Khan
A stately pleasure-dome decree:
Where Alph, the sacred river, ran
Through caverns measureless to man
Down to a sunless sea.

As it turned out, encrypting my spell was the correct thing to do. For Turing was thus free to unpack it at precisely the right time. The next day he went and crawled inside the V-bomb device, decrypted my message, and turned himself into a matter wave that pulsated in the magical, discordant rhythm that I'd unearthed. When the V-bomb was ignited, Alan overlaid the deskugging signal upon the V-rays—with socially beneficial results.

This really happened.

Why aren't schoolchildren taught that William Burroughs and Alan Turing saved the world? There are several reasons.

First of all, we're queer.

Second of all, due to Turing's odd manipulations, the V-bomb *imploded* rather than exploding. It didn't send out the customary annihilating and highly conspicuous fireball. Instead it shrank down to the subatomic level, tore a hole in space and, one assumes, burbled into the void. Like the river Alph, eh? Life is all of a piece.

The doctored V-rays cancelled out the vibrations of all the skugs, whether they be free-ranging or nestled in the flesh of their human hosts. And therefore all skuggers reverted to being normal humans, more or less. No trace of the skugs remained.

As an extra fillip—and this is the third reason why we remain uncelebrated—Turing modulated his V-rays in a most cunning way. Not only did the V-rays cancel out the wave functions of the *skugs*, the rays removed all *human memories* of the skugs and—so malleable is our frail reality—the V-rays vaporized all *material records* of the skugs. In short, Alan Turing pulled after him every possible trace of skug.

Well, not quite *all* traces were removed. In his incomparable genius, Alan had so fine a psychic touch that he was able to leave your humble narrator's own memories intact.

Adding to my store of info, in recent months, I've had several personal contacts with Turing's ghost. And this is how I've come to know the particulars of his final moments on Earth.

Where is Alan now? Call it paradise.

I'm nearly done. Let me only remark upon the salient lesson that I draw from my adventures with Turing. *The world is magic.* We never needed any scientific mumbo-jumbo. The lectures of a Harvard physicist teach no more than the crooning of a drunken shaman in a rayon sport shirt. Science is but an insipid style of sorcery.

At least that's how I see it. And now I'm turning off the machine.

afterword

Why did I write a beatnik SF novel about William Burroughs and Alan Turing? In short, I'd come to think of them as my friends, and I wanted to show them a good time.

Would Turing mind? Late in his life, at the suggestion of a therapist, Turing actually made a start at writing a semi-autobiographical science-fiction tale. To some extent this allays any uneasiness I might feel about dragging the man's name into the mud of transreal SF! As for Burroughs—hell, looked at in the right way, the man was an SF writer like me. He definitely would have liked skugs.

Turing was a heroic and inspiring figure, well ahead of his time. He worked on deeply fascinating things without getting lost in in the merely technical.

He created the idea of what's called the Turing machine, which is a simple abstraction of a computer. And then he proved it's impossible to create a general program that will predict how long all the other programs will run. That is, there's no master computation that knows in advance what all the other computations will do.

To my way of thinking, this connects, in a roundabout way, with the fact that, if you're an author working at the limits of your power, it's impossible to predict where your novel is going to go. Your mind is a computation, but you can't predict what it'll do.

Turing is especially well-known for his 1950 paper, "Computing Machinery and Intelligence." It's a non-technical essay in which he describes a test for AI knows as the *Turing imitation game*. The idea is that a program is intelligent if you can't tell it from a human when you're conversing with it. A significant footnote: Turing initially framed his "imitation game" in terms of a man trying to convince a listener that he's a woman.

During his life Turing had a way of switching subjects. He helped to design and build some of the first wires-and-vacuum-tube computers. He was involved with a code-breaking effort in WWII, cracking the German Enigma code. And near the end of his life, he was looking into how certain biocomputational mixtures of chemicals will produce patterns, such as the ones you see in the coats of animals.

In this vein, he wrote a paper, "The Chemical Basis of Morphogenesis," where he did an immense calculation—and his output was a single black blob, like you'd see on the back of a cow. This makes me love Turing— the image of the great mathematician doing a huge computation by hand.

Another compelling aspect of the Turing story is that he was openly gay, was persecuted for it, and had a strange, tragic death—which is usually described as a suicide.

Turing was a fan of the movie *Snow White*, with the poison apple. He was said to have danced down a university corridor singing songs from the movie. And he was found dead with an apple that had cyanide on it. The authorities announced that Turing put the cyanide on the apple himself. A weird way to kill himself.

I've always felt there's a possibility that Turing was in fact assassinated by agents of the British government. This seems somewhat plausible, given that Turing was involved in that top-secret code-breaking effort during World War II. Keep in mind that he died in the 1950s, when there was a collective hysteria over homosexuals being security risks.

Before I began contemplating my novel, I'd read some stories and plays about Turing. But I didn't feel that any of these works captured the vibrant, quirky image of the man that I wanted to project. Some works depict homosexuality in a lugubrious tone—as if homosexuals were pathetic victims of a genetic flaw. I finally found the key to Turing's personality in *Alan Turing: The Enigma*, a wonderful biography by Andrew Hodges.

Turing was anything but secretive or downcast about his predilections. He was stubborn, unrepentant, impulsive, and warm. And, like many mathematicians and computer scientists, he was socially unaware. He'd say whatever he thought—he might even say to a man, "I'm a homosexual. Would you like to have sex with me tonight?" In the 1950s, in England, this was not done. Alan is a great character to write about.

So in the spring of 2007, I wrote a short story about Turing, "The Imitation Game." He escapes his assassination. This story came to be the first chapter of *Turing & Burroughs*. By the way, my story predates—and has no connection with—the Turing movie of the same name. Nor does it relate to the earlier play with the same title.

After my "The Imitation Game," I wrote a second story, "Tangier Routines." Turing meets up with Burroughs in Tangier. Two brilliant men, gay, outcast—they hit it off. In my story, Turing intensifies his biotech to the point where he can turn his body into a huge slug, or *skug*, that slimes around. And his condition is contagious. It's vintage 1950s-style mutant invasion SF.

I'm a huge Burroughs fan. I started reading him in high school, and his epochal *Naked Lunch* made a huge impression on me. I've always liked his attitude—so completely in your face, with no compromise. "Homosexuality is what I like." And he was funny about it. The same with the drugs. I've studied Burroughs's works very closely over the years, and I wrote "Tangier Routines" in the form of a series of letters I'd imagined him writing.

My story was so gleefully scabrous that I didn't bother sending it to any magazines, science-fictional or otherwise. Instead, in the fall of 2008, I printed it in the SF webzine *Flurb* that I ran for a few years, and it eventually became the third chapter in *Turing & Burroughs*.

One of my challenges in writing a William Burroughs character was that I had to deal with the fact that, a couple of years before the start of my novel, Burroughs had shot and killed his wife Joan in Mexico City. At first I felt like this was too explosive and difficult to write about directly. But then I realized that I had to face the killing.

So my versions of Turing and Burroughs end up going to Mexico City, resurrecting Joan, and letting her run some routines on Burroughs. I wanted to give Joan a voice, and to give her a chance to get even. I wrote the Mexico City chapter from the Burroughs point of view, writing very fast. It was like I was possessed—but in a good way. The experience was heavy and ecstatic. I'm always happy when I'm emulating Bill Burroughs. He didn't give a fuck. And neither did Alan Turing.

As I already mentioned, for the main SF element in *Turing & Burroughs*, I introduced the skugs, made of a kind of programmable flesh. Burroughs himself actually wrote about this substance in his novels, referring to it as UDT or "undifferentiated tissue."

My agent sent my manuscript for *Turing & Burroughs* to a number of publishers, and they all said, "This is well written, but we don't want it." Maybe they thought it was too outrageous?

So I self-published the first edition under my Transreal Books imprint back in 2012. It was a lot of work. But I'm a computer guy, so I figured out how to make ebooks and paperbacks, and how to sell them online—although it *did* take me seven months.

The Transreal Books *Turing & Burroughs* had good sales and was well reviewed. And now Night Shade is putting out a beautiful new edition! Many thanks to Jeremy Lassen and Cory Allyn for making it happen.

When I was in the middle of writing this novel, I happened to see a video of Burroughs at his house in Lawrence, Kansas, shot a year or two before he died. I knew right away I could use this scenario for the last chapter of my novel. Bill's final sentence?

"And now I'm turning off the machine."

I like that. You might say it captures the theme of my novel. You can turn off the machines and get wiggly. Especially if you're Burroughs, and even if you're Alan Turing.

Long may they wave.

Rudy Rucker
Los Gatos, California
October 3, 2018.

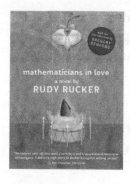

mathematicians in love
a novel by
RUDY RUCKER

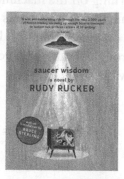

saucer wisdom
a novel by
RUDY RUCKER

white light
a novel by
RUDY RUCKER

million mile road trip
a novel by
RUDY RUCKER

the big aha
a novel by
RUDY RUCKER

spacetime donuts
a novel by
RUDY RUCKER

jim and the flims
a novel by
RUDY RUCKER

the sex sphere
a novel by
RUDY RUCKER

the secret of life
a novel by
RUDY RUCKER

also from rudy rucker
and night shade books

Night Shade Books' ten-volume Rudy Rucker series reissues nine brilliantly off-beat novels from the mathematician-turned-author, as well as the brand-new *Million Mile Road Trip*. Conceived as a uniformly-designed collection, each release features new artwork from award-winning illustrator Bill Carman and an introduction from some of Rudy's most renowned science fiction contemporaries. We're proud to make trade editions available again (or for the first time!) of so much work from this influential writer, and to share Rucker's fascinating and unique ideas with a new generation of readers.

Mathematicians in Love
$14.99 pb
978-1-59780-963-4

Saucer Wisdom
$14.99 pb
978-1-59780-965-8

White Light
$14.99 pb
978-1-59780-984-9

Million Mile Road Trip
$24.99 hc
978-1-59780-992-4
$14.99 pb
978-1-59780-991-7

The Big Aha
$14.99 pb
978-1-59780-993-1

Spacetime Donuts
$14.99 pb
978-1-59780-997-9

Jim and the Flims
$14.99 pb
978-1-59780-998-6

The Sex Sphere
$14.99 pb
978-1-94910-201-7

The Secret of Life
$14.99 pb
978-1-94910-202-4

Rudy Rucker is a writer and a mathematician who worked for twenty years as a Silicon Valley computer science professor. He is regarded as contemporary master of science fiction, and received the Philip K. Dick award twice. His forty published books include both novels and non-fiction books on the fourth dimension, infinity, and the meaning of computation. A founder of the cyberpunk school of science-fiction, Rucker also writes SF in a real-istic style known as transrealism, often including himself as a character. He lives in the San Francisco Bay Area.